Elizabeth Waite was born in Tooting and lived there until she was thirty-four years old. During the war she worked as a bus conductress at Merton Garage. In 1956 she and her husband moved to Devon and bought their first guesthouse.

Now retired, they live in East Sussex.

LIFE'S FOR LIVING

ELIZABETH WAITE

sphere

SPHERE

First published in Great Britain in January 2005 by Time Warner Books
This paperback edition published in April 2006 by Time Warner Books
Reprinted by Sphere in 2007
This paperback edition published in 2010 by Sphere

A CIP catalogue record for this book
is available from the British Library.

ISBN 978-0-7515-4566-1

Printed in Great Britain by Clays Ltd, St Ives plc

Papers used by Sphere are natural, renewable and
recyclable products sourced from well-managed forests and certified
in accordance with the rules of the Forest Stewardship Council.

Mixed Sources
Product group from well-managed
forests and other controlled sources
www.fsc.org Cert no. SGS-COC-004081
© 1996 Forest Stewardship Council

Sphere
An imprint of
Little, Brown Book Group
100 Victoria Embankment
London EC4Y 0DY

An Hachette UK Company
www.hachette.co.uk

www.littlebrown.co.uk

Bob

There is never a day
that I don't miss your love,
your companionship and all the ups
and downs that make a marriage.

Human beings can live for quite a while
without water or food, but they cannot
withstand loneliness.

It is the worst of all sufferings.

Chapter One

SOUTH LONDON, 1926

MR GILBY, THE RENT COLLECTOR, was having a bad day. He was smartly dressed: dark suit, the trousers pressed to perfection, worn with a sparkling white shirt and a dark blue tie. He also wore a bowler hat on his head. Usually he was in complete charge of any given situation. But not today.

'You've had enough warnings, Mrs Brown,' he said, doing his best to remain calm, 'and it won't wash any longer. Seven days and you pay in full or you and your whole family will be evicted.'

Martha Brown lost her patience. 'My husband is on short time at the foundry and this last four weeks is the first time in all the years that we've lived here that I haven't had my rent ready and waiting for you.' She stuck a finger within an inch of his face. Mr Smart-arse, as the locals had nicknamed him, gasped and took a step backwards. Martha wasn't finished, not by a long chalk. 'You might frighten some of the poor old souls round 'ere but you don't frighten me. I've told you, as soon as my man is set on full time again you'll get every penny that's owing. Meanwhile, if you dare t' threaten me again I'll go straight up to Ensign's offices and ask t' see the owner of these properties, 'cos

1

you're not the organ grinder by any means. You're only the employed monkey.' Martha's voice was set with emphasis. 'You wanna remember, two-thirds of these houses in all these three streets are occupied by my relatives and Ensign's know we've always been good tenants.'

The collector looked at her as if she were someone from the gutter. 'Yes . . . well, I'll be here as usual next Monday.'

Martha closed the door in his face and pressed her aching head against the solid wood. She closed her eyes and thought of her children, but mostly of Rose, her only daughter.

Her two sons, Lenny and Bernie, were good lads and she loved them both dearly. Lenny, nineteen years old, was the image of his father, and Sid Brown was a big man. In his stockinged feet he stood six foot one, though these days his back was no longer ramrod straight. From the day he'd left the East End of London where he had been born and bred to move south of the Thames, he'd held down an un-believably hard job at Merton Foundry, where massive furnaces were kept going day and night in order to separate metal from ore. Broad-shouldered and thick-set, he had grown tough over the years. It was said of him that he could fell a man with one blow from his huge fist. Lenny was quite content to walk in his father's shadow. He'd worked in Wandsworth Brewery since he was fourteen years old and was never happier than when rolling the huge barrels of beer down the ramps which led to the cellars of various pubs. His pride and joy were the enormous dray horses which he always groomed with the greatest of care.

Bernie was different. Just one year younger than his brother, he was always frustrated. He wanted so much more out of life than his parents had. He'd grown up with misery and poverty, and he yearned to be educated. Although he was not quite as tall or as muscular as his father and brother he was still well-built and strong – and the best-looking one of the family. His striking good looks would always be a powerful asset. He worked in Paines' firework factory and hated every minute that he had to spend there.

Third time lucky, Martha and Sid had said when their lovely daughter had been born. 'As beautiful as a rose, and well worth waiting for,' Sid had exclaimed. Martha had never known her husband to show such emotion and immediately decided that would be her baby's name. Rosie, with her blonde curly hair, pale skin and wide blue eyes, was the opposite of her brothers who both had dark hair and sharp brown eyes. Most definitely Rosie took after her side of the family.

Rose was a gentle child, endearing herself to people by smiling readily and chatting away nineteen to the dozen. It was said that she could charm the birds out of the trees. She'd learnt to twist her big brothers and her father around her little finger. Her cheeky, expressive face with those big, innocent-looking blue eyes always captivated them completely. Almost every Saturday one of them brought her something: a colouring book and crayons, a pretty hair slide, a bag of sweets, even a skipping rope with colourful painted handles. The fact that just lately she had changed so much was worrying Martha more than she would admit. At first she had supposed that turning thirteen and becoming a teenager a couple of weeks ago had made the difference. She'd changed so suddenly, one minute behaving as if she were afraid of something and the next, without warning, back-answering and acting too big for her boots. It was as if now there was a different side to her; she'd become deceitful, cunning and wilful.

Slowly Martha walked into her scullery, filled the tin kettle from the single cold tap at the brown-stone sink, struck a match and lit one of the four rings on the top of her enamel gas stove. Having placed the kettle over the flame she walked into the living room and sat down to wait for it to come to the boil. After that rumpus with that pompous old git over the rent she badly needed a cup of strong tea.

She sighed heavily and murmured, 'Oh, Rosie, Rosie, Rosie. Why won't you talk to me?' Even a blind man would be able to tell there was something wrong and she was ninety per cent sure that she already knew what it was. If half of what she feared was true there was no way she could shift the blame. It would all fall on her shoulders and Sid would do his nut. She'd had a hard enough job persuading him to let their little girl do a favour for her Auntie Joan in the first place.

Joan was Martha's elder sister by two years. Despite being up at the crack of dawn every morning to catch the tram which would take her to the city where she cleaned offices, Joan had got herself an extra job making lampshades. It worked out very well because she could work from home. Trouble was she had to report to the factory twice a week between four and six o'clock in order to deliver her finished work and collect a fresh set of lampshade frames and material. Her mother-in law lived with Joan, had done from the day she'd been married, and Joan loved her dearly. Sadly, in the latter years, the old lady had become ill. Sick in the mind as much as bodily ill, but Joan cared for her to the best of her ability. Which was more than could be said of her son.

Daily Joan washed and fed the old lady, and if she had the time she would give her a blanket bath, dress her and get her settled in a chair by the front window to enable her to see folk passing by. She could never be left on her own, because her movements were jerky and disjointed and she often fell. Martha helped her sister as much as she could and many a good neighbour came in to sit with the old lady when Joan needed to go to the shops for a bit of shopping. But the evenings when she had to go to the lampshade factory were awkward. Martha had to have dinner ready on

4

the table for Sid and her own two sons when they came home from work and it was the same for most local women, and so she had agreed that Rosie would go round, only into the next street, for those couple of hours and sit with the old lady just to make sure she didn't get out of bed.

Poor Joan! Christ knows she needs the money. Martha shook her head in disgust. Married to Bill Baldwin, Joan had not found life a bed of roses. Lazy sod he was and always would be. Work was something other people did, not him.

Through the open door Martha saw that the kettle was steaming. She got to her feet, poured some water into the brown china teapot and swilled it round before throwing it into the sink. She would have liked to use two heaped teaspoons of leaves because she liked her tea hot and very strong, but it was the middle of the week and the way things were going there would only be the few shillings that her sons gave her coming into her purse this weekend, so she sighed and made do with just one level spoonful. 'Don't drown it,' she muttered as she poured on the boiling water.

Settled back in what was Sid's wooden armchair, she sipped at her tea. She'd bet her last penny that the way young Rosie was acting up was something to do with Bill Baldwin. Quite unexpectedly Martha felt tears sting the back of her eyes. She swallowed hard. She hadn't cried in years, but now memory had her mind jumping back far into the past.

She'd been fifteen and flattered that her big sister's boyfriend had paid her attention. Bill Baldwin had been twenty-one, six years older than herself and four years older than Joan. She had gone for a walk across Tooting Bec Common with him and he'd taken her into a pub, where he'd had a pint of beer and bought her a shandy. She shouldn't really have been in a public house because she wasn't old enough but the experience had made her feel very grown up. And Bill Baldwin had acted nice, holding her hand as they walked back across the common, but when they were almost home he'd tried it on.

'God forgive me,' she muttered beneath her breath. He'd almost got there. His kisses had been lovely to begin with and she hadn't given a thought to the fact that he was walking out regularly with Joan. It was only when he'd tried to get his hand up the leg of her knickers that she had come to her senses.

She'd kicked him in the shins and run like the devil, never once stopping until she reached the safety of their porch. Even then, for a good many minutes she hadn't been able to pull the string through the letter box which held the key to the front door. She'd had to get her breath back and straighten her clothing before she could face her mum and dad.

For months afterwards she'd been nervous whenever Bill Baldwin was in their house. She hadn't been able to tell anyone, her sister least of all, because only days after she'd gone for a walk with Bill he had given Joan a ring and they'd become engaged.

It had been an awful situation. Joan would be sitting snuggled up to him on the sofa and he'd look over the top of Joan's head and wink at her. Nothing had ever been said but the looks he gave her on the quiet made her flesh crawl.

But all that had been donkey's years ago. She and Sid had been married for almost twenty years. They'd had their ups and downs but they'd weathered them and, thank God, they had three healthy children. The same could not be said for her sister. Joan had had one hell of a life. Although it was Bill's mother whom Joan loved and cared for he never lifted a finger to help. Any money that did come his way went into either a publican's pocket or that of a bookmaker. Three times Joan had been pregnant and each time she had miscarried. No one could tell Martha that the cause of her sister's being unable to carry a baby to full term was not down to that bugger of a husband of hers. She knew, when he had had too much to drink, or even when he hadn't, he would think nothing of using Joan as a punch bag.

'Why the hell does your sister stay with him?' Sid had often asked. Martha was sure she knew the answer. If Joan didn't take care of old Mrs Baldwin, then who the hell would?

Half the trouble was that Joan appeared to come from a different mould from the man she had chosen to marry. But in those long-ago days when a whole host of East-Enders had moved to South London because both houses and employment were more plentiful there, Joan had been deemed old enough to be put into service. Having had hardly any schooling she started at the bottom, but as it turned out that period of her life had been a blessing in disguise. Her employers had been taken with this girl who came from such a poor background. As a worker they thought of her as a little wonder. As to her looks, she was a beauty, even if it was an unusual sort of beauty. Quiet and peaceful was how the mistress described her. She was small and slight, with soft features, a gentle nature and long soft golden-brown hair which she mainly kept rolled up in a bun, which was a shame, Martha thought, because it caused her, at times, to look stern. She had given her name as Joanie, but that was not how they referred to her in that posh household. Always Joan. Her own way of speaking had soon altered, and not only that, she was taught manners and that there was a right way to do everything one was asked to do. After proving that she was willing to learn she rose from being a kitchen maid to a parlour maid, and finally she'd been promoted to the position of lady's maid. It was during that time she had learnt about clothes. Indeed she had. Even today Joan's handiwork with a needle was something to be admired.

Joan had quickly seen the vast difference between life at

Morley House and life for lower-class families. The pampered Morleys wanted for nothing, totally unaware of the harsh realities of the lives of their employees, especially when the man of the family was unable to find work even though he tramped endless miles searching for it, willing to do the meanest of jobs if he could only earn enough to keep his wife and children in the bare essentials of life. It hadn't taken her long to realise that money bought not only necessities, but so much more as well. How many times, Martha wondered, had Joan told her that her mother-in-law needed medicines and nourishing food, not to mention spare clean bedding. It was at such times that the pair of them had readily agreed that money is the answer to everything.

Martha decided that she was going to have to put some direct questions to Rosie. She had done her best to talk to her, and although her daughter always avoided giving straight answers, on one occasion she had blurted out that her Uncle Bill had been in the house when she was supposed to be on her own looking after Granny Baldwin.

Martha felt betwixt and between. Should she stop Rosie going round there? That would only be victimising Joan. Whatever was going on couldn't be Rosie's fault. What did she know at her age? She's always got on well with her Uncle Bill. He tickled her, made her laugh, and as far as Martha was concerned, up until now, there had not been any reason not to trust him. She decided, at least for the time being, she was going to have to keep her suspicions to herself. She couldn't bear to think that there might come a time when she would have to tell her husband, which would involve her two sons at the same time. Then God help us. Things might get out of hand.

Rose came down the stairs just as the front door opened and her father walked in. 'Daddy,' she shrieked, totally forgetting that her mum had allowed her to stay home from school because she'd pleaded an awful headache. She ran down the passage, her face wreathed in smiles.

Sid eased his great body towards her and swept her, the apple of his eye, up into his brawny arms, swung her round several times until the walls whirled before her eyes, and then held her tenderly as he carried her into the living room.

''Allo, my luv,' he said to his wife. 'I'm sure we've got the prettiest daughter in the world. But what I can't make out is why she's so small and dainty when our two boys are such great big louts.'

'I've told yer often enough. You've only got t' look in the mirror to see who Lenny and Bernie take after, while our Rosie looks a bit like me but much more like her Auntie Joan.'

Sid put Rosie down and walked over to Martha and took hold of her arm before planting a kiss on her cheek. 'You're nice an' plump 'cos you're 'appy an' well cared for whereas your sister, Gawd bless 'er, ain't nothing but skin an' bone 'cos she spends 'er entire life slogging away to keep that useless sod she married an' his mother.' When Martha didn't answer he looked intently into her eyes and asked very quietly, 'What's the matter, gal? Is something wrong?'

She didn't answer, but turned her face away.

'Why isn't Rosie at school? There is something wrong, isn't there?' he said again, more loudly, at the same time catching hold of her arm.

She shook his hand off. 'No, nuffin's wrong. She wasn't very perky this morning – said 'er 'ead ached, that's all.'

'But you look worried. An' yer jumped when I touched yer arm.'

'No I didn't. I was just surprised to see you 'ome so early.'

'There was nuffin' doing. They've even let two of the furnaces burn out an' I ain't ever seen that 'appen before.' He turned away, realising he wasn't going to get any answers

9

from her at the moment. He'd leave it for a bit. But for days there'd been a funny uneasy atmosphere. Why couldn't he put his finger on it? Before this day is out I will, though, he vowed to himself. I'll get Martha on her own and I *will* find out what is going on.

He wandered over to where Rose sat and, doing his best to be gentle, he sat down on the floor at her feet and looked up at her. 'Do you feel better now, luv?'

'Yes, Dad,' Rose said quietly.

'You would tell me if there was something troubling you, wouldn't you, babe?'

Martha held her breath.

'Course I would,' Rose murmured, hanging her head.

Her father got to his feet and took hold of both of her hands. 'Rosie, I know everything is not all right with you. Are you gonna tell me about it?'

She didn't raise her head, merely shook it and muttered, 'Ask Mum.'

It took a lot to make Sid Brown lose his temper but when he did, God help the person who had upset him. He took a very deep breath as he turned his gaze on to his wife and instinctively was aware that she knew more than she was letting on. This wasn't a bit like his Martha. Even when times had been really hard, with five mouths to feed, food and clothes to buy and money to be found for coal because the kitchen range was the only heating in the whole house and there was times when the weather was so cold that ice formed on the *inside* of the bedroom windows, his Martha had never let her feelings show. He couldn't remember when he'd come home and Martha hadn't had a smile on her face. He clenched his fists in frustration. No matter what he said or did he was being balked at every turn. He knew full well he wasn't going to get anything out of either of them just yet but he couldn't resist saying, 'Well, it'll take a bit more talking to convince me that

10

something 'asn't 'appened to upset the apple cart in this family.'

Martha didn't like the way Sid was scowling. 'I've got to get the meal on. Let's leave it till the boys are 'ome an' we've all eaten, shall we, Sid?' She smiled, but there was no mistaking the note of pleading in her voice as she looked at her daughter and added kindly, 'You're all right now, aren't you, pet?'

Sid's face was set straight, no answering smile. 'All right,' he said gruffly, letting her know that nothing was settled until she had told him the truth.

There was no way out. Martha knew that she would have to voice her fears to her husband. He'd get the truth out of Rosie and he'd know what to do, he always did. But there was one point she was going to make. Joan mustn't know about this. Every time Bill Baldwin got himself in a bit of bother it was always left to Joan to sort it all out. What with looking after old Mrs Baldwin twenty-four hours of every day and trying to keep up with two jobs, Joan was almost at the end of her tether; certainly she was in no fit state to take on more worries. She had no children of her own and Rosie was the light of her life, and if she thought that her Bill had hurt the child in any way she would probably go berserk.

As Martha went towards the scullery, Sid stepped in front of her and said firmly, 'Remember what you've promised. As soon as we've eaten we're getting this matter sorted. No matter what it is. Do you hear me?'

She nodded.

The vegetables she was preparing for their evening meal were done in next to no time because as she peeled potatoes and scraped carrots she was venting her fury by muttering over and over again, 'Bloody Bill Baldwin.'

Chapter Two

'BUT, DAD, I LIKE sitting with Granny Baldwin. I tell her
all about what we do at school and Auntie Joan always leaves
us some sweets and an apple or an orange which we have
half each of. You won't stop me going round there, will you?'
Rosie's eyes were imploring.

Big Sid's face was creased with worry. He was sitting
opposite his daughter, and now he stretched out his hand
and took hold of hers and sighed deeply. Rosie was
especially dear to him, as she was to all of them, and she
would for ever be regarded as the baby of the family. Yet
the relationship she had with Granny Baldwin was
amazing. She had the ability to listen, to care, and to show
kindness to the old lady – unlike the do-gooders who, when
Joan had asked for their help, had only come up with the
suggestion that Mrs Baldwin would be far better off in a
council home. The last thing he wanted was to forbid Rosie
to go and sit with the old lady. Besides, Martha would
raise hell if he even suggested it. Martha was never one to
mince words or hesitate to go where even angels would
fear to tread. All the same, he knew he and his two sons
had to sort something out, and soon. If it weren't for the

fact that Joan was Martha's sister he wouldn't be hesitating: he'd be round to Baldwin's place and he'd make damn sure the bastard wouldn't be able to walk for weeks on end.

It was Bernie, the quietest of his two sons, who had gently got most of the story out of their Rosie.

'Just tell me why you've suddenly gone off yer Uncle Bill,' he had asked, his manner not accusing, just soft and soothing. He smiled at her and his sister had smiled back and looked at him with utter trust. 'Don't you like him any more?'

Rosie seemed to be struggling to find an answer. Then quietly she said with complete honesty, 'Not really, no. He gives me the creeps.'

'Get on with it,' Lenny chipped in irritatedly. 'I don't know why we don't just get round there an' knock the bloody 'ell out of him.'

Martha's faced paled. If this all blew up into a full scale fight it would be poor Joan who would come off worst in the end. 'Don't be so damned stupid, Lenny,' she snapped. 'We don't know the 'alf of it yet and we won't unless Rosie tells us the truth.'

Rosie wasn't daft. No different from most of the girls in her class at school. It was just that she had two elder brothers and her dad was a great big man and she knew exactly where she stood with them. If the three of them had their way they wouldn't let the wind blow on her. They were always questioning her as to where she was going and whom she was going with.

A lot of her friends plastered their faces with cheap make-up and some even smoked when they could cadge enough pennies to buy a packet of fags. Two girls she knew had big breasts and they boasted about how they let the boys touch them. She was probably the smallest girl in her class and her breasts were scarcely formed. She'd asked

13

her mum to buy her a brassiere but she'd only laughed and told her to give herself a chance to have something to put into it first. For all that, she liked boys as much as the other girls did; they could be great fun at times. But this thing with her own uncle . . . well, it wasn't the same. It was nasty.

'I dunno why Uncle Bill keeps wanting to touch me.' She suddenly opened up. 'He always used to be out somewhere when I first started going to sit with Gran, but not now. He's always there. Granny Baldwin saw him come up behind me the other night when he pulled my dress up and put both his hands on my bottom. I yelled 'cos he made me jump and Granny said he was a dirty twisted git. I thought he was going to hit Gran and that's when I told him I was gonna tell Auntie Joan.'

'And did you?' her mother asked, cagily.

'No, I didn't, 'cos Auntie Joan 'as all sorts of things to worry about. She works all the time. She's always changing Gran's clothes 'cos sometimes she can't get to the lav quick enough an' she wets herself. And she dribbles an' drops her food down her jumper. She can't 'elp it, though – her hands shake. Loads of washing Auntie 'as t' do yet she still cooks lovely meals, but Uncle Bill moans and shouts at her all the time and . . .'

'*And what?*' Her father and her mother bawled the question simultaneously.

Rosie shrank back into her chair, wishing she didn't have to answer, but one look at her father's face told her she had to. 'Uncle Bill hits Auntie Joan,' she said, trying not to cry.

Martha shook her head sadly, thanking God that she had a good man and wondering how Joan managed to put up with the life she had to lead.

'I can't believe I'm hearing this.' Sid's anger was choking him. 'Come on, Lenny. You too, Bernie,' their father said, standing up and straightening his shoulders. 'It's about time we paid that relation of ours a visit and believe you me by the time I've finished with him he'll think he's been hung, drawn and quartered.

Bill Baldwin was feeling very proud of himself as he glanced in the mirror that hung over the fireplace. He'd used brilliantine to smooth down his thick mop of jet black hair and as he rolled down his shirt sleeves he was well pleased with his brawny arms which from wrist to elbow were covered in tattoos. He thought and acted tough and as he shrugged his jacket on he was thinking he was well able to take care of himself. He'd only had to give Joan a couple of slaps around the head and she'd opened her purse and given him a ten bob note. Why the hell hadn't she given it to him in the first place? She knew it was pointless arguing with him. He had to have a drink; any man was entitled to that and he hadn't got a penny to his name. He was whistling away, happy as a lark as he walked down the passage and opened the front door.

The flat of Sid Brown's hand was shoved straight into Bill's chest and he had no option but to stagger backwards down the passage. To say that he was dismayed to see this great brute of a man was to put it mildly, but when he looked beyond and saw Lenny and Bernie behind their father he knew he was in deep trouble and the colour drained away from his face. Already he was conscious that if he made a wrong move or uttered a wrong word these brothers and their father would beat him so badly it was quite possible that they might even kill him.

Sid was pleased to see Bill's scared expression. Grabbing his tie and glaring into his eyes he yelled, 'You're a sodding coward, yer pick on women, yer ignore the needs of yer own mother, yer've never done an 'ard day's work in yer life but my God you've gone too far when you start puttin' yer filthy 'ands on my Rosie.' By now Sid's fury had got the better

15

of him and without giving it a second thought he drew back his arm, clenched his fist and used brute force to land a punch square on Bill's face, breaking his nose and sending blood splashing all over the place.

He stepped aside and Lenny aimed his punches well, one in Bill's kidneys and one in his belly.

Bernie went for his legs, kicking his shins with his steel-toecapped boots. As Bill Baldwin hit the floor, Sid stood over him spattered with blood that was not his own.

Joan watched the commotion from her kitchen doorway. Bernie stared at her. She was wearing a thin cotton dress and an old cardigan. She looked a mess. Her face was a mass of bruises and the side of her head was streaked with blood.

'You all right, Aunt Joan?' Bernie really liked his aunt and tonight he felt especially sorry for her.

Joan had heard her husband scream once and now it seemed as if his loud moaning was coming from far away. She had no idea why her brother-in-law and his two sons were here, giving her Bill a right good going over by the looks of things. She thought it must be about money, although she knew of old that Sid was wise enough not to listen to her Bill's hard luck stories.

Then it came to her what these three men were threatening Bill with and her heart came into her mouth. Oh, no! She didn't want to believe what she was hearing. Lovely young Rosie! Christ almighty, she's his niece! She had good cause to know that her husband was selfish to the core, no good to man nor beast. But this! Even he couldn't have sunk so low. Could he?

It was Lenny who manhandled his uncle to his feet and dragged him outside into the street. Bill was in such a state that they had to let him slide down until he was sitting on the pavement with his back propped up against the front garden wall, head hanging limply, chin resting on his blood-splattered chest.

Sid waved his two sons aside. He was going to be the one to make sure that this lousy sod understood that what he was about to say was not empty threats or intimidation but that every word was for real. 'This won't be the end of the matter, Bill, you realise that, don't you?'

Bill was frightened and he didn't try to hide it.

'I can't think what possessed you to think you'd get away with mucking about with our Rosie.' Sid was in full steam now and he bent over and hollered, 'While we're about it we may as well sort a few more things out that should 'ave been dealt with years ago. Your wife works like a slave. She's a decent woman. A bloody kind woman. Too good for the likes of you. Where would your mother be if it weren't for Joan? You've never brought a wage packet home in yer whole life. You're no better than a scavenger. Left t' you she'd bloody starve, that's for sure, or even worse you'd 'ave shoved 'er away in some lousy institution. From now on me an' my boys will stop at nothing to see that you start pulling your weight. You get yerself a job, you bring yer wages 'ome every week an' you take care of Joan and your mother.'

As Bill tried his best to raise himself on to his elbows, Lenny pushed his father out of his way. 'My dad might be finished with you but I'm not.' By now quite a few neighbours had come out into the street and Lenny's booming voice took them all by surprise. 'What goes on in your married life is your own business but from now on there are a couple of things you'd do well t' remember. One, your wife is our relation, part an' parcel of our family, and two, you so much as lay a finger on our Rosie and you're a dead man. Don't even look at her. Got it? I'm not threatening you, matey, I am pure an' simply stating a fact an' you'd better believe it.'

Bill could hardly see through the blood that covered his face but he was well aware that the words spoken by Sid and his elder son were well and truly meant. He would have dearly loved to tell this bullying brother-in-law of his where to go but he knew better than to put on an act of bravado. So when he did manage to speak, his words came out very meekly.

'I've tried t' get a job, honest I 'ave, Sid. There just ain't any work about.'

'Try harder.' Sid taunted him. ''Cos this visit ain't a one off by any means. Me an' me boys are gonna pay you a weekly visit t' make sure Joan is getting regular housekeeping money and that your dear old mum is being well looked after. Oh, and by the way, our Rosie is still coming round to your 'ouse 'cos she loves Gran Baldwin; an' her auntie, but where will you be, Bill?' he asked sarcastically. 'You'll be at work. Won't you?' The last two words were hollered into Bill's ear.

Sid and his two boys backed off, watching as Bill slowly got himself up until he was kneeling on all fours. That was when Sid's booted foot kicked his backside and he fell flat on his face this time. Bernie bent so low his face was almost touching the back of his uncle's head. 'Don't forget,' he said mockingly. 'Mend yer ways, you spineless bastard!'

Sid and Lenny turned to go, but Bernie seemed to have an afterthought. Bending his knees and leaning close to make sure that Bill could hear his words he said, 'Oh, and by the way, we'll be round next week to see if you've learnt anything tonight or if you will be needing another lesson.'

Bill Baldwin stayed put. He listened to his neighbours moving away, heard their front doors closing. The ring of heavy footsteps as Sid and his two sons walked the pavement. At that moment he was wishing he could be miles away. There had never been a time when he had needed a drink more badly than he did right now. There was a boozer on the corner of the street but it might as well have been at

18

the furthest corner of the world because he couldn't even bloody well crawl there.

Let alone walk.

Chapter Three

JOAN WAS FEELING VERY THOUGHTFUL as she walked down Mitcham Road and turned right into Welford's Dairy. Her basket already held a warm cottage loaf, and now she was going to buy a half-pound of Welford's speciality, a really strong Cheddar cheese. Then she was going to get on the tram, only today she was not going straight home but calling in to see her sister. A crusty knobby off each end of the top half of the loaf, a lump of cheese and a couple of Martha's famous pickled onions washed down with a good hot strong cup of tea plus a good old natter would set them both up for the day.

Just lately she had felt she had much to be grateful for, and one of the many blessings she counted was having a little time to herself. And the way her life had changed for the better was all down to her sister's husband and his two sons.

Things wouldn't have altered if it weren't for the fact that the three of them had kept their word. She had to smile as she thought back to the first week after they had given her husband a beating. Bill had really kidded himself that the subject was over and done with. They had made their point and to him that had been the end of the matter.

Not so!

Sid and his sons had turned up that weekend and the first thing they saw as they stepped into her living room was Bill stretched out on the sofa, fag hanging from the side of his mouth, reading the *Racing News*.

In two strides Sid had crossed the room and was towering over Bill. 'Got a job then, 'ave you?' he had asked, his voice quiet but menacing.

It had certainly been a shock to Bill's system just to stare up at his brother-in-law, whom he'd freely admit he was terrified of. From the position he was in Sid Brown appeared to be even bigger in stature than he was because of the largeness of his frame, his broad shoulders and his powerful arms. He might be brawny and well built but there was no excess flesh on him. He was all muscle and sinew and Bill had had first-hand experience of his unbeatable strength.

Sid grabbed him by the hair, pulling him to a sitting position. Bill let out a piercing scream which scared his mother, whose bed was in the corner on the opposite side of the room.

'It's all right, Mrs Baldwin,' Bernie softly soothed her.

And it was. Bill hadn't made another sound because Lenny had stuffed his mouth with pages from the sporting paper he had been reading. They only gave him a few slaps around his face and head before saying, 'We'll see you same time next week an' if you 'aven't got a job by then, well, we'll just say no more warnings, shall we?'

Joan grinned to herself at the memory. That had been eight weeks ago and after a third visit from Sid and his boys Bill had shifted himself and got a job. Not much of a job, it had to be said, but Bill now knew better than to refuse it. He was night watchman at Young's Brewery which was situated in Wandsworth High Street. The few shillings he now gave her regularly every Friday had made a huge difference, especially where his mother was concerned. Poor

Granny Baldwin – she couldn't last out much longer. Worn out as she was by the struggle to survive, riddled with consumption, undernourished and constantly racked by a terrible chesty cough, she was beginning to fade. At least now Joan was able to buy new-laid eggs and fresh fruit with which to tempt the old lady. Strange, wasn't it, was Joan's daily thought, that she herself, related only by marriage, had come to love Gwen Baldwin so much, whilst her only son didn't give a hoot as to whether she lived or died.

Having finished her shopping, Joan boarded the tram at Tooting Broadway and sat smiling to herself as she thought of the welcome she would get from her sister.

'Cooee,' she called loudly as she opened the door, using the key that hung on the length of string behind the letter box. It was the first week in October and already there was a nip in the air, but the sight that met her as she opened the door to the living room was heartening. A fire was burning brightly and there was a smell of baking coming from the oven which was part and parcel of the kitchen range. 'Anyone in?' she called again, as she took off her coat and scarf and hung them on the hook on the back of the door.

There was a thump, thump of footsteps coming down the stairs and within seconds a beaming red face appeared round the door. 'I 'eard yer the first time,' Martha said. 'I was expecting you, anyway – that's why I've got an enormous bread pudding in the oven.'

Joan giggled at the sight of her sister but nevertheless she threw her arms round her bulky frame and hugged her close. Martha, in her late thirties, was two years younger than her sister Joan but the way she dressed and neglected her overweight body made her look much older. Joan was still giggling as she released her hold and stood back. 'Don't you ever wear anything different?' she asked, her voice full of laughter.

'Give a body a chance,' Martha snapped. 'I've been turning the boys' rooms out an' believe you me there ain't much room to turn round in there.'

Joan shook her head, doing her best to control her merriment. Martha was wearing a long grey dress over which she had tied a floral wrapround pinafore. Her hair was covered by a pink scarf tied to look like a turban and peeping out here and there was a mass of metal dinkie hair rollers.

'Ain't yer put the kettle on yet?' she demanded as she dumped an armful of dirty bedlinen down on to the floor. 'Don't yer want a cuppa? Christ knows, I could do with one.'

'Give us a chance. I've only just got 'ere. But I have bought a few bits in for our midday snack.'

'Good on yer, luv, that's what I like to 'ear. Got t' keep our strength up.'

It wasn't long before Joan had set two ploughmans down on the table and fetched two great breakfast cups filled with scalding tea from the scullery. 'Come on, Martha,' she yelled. 'Come and take the weight off yer feet and feed yer face.'

Her sister was out in the outhouse where a stone copper had been fitted. This makeshift building was next to the lavatory shed. Only cold water was connected and a fire had to be lit in the metal container which was fixed to the bottom of the copper in order to heat the water before the washing could be done.

'All right, luv,' she yelled back, 'just finishing poking these sheets in an' I'll be with you.'

The two sisters got on so well together, yet in a funny sort of way they were entirely different. Everyone took Martha to be the older of the two. She was always happy and contented and with three great men and one little girl to feed and take care of she was endlessly cooking and cleaning, so perhaps it wasn't unreasonable that she had let herself go a bit.

Joan had the harder life. Even now, with Bill working, who was to say how long it would last? Yet she appeared neat and tidy at all times. Most of her clothes she made herself. More often than not a dress or even a coat bought off a top barrow or at a jumble sale would be patiently taken to pieces and remodelled. Her most precious possession was her Singer treadle sewing machine. There had been times when Bill had sold almost everything of any value that they possessed, but even he knew it was more than his life was worth to touch her machine. Every piece of secondhand calico or linen that she came across Joan would haggle a price for in order to be able to run up spare nightdresses for Granny Baldwin and draw-sheets for her bed. If on the odd occasion her sister queried her devotion to her mother-in-law, Joan's reply would always be the same. 'I'll be old some day and perhaps need help myself.'

'Not from strangers if I'm still around,' Martha would reassure her aggressively.

When their plates were empty and their cups drained Martha could not hold back her curiosity any longer.

'So how's your Bill been getting on at Young's? Can't be that the work is too 'ard 'cos he's been there now, what, over two months, ain't it?'

Joan grinned. 'I wouldn't have laid bets on him staying there two weeks, not at first, that's for sure.' She shrugged her shoulders. 'Now, well, I wouldn't say he is over the moon but he's changed some, I have t' give him that much. He doesn't tell me a lot but then he never was much good at holding a conversation.'

'Except about racing.' Martha laughed loudly. 'The times he's told me he's been on to a dead certainty and the next day he'd be scratching around for someone t' lend him a couple of bob.'

'Tell me about it,' Joan muttered. 'He wore that one out with me years ago and yet still he'll try it on if he thinks

24

he'll get away with it. Everyone seems t' know that there was a bit of trouble the first week my Bill started at Young's, but no one's ever told me the extent of it. I do get the feeling he doesn't like Mr Grant, who's the general manager, but on the other hand I'm pretty sure that Bill will do his best never to get on the wrong side of him.'

Martha giggled. 'My Lenny told me about Mr Grant. Said he's not over tall but by God he's got a head like a bull on his very thick neck and real broad shoulders. The saying goes he could fell an ox with his bare hands.'

'Well, I know for a fact that when Mr Grant is not around Bill doesn't think he has t' graft so hard, which sits well with him, but before he gets his head down for a snooze about midnight he tells me he has to groom the big dray cart horses, and yer know what? He went on an' on about how much he liked doing that job.'

'Must be a smattering of good in him somewhere,' Martha sneered, 'though I bet a blind man would be glad t' see it.'

The two sisters looked sadly at each other. Joan was the first to compose herself and with a note of sensitivity in her voice said, 'Well, if there is I've never seen sight nor sound of it, at least not since we've been married I haven't. I wouldn't mind so much for myself if only he would spare a thought now and again for his mother. It's such a shame. Honestly, Martha, you wouldn't believe some of the horrible things he says to her. Especially if she has an accident and messes her bed. There are times when I could cheerfully murder him. He leaves her in no doubt that she's nothing but a burden to him and anyway that's not true 'cos he does sod all for her. God forgive my language. I know it's not the best situation, her having to be in bed most of the time and the fact that her bed is in our living room, but there'll come a day when . . . oh, I don't know. I daren't leave her on her own with him, though.'

Joan was close to tears at that moment. She shook her

head fiercely, her temper rising, and her face was twisted with a mixture of loathing and deadly intent. Suddenly Martha felt afraid. More so when Joan said, 'He hasn't got a spark of humanity in him! His own mother!' Her limbs were shaking, and her face now showed confusion but also disgust.

'He really is a nasty bugger,' Martha agreed passionately, at the same time wondering to what lengths he would eventually drive her sister. The very thought that Bill Baldwin might hurt his mother and that Joan might retaliate and do something she would bitterly regret brought a sharp stab of pain to her heart. It took a moment or two for her to compose herself. Then she took a deep breath, moved to take hold of her sister's hand and say, 'It's all right, luv. God 'as a way of paying His debts without any money.' Then as an afterthought she added, 'Why don't Sid an' me come round one night and sit with Mrs Baldwin? You could take yerself off to the pictures or t' the Hippodrome. A night out might do yer all the good in the world.' Beneath her breath she muttered, 'Christ knows yer deserve a break.'

'No, thanks all the same, Martha. I appreciate yer offer, but I don't have the money to spare for one thing and another reason is Granny would get in a state if I weren't there t' take her to the lav. Mrs Bradshaw is with her now – brings her ironing over to do at my place and talks away to Gran and Gran don't mind her so much 'cos she's used to seeing her. There's nothing t' stop you and Sid coming round, though. We could have a game of cards.'

Martha gave her sister a thoughtful look. 'How about when our Rosie used to sit with her?'

'She's got a lot worse since then and I've given up that lampshade job since Bill started handing over a regular wage to me.' She grinned. 'Only 'cos he knows I'll tell your Sid if he don't.'

It was galling for Martha to see what was happening to

her sister. Poor Joan! What made it worse was the fact that Joan had seen both sides of the coin. Having been in service she knew there were other ways of living where one had lovely clothes to wear and really good food on the table at each and every mealtime. Now she was nothing more than a drudge. She led such a monotonous life, scrimping and scratching around to make every penny go a long way, and for what? Certainly no thanks or even a kind word from that rotter of a husband of hers. It wasn't as if she had any company, any children to lighten up the place, just day in day out she seemed to be at the beck and call of Mrs Baldwin with no help whatsoever from Bill.

'God knows how long it will last.' Joan muttered her thoughts aloud. 'Never in my wildest dreams did I think my Bill would have held down a job this long, and it's only down to your Sid that he has, but . . .'

'But what?' Martha cried quickly.

Joan sighed heavily, wishing she hadn't mentioned her doubts, but it was too late. Martha had cottoned on to the fact that not everything had changed for the better in her sister's life and she wouldn't rest until she got to the bottom of the matter. So Joan took a deep breath and blurted it all out.

'Bill's still drinking more than he should and he's gambling. Got in way over his head this time if what I've been told is true.'

'Oh yeah, an' who was the kind person who gave you that information?' Martha's voice was full of sarcasm.

'Well, if you must know it was Mabel Richards, and I believe her, Martha. Not that I want to, but I think she has got her facts straight and she sounded very convincing to me.'

Martha leant forward and looked quizzically at her. 'Mabel Richards? Ain't 'eard tell of 'er for some time, let alone seen 'er. She moved down to Tooting last I 'eard an' at the time there was more than a few of us remarked we'd 'ave t' buy the bloody local paper now she wasn't around to pass all the gossip on. Try telling me what she's told yer and see what my feelings are. Not that either of us should really be surprised. Like you say, if my Sid and my boys didn't keep a check on your Bill there's no way he would still be working at that brewery.'

Martha was like a dog with a bone. She wouldn't let it go until she'd got some answers. Sighing again, Joan sat on the edge of her chair and began.

'You know where the back end of Tooting Market comes out in Totterdown Street?'

Martha nodded her head, showing she was all ears.

'It appears Mabel's got herself a job there, on the very last stall, which faces the roadway. Greengrocery and fruit is mainly what they sell. Anyway, she gets to see everyone who comes and goes or is just passing, an' you know what? They've opened a club upstairs over the top of the market.'

'Oh, fer Christ's sake get t' the point, Joan,' Martha moaned. 'The way you're going on we'll both be 'ere t' the middle of next week.'

'It's not only a drinking club, it's a gambling club as well.'

The bitterness in her sister's voice was like a red rag to a bull where Martha was concerned. 'You don't 'ave t' say any more. I can guess. That's where your Bill 'as been spending his afternoons, isn't it?'

'Got it in one,' Joan muttered.

'You said he's over his 'ead in debt. Did he tell you that himself?'

'As if he would! Mabel Richards said she heard the Riley brothers talking an' everyone knows you don't mess with that lot.'

''Ave yer asked Bill about it?'

'Not likely. I do my best never t' wind him up. I just listen, if ever he talks to me, which is not very often. But how he's going t' get out of this mess God only knows.' Joan's voice was low with fright.

Martha shook her head impatiently. 'That's his worry not yours. Your 'usband is a stupid ignorant fool an' he'll never change. Leave him t' get on with whatever mess he's in. After all, it's of his own making.'

'I know, but for all he's no good I don't want to see him really hurt. Those Riley brothers won't stop at a warning if he owes them a packet.'

Martha got to her feet and hugged her. 'Come on, cheer up. I'll put the kettle on an' we'll 'ave another cup of tea and a lump of hot bread pudding, 'ow does that sound?'

'Well, if it tastes as good as it smells I'm all for it.'

Martha was halfway to the scullery when she stopped and turned to face her sister. Her shoulders were heaving and her face was creased up with laughter.

'What the hell has tickled you?' Joan asked, sounding bewildered.

It was a job for Martha to get the words out but eventually she said, 'Don't know what we're doing worrying ourselves over your Bill. The devil takes care of his own, an' come t' think of it, if Bill Baldwin fell down a sewage drain he'd come up smelling of roses.' Martha let out a hearty chuckle and Joan couldn't help herself. She joined her.

Chapter Four

MARTHA STOOD AT THE FRONT DOOR and could not believe what she was hearing. Joan was screaming and shouting as if all hell had been let loose. Joan, the quiet one, the one who looked after her mother-in-law day and night and was never heard to grumble, the one who did all the cleaning and cooking and loads of washing and would bend over backwards to keep the peace.

Martha put her hand over her face to smother her smiles. If she was shocked she'd have loved to see her brother-in-law's face. Wondered how he was feeling knowing the worm had turned at last. She waited a few seconds before coughing loudly as she went down the passage and walking into the kitchen with a big smile on her face.

''Allo, everyone. Everything all right?'

Joan was white-faced with anger as she pointed her finger at her husband. 'He hit his mother! Can you believe it, Martha? He actually struck his mother, an' when I tried to reason with him he slapped me one and then kicked me.'

'You asked for it, you lying cow. You said you've got no money and I know for a fact you're lying through yer teeth.' Bill was red-faced and roaring with temper as he clenched his fist and stepped towards Joan.

Martha got between them. She was worried now. Her sister was not normally an aggressive person and in many ways that was more than half the trouble. She had let Bill get away with far too much. Allowed him to see that she was frightened of him. Whatever had set her off today it must have been serious and Martha would bet her last penny her sister was in the right.

Joan pushed herself past the pair of them and leant over the single bed where Granny Baldwin was lying. The poor old soul's face was so white she looked deathly. Her eyes were closed and there was a trickle of dark blood running down the side of her face.

'Oh, you didn't deserve that, you poor darling.' Joan was dabbing at the blood with a piece of white rag and she was nearly crying with frustration and anger.

'Oh, going to put on a show for yer sister now, are we?' Bill shouted. 'Playing for her sympathy? Well I'll tell yer this much, I've 'ad it up to my back teeth with the bloody pair of yer. You're a mean pair of bitches, you and me mother; all you do is make my life a misery. And you coming 'ere don't 'elp, Martha. If it weren't for your heavy-handed mob my life would be a damn sight more simple. Always were a nosy lot, you Browns.'

With an effort, Martha held her tongue between her teeth as she watched Bill shrug himself into his coat and storm out of the room. She didn't really need to ask what had started this shemozzle: the smell coming from the old lady's bed said it all.

'Take a few deep breaths, Joan, an' calm down,' Martha pleaded. 'I'll put the kettle on, get a nice bowl of hot water while you take Gran's nightie off, and between us we'll give her a good wash and a nice clean bed.'

'Ah, thanks, Martha, but you don't have to do it. I can manage,' said Joan, her voice still trembling.

'I know I don't *have* to, but I'm going to. I'm just glad I came round this morning. The way you were going on you might have done your old man a real mischief.'

'You're dead right, sis. I don't think I've ever felt so mad in my life before. Fancy, a son hitting his own mother! Bad enough if she were up and about on her own two legs, but lying there utterly defenceless— Only a spineless git like Bill would do such a thing.'

'Wanting money, was he?'

'Isn't he always?'

Martha nodded and they both sighed.

'Well, let's get cracking.' Joan took hold of her mother-in-law's hand. It felt very cold and lifeless. 'Mam, my sister Martha is here and between us we are going to clean you up and make you nice and warm and comfortable.'

Gwen Baldwin opened her eyes slowly, as if to lift her lids was too much effort. 'Thanks, Joan, luv,' she said weakly. She attempted to touch her daughter-in-law's face, but she was too exhausted and her hand dropped limply back down on to the bed.

The two sisters worked well together. They tenderly washed her from head to toe, powdered her bottom and slipped a clean nightdress over her head. Each guided a thin bony arm into a sleeve. Lastly, they gently sponged her thin white hair and softly ran a comb through it. At last, when a piece of white lint and a plaster covered the gash on her forehead and she was propped up by three pillows covered with snow-white cases, Joan whispered, 'Here's the final touch, Mum.' Showing her a bottle of Yardley's lavender water, she dabbed a spot of the scent behind each of Gwen's ears.

'Ah.' The old lady sighed deeply as her head rested back. 'That feels so lovely. Yer a good girl, Joan.' She paused, as if talking was too much of an exertion, but after a minute or two had passed she roused herself. 'Joan, when I go don't stay with my son. You deserve a much better life.'

Joan felt quite stunned, and she had to control her feelings before she was able to say, 'You're not going anywhere yet, and neither am I. I'm staying here and I shall look after you.' Tears rolled silently down her cheeks as she leaned forward and kissed her mother-in-law's forehead. 'Go to sleep now. I'll have a nice bowl of soup ready for when you wake up.'

Gwen Baldwin did wake up and she did manage to eat some of the soup which Joan had made. She also lived another three days.

It was the very early hours of the morning. It had not been a peaceful night. Joan had called the doctor the previous evening. He had been very sympathetic but as Joan had gone to the front door with him he had shaken his head and held her hand for longer than was necessary before saying, 'I know it is sad, but the poor woman has no fight left in her. She is very much weaker than when I last saw her.'

Joan had sat the rest of the night beside her bed and in the very early hours of the morning, when she saw Gwen stir, she asked if she fancied a cup of tea. Gwen struggled to sit up. 'No thank you, Joan dear, you've done enough for me. Nobody could have done more,' she said.

Her voice was so clear and so strong that Joan was startled. She caught her in her arms as she fell back. Gwen's eyes were wide open as she looked at her daughter-in-law. A loving smile briefly came to her lips and her bony hand came up and stroked Joan's cheek. She half smiled; sighed heavily.

And then she was still.

By the time Bill Baldwin returned from his shift at the brewery, he found his wife and sister-in-law just putting the finishing touches to laying his mother out.

'Yer mum died peacefully,' Martha told him.

He drew in his breath sharply and stared at her, then looked across the room to where his wife was kneeling beside his mother's bed. Joan raised her head and said quietly, 'I am so sorry you weren't here, Bill.' The look she gave him was full of sadness and her shoulders drooped.

'Oh my God!' he exclaimed as he took off his coat and threw it on to a chair. 'We ain't got t' live fer days now with nothing but gloom an' doom, 'ave we?' When neither his wife nor her sister answered he said, 'Why don't yer stop being a pair of hypocrites? She's a darn sight better off dead than lying there all day, ain't she? At least with 'er out of the way we might manage t' have a decent Christmas. By the way, 'ave yer looked for 'er insurance policy? I know she 'ad one an' all I hope is that it will pay out enough t' bury her.'

Joan was up and on her feet. Sadness, for the moment, had been swept away and she was seething with anger. Martha got in first. Shaking her head in disbelief she said, 'You're something else, you are, Bill. Your own mother is lying there an' you can't be bothered to cross the room and even look at her.'

'Leave him be, Martha. He's a cold-blooded sod. Never has had a decent bone in his body but I never realised until now just how callous he can be.'

'I don't 'ave t' take all this hassle from you two,' he bellowed, as his attitude changed and became threatening.

It was at that moment that a discreet cough was heard and a cautious voice called out, 'The door was open. Is it all right to come in?'

Joan had asked a neighbour to go for the local undertaker and he could not have arrived at a more opportune moment. He and his men went about the grave task of preparing to take the body of Gwen Baldwin to their chapel of rest, and her son sussed out that it was a good moment for him to

34

scarper. Joan and Martha were left to surmise what evil they might have done to Bill if there had been no intervention.

'Perhaps it is just as well that Bill took himself off,' Joan said tersely when she and her sister were finally alone. They had both collapsed on to what had been Gwen's bed, each quietly crying, whether from sadness or temper they couldn't have said at that moment.

'Yer can't believe that 'ard-hearted bastard, can yer?' Martha muttered.

Joan sighed deeply. 'I really could have killed him today. I didn't realise how much I've come to hate him. When Gran's funeral is over I am going to get away from this place and from him. There must be more to life than this.'

Martha couldn't answer her. There was nothing to add.

Joan had spoken the truth.

Chapter Five

MARTHA LOOKED AROUND her sister's neat living room and said admiringly, 'My, you must 'ave worked yer socks off. Made quite a difference, ain't yer?'

'Well, without Gran's bed it's given us a lot more room.' Joan sounded funny and Martha moved nearer and looked at her hard. She gasped, then stood white-faced and silent. It was only a few moments before she felt her temper rise and her face burn with rage.

'How the hell? When? Why?' Her questions poured out.

'Please, Martha, leave it. Go and put the kettle on and we'll have a cup of tea.'

'Plenty of time for tea later.' Martha's voice was trembling with anger. 'Sit down and tell me what 'appened 'cos I ain't moving from this spot till I get some answers.'

Joan stood still like a statue against the wall. Her eyebrow had been split open, and there was dark bruising and a huge discoloured patch that ran from below her ear to her jawline. Martha couldn't find words to say. That bugger must have given her a couple of really hard punches.

The next thing Joan was aware of was her sister pulling her across the room and pressing her down into an armchair.

'I'm going t' make that tea. I brought some doughnuts with me and when we've had that I'm off t' the chemist to see what he thinks we should put on your face.' Martha knew she was prattling, but the sight of her sister just sitting there utterly listless was heartbreaking. She walked through to the scullery and went through the motions of filling the kettle, lighting the gas and making a pot of tea.

Her mind was in a turmoil. If her bloody brother-in-law were here now she'd throw the whole kettle of boiling water over him and stand and watch as it scalded him. Only a bully would attack a defenceless woman. But why in the name of God did Joan never retaliate? *If he went for someone the likes of me it would be a different story. Christ knows he'd only ever do it the once. He'd never get a second chance.* Why was there so much difference between herself and Joan? Was it because Joan had been in service, learnt to live with the nobs? Surely not. Maybe the men in those big houses were gentlemen but they were still human beings so doubtless they lost their tempers sometimes. Did ladylike women learn to take it in silence? *God knows!* She answered her own question. Whatever, the kind of life Joan was leading couldn't be allowed to go on.

As Martha carried the tea tray through, her thoughts were muddled and fearful. Someday something terrible would happen. It was quite possible that blighter might end up killing Joan. It crossed her mind that if that happened there would be total disaster. The whole family would get involved. It would be the end of Bill Baldwin, that's for sure.

Joan only nibbled at her doughnut but she gratefully drank her cup of tea. Martha hesitated to ask questions but the need to know was great. Joan looked a shadow of her normal self and as she placed her cup down on the saucer Martha could see that her hands were shaking.

'What started him off this time, Joan?'

Joan sighed. 'What does it ever take?'

Martha drained her cup and kept silent, knowing Joan would tell her in her own good time.

A loud knocking on the door made both of them jump with fright. The look that passed between them was dreadful and the expression on Joan's face told Martha that she was terrified.

'Who do you think it is?'

'How do I know, Martha? It could be anyone. But one thing's for sure – they'll be after Bill for money, 'cos he owes left right and centre.'

The loud knocking was repeated.

'Come on, I'll come to the door with you.'

Opening the front door, Joan breathed a sigh of relief on seeing not more heavy-set thugs after her husband, but the owner of the funeral parlour. He had removed his tall hat and was twirling it nervously between his hands. However, his voice was firm as he said, 'Good morning, Mrs Baldwin. I should like a word with your husband if it is convenient, please.'

His tone of voice might have sounded firm but somehow he looked nervous as he stared at the two women standing side by side.

'I'm afraid he's not in,' Joan answered. It was just as she had thought. He might not be one of the great brutes who were after Bill for gambling debts and what have you, but he was still someone to whom Bill owed money. It wasn't fair. While she had been sitting at home worrying herself sick, he had been spending his mother's insurance money. Nevertheless, her conscience was bothering her. After all, this gentleman and the men who had acted as pall-bearers had given her mother-in-law a very respectable send-off, and he was entitled to have his fee paid. 'Has he not been in to your office to see you?' she asked timidly.

The poor man suddenly looked extremely embarrassed. Perhaps it was the sight of Joan's swollen, bruised face. He shook his head. 'No, I'm afraid he hasn't.'

She sighed then, a long weary sigh. 'I am sorry. I will talk to my husband as soon as he comes home and I will do my best to settle our account with you before the week is out.'

'I would be more than obliged, Mrs Baldwin.'

The two sisters watched as the somberly dressed gentleman walked away from the house. Back in the kitchen, Martha shook her head impatiently. 'Are you going to tell me what's going on?'

'I just don't understand how my Bill could act the way he is.'

The bitterness in her older sister's voice made Martha want to shake her, and she turned on her.

'You're covering up for Bill each and every way and what thanks 'ave yer got? All I can see is that he's given you a bloody good hiding and still you sit there and take it. The sad thing is, he's not worth it. All he's ever done is bully you an' cause yer heartache.'

'I know, I know,' Joan murmured, and Martha was amazed to see her eyes brim with tears. This was all she needed. She so much wanted to help her sister and yet at this moment she felt utterly useless.

'I suppose you're still waiting on him 'and foot an' finger even though you're still his favourite punch bag.'

Even Joan had to smile at that. 'Since his mum died he's been ten times worse. Hasn't been near nor by me for the last two days and whenever I have set eyes on him he's always been the worse for drink. I'm terrified by the blokes that have been here looking for him. You wouldn't believe what rough types they are.'

'I wouldn't worry about him, Joan,' Martha said. 'Whatever they are after him for he's brought it all on himself, and he'll 'ave t' learn that there's a price t' be paid for everything.' She leaned across the table and squeezed her sister's arm in a reassuring way.

Joan shook her head. 'He's so downright deceitful. Never

wants to discuss anything with me. You want to know something, Martha? He's never let on to me how much the Prudential paid out on his mum's insurance. It couldn't have been bad – I came in when he had the cheque in his hand and his face was wreathed in smiles. Shoved it in his pocket quick enough and was out of that front door like greased lightning.'

Martha sighed. She'd only popped in for a cuppa, and the conversation was beginning to irritate her. She threw her sister a furious glance, and said harshly, 'Leave it out, Joan. You never expected anything different, did yer? You've wasted enough of yer life worrying over that rotter. You did all yer could and more in looking after his mother, but now's the time to start thinking about yerself and what *you* are going to do.'

'Easier said than done,' Joan snapped.

Martha looked at her and sniffed. 'I expect it will be 'ard, but yer won't know till yer try, will yer?'

Joan looked startled, for it was unlike Martha to be so unkind, but before she could answer the kitchen door was thrown open with such a crash that it bashed against the dresser and caused the china it held to rattle.

'Tongues still wagging?' asked Bill, glaring at both women with open hostility. 'Pity yer ain't got nothing better t' do.'

Joan shivered involuntarily. She could smell the drink on her husband's breath from across the room. 'I'll get you something t' eat,' she said nervously.

'You'll do a bit more than that,' he shouted. 'I've got a job t' go to, so move, yer lazy cow, and get me a clean shirt. And I'd like some boiling water 'cos I'm going t' have a strip wash and a shave.' He turned and outstared Martha. 'And unless you want t' stay and watch the show yer can sling yer hook right now. Yer spend more time in my 'ouse than yer do in yer own.'

He was shouting and crashing about with such violence

that Martha was afraid to leave her sister alone with him. 'You're a selfish pig, you know that, Bill Baldwin? You think of nobody but yer bloody self. *And* you're a bully. Take a good look at my sister's face. Proud of yerself, are yer?'

Bill snarled. 'Go 'ome, Martha, before I do something you'll be sorry for. I ain't in the mood for your preaching today.' He shoved her hard in the chest and she almost lost her balance. She clenched her fists and was about to retaliate when she saw her sister was quietly crying.

'All right.' Her voice was harsh with hatred. 'I'm going, but just you remember all of this is only lent. I'll 'ave my day with you, you see if I don't.'

'Shut yer mouth. An' if you ain't gone in two minutes, I'll bash the pair of yer.'

Knowing he meant what he said, Martha rose quickly to her feet. She'd have her day with this bully, she vowed, but now was not the time. Joan fetched her coat and held it for her and together they walked down the passage to the front door.

'You going t' be all right, love?

Joan half smiled and nodded her head. When Martha rumpled her hair and kissed her in her motherly fashion, Joan's thin arms went round Martha's neck and she nuzzled against her affectionately. 'Stop worrying about me.' She kissed her plump cheek. 'Thanks for always being there for me. I love you, Martha. Ever so much,' she whispered.

'I luv yer, too, Joan,' Martha answered, hugging her tightly. 'Think on what I said. I'll be back later when I've been to the chemist an' he's out of the way. Meanwhile you take care.'

'I will, I promise,' Joan said, watching until her sister stopped at the corner of the road and waved before she slowly closed the front door.

Joan cursed under her breath as she worked. She had laid

41

out clean underwear and a neatly ironed shirt on the double bed she shared with a man she had grown to dislike. From the top drawer of the chest of drawers she took out a pair of navy blue socks and a white handkerchief. Let him choose his own tie; whichever one she picked was bound to be wrong. Getting down on to her knees she pulled open the bottom drawer, which was twice the depth of the other five, and the minute her eyes rested on the two neat piles of jumpers and cardigans that lay side by side she felt tears prick at the back of her eyelids. Every article had been hand-knitted by Gwen Baldwin. Such intricate patterns! At the time of their making, when Gwen had been a lot younger and fitter, every stitch had probably been knitted with love. And how had that only son of hers repaid her? Certainly not with any show of appreciation. Martha was right. He hadn't got an ounce of love in him, except for himself.

She selected one of the heavier jumpers, for it was bitterly cold outside. During the previous night there had been a slight fall of snow followed by a really heavy frost. The pavements were slippery and the roads treacherous. Bill would have the luxury of a brazier with no lack of either coal or wood to burn but his duties did not permit him to sit by it all night. Whether or not he did was another matter. At least, since he'd bothered to come home today, she would send him off well wrapped up, with a good pile of sandwiches in his tin and a flask of hot tea which should see him through the night.

His overcoat was quite scruffy – even the edges of the sleeves were ragged – but apart from that he looked quite presentable as he settled his cap on his head, tucked his scarf round his neck, picked up the evening paper and the carrier bag which held what Joan had prepared for him and walked out of the door without so much as a goodbye, let alone a thank you. When he had gone, Joan stood stock still staring into space. She was a fool for putting up with the way he treated her. She needed no one to tell her that.

The sound of a faint, hollow voice came back to her, and she heard again the words her mother-in-law had said to her only a few days before she died. She remembered them so clearly.

'Don't stay with my son, Joan. You deserve better.'

Granny Baldwin had known a lot more about what went on than Bill gave her credit for, Joan thought. *She knew how unhappy I was.*

She gripped the edge of the table and closed her eyes. She shouldn't have to take this. She didn't feel that she could. There and then, she made a vow to herself that never again would she allow a man to use her, least of all a rotter like the man she had married.

Such high hopes she had had on her wedding day. If anyone had told her then that he would use his fists on her whenever he felt like it, keep her short of money and deny her children, she would never have believed them. But although she had never admitted it aloud before now, those three miscarriages hadn't come about naturally. He had had no respect for her at any time, and the months she had been pregnant had made no difference. If anything, he had treated her worse. She was the one who was out at five in the morning in all weathers, scubbing and polishing offices up in the West End, and ten to one Bill would still be lying in their warm bed when she came home at midday, expecting her to cook him a meal. And like a fool she always had.

Well, not any more. It was a dreadful thing to admit, but it was the truth: she had not only stopped loving her husband, she had come to loathe him.

She was going to have to leave him. Good. She was at least halfway towards making a decision. Then doubt crept in and she fell to wondering how she would manage on her own. What would she do? Where would she go? She didn't know, but at this moment she didn't care. She only knew beyond a shadow of doubt that very soon she was going to have to leave. If she stayed her life would not be worth living.

Later that night Bill Baldwin strolled across the cobbled brewery yard, a contented expression on his face. His luck had certainly changed for the better since the death of his mother. At least one good thing she had done for him: named him beneficiary of the few pounds there was to come from her long-term insurance policy. Two days running he'd had a good little earner. He'd won on the dogs at Wimbledon, and on the second day he had taken a chance on the gee-gees and placed a triple bet. It was a long shot, but it had paid off handsomely. He laughed to himself. Good job he'd used a betting shop in Wandsworth. If he'd placed the bet in the club at Tooting they'd never have paid out. They'd have hung on to his winnings against what he owed.

He hadn't given so much as half a thought to paying the undertakers for his mother's funeral, but there again he hadn't arranged for them to bury her. Joan had taken it upon herself to see to everything. Let her pay them. Even the collection the neighbours had contributed to, Joan had hung on to. She'd used part of that money to put flowers on the altar in the church so his mum's coffin could be near them. Did you ever hear of anything so bloody daft in all yer life? When you're dead you're dead. You can't see and you certainly can't smell. So why waste the money? According to him, he'd done what most men would have done. Had a drop of good whisky, toasted the old gal and hoped she'd gone to that wonderful heaven she was always talking about.

His thoughts stopped wandering when he reached the horses tethered in their stalls. He petted his favourite, big old Dobby, then continued along the line, stroking, petting and holding a knob of sugar in the flat palm of his hand for each of them. He enjoyed watching their big wet mouths and the saliva which dribbled from their long tongues because of their eager anticipation. These carthorses had become his best friends. He felt different when he was with these huge creatures and he felt it to be a privilege to have been put in charge of them. He took his time in grooming them, almost two hours. Not that he didn't stop every so often to make a roll-up and have a smoke, and of course every now and again he needed a swig from the half-bottle of Johnnie Walker which he had in his pocket.

In spite of the cold outside he was sweating and felt he needed a breath of fresh air. Walking to the end of the stables, he used all his strength to open the heavy wooden door a few inches. It was pitch dark and bitterly cold, and the strong wind was biting. He put one foot outside and heard the crackle as his heavy boot hit the ice on the frozen cobbles.

'Blow that for a lark,' he muttered, heaving hard with his shoulder in order to get the door closed again. 'I'm better off staying in here.'

He knew full well he should check on the warehouse, but more than likely his brazier would have burnt out, and in any case he didn't care. He'd had the presence of mind to bring his carrier bag over to the stables with him. He'd snuggle down between two bales of hay, eat the grub Joan had put up for him, have a cup of tea with maybe a drop of the hard stuff in it and read his paper, and he would be set for the night.

The whisky bottle lay empty at his side and Bill Baldwin was too far gone to notice the little whirls of smoke that were gathering speed as he slept. It was only when the horses began to whinny and stamp their great hoofs that he came to and smelt it. He sniffed hard, struggled to his feet and to his horror saw smoke wafting up towards the rafters. He caught his breath, suddenly aware of the heat. The dry straw on each side of him was smouldering and he crawled away to get clear.

It was pure instinct that made him run towards the main door. Fear was making him tremble as he began tugging at the latch. This way, that way. No matter which way he tried to wrench it, it would not budge. He swung round to go back and was met by the tremendous heat. Turning again, he continued his fumbling efforts to open the door and finally managed it.

Should he run? Whatever, he couldn't save all of the horses, but he'd have to try and big Dobby had to be first. At the far end of the stables bales of hay and bags of winter feed were stacked one on top of the other on wooden platforms. By now they were blazing furiously, one by one catching light in rapid succession.

Thank God Dobby was the nearest to the door. It seemed to Bill to take for ever to open his stall door, untie the rope which was restraining him and lead him towards the exit.

'Go, go, run,' he screamed, slapping Dobby hard on the rump. For a moment he stayed in the yard, yelling, 'Fire! Fire! Help, someone!'

For a split second he had the urge to run himself. His good sense said he must try to get the other horses out, but instinct was urging him to save himself. For a moment he hesitated, staring into the stables. He was scared stiff but for once he told himself he had no choice.

The next horse whinnied loudly and pranced like a mad thing, and Bill suffered a painful kick in the shin from the horse's hoof as he tried to free him. Bill wanted to drop where he stood. The heavy smoke was choking him, and his vision was blurred because his eyes were watering. With the rope freed he slapped the second horse's rump really hard and breathed a sigh of relief as it galloped towards the fresh air.

46

So far it was only the end of the building where Bill had been sleeping that was going up in flames, but sparks and embers were flying all over the place and the billowing smoke was getting more dense by the minute. He had to try to get at least one more horse out. He knew it would be the last no matter how hard he tried. He'd got the main door wide open but that had only made matters worse for the terrific wind coming in now was fanning the flames. Suddenly the heat was unbearable and the smoke overpowering. He could hear voices yelling, the clanging of the bells on the fire engines. Thank God! He spluttered. He was coughing harshly and could barely see through the thick smoke. But he made himself go forward. He flinched as the heat of the bolt on the third stall seared his hand but he held on, and managed to slide it open. The animal was terrified, wouldn't come forward, was not whinnying but whimpering plaintively. Bill got behind it and beat on its flank. He sighed thankfully when at last the horse ran like a bat out of hell through the smoke and out through the open door. He staggered after it. He could do no more.

At that moment one of the high platforms sagged, disintegrated and collapsed. Bill looked up in horror. Bales of burning hay were falling haphazardly. He saw one coming, bent over double and covered his face with his hands. One of the flaming bales landed on top of Bill's back, knocking him to the ground. The fire immediately ignited his clothes and his flesh began to burn. Heaving, twisting and kicking, he struggled hard to throw off the flaming bale. Pain tore through him. Choking on the smoke he had inhaled, he wanted to scream but no sound came. All he felt was excruciating pain, and then, mercifully, he lost consciousness.

Joan sat with Martha and Sid and their two sons, Lenny and Bernie. She could not have faced the inquest on her own. A neighbour had kindly suggested that young Rosie remain at home with her and her children.

The coroner was a well-dressed, handsome, smooth-talking man who, on the surface, seemed cordial enough. Yet for reasons she could not fathom Joan had disliked him from the moment he opened the proceedings. Mr Grant, General Manager of Young's Brewery, was the only person to be questioned.

The coroner started by reading from the typed report he had been handed by the chief fire brigade officer, who had gathered evidence from the team of fire-fighters who had attended the blaze at the brewery.

'I'm given to understand that the bales of hay were already smouldering when Mr Baldwin opened the main door of the stables, and that the draught from the door obviously fanned the flames. May we ask your opinion as to how you think the fire was started?'

Mr Grant cleared his throat. His face was bright red and he could feel the sweat running from his armpits. His manner was very stern. 'Well, sir, I could hazard a guess.'

The coroner leant forward and stared at Mr Grant. 'Speak up, then. You've obviously given this matter some thought.'

Mr Grant scowled. 'Mr Baldwin, the man I took on as night watchman, had himself too much to drink, lit a cigarette, fell asleep and did not notice that the cigarette had fallen from his lips whilst still alight. The bales of hay were very dry; it would only have taken a spark to set . . .' He couldn't continue.

The coroner sighed, and took a sip from the glass of water that had been placed on the table in front of him. Then he looked Mr Grant squarely in the eye. 'Should Mr Baldwin have been in the stables in the early hours of the morning?'

Mr Grant hesitated. He knew damn well that Baldwin had caused that fire. In his mind he had been over and over the facts for hours on end. He felt he could say a great deal but he had to be cautious when voicing his opinion. He nervously cleared his throat again. 'No, sir, he should have been back at the warehouse. But, well, sir, if there was one thing that Mr Baldwin did exceptionally well it was seeing to the grooming of the horses. He took his time over them, liked being with them. Thinking back, it was a terrible night, and the stables would have been . . .' He had been about to say the warmest place to be, but decided it would not have been an appropriate turn of phrase.

The coroner looked thoughtful, reflecting on Grant's words. Then he said, 'Sadly, what you're saying is along the lines of the chief fire brigade officer's report.'

Mr Grant composed himself. Quietly, he asked if he might add something to what he had already said. The coroner drew himself up straight and looked very pompous.

'If you think it is relevant.'

Mr Grant did not shirk what he considered to be his duty to the dead man. He cleared his throat and spoke loudly. 'Mr Baldwin might have been a lot of things but it should be remembered that he stayed there in those stables and freed three horses. Because of that he lost his own life.'

Joan clutched Martha's hand. Tears were streaming down her cheeks. Very quietly, she said, 'Nice, that at the end somebody had something good to say about him, isn't it?'

Martha sighed as she nodded her head. Everything else was better left unsaid.

Chapter Six

MARCH 1927

JOAN WAS SITTING STARING into the fire, doing her best to convince herself that she was feeling better and knowing that she should be grateful to her sister and brother-in-law for having taken her into their home, and for all their kindness. But no matter how hard she tried she didn't seem able to come to terms with all that had happened during the past miserable months. She had had to give up her house because she had no means of keeping up with the rent, yet only last night Sid had told her that she would feel better given time, that she must put the past behind her because things could only get better for her. Then he had said that the only road open to her was forward.

Forward to where? It was a question she had asked herself over and over again. She hadn't a penny to her name, and nowhere to go.

It had stayed freezing all through January, and February too. Biting winds and even a week of snow. Try as she might, Joan couldn't feel optimistic about the future. She helped Martha with the housework, even did some of the cooking, but whatever she attempted held little interest. Even books could not hold her attention for long. The days dragged by and the hands on the clock seemed to move more slowly than usual. She couldn't be a burden on Martha and Sid for much longer.

'Can Auntie Joan stay here with us for ever?'

Oh, dear God. Joan wished young Rosie hadn't asked that question. Worse still, she saw a flicker of uncertainty in her sister's eyes.

'Come an' sit by me an' give yer old mum a cuddle,' Martha patted the horsehair sofa, 'and you, me and yer auntie'll 'ave a little talk.'

Rosie was as bright as a button. She might be only thirteen years old but there wasn't much going on that she missed. Joan's heart plummeted. She knew it wasn't a case of wearing out her welcome: there just wasn't room for her to stay in this house for much longer. Sid and Martha had Lenny and Bernie besides young Rosie to consider. Yes, there were three bedrooms, but one was only a boxroom, just about big enough to take a single bed, and it was normally used as Rose's bedroom. The two lads were grown men now but they still shared a room. Since Sid had been so kind-hearted and insisted that Joan stay with them until she got herself sorted, Rose had slept on a truckle bed in her parents' room and Joan had been occupying the boxroom. With no bathroom it was a scramble every morning for everyone to get washed and the men to shave, all at the stone sink in the scullery. On top of all that there wasn't enough money coming into the house to enable her sister to go on feeding her for ever. Deep down Joan knew she should have shifted herself a while ago, but her feelings were still mixed up and being with her family these last weeks had been so comforting.

Martha did her best to spell things out kindly to her daughter. 'Poor Auntie Joan wasn't feeling too well, what with one thing an' another, as you well know. Now, though, she's gonna pick herself up, get a nice job and start to live

51

her own life. She'll never be far away and you'll see ever such a lot of her still. When she gets a little flat or whatever, you'll even be able to go an' stay with her.'

'Is that true, Auntie Joan? Will I be able to stay with you? 'Cos otherwise you'll be ever so lonely.'

Joan forced herself to smile reassuringly. She didn't want to make any promises she wouldn't be able to keep. 'If it works out the way your mother says it will I'll buy a new bed just for you so you can stay whenever your dad says you may.'

Rosie broke free from her mother's arm, which was round her shoulders, and sat up straight. 'What do you mean *if* it works out? Why won't it?'

Martha gave her sister a tense look but Joan had her answer ready. 'I can't say what will happen for certain. You see, pet, it's hard for women to get work. Before I was married to your Uncle Bill I worked in a great big house where they had servants and I might have to consider doing something like that again.'

'Were you happy there?' Young Rosie's face was puckered with concern.

'Oh, Rosie, leave yer poor aunt alone,' her mother implored.

'It's all right, Martha.' Joan smiled. 'She's always been inquisitive, and that's a good thing. It broadens a child's mind.'

'I'm not a child. I'll be able to leave school next year,' Rosie protested loudly. 'But please, Auntie, tell me what you had t' do in the big house.'

'I'm going to put the kettle on an' leave you two to it,' Martha said, struggling to her feet.

Joan moved to sit in the place that Martha had quit and Rosie snuggled up to her. Rosie was the light of Joan's life. How often had she wished she had been able to have a little girl like her. Too late now. She would soon be forty-one.

Jesus, it didn't bear thinking about. Who in God's name was likely to offer her a job?

'Come on, Auntie, tell me some things before Mum comes back with the tea, 'cos she'll only grumble if I ask you a load of questions.'

Joan looked down at her niece. She was, as her father was fond of saying, 'as pretty as a picture', with her slender frame, golden-fair hair and skin that could be described as peaches and cream. And as for those wide blue eyes . . . There would come a time when this young lady would break a lot of young men's hearts.

'The family I worked for were very nice,' Joan began, 'but I hated every moment when I first went to work there. The place was so big and scary, and there was always so much to do.'

'Such as?' Rosie interrupted.

Joan laughed. 'Mountains of washing up for a start. Huge great saucepans to scrub and baking tins to clean and God help you if Cook found one that didn't shine.'

She paused, letting her mind wander back over the years.

'I had to be downstairs every morning at a quarter to six. Rake the fire out first then go down the steep stairs into the cellar and make sure the coal scuttles were full. That wasn't too bad, though your aprons did get dirty shovelling the coal. I was supposed to pin a clean sack round my waist but more often than not I forgot. It was the lugging of the filled coal scuttles back up the stairs that used to almost break my back.'

'That must 'ave been 'orrible,' Rosie murmured. Then, sounding indignant, she asked, 'What about the men that worked there? Weren't they supposed to do jobs like that?' Her solemn blue eyes regarded her aunt steadily as she waited to hear her reply.

Joan's voice was strong but cold as she said, 'The only men employed inside the house were the butler and . . .'

She laughed. 'Two cellar men, but before you ask they never went near the coal cellars. They were employed to take care of the wine cellars, which were vastly different. Outside of the house there were a number of male employees, men and boys.'

'And what did they do?'

'Some were grooms, who looked after the horses.' That thought brought Bill's untimely death to mind and she struggled for a moment before going on. 'Some were stable lads; they got all the dirty jobs. Others were known as groundsmen.'

'What does groundsmen mean?' inquisitive Rosie cut in again.

Joan chuckled. 'Posh word for the gardeners.'

Rosie giggled. 'You like posh words, don't yer, Auntie?'

'It's what you get used to. It's a very long time ago that I lived like that, and anyway I think that the way we speak is all to do with surroundings. And before you ask, I mean that the people one lives with, the community, in all different parts of the country have their own way of talking. If you stay long enough in one place you are bound to pick up a certain amount. On the other hand I do think that you never lose the accent from the place where you were born and brought up.'

'I know what yer mean, Auntie Joan. Sometimes you let slip an' talk like me mum. An' there's a boy in my class who is a right laugh. When he first came to London none of us understood 'alf of what he was saying and even now if we make faces at him he goes all daft like an' says, "Cows chew grass, clouds bring rain, price of milk's gone up again."'

'I can see you like this boy,' said Joan.

'You've got funny eyesight, then,' said Rosie. 'But get on with telling me what you had t' do once yer'd got the fires alight.'

'Help Cook get everyone's breakfast, and once that was

over there was tons of vegetables to scrape, peel and chop. Then came polishing and dusting, then beds had to be made and chamber pots emptied.'

Rosie made a terrible face. 'Eeh, you didn't really have to empty other people's pots, did yer?'

'I certainly did. But the worst thing was the times the staff had to go up and down the great staircase. I'd be rich if I had ten shillings for every time I've dragged myself up those stairs, and loaded like a donkey most times.'

'Didn't you get any nice jobs? Not even one?'

Joan didn't have to stop and think. She let her mind wander back again and she dreamily said, 'Afternoon tea was lovely. I had to change my working uniform for a black dress, a white frilly apron and a white mobcap before I could go into the drawing room and serve the tea. Tiny sandwiches with all the crusts cut off the bread. Scones and strawberry jam, cake stands that had four and sometimes five tiers which held every assortment of dainty cakes and slices of the richest fruit cake you could imagine.'

'What's a drawing room?'

'A very posh front room.' Joan giggled at the thought and that set Rosie off.

'I thought you meant people had paper and coloured pencils and drew pictures in a special room.'

'Oh, Rosie, I love you.' Joan tickled her and when she wriggled she kissed the top of her head.

'Why did you stay there if it was so bad?' Rosie's bright blue eyes were sparkling with merriment. 'I mean, I do feel sorry that you had to work so hard, but couldn't you 'ave come 'ome t' yer mum?'

Joan shook her head. 'It wasn't like that in those days. My mother had two girls, your mother and me. I was the eldest and I had to be sent into service. We had three brothers, one, your Uncle Tom, who is in the Merchant Navy, I'm sure you remember him – it's not so long ago that he came home. He's never married. Another brother died when he was only five years old and the last one died in a pit accident.'

'I know about that uncle. Dad told me. He worked down the coal mines in Kent, didn't he?'

Joan nodded her head and there was a pause before Rosie came up with her next question.

'You said you hated it when you first went into service. Does that mean that later on you got to like it?'

'That's quite right, Rosie. Thinking about it I'm very grateful that my mother sent me away into service. I learnt so much, especially after I got promotion, and got given a very nice little bedroom all to myself. At first there was four girls sleeping in one attic room.'

Rosie looked baffled for a moment. Then she laughed and it was a joy to hear her and watch as she tossed strands of her long blonde hair back from her face. 'What was the best thing you learnt?'

Joan thought hard for a moment. 'Being taught to sew, I think. I loved it. Took to it like a duck to water, and you know what, Rosie? You know my old sewing machine that is in your dad's shed at the moment?'

Rose nodded her head.

'Well, that is the machine that I first learnt on, and when I left to get married to your Uncle Bill, Mr and Mrs Morley, my employers, gave it to me as a wedding present.'

Rosie had the fidgets. She spun round until she was able to look up into her aunt's face. 'I know some more things you learnt by working in that big house.'

'Do you now? Well, let's hear them.'

'I already told yer. You talk different.'

'Do I? Different in what way?'

'You don't talk like what we do. Mum an' Dad an' Lenny an' Bernie, we all say ain't. You don't. My teacher at school is always telling us that there isn't any such word as ain't

56

'cos it ain't in the dictionary. And you dress different an' all, an' another thing, you always lay the table nice.'

Joan was saved from having to comment because Martha was pushing the door open with her hip. Joan nudged Rosie out of the way, got to her feet and cleared a space on the table for the heavy tray that her sister was carrying.

'Well, 'ave yer had yer natter?' Martha grinned at the pair of them.

'Yeah, we 'ave. Auntie Joan learnt to talk posh 'cos of when she was in service,' Rosie answered, her voice riddled with laughter. Then she looked at the laden tray and asked, 'What yer got t' eat, Mum?'

Martha whipped off the cloths that were covering two large plates. 'Victoria sponge, and I was gonna say rock cakes but perhaps I'd better think of another name. And seeing as we're going all posh you can move yerself, young lady, and go and fetch three small plates off the dresser, 'cos I ain't 'aving crumbs all over my best rug.'

Rosie and her aunt looked at each other. They each managed to keep a straight face, but when Martha looked at Rosie and asked, 'Well, are yer going for the plates or ain't yer?' they both had to smother their laughter. Fortunately, Martha had her back to them as she poured milk into the cups, and by the time she turned round again Joan had put her finger to her lips. Rosie went to fetch the plates without saying a word.

It rained solidly for the next two days and the horrible view of endless small grimy houses with a gigantic factory at the end of the road did nothing to make anyone feel cheerful, least of all Joan. But on Thursday morning the rain had stopped, and watery sunshine was doing its best to shine through the clouds. Joan had finished washing up the breakfast things and tidied the kitchen and scullery. Suddenly she made up her mind to walk to the Labour

Exchange and see if there were any jobs on offer which might be suitable for her. If she were going to get her own place to live she would have bills to pay besides buying food and other necessary commodities so she would need a decent wage. At this moment that seemed too much to ask for.

It was just after half-past ten when she stepped out into the street, looking businesslike in a navy blue straight skirt, the hem of which just reached her ankles. The knee-length jacket, made of the same heavy material, had a velvet collar and was nipped in at the waist, and her white blouse had a ruffled collar which stood high round her neck. All three articles she had made herself, albeit a very long time ago. She had also retrimmed the black felt hat she had worn for Bill's funeral, and she carried a small handbag. Her hands were warm and snug in hand-knitted white woollen gloves.

As she closed the gate her sister yelled, 'Good luck, gal.'

Joan knew she was certainly going to need it. Her thoughts were sombre as she walked and tried to weigh up her situation. On the plus side, she spoke well, could write a good hand and was intelligent if not well educated. Now for the minus side of things. Her clothes, although clean and well pressed, had seen a lot of wear and were hardly up to date. She looked down at her boots. Half an hour she'd spent polishing them, but the shine did not hide the fact that they were shabby and well worn. Looking as she did now she wasn't going to be offered the best of jobs if she was offered anything at all.

She was on a treadmill, and until she found a way of earning enough money to buy some decent clothes, or material to make them, she thought it highly unlikely that she would be able to get off it. She'd hit rock bottom and did not know which way to turn. Everyone had been so kind, but no one who lived around these parts had long pockets. Neighbours had given generously when Gwen Baldwin had died, and with a struggle and a bit of help Joan had managed to pay off the undertaker, for the old lady had been well liked and respected. The same could not be said of her son. Joan felt it was only because the local paper had made such a good story of the fact that Bill had lost his life because he had gone back into the burning stables and saved three horses that the owners of the brewery had paid for his quiet funeral.

She had reached the drab building that was known as the Labour Exchange. The inside walls were painted in two colours, the top half dark brown and the other half dark green, making the inside of the building no more welcoming than the outside. The far wall was divided into sections. A thin wooden partition between each booth allowed for some privacy.

Joan took a seat and soon cottoned on to the fact that whenever a clerk called out 'Next' a person went forward and everybody else moved up one seat in the row. She seemed to have been waiting for ages. Her hands felt sticky, and because she had washed her hair last night it was so soft it was falling loose from the pins she had used to put it up into what she had thought was a very neat long pleat. She took a minute or two to tuck up the stray strands beneath the rim of her hat. Her hair used to be her best feature. People thought her face was beautiful, and her brown hair with its golden glints framed it well. It was only these latter years, when her marriage had become so hard to cope with and she had had to manage alone with the failing health of her mother-in-law, that she had let herself go a bit. It wasn't laziness on her part. There just hadn't been the money to spend on herself, let alone have her hair done or buy new clothes.

What did she look like today? Passable, she supposed, but only just. She wondered if there were any lavatories in this place where she might go and tidy herself up, but she was afraid to ask.

'Next.' A nudge from the girl sitting next to her made Joan realise she was at the end of the line. She went forward and was surprised to be greeted with a smile from a sweet-faced young woman who looked about thirty. Joan gave her name and address and started to explain that she had come to enquire if there were any suitable vacancies on the books as she needed to find work.

'Whoa, not so fast,' the young woman cautioned. 'Is this your first application?'

'Yes. Yes, it is,' Joan stammered.

'In that case you have to see Mr Thompson. He will fill out a form with all your details.' Seeing the colour drain from Joan's face, she very quickly assured her, 'Mr Thompson is a very nice understanding gentleman.' She leant forward over the counter and whispered, 'He doesn't bite. Just go to the far end of the room. I'll let him know you are waiting and he will open the door for you.'

'Thank you,' Joan said, thinking what a kind, considerate person she was.

She was startled by the office she was led into. It was a lovely light room with just one big curtainless window, one enormous desk and two upright chairs, one standing in front of the desk and the second one behind it. She turned to look at the man who was closing the door behind her.

'I'm Mr Thompson,' he said, holding out his hand, 'and you are?'

Joan shook his hand and murmured, 'Mrs Baldwin.'

Mr Thompson was smartly dressed, aged about fifty, with stooped shoulders and a happy-looking face. He pointed to the nearest chair. 'Please sit down,' he said, going behind the desk and seating himself.

He was so courteous Joan forgot her appearance and her anxiety for a moment. He asked all the normal questions she had been expecting, and she began to relax and to feel extremely comfortable in his company. He told her how the

Exchange worked and that if they sent her after any position she would be given a green card to present to the employer. But he wasn't a know-all type, nor was he overly officious. He prompted her to speak about her own life, and why at her age she so badly needed to find work.

She told him how her husband and her mother-in-law had recently died. She even told him how she had nursed Gwen. Then there was the fact that she had had to give up her own house and was temporarily living with her sister and her brother-in-law.

'What kind of work have you done, say before you were married?' he asked.

'I was in service to a Mr and Mrs Morley.' She went on to tell him roughly what her duties had been.

The time flew by, and suddenly he looked very serious. 'So, what it boils down to, Mrs Baldwin, is that you need not only a job but somewhere to live.'

Joan's only thought was that Mr Thompson had summarised her situation very promptly. Mr Thompson, on the other hand, was afraid it would be a hard task to find a situation that would be suitable for this lady. As he continued to stare at her he guessed she was under-nourished. Her neck was thin, her face looked peaky, and the costume she was wearing was shabby. But he also saw something else: her lady-like attitude, the proud way she held her head, her soft manner of speaking. She had known better days, of that he was certain. Lately? Well, his guess would be a life of drudgery and a lot of grief. Grief that still showed in her beautiful brown eyes.

Reluctantly he rose to his feet and quietly said, 'I am sorry that at the moment we do not have anything suitable on our books. However, Mrs Baldwin, you may rest assured that I shall do my best to find a position that will be entirely suitable for you.'

Joan smiled grimly to herself as she pulled on her gloves.

61

'We shall keep you informed,' he said as he held the office door open for her.

I'll believe it when it happens, she almost replied, but stopped herself in time.

She walked the streets slowly, in no hurry to go back to what was her sister's home but not hers. She had no home of her own. Mr Thompson had been discreet and attentive, but would he be able to find her employment? As she knew only too well, life in general was full of broken promises.

Chapter Seven

JOAN WAS AMAZED. She was actually window-shopping in the beautiful royal town of Tunbridge Wells.

She had been working at Mulborough House for two months and this was her first full day off. The first four weeks she had been on trial and only allowed two half-days.

Mr Thompson had come up trumps. Three days after her visit to the Labour Exchange a postcard had arrived requesting her to call in to see him as soon as possible, and within two hours of receiving it she was once again seated in that bare office.

Mr Thompson returned her gaze, smiling broadly. 'You did not expect to be seeing me again quite so soon, did you?'

Staring at his open, friendly face, Joan took in his warm smile and the somewhat mischievous glint in his eyes. Her hands were trembling, he noticed, and with quick sympathy he said, 'I think we may have come up with a solution to many of your problems.'

For the life of her Joan didn't know what to say, so she nodded her head and waited for him to go on.

'The kind of position that would be suitable for you, Mrs

Baldwin, is very rare in this neighbourhood, as you well know. However, my colleagues have been very helpful and here on my desk I have the details of a vacancy for a housemaid. With your past experience I thought it might be worth your while to go for an interview. The house is in Kent, at no great distance from Maidstone and Canterbury, but the address I have been given is Tunbridge Wells. The whole area has quite a history. Did you know, for instance, that those born west of the Medway are called Kentish Men, while the inhabitants of the eastern part are known as Men of Kent?' He smiled, doing his best to ease the tension, but Joan did not react. He looked uncertain as he lowered his gaze and silently reread the papers that lay in front of him. He decided honesty was the best policy.

'The lady of the house had been made aware of your age. Nevertheless, she has agreed to grant you an interview.' Seeing Joan's downcast eyes, the drooping of her mouth and the sad expression that swept across her face, he hastened to add, 'You've nothing to lose by going to apply for the job. It isn't too long a journey, only about thirty-five miles from London.'

Joan was speechless, and the colour had gone from her cheeks.

Mr Thompson guessed straight away what was troubling this quiet lady. Quickly, he added, 'Of course, it is entirely up to you to decide as to whether or not you go for this interview, but I should tell you that all expenses will be paid by this Exchange. You would be given cash to get you to the railway station, and a travel warrant for your return journey.'

He recognised the relief on Joan's face, and knew that his insight had been right. She hadn't the money to pay the fare to Kent herself.

Her job description was that of housemaid and while she

would be the very first to admit that she had fallen on her feet, not everything about her new life was wonderful. But then she shouldn't expect it to be so, she often chided herself. Mrs Hamilton was a real lady and had freely admitted at Joan's interview that she had expected the applicant for the position to be a much younger person. Joan hadn't held it against her because that very doubt had been uppermost in her own mind since Mr Thompson had broached the subject. Then this gracious lady had thought hard for a moment and said, 'Shall we give each other a trial period? After all, you won't want to be climbing out of windows and scampering off to meet young men late at night, will you?' They had smiled together at the thought.

At first sight, Joan had been overawed by the dignified splendour of Mulborough House and had almost turned away. She stood at the foot of the wide front steps, sure she would never find the courage to walk up them and ring the shiny brass bell beside the huge front door.

While she was wondering what to do a young man came round the side of the house wearing a green baize apron, his shirt sleeves rolled up above his elbows. He smiled and raised a hand in greeting to Joan, which certainly helped to settle her nerves.

'Come on, miss. Don't look so troubled. I'll take you round the back. Not many other than the family use the front entrance.'

Joan had followed the lad through an archway and she'd gazed in surprise at the beautiful green lawns and flower beds that seemed to stretch for miles. She wondered how he knew what she was there for. It hadn't taken much thought for the reason to hit her.

She wasn't exactly dressed as a visitor might be.

June had come in with a heat wave. The sunshine was brilliant and the sky clear and blue, and the clothes she was wearing were hardly appropriate. She had no decent summer dresses, but when she had started out from Merton early that morning her navy blue suit had seemed to be passable. Now it felt hot and cumbersome.

She might have entered Mulborough House through the back door but she certainly had not been disappointed. Even the rooms below stairs were enormous and airy. And the welcome she had received from the cook had been so unexpected that all she could do was mumble her thanks. She had also been very impressed by the size of the kitchen and the massive, coal-burning range with its two ovens. In fact, since she had started working there she had been stunned by everything she saw. There had been new surprises each and every day.

Mrs Hamilton, the mistress of the house, was kindly but firm, but her husband's behaviour baffled Joan. Cook had told her that he just had not been the same since he had returned from the war in 1918. It seemed to Joan that all the spirit had been knocked out of the poor man, because he was given to quiet, withdrawn moods. He would often sit for hours, never moving, not answering anyone who spoke to him, staring vacantly into space like a lost child. At other times he would erupt into sudden almost uncontrollable anger over the simplest of things. Sometimes she wished she could grab hold of him and take him for a walk in the grounds. She was too small to cope with him. He was a huge man with a strong body and she wished it were possible to make his life somehow more worthwhile.

It was such a pity.

Of all the people who constantly came and went Joan felt the best friend she had made since coming to Mulborough House was the cook, Kathleen O'Leary. Round, fat and jolly, just as a cook should be. There was happiness in every line of her face. She was a kind person who saw only good in everyone, and a marvellous cook to boot. During what little free time they did have, and always while drinking a cup of

Kathleen's strong brew, Joan had learnt that the cook was fifty-six years old and had been a widow for the past twelve years.

Joan had been wandering along the Pantiles, an avenue of very smart and different kinds of shops, and now the smell of freshly ground coffee was tempting her to enter a very luxurious-looking tearoom. Before she had become housemaid to Mrs Hamilton the only coffee she had ever tasted came from a bottle. Fresh coffee was something she had quickly learnt to enjoy very much.

Yes, Joan suddenly decided, she was going to splash out and treat herself to an iced bun and a cup of coffee. So before her confidence faded she opened the door, smiled as she heard a bell tinkle and made her way to a corner table that was not only covered by a white linen cloth but had a delicate lace one draped three-cornerways on top. A glass vase that held a few brightly coloured and highly perfumed sweet peas had been placed in the centre.

She removed her gloves, and gave her order to a friendly waitress who appeared to be a few years older than herself. Considering her fellow servants at Mulborough House, she wondered whether Tunbridge Wells favoured older employees. Certainly the housekeeper, Miss Reid, was elderly, nearer sixty than fifty. Janet, who only worked part-time as a chambermaid when the spare rooms were occupied by guests, was about thirty-five. Mr Farrant, the butler, wore an impeccably cut suit when he was above stairs, which helped to hide his big belly, and even his bald head gave him an air of distinction, but as to his age she wouldn't like to hazard a guess. All she really knew about him was that he lived with his wife in a cottage in the grounds, although to Joan he never seemed to go home, for whatever job she was doing Mr Farrant was always nearby. The only two youngsters who were employed inside the house were the kitchen maid, sixteen-year-old Mabel, and seventeen-year-old John, whom she had met when she came for her interview. John seemed to spend most of his time cleaning shoes and boots or polishing silverware – and God knows there was enough silver in that household.

Joan was well aware of just how good her life was now. But for all that she had landed on her feet, there was always something missing: her sister and her family.

To begin with the nights had been awful. Having one's own bedroom was nice but when it was dark outside she could hear all the strange sounds of the country. She missed the noise of the traffic, missed knowing that she had good neighbours next door and friendly folk close by. She even felt the loss of hearing men singing on their way home when the pubs turned out. Mostly, though, tears stung the backs of her eyes when her thoughts were of her dear sister Martha, and young Rosie. Oh, God, how she missed that girl. *She'll be all grown by the time I get to see her again.* Joan sighed to herself as she sipped her coffee from the dainty bone-china cup.

All her toughness and determination to get on with her new life dissolved when her thoughts turned that way. She found it particularly hard when she was helping to serve a meal to a room full of people, all related, each a member of a close-knit family. Then she felt bleak and lonely. If only she had some relatives living nearby. During the first few weeks, alone in her room, she had often shed tears of despair, afraid that she would never stick it. But whenever she was tempted to quit and take herself back to London she made herself stop and think. What had she to go back to? Where would she live? How would she live? She certainly couldn't plant herself on Martha and Sid again, though the thought of those small rooms and the crowded table as they'd eaten together, laughing and chatting . . . it didn't pay to look back. She should count herself lucky and count her blessings, she often chided herself. Then she would think of the freshness of the home-grown vegetables, newly laid eggs and farm produce that everyone in Mulborough House took for granted. Martha's eyes would pop out of her head if she saw some of the meals that Kathleen O'Leary was able to turn out.

The waitress came back and with a friendly smile asked Joan if she would like her cup refilled. The waitress was wearing a black dress and a frilly white apron, much like the ones Joan wore of an afternoon in the big house, though she'd be the first to admit the uniform fitted this waitress far better than the dress she had been given fitted her. She'd give a lot to be able to buy some decent material and make her own. Several reasons stopped her. For one thing, since the wages were paid once a month, she'd only been paid twice. She got twenty-five shillings a week and all found, and the first five pounds she had posted straight off to Martha and Sid. After all, although Sid was back on full time at the smelting works they owed a few bob here and there and some of their debts had to be because she had lived off them for a considerable time.

She smiled, remembering. Martha had written her such a lovely letter. Five pounds! Think you're lady bountiful, do yer? Rosie, too, had written to her. Her mum had given her and her friend the money to go to the Saturday morning pictures at the Central Hall in Tooting, and she'd told Rosie that her Auntie Joan had sent the money especially for her.

Joan finished her snack, paid her bill and gave the waitress a threepenny bit as a tip.

'Come in and see us again. We do lovely lunches,' the friendly waitress said as she opened the door for Joan.

Joan was tempted to say, So do we up at the house and I don't have to pay. Instead she nodded her head and said quietly, 'Thanks. Hope to see you soon. 'Bye for now.'

For a while Joan continued to walk round the shops. She looked at clothes and at beauty products, wishing there was a market here like the one in Whitechapel Road in the East End of London where she could buy remnants of really good material for next to nothing. However, even if that had been possible she didn't have her sewing machine, which was still lying in Sid's garden shed, more's the pity. Of course she could sew by hand and in the past had done, many a time, but that would take time and that was something she didn't have a lot of to spare.

In the end she decided there was nothing she needed to spend her money on. Everything was provided for her, even down to soap and tooth-cleaning powder. Time had certainly brought about some changes since she had been in service all those years ago. Her days were still long, and she still only got a half-day a week off and a whole day once a month, but the tasks she was asked to do were nowhere near so hard as they were in days gone by.

Joan looked at the big clock that was on a high plinth and decided it was time for her to catch the single-decker bus which would set her down within about half a mile of the house. By the time she'd strolled down between the leafy trees on each side of the lane she'd be hungry; she'd be more so when she smelt all the good things that Cook would have ready for the evening meal. Besides, Mr and Mrs Hamilton's two daughters were expected home from abroad today and their only son and his wife were due to arrive tomorrow. There had been talk about some kind of celebration but nothing definite had been settled yet. Joan had made up the beds for the daughters yesterday, hung big white fluffy towels each side of the washstands and made sure that toiletries were set out in the enormous bathroom. In her mind she knew that although it was her day off Cook would be more than pleased to see her. Ten to one there would be some job that she'd beg her to do before dinner. She wouldn't mind. Cook did her many a favour.

Joan's assumption wasn't wrong!

'Ah, lass, am I glad t' see thee, so I am,' was the greeting that met her as she stepped into the kitchen. Cook was red in the face and the starched white cap perched like a crown on top of her thick mop of hair bobbed about as she moved. 'I know it's yer day off, me darling, but I could surely use a hand. Would you mind seeing to the joint of beef I've got in the oven? It needs basting and I can't be leaving these egg whites I'm whisking.'

'Of course I'll be only too glad to help,' Joan cried as she ran across the kitchen, pulling off her jacket and hanging it over the back of a chair. With one of Cook's large aprons tied twice around her slim waist she was soon on her knees, thick sacking oven gloves protecting her hands as she pulled the baking tray towards her and slowly and carefully ladled the juices from the bottom of the tray over and over the joint. Cautiously she slid the tin towards the back of the oven once more and carefully closed the door.

'It's fine, Cook. Won't be long and it will be done to a tee.'

'Ah, I send thanks to the blessed saints for the day that you came here, Joan, so I do.'

'Get on with you.' Joan chuckled. 'You manage fine, but do you want to tell me what all the haste is about and why you are working yourself into a fine old lather?'

Cook's eyes flashed with indignation. 'At noon today I was informed that there would be eight for dinner tonight. Besides Mr and Mrs Hamilton and their daughters Fiona and Delia – who, by the way, have arrived – Bruce and his wife are coming from London today not tomorrow and they are bringing two friends with them. It's no wonder I'm in a devil of a mess.'

At that moment Miss Reid appeared. 'Ah, you're back, Joan. How very fortunate for us. I presume you will have no objection to stepping into the breach. It would be so helpful if first off you'd see that extra place settings are added to the table.'

Joan ignored this friendly greeting. Frosty-face was the nickname she had given to the housekeeper right from the word go. Trying hard not to let her embarrassment show, she said, 'I don't mind in the least doing the dining room, Miss Reid, but I cannot be in two places at the same time. Has anyone thought to tell Janet that extra guests are expected and that her services will be required today?'

'I thought you had made up the bedrooms yesterday,' the housekeeper replied starchily.

'Yes, Miss Reid, I had, for Mrs Hamilton's two daughters, but I was advised that young Mr and Mrs Hamilton were not arriving until tomorrow and that Janet would be here by then. No mention was made that two extra guests were accompanying them.'

Had Mr Farrant been eavesdropping? It would seem so.

He barged in quickly, pouring oil on troubled waters. 'I'll send young John off on his bicycle to inform Janet that she is needed for this evening.'

Miss Reid huffed, turned on her heel and left them to it.

Kathleen O'Leary was smiling to herself as she bustled around the stove, clattering pan lids, peering at the contents of her boiling pots. Miss Reid always irritated her, thought she was a cut above everyone else. She looked across at James Farrant and he rewarded her with a sly wink. They were both thinking the same thing. Glad that Joan Baldwin had found the guts to stand up to that one. After all, it was her very first day off and she hadn't uttered one word of complaint at being asked to work the minute she'd stepped into the kitchen.

Miraculously, everything in the kitchen was well under control, and although Cook was flushed and perspiring she was presiding over all the preparations and the dishing up with a certain amount of pride and a smile on her chubby, rosy face.

Joan rinsed her hands under the running cold tap and said, 'If you don't need me for anything else, Cook, I think I'd better go and get ready to wait table.'

'All right, Joan, me darling.' Cook beamed at her. 'Everything's fine here now. Thanks for your help, love. I hope it's plain sailing upstairs for you tonight, but you don't want to let them get away with forgetting that you are owed some free time. Ain't many as would have worked on their night off.'

Mabel, who was polishing some serving spoons that Joan had brought down from the dining room, looked up and grinned. 'When I've finished these I'm going to make a pot of tea for me an' Cook, so if you've time when you're dressed pop down an' have a cup. I'll put cosy on the pot t' keep it hot.'

Joan returned her smile. 'Thanks, Mabel. I'll see you later.'

She climbed the back stairs that led to the staff quarters, and smiled as she entered her room. It was a pretty sight with its single bed and the pale pink bedspread that matched the curtains. She stood at the small window for a few minutes, thinking how wonderful the view was. She could see the sparkle of the panes of glass in the greenhouses in the nearby kitchen gardens, and she told herself what a lovely summer's day it had been. Bet it was hot and dusty in London, she thought.

She moved to the marble-topped washstand, poured cold water from the enormous jug into the large floral-patterned bowl, and then quickly undressed and washed herself from head to toe, leaving her face until last. For this she cupped fresh water from the jug to splash her face, leaning over the bowl and rubbing her skin with her face flannel until it felt really fresh. She spent some time brushing her dark hair, then twisted it cleverly into a thick plait before winding it into a bun that sat at the nape of her neck.

She sighed as she laid out her dining room uniform. It

was supposed to be for the summer, but the material was a heavy crêpe and the dress had been made for someone considerably bigger than herself. She did her best to fold the sides of the dress into a pleat, hoping that if she tied the frilly white apron tight enough round her waist it would hold the surplus material in place. It often didn't. The white cotton collar looked very nice but as the sleeves of the dress were a couple of inches too long she had to fold them back, which made it hard to keep the separate white cuffs in place. Joan stared at her reflection in the mirror and was not at all pleased by what she saw. Sighing again, she picked up the white band of linen which was worn of an evening in place of the daytime mobcap, and secured it round her forehead. At least that fitted, and it kept the odd strand of hair from falling into her eyes. Finally, slipping her feet into her black shoes with their paper-thin soles, she promised herself that that was the first thing she was going to buy. A brand new pair of shoes.

She made her way down the main staircase. When she reached the hall she heard her name called and turned to see Miss Fiona and Miss Delia, who greeted her quite eagerly, she thought, considering she had only met them once before and then only briefly, when they had come down from London just for the day to see their parents. She was surprised at how well and suntanned they both looked, but then she remembered they had been on holiday abroad.

'How have you settled in, Joan?' asked the younger sister, Fiona.

'Very well, thank you, miss.'

'Good,' they both said in unison, but Delia gave Joan a funny look and added, 'Would you turn round, please, Joan?'

Joan did as she asked, feeling very awkward.

'Joan, is that the uniform my mother gave you?'

Joan felt her cheeks flush up and to her dismay she saw

that one of the folds she'd made in the sides of the dress had worked its way loose as she had come down the stairs and the extra cloth was hanging over the edge of her apron. Feeling very embarrassed, she answered, 'Yes, miss.'

'Well, don't look like that, Joan,' Delia said kindly. 'It's not your fault.' Then, turning to her sister, she said, 'I don't know what Mother could have been thinking of. Does she think one uniform fits all staff?'

Fiona had been studying Joan, and now she said, 'First thing in the morning we'll sort you out. Delia will take your measurements and she and I will go into Tunbridge Wells and have a good old forage around. One of the department stores must sell uniforms, surely.'

'If not, we'll go on to Maidstone,' Delia said forcefully.

Joan spoke up. It was something she had been dying to say ever since she had tried the first dress on. 'Excuse me, Miss Delia, and you, Miss Fiona, I could make my own uniforms, both sets, if I were given the material.'

The girls looked at each other and raised their eyebrows.

'Sorry if you think I'm speaking out of turn,' Joan mumbled self-consciously.

'Not at all.' Fiona hastened to reassure her. Then, almost as an afterthought, she asked, 'Have you ever used a sewing machine?'

'Yes, quite a lot,' Joan said quietly. 'Before now I have cut out a pattern from my own drawing and made up dresses for a few ladies on my own treadle sewing machine.' Hurriedly she added, 'They paid me for my work.'

The two sisters chuckled. 'Did they indeed? That's excellent. Did you know our old schoolroom at the top of the house was at one time used as a sewing room?'

Joan shook her head.

'We'll have a word with Mother later on,' Delia promised. Then, turning to Fiona, she asked, 'Is there a sewing machine up there still?'

'I haven't the faintest idea, but I'm sure Miss Reid would know.'

Joan's heart sank. She knew she was not the housekeeper's favourite person. Old Frosty-face wouldn't do anything to help the housemaid look smarter.

'Well, I'd better get on. Thank you both, very much.' She nodded her head and hurried across the hall to the dining room.

She did not see the look that passed between Fiona and Delia Hamilton, nor was she mindful of just how shabby she looked and how much sympathy she had aroused in those two young ladies. She was unaware that she had set in motion a chain of events that in the end would make a world of difference to her life.

Chapter Eight

THE NEXT DAY was one of the happiest that Joan had spent since arriving at Mulborough House. First thing after breakfast Miss Reid had asked Joan to follow her, saying she had orders to show her what had once been the sewing room. Undoubtedly, Miss Fiona and Miss Delia had discussed their conversation with their mother.

'Well, Joan, I've been given to understand that you are pretty good with a needle and are to be given free run of the old sewing room.' The housekeeper spoke over her shoulder to Joan as they climbed the back stairs. Her voice sounded friendly for once, even though she added, 'I hope you know what you are letting yourself in for.'

Walking behind her, Joan smiled to herself, and there was a flicker of satisfaction in her eyes.

Miss Reid opened the door to an attic room and stood back to allow Joan to enter before her. The first sight that met Joan's eyes was a collection of long forgotten toys: a doll's house and an assortment of dolls; a toy-sized perambulator; a huge rocking horse with a real leather saddle and silver stirrups. Against a side wall there was a complete set of drums and further along two well-worn desks, each

77

with one drawer and a sloping top, and a child-sized chair tucked beneath it. It was only as she walked further into the room that she let out a peal of laughter. There, right at the end of the room, was everything that she could desire.

Joan felt they had discovered Aladdin's cave. Placed on a long trestle table was a sewing machine that one worked by turning a handle. Further along was an exact replica of her own treadle machine that was lying idle in her brother-in-law's garden shed. And, 'God above,' Joan cried, 'will you look at those? Two tailor's dummies.'

'The whole place will need a fair bit of cleaning,' Miss Reid said, sighing heavily, 'and as for those two stuffed dummies you're getting so excited about, they are so thick with dust the only place for them is on a bonfire.'

Joan concealed another smile. Over my dead body, she only just stopped herself from saying.

That evening, Joan knew without a doubt that her making known the fact that she could sew and being told she could have the run of the sewing room whenever she had any free time was as good as finding a gold mine.

'Miss Delia is asking for you, Joan.'

Joan looked up from laying the dining table in readiness for the evening meal to see Miss Reid standing in the open doorway.

'Go along, Joan, quickly. I'll finish laying up for you.'

Joan couldn't believe what she'd heard and had a job to stop herself from raising her eyebrows in complete surprise. As she climbed the stairs she was thinking that it was a nice change to have Miss Reid speak to her in a friendly tone. She couldn't help wondering why the housekeeper had appeared to regard her as the enemy almost from the day she arrived.

Miss Delia had worked herself into a fair old state and Joan had hardly set foot in her bedroom when she burst out, 'Joan, please, can you do anything with this dress? I thought it looked great in the shop this morning when I tried it on, but now . . . just look at it.'

'Please, stand still,' Joan said as she slowly walked round Delia. It was indeed a beautiful dress, calf length, the colour of rich port wine. She spotted the trouble straight away. The actual material of the dress itself was a soft, shimmering chiffon, and the slip lining was of heavy satin.

'You say you tried the dress on in the store, miss?'

'Yes, I did. It fitted perfectly. Fiona said it could have been made for me.'

'It won't take me a few minutes to set it right, if I can just pop upstairs and hopefully find a reel of silk thread that will be near enough a match. And I'll need a pair of sharp scissors. Will you carefully slip the dress off, please, miss.'

Minutes later Delia watched as Joan turned the dress inside out and snipped at a few stitches of the inner lining. Then, having threaded a needle with a length of dark Silko, she began to sew along the side hem of the heavy satin using tiny neat stitches.

'Are you sure you know what you're doing?' Delia asked nervously. 'What's wrong with the dress, anyway?'

'Hardly anything at all, Miss Delia, as you pulled the dress over your head when you were in the fitting room one of your rings probably caught the two materials together, and the chiffon being so much lighter in weight than the underslip they joined together and caused the whole side of the dress to ruck up.' Seeing the look on her young mistress's face she added quickly, 'Of course, it could have been the fault of the young lady assistant when she was packing the dress. Anyway, it's fine now.' She cut the thread, stood up and carefully turned the dress back to the right side, giving the whole garment a gentle shake. 'Hold both your arms straight up in the air and I will slip the dress over your head.' Joan spoke nervously, hoping against hope that she had cleared the problem to the satisfaction of her young mistress.

Seconds later Delia was smiling broadly, and as Joan held out the matching bolero for her to put her arms into she stared at her reflection in the long mirror and visibly brightened. Joan breathed a sigh of relief, just as Fiona burst into the room and let out a long, low, unladylike whistle.

'Wow, I told you that dress had been made for you, Delia.'

It was true. The rich dark colour accentuated the creaminess of her skin and the golden glints in her shoulder-length hair.

'Joan, you are a marvel.' Delia nodded appreciatively. 'I cannot thank you enough.'

'You're welcome, miss.'

Flying down the staircase to catch up on her duties Joan had the foresight to recognise that fate had been on her side this evening.

From little acorns great oak trees grow.

As time passed even Miss Reid had cause to be grateful for Joan's hidden talent. Accordingly, she made it possible for Joan to work in a more efficient and orderly manner. Some days she would even reduce her workload, and thus Joan was able on a few afternoons a week to retire to the sewing room and work on the household linen, some of which was badly in need of repair. She herself also looked a whole lot better in the well-fitting uniforms she had made for herself, and as a result she felt better.

She had been congratulated several times on having achieved such a skilful result.

It wasn't long before she was being asked to alter or repair clothes for Mrs Hamilton and both her daughters. Even Miss Reid had approached her, somewhat timidly it had to be said, but nevertheless she had brought some fine underwear to Joan, explaining that the petticoats were too long and showed below her dress, so she had never been able to wear them. Would Joan be so kind as to shorten them?

'Only too pleased to,' had been Joan's reply, and she had taken the time to hand-sew the delicate fabric using the finest of needles and making sure that each stitch was perfect. Joan felt she needed Miss Reid as a friend. After all, the housekeeper was responsible for how much free time Joan was allowed in order to pursue her sewing.

There came a time when even more progress was offered.

All the family were in the drawing room and Joan was serving afternoon tea. The French doors were wide open, for the summer was stretching out well. The lawns were an emerald green and the gardens were still a blaze of colour, with tall stone pots filled with great bushy geraniums spaced along the edges of the pathways. In the hearth of the white marble fireplace stood a lovely floral arrangement, the flowers filling the room with a soft perfume. That in itself was a bonus. All this lovely sunny weather meant no fires had to be lit and no grates had to be cleared of ashes every morning.

Even the old gentleman (as Joan always thought of Mr Hamilton) was brighter today and seemed to be listening with interest to the conversation. Joan had served everyone with a cup of tea and seen that everyone had a plate, a napkin and a cake fork before pushing the laiden tea trolley to the centre of the room where it would be within easy reach of every member of the family. She was about to leave the room when Mrs Hamilton asked her to stay.

'Joan, my daughters and I have a proposal which we would like to put to you. First, though, I must compliment you. Indeed I must. Not only are your uniforms a credit to you, Miss Reid tells me you have been through every article in the linen cupboard, hemming napkins, repairing torn pillow cases and sheets, and restitching the edges of frayed tableclothes. It would seem we have found a treasure in you. You certainly are a talented woman.'

81

Joan was delighted with the knowledge that her efforts had been successful, but she managed to conceal her smiles as Mrs Hamilton went on.

'It will be autumn soon, and Christmas won't be far behind, and we thought it would be wonderful if you would design and make at least one dress for each of us. During the winter months we attend many functions and it would delight us to know that we were wearing something different. A dress or a two-piece that one would not be able to purchase even in the London stores.'

Joan was flabbergasted.

Mrs Hamilton smiled at her. 'You're probably wondering how you would ever find the time to fit in this extra work alongside all your other tasks. We were of the same mind to begin with. However, we have hit on a solution. We will hire another girl, someone from the village who would not need to live in. If you are of a mind to take on this dressmaking we shall pay you separately for the work. I would insist on that.'

Joan's head was buzzing. It would be work she would relish *and* she would be able to save some money. Having a bit put by wouldn't be a bad thing, because the way things stood now if she were to lose this job tomorrow she would have nowhere to live and no savings to fall back on. Could she do it? Well enough to satisfy not only Mrs Hamilton but the very fashion-conscious Miss Delia and Miss Fiona? She could give it a go. After all, there were enough magazines coming into the house that she could get ideas from. Even more likely, the two girls would probably bring patterns down from London.

What if they did? She was a dab hand at cutting cloth. Not so long ago she had been making every stitch that young Rosie put on her back. Even her school uniform. And that was besides the dressmaking that she sometimes did for neighbours. Word had got around years ago that Mrs

Baldwin did alterations and repairs, from shortening or lengthening skirts and trousers to turning a well-worn shirt collar. But then nobody would have moaned at her had she messed up any article she was working on. God almighty! This chance was a very different kettle of fish!

'Are you going to stand there all night, Joan?' Fiona laughed as she asked the question. Delia was quick to urge her to agree.

'Please, Joan, think what fun it will be choosing all the lovely colours and the different materials.'

'And while you are busy making our outfits we'll scour the shops for shoes and evening bags to exactly match what we have chosen.' Fiona sounded excited and it was infectious. Soon even Mr Hamilton was smiling and nodding his head with approval.

'Please, Mrs Hamilton,' Joan begged, 'may I think about this? I wouldn't want any of you to go to the expense of buying material all at once. May we talk more tomorrow morning? I am honoured that you trust me so much, truly I am, but perhaps I should take it slowly. Make just one outfit, then you can be the judge of whether I should carry on or not.'

'That is an excellent idea, Joan. We shall talk again tomorrow. Meanwhile you are not to lose any sleep tonight worrying over this. You promise, now?'

'Yes, I promise, and thank you, ma'am,' Joan mumbled before she made what she hoped was a respectable retreat. The idea was so sudden and incredible. Could she pull it off?

As she lay in her bed that night Joan felt she was inadequate to tackle such a task. She felt that everything that was happening was slightly unreal, as though she was dreaming it all. It seemed ages since anything good had happened to her, and now that it had she couldn't make herself believe that she would be able to cope.

First thing next morning she was greeted enthusiastically by both Fiona and Delia. 'You are going to do it, aren't you?' Delia smiled.

Joan shook her head. 'I still haven't taken it in. It's very exciting but you two young ladies and your mother are in a position to buy your clothes from any of the great fashion houses. Why pick me to make an outfit for you?'

'Because we want to be different,' Fiona cried. 'I've seen some of the sketches you've left lying about in the kitchen. They are unusual, to say the least. We could put our heads together, you sketching and us commenting, and together we might come up with an exclusive design. Please, Joan, say you'll give it a try.'

'I can see it working just as well as my sister has described, but there is one thing I am afraid of,' Delia said, but her eyes were flashing mischievously. Seeing the smile fade from Joan's face, she said quickly, 'Hey, I was only joking. I was going to say that we'll be the belles of any ball that we get invited to. Ladies will plead with us to tell them where we bought our original dresses, and should we be so silly as to tell them word will get around and you'll be whipped off to Paris before you know what is happening and we shall lose you.'

'Oh, don't be so daft!' Joan's fingers flew to cover her mouth. For a moment she had forgotten who she was talking to.

At that moment Mrs Hamilton put her head round her bedroom door and looked amazed to see her daughters hugging each other and laughing fit to bust. 'What on earth?' their mother cried.

It was a minute or two before the girls were able to speak and by then Joan had taken herself off into the dining room.

'It's all right, Mother. We have not taken leave of our senses but we do believe we shall be able to persuade Joan

84

to go along with our scheme.' Fiona nodded merrily at her sister and added, 'Right, Dee?'

'Dead cert, I'd say. Besides, Joan is a likeable and clever lady and she will be far happier using her talents than merely being a housemaid. Given different circumstances I believe she could have a different life, and what's more I believe she is the kind of person who deserves it.'

Their mother's eyes widened in admiration, and Delia was puzzled at the smile on her face. 'What is it – did I say something funny?'

'No, no,' said Mrs Hamilton hastily. 'I agree with both of you and it is nice to hear that you are willing to help someone who has not been so fortunate in life as you have.'

'Is *that* all?' Delia laughed and looked at her sister.

'So now we are being thought of as angels of mercy.' Fiona laughed back.

'Oh well. I guess we can live with that. Come on, let's go and have some breakfast.'

Everything had been set in motion.

Joan told herself time and time again how lucky she was. Oh, how she loved the room that had been transformed for her at the top of the house. The cleaning and oiling of both machines had given her no problems at all and there weren't many afternoons that the whirr of machinery couldn't be heard.

Two extra tables had been found and more often than not were filled to overflowing with paper patterns, reams of brown paper that Joan found useful to use when making the first cut-out pattern. Whether it be a blouse, skirt or dress it was always made up in stiff brown paper before she allowed herself to put scissors to cloth.

Best of all were her tailor's dummies. They were not a perfect fit for the three females she was making clothes for, but absolutely indispensable when the first stages of any garment were only held together by tacking stitches.

There was only three weeks to go until 25 December.

Mrs Hamilton had kept her word and had hired another girl, Mary, from the village, whom Miss Reid was doing her best to train as the between maid. This gave Joan more time to sew, and the domestic routine was kept running so smoothly that Joan thought at times it was all too good to be true. Each night she prayed that it would last. In the sewing room there now hung two evening dresses, and one two-piece for Mrs Hamilton that had a skirt that reached the floor. All three outfits needed just the finishing touches. It had been grim determination that had kept Joan Baldwin going as summer had turned into autumn and winter had not been far behind.

Mrs Hamilton was easy to please. Delia and Fiona changed their minds so many times as to how they wanted their very different dresses to hang, and what adornment they preferred, that some days Joan was tempted to throw her arms up in the air and suggest that they finished the work themselves.

If only her sister lived nearer. She so much missed being able to talk to her. Martha wrote regular letters which told her about the neighbours, what Lenny and Bernie were getting up to, how Sid always took her to the pub for a drink on a Saturday evening. Every letter ended by saying how Rosie was growing, how much she missed her Auntie Joan and how she was constantly asking when was she coming home for a visit. You'd think that Martha would be a bit more thoughtful. She didn't stop to think, that was her trouble. Surely she realised that Joan didn't work just a few miles away, and that she would dearly love to come home if she could.

Most of the time Joan felt happy enough, but at the back

of her mind was always the fact that she wasn't here by choice. After all, she was no spring chicken. By rights she should be happily married with children of her own to care for and love. Life wasn't fair. But come to think of it, who ever promised that it was going to be?

Chapter Nine

TOMORROW WOULD BE Christmas Eve.

Joan had spent all morning helping to put the finishing touches to the decorations in the hall and the dining room. For the past week a huge tree had stood at the far side of the drawing room shimmering with tinsel and exquisite glass ornaments. Whenever possible she had also lent a hand in the kitchen. Joan shook her head and grinned as she thought of Kathleen O'Leary. One could be forgiven for thinking that she had been asked to prepare enough food to feed an army. She certainly was an amazing woman. It was not only the quantity of the food that she was preparing, but the variety and the quality.

'Joan, be a dear and check this list that Miss Reid has given me.' Kathleen sounded flustered, which was unusual. Normally she took everything in her stride.

Joan took the sheet of paper and quickly ran her eyes down the list. 'It's just the numbers, including guests, who will be in the house over the holiday. It's no different from what we were told three weeks ago.'

'I know that, Joan, but first someone tells me one thing and then along comes someone else saying something different. With all the blessed saints on me side I don't get the same number no matter how many times I tally it up.'

Joan did her best not to laugh. 'Come on, Cook, we'll do it together.'

Kathleen, who already had a sheet of paper in front of her, slipped on her steel-rimmed glasses and, having licked the end of the pencil she was holding, looked across to Joan and said, 'Right.'

'Shall we start with the family?'

'Yes, that's a good idea,' Cook agreed.

'First off there is Mr and Mrs Hamilton – that's two. Bruce, their son, will be bringing his wife Pamela with him. They haven't any children, have they?'

'No, more's the pity,' Cook answered with a wry little smile.

'Well, that's another two.'

'Then there's Delia, and the youngest is Fiona. If you ask me, Joan, which I know you haven't, but all the same my opinion is that those two young ladies are very sweet and nice when they want to be but they are flibbertigibbets, the pair of 'em, an' I can't be seeing either one of them pushing a pram with a bairn of their own in it.'

'So that's another two,' Joan said cheerily, thinking it was always the best policy to let Cook have her say. She studied the list that had been handwritten by Miss Reid and commented, 'All that is written after the family names is "Six guests, i.e. three married couples". No names are given.'

'That's what I'm on about,' Cook answered abruptly. 'Preparing meals for folk with no names.'

Now Joan could not stop herself from laughing. 'What difference does it make? It adds up to twelve upstairs for the holiday, and Miss Reid will see to the names on the place cards.' But Joan just could not resist teasing Cook. She murmured softly, 'Of course, the family and their guests will be going to watch the hunt on Boxing Day, or so I've been told, which means God alone knows how many folk they might invite back for lunch.'

Cook was about to explode when the merriment in Joan's eyes caused her to pause. 'Get on with yer,' she said, playfully swiping Joan around the head. 'You've come out of your shell these past few weeks. Wouldn't have said boo to a goose when you first set foot in my kitchen.'

'Only teasing, my fair Kathleen. I wouldn't be hurting you 'cos I know you'd set the Irish little folk on to me, so you would.'

'Let me tell you, young lady, you're getting too saucy for your own good, and for your cheek you can put the kettle on and make me a pot of tea for a change.'

'Yes, ma'am.' Joan smiled and gave Cook a mock salute.

As she waited for the kettle to come to the boil she pondered on how a certain kind of comradeship had developed between Kathleen and herself in the last few months. Different as they were in background and age, they were curiously at ease with each other. Although they never talked about their previous lives, and no questions were asked, there was still a caring understanding. Without words being said they both knew the feeling of friendship was very real.

Joan had had her work cut out to make last-minute alterations and put finishing touches to the two evening dresses she had made, plus the evening suit which Mrs Hamilton insisted on saying was a work of art. It was with a sigh of relief that Joan tidied up the room, clearing the tables of reels of cotton, skeins of embroidery silk, scraps of material, and small tins and boxes which contained pins and needles of all shapes and sizes and several different-sized thimbles. Three different pairs of scissors and one pair of pinking shears were carefully wrapped separately in squares of white linen before she placed them in the huge wicker basket, overflowing with paper pattern and fashion magazines, that had served so faithfully as her sewing basket over the last few months.

Delia's dress could only be described as sophisticated. Black taffeta, it had a tight bodice with two wide shoulder straps, a very full skirt that fell in folds to the floor, and as the only decoration a small single red rose sewn into the right side of the waistband. To wear with it Delia had chosen red shoes with a small heel.

Fiona's dress was entirely different: a simple cream silk. Joan touched it tenderly. It was so elegant, and undoubtedly the one she was most proud of. It could easily pass as a wedding dress. The bodice was cut straight across in a wide band that fastened at the back with a row of silver buttons. There were no shoulder straps and no sleeves. The front of the dress was perfectly plain, while the back of the skirt was a mass of tiny pleats that fell skimming over the hips and falling in a straight line to the floor. Fiona's choice of accessories had been pale rose pumps and a small evening bag to match. To cover her bare shoulders Joan had made a long, wide stole of the same soft material and had edged the bottom of each side with a heavy rose-coloured silk fringe.

Mrs Hamilton's outfit was coffee and cream. Joan had copied the pattern from a sketch that Delia had drawn, and when their mother had had the final fitting both her daughters had declared that Joan had done so well it was perfection personified. The beige skirt was long and straight, with a slit in the centre of the back to make walking, even dancing, that much easier. The hip-length loose jacket was of the same heavy beige silk, with the collar, revers and wide turned-back cuffs all edged with a rich, dark brown velvet. The piping on the cuffs of the sleeves was embroidered with tiny pearl and crystal beads. Joan had also made a high-necked sleeveless vest to be worn beneath the jacket. Very plain but extremely smart, as befitted the lady of the house.

It was the kind of Christmas most people love to dream about, bitterly cold but bright and sunny. Earlier there had been a light fall of snow, then severe frost had covered the lawns, giving the grass a silver carpet. Icicles hung from the bare branches of the deciduous trees, whereas the evergreens were coated as if with white paint. From every window she looked out of Joan was enthralled by the view.

Everyone, including all the staff, enjoyed the magnificent dinner that Kathleen O'Leary had provided and drank wine from Mr Hamilton's vast cellar. During the evening the sounds of great merriment came from the drawing room as the family and their friends played charades, while downstairs in the huge kitchen four members of the indoors staff played cards: Cook, Miss Reid, Joan and Mr Farrant.

Just as they were about to start a hand of bridge, Mrs Farrant came to join her husband. 'Brr, it's cold out there,' she said, removing her gloves and rubbing her hands together.

Moving swiftly, Mr Farrant was on his feet, helping his wife to take her coat off. 'You said you weren't going to come over to the house, dear. I would have come for you if you had said.'

'I changed my mind, and it's only a few minutes' walk, and I knew the company would be good.' When an introduction had been made, Joan looked at the thin lady whose hand she was shaking. Mrs Farrant was very attractive. Pretty was not the right word. Dazzling would have been better, and Joan wondered how portly Mr Farrant had found himself such a beautiful wife.

'Please take my place, Mrs Farrant,' Joan said, moving hastily away from the table.

'Certainly not, my dear. I'm quite happy to sit and watch.' Even her voice was pleasant to listen to.

'You would be doing me a favour,' Joan insisted. 'I have never played bridge in my life, but as Cook said they needed two pairs of players I was going to give it a try. I'm really glad not to have to. Truly I am. I'll sit by the fire and maybe learn a thing or two.'

Mrs Farrant was gracious in her thanks as she took Joan's place at the table. Now Joan was seated in Cook's favourite armchair close to the fire and she began to try to convince herself just how lucky she was and what a happy Christmas Day it had been. There was a bowl of fruit in the centre of the table, as well as sweets and chocolates which had been given as presents to the staff. A huge fire burned halfway up the chimney, chestnuts roasted and popped on top of the range and there was plenty to drink. What more could anyone ask for?

All the same, Joan was relieved when the day was over and she was able to go to her own room and let her thoughts run freely. Taking off her clothes she slipped her nightdress over her head, washed her hands and face in cold water and got into bed. Why, oh, why did she feel she wanted to lie there and cry her eyes out? It had been a good Christmas, but even with the house full of people she had felt lonely. Who did she have to wish her a happy Christmas? Not one single person of her own. Here at Mulborough House she had had everything good that money could buy, but today she would so dearly have loved to be at Martha's. To sit round a crowded table, all of them wearing cheap but colourful paper hats. To know that she was among people who loved her. Wanted her, because she was family. True, she felt secure here. She wanted for nothing. But . . .

She missed her sister and the whole of Martha's family. She missed the children who lived in the same street. They'd have been knocking on her door this morning, bringing her small gifts, and she would have managed to wrap up a gift for each and every one of them. Most of all she missed

Rosie. What would she have given her if she'd been at home? Not toys any more, that's for sure.

She missed Sid and Lenny and Bernie. Their teasing, their warmth and their laughter. Maybe each of the lads had a girlfriend by now and big-hearted Martha would welcome them into her home, pleased that she would have even more folk around her to mother. Working here, she led almost a life of luxury. But what good did it do her? She had no one to share her day off with. Nowhere in particular to go to. Letters were her only link with her family. She read and reread them, only to find that they made her feel even more lonely. Almost unwanted. Always the odd one out.

Sometimes Martha wrote about having gone to the school to see Rosie acting in a play. If she'd been there she would probably have made the costumes for all the children. Was this how it would be for ever? No. Because soon she'd be too old to be a housemaid. Kind as the Hamiltons were, they weren't going to house and feed her if she wasn't able to do her work or became ill and needed medical attention. Were they?

She had thought it was really nice when first she had been given this bedroom with its glorious view of the gardens and the countryside beyond, but at this moment she would have given a lot to be back in her old house in London taking care of poor old Granny Baldwin, even though it had entailed a great deal of hard work and money had been so short. Why, oh, why had Bill been as he was? Why couldn't he have taken a little more care of his own mother? *And why couldn't he have loved me?* He had done once. When they had first met he had often told her that he adored her. So what went wrong? Folk were wont to say that when poverty came in through the window, love went out of the door. Not true. At least not in every case. God knows Sid Brown had had his share of hard times but he'd walk miles to earn a shilling before he'd let Martha and his three children starve.

The more she thought about London and the people she had left behind the more lonely she felt. She sighed, then speaking out loud she said, 'I never thought I would miss my folk as much as I do.' She was tired, too. Tired of hoping that one day everything would come right for her. She turned over and buried her head in the pillow and cried bitterly.

It was in the early hours of the morning, when she had no more tears left in her, that Joan came to a decision. She would let the remainder of the holiday go by but as soon as the guests had left the house and things were back on to a normal footing she was going to ask Mrs Hamilton to let her have a whole week off. She had put in a good many more hours than she was paid for, and in fact for the three weeks leading up to Christmas she had not even taken her half-day off. She had been too busy sewing. She had quite a nice little nest egg put away, what with her wages and the money she had received for making the three outfits. Mrs Hamilton had given her five guineas. She supposed that was for seeing to the linen as well as making her outfit. Miss Delia and Miss Fiona had each given her two pounds. She now had enough money for her train fare and to buy each member of her family a nice present. They'd have a party while she was there. Better still, she'd write and ask Martha if they could have another Christmas Day. One that she could share in, when she would feel wanted and be part of a family again.

With that final thought she felt happier and at last fell into an exhausted sleep.

Chapter Ten

JOAN STOOD STILL and stretched her arms above her head. The effort helped to ease the pain in her shoulders. Her legs ached and her feet were burning. What a New Year's Eve it had been. They had had to bring Mabel upstairs to take coats from what seemed like a never-ending stream of arriving guests. Mr Farrant and herself had struggled through the evening meal, when twenty people had sat down to dine. Even when Mr Bruce had suggested the diners retire to the drawing room, it was not all over. Time and time again Joan had climbed the stairs in Mr Farrant's wake as they carried up trays of tasty morsels, all prepared and decorated by Kathleen. Surely the family and their guests wouldn't want to go on eating all evening? Some of the elderly folk, including Mr Hamilton, had settled themselves in front of the fire. The younger ones, led by Delia and her brother Bruce, were dancing to the loud music coming from the gramophone. At the far end of the room Fiona and her sister-in-law, Pamela, were plotting with others as to how they would put on the very popular game of guessing the names of famous people, the participants having been given very few details. Mr Farrant had poured drinks for everyone and even now was replenishing glasses. At last, Mr Bruce took him aside and told him, in no uncertain terms, that he had done enough for one day and should retire downstairs. 'And take Joan with you. She looks fit to drop,' he added.

Mr Farrant placed the whisky bottle and soda syphon on a side table with the utmost care and thankfully murmured, 'Thank you, sir.'

In the kitchen the atmosphere was warm and friendly. Mr Farrant and John, being the only two male members of the party, had made sure all the females had a drink and plenty to eat. Mrs Farrant was there, Miss Reid, Joan, Cook, Mabel the kitchen maid, and Mary the in-between, who had written permission from her parents to stay the night at Mulborough House.

Kathleen took a good swig from her glass of Guinness, looked at the clock and called loudly, 'Open the door wide, Mr Farrant, there's only two minutes to go.'

Each of them got to their feet, glass in hand ready to be raised, and not a word was spoken until the sound of Big Ben striking midnight could be heard coming from the wireless in the upstairs drawing room.

'Happy New Year,' all the members of the staff chorused. Everyone hugged and kissed each other on the cheek. It was 1 January 1928.

A sudden thought struck Joan. There had been no tall dark man entering the house bringing a lump of coal. Perhaps this household did not believe in first-footing. After all, she said to herself, they aren't Londoners, are they? And they certainly aren't Scottish. Every house in Scotland would have a first-footing tonight.

The new year brought Joan some unexpected good luck.

It had taken the staff two days to set the house to rights.

Beds had been stripped and laundry hampers filled with dirty linen. That was one blessing about this house: only smalls were washed. Everything heavy was sent to the Sunlight Laundry or to one of those new-fangled dry-cleaning premises. Joan thought they were a godsend. Still, there was furniture to dust and polish, baths and wash bowls to be cleaned. The smallest of the carpets were carried out into the back yard by the gardeners and hung over the clothes lines, where Mabel or Mary beat the dust from them using a bamboo beater shaped like a large paddle.

It was on the third day after the holiday, when Joan was preparing afternoon tea in the drawing room, that Mrs Hamilton entered the room on her own and Joan managed to pluck up enough courage to speak to her.

'Please, ma'am, would you consider allowing me to take a week's holiday? I would dearly love to see my sister and her family,' she said wistfully.

After a moment's thought Mrs Hamilton asked, 'How would you intend to travel, Joan?'

'By train to London and then a tram to Wimbledon, ma'am. I can walk from there.'

'Hmm.' Mrs Hamilton looked thoughtful. 'Of course you may have a break, Joan. You have certainly proved your worth. As to travel arrangements, leave it with me for the moment and I will see what we can come up with.'

'Come up with?' Joan was puzzled, not having the least idea what her mistress was thinking of.

Long ago, Joan had come to the conclusion that she had been unlucky where men were concerned. God knows Bill had hurt her enough. Now, as she stood facing Mr Hamilton and listening to what he was saying, she could hardly believe her ears. It seemed odd, because Mr Hamilton, although always a gentleman and appreciative of anything that she did for him, hardly ever spoke more than a few words at any one time. At the moment, however, his speech was quite fluent.

'Please, Joan, don't feel that you are obliged to accept my son's offer, but be assured he would not be going out of his way. Unless, of course, you would prefer to travel by train.'

Bruce Hamilton was standing beside his father's chair. The first time Joan had set eyes on him she had thought him a handsome young man. His hair was thick and dark, as his father's must have been before it turned white. 'What's the matter, Joan? Don't you trust me?' he asked, but his brown eyes were smiling. 'As my father has told you, I shall be leaving here on Thursday, which will give you two days to get yourself ready, and I can drop you off at any point in London that you care to suggest.'

Still, Joan's mind was in a complete whirl. A lift in a motor car! All the way to London. And the offer being made by the son of the house.

Having studied Joan's face for a moment or two, quite suddenly Bruce burst out laughing. Bending to speak to his father, he said, 'The penny has just dropped. We haven't explained to Joan that Pamela will be travelling with me.'

Joan knew her face had flushed, because he had read her thoughts. She knew darn well housemaids did not travel in a car with the young master of the house. Not on their own they didn't!

'Oh, Joan, I am sorry. I really haven't made myself very clear.' The old gentleman sounded so conscience-stricken that had the circumstances been different she would have thrown her arms around him and given him a hug. She had to restrain herself. 'What I should have said in the first place was my son and his wife will be going home, and as they have no passengers you could travel in the back of their car in comfort.'

Bruce leapt in. 'Well, now all has been made clear, are you going to travel with my wife and me? Oh, by the way,

I must mention that we shall be leaving at six in the morning as I have an early appointment in town. Is that all right?'

More than all right. It's bloody marvellous, Joan felt like saying. What she did say was, 'Yes, thank you, sir, and I am very grateful.'

'No need for you to feel you are under any obligation, Joan. I assure you, what my father said is true. You will not be taking me out of my way. Not in the least.'

Joan had never been in a car before. Oh yes you have, she reminded herself. On the day that they had buried her husband. Mr Young from the brewery had paid for one car to follow the hearse and she, Martha, Sid, Lenny and Bernie had travelled to the church in a large black limousine.

She didn't want to remember that day. This was different. As she slipped into the back seat and Bruce closed the door her heart was beating nineteen to the dozen with excitement. The smell and feel of leather . . . it was going to be a real adventure.

Pamela Hamilton half turned from where she sat in the front passenger seat and asked, 'Are you comfortable, Joan? If you should feel cold there is a travelling rug on the seat beside you.'

'I'm fine, Mrs Hamilton, really I am, more than fine, thank you.'

At such an early hour there was not much traffic on the road. The only hold-up they were caught up in was when Bruce tried to manoeuvre his car round a herd of cows that a young farmer, with only the help of a long cane, was urging to move off the roadway and pass through an open gate and into a green field that lay beyond.

As they neared London, Bruce glanced into his mirror. Speaking to Joan's reflection, he asked, 'Joan, is there anywhere in particular you would like me to set you down?'

'Wherever suits you, sir. I know London quite well – I shan't get lost.'

Pamela laughed. 'Well spoken, Joan. From the few times we've met I've never had you down as a country bumpkin.'

'How about the Elephant and Castle, then?' Bruce asked, smiling.

'Spot on, sir. Thank you. That will suit me fine.'

Joan stood a moment or two on the pavement after she had waved to Pamela and watched Mr Bruce drive away. She took a huge breath. Even the air smelt different. It wasn't quite eight o'clock in the morning yet the streets were full of people. Looking about her, she felt she had entered another world. 'You'd think I'd been away for years instead of only months,' she muttered as she watched the costermongers set up the market and the young boys their barrows. Big brawny men, their strong powerful arms steadying the loaded boxes they were carrying either on their shoulders or on top of their heads.

'Out the way, luv.' 'Shove over, me darling,' they called cheekily as they shouldered their way through. This was London and it would never change. Joan smiled broadly as one strapping great man brazenly winked at her. She didn't mind; in fact she felt flattered. After all, it was not so far from here where I was born, she was thinking as she wandered along to the nearest bus stop. She only had a few minutes to wait for the bus and when it came she decided to climb the stairs. From the top of the double-decker she would be able to see so much more.

Through the city, already bustling with activity, past Lambeth Palace and its gatehouse, over the bridge, looking down the dear old River Thames and seeing the brightly painted barges and the dirty sooty freighters which had brought coal down from Newcastle. As the bus neared Victoria station she gripped her small attaché case and slipped the strap of her handbag over her wrist, descending the stairs her mind was going way back into the past.

When she was on the pavement once more, for a moment or two she could not move. She was lost in thought. How different Bill had been before they had been married.

There had been days when he had brought her to Kensington Gardens and shown her the statue of Peter Pan, and they had stood holding hands, gazing at Kensington Palace. Another day they had spent time in Hyde Park. Bill had hired a boat and taken her on the Serpentine. It had been there that he had asked her to marry him. She had been so happy and excited, believing that the world was her oyster and that they would both live happily ever after.

She shook herself. Why, oh why, was she trying to relive the past? It was gone. Done with. And life with Bill had not been the happy time her mind was picturing now. She was looking through rose-coloured glasses, that's what she was doing. She shuddered, suddenly aware of the biting wind, which was blowing straight through her thin coat, getting right into her bones. She tugged her hat down tighter over her ears and pulled her scarf more securely round her neck. Her teeth chattered and her eyes watered from the icy blasts and she couldn't get to Martha's warm kitchen quickly enough.

Rosie had been in and out of the house like a jack-in-the-box for the last half-hour, looking for her Auntie Joan. Martha came to the gate. 'Still no sign of her?' she asked her daughter.

'No, not yet.' Rosie crossed her arms over her chest and shivered.

'Well, come on in.' Her mother waved towards the house. 'You'll catch yer death if yer stand here much longer, 'sides letting all the cold air into the 'ouse. Come on now, inside.' She put her arm round Rosie's shoulders and edged her towards the open front door.

They were almost inside when Rosie turned her head,

broke away from her mother and yelled, 'She's here! She's just turned the corner!'

Never mind the cold, with the wind behind her Rosie went flying up the street. Joan put her case down and stood still with her arms wide open and Rosie flew into them. Martha, watching them hugging as if they would never let go of each other, felt tears sting the back of her eyes and she lifted the corner of her overall to wipe them away before she bellowed, 'Are yer mad, the pair of yer? It's cold enough to freeze the brass balls off the pawn shop. Come on, get yerselves in 'ere before I shut the door an' leave yer there.'

Still holding tightly on to each other, aunt and niece were stepping over the front doormat when a young voice called, 'Oi, Mrs Baldwin, yer left yer case up the road.'

Martha looked at her sister and, half laughing but still half crying, said, 'You 'aven't altered. Lose yer bloody 'ead if it weren't screwed on.'

Joan took her case from the lad, thanking him, then she hesitated. 'Are you Johnny Carter?'

'Course I am, Mrs Baldwin. You come 'ome now? Me mum was saying you'd been gone a long time.'

'I'm going to have a little holiday, Johnny. Tell your mum I'll pop in and see her tomorrow.'

'All right, missus. Ta-ta.'

'Can we shut the door now?' Martha asked sarcastically.

Joan and Rosie both burst out laughing and would have hugged again but Martha pushed her daughter out of the way. 'You've had your turn,' she said. Then, turning to her sister, she spoke softly. 'God alone knows 'ow much I've missed you. You're a sight for sore eyes. Come here.'

Joan went willingly into those fat wobbly arms, laid her head on Martha's ample bosom and burst into tears. Martha stood holding her and rocking her for a good few minutes before she said, 'We must be mad. I've got the fire burning 'alfway up the chimney and the kettle has boiled dry twice and there's us standing out 'ere in this drafty passage! We must be a right pair of lunatics.'

The pleasure of that afternoon would stay with Joan for the rest of her life. The warmth of that small but sparkling clean living room, the tasty shepherd's pie Martha had cooked for their midday meal, telling Joan that they'd all have their proper dinner tonight when Sid and the boys got home.

The difference Joan noticed in Rosie was unbelievable. How could she have changed so much in nine months? She would be fifteen this year, probably going to leave school come Easter. She was taller, still slim and fresh-faced, with a mop of the fairest curly hair you'd hardly ever see the like of. And she spoke nicely, which pleased Joan a great deal. Not that her thoughts were knocking Martha. To her there had never been another person in the world like her sister and there never would be.

They chatted non-stop and it was a miracle that dinner was ever produced at all. When the menfolk came home it was sheer pandemonium. How a room the size of Martha's living room could hold so many people Joan didn't know. Sid was first through the door. His massive hands went straight round Joan's waist and she was lifted up to his face level where he held her and kissed her over and over again. When he did let her feet touch the ground once more he held her at arm's length, looked into her eyes, and asked, 'You been all right gal? 'Cos if you ain't then yer looks don't pity yer. Fattened you up a little bit, ain't they? And there's a bit of colour in them cheeks. Must be the country air.'

'Something like that I suppose, Sid, but you'll never know what coming home to this house and such a welcome means to me.'

'Well, gal, I've said it before and I'll say it again, home is where the heart is an' as long as me an' Martha have got a roof over our 'eads then you've got a home.'

Joan couldn't answer, she was so choked up. She had known she would be made welcome but she hadn't anticipated anything like this.

Now Bernie and Lenny were standing facing her.

'Goodness me, what a pair of good-looking fellas.' Joan felt quite shy of her nephews.

'Yeah,' Sid said proudly. 'Right chips off the old block, wouldn't yer say?'

There was only a year between them but the difference was visible, at least to Joan. Lenny, twenty years old now, was tough-looking, well over six feet tall and broad-shouldered. Bernie was not quite so tall, still well-built and strong, but he had an eager studious look about him and there was no arguing that he was well and truly strikingly good-looking. Both lads had large brown eyes and at this moment they were twinkling with merriment as they watched their aunt sum them up.

'Well, Aunt Joan, do we pass muster?' Lenny grinned cheekily.

'You know darn well you do. You're only fishing for compliments,' Joan told them.

'If you've all finished telling each other how wonderful you all are, I've a dinner ready to put on the table, so wash yer 'ands and sit yerselves up,' Martha said, doing her best to sound stern, but her happiness showed through. She had all her family round the table tonight and that gave her the greatest of pleasure.

But no more than it did Joan.

How she'd dreamed of sitting round this large kitchen table, staring at the old black-leaded kitchen range that wasn't half the size of the one at Mulborough House. But in front of Martha's was a massive steel fender with a lidded box fitted to each end, and now Joan was remembering the times she had sat there toasting bread on the end of a long toasting fork. Oh, it was so good to be home.

Her heart was swelling with love as they all enjoyed a homely meal. Only when it came time to say good night did a little doubt creep in. This was not her home. She was sleeping in Rosie's little room. To be honest, whichever way you looked at it she would be forty-two years old this year and she had no home to call her own.

Chapter Eleven

THE HOUSE WAS STILL DARK when Joan woke up, dark and cold. She couldn't hear anyone moving about and she hadn't any idea of the time. Martha had put a box of matches on the chair beside her bed so that if she wanted to get up in the night she could light the gas mantle. She pulled the blankets and the eiderdown up to her neck and snuggled down again, deciding she would have a little extra time in bed seeing as how she was on holiday. She didn't go to sleep again, though, because the street was coming alive and it was bringing back so many memories. The clip-clop of the horses drawing the milk cart, followed by the clinking of milk bottles as the milkman stood them on folk's doorsteps. Joan grinned when she remembered how men who had allotments would be out with buckets and shovels before they went to work. That is if the horses had obliged and done their business in the middle of the road. The steaming dung never lay there for long. Next came the paper boy, whistling as he delivered the daily newspapers, and then the clang of letter boxes as the postman did his first round of the day.

Better get up now. Too late – her bedroom door was being

pushed open and a smiling Martha came in holding out a steaming cup of tea.

'Sit up. I thought I'd spoil you for a change. Bet you don't get tea in bed in that posh house where you work.'

No, Joan thought, it's me that takes it to other folk, but then she chided herself. *That's all part and parcel of what you get paid for.*

She wriggled herself up and Martha put the tea down on the chair and plumped her pillows behind her shoulders. Then she kissed her, gave her a hug and told her, 'Stay there till the men are out of the way. Rosie will be in to see you before she goes to school. Mind you, I'm 'aving a helluva job to make her go. Says she don't feel well!'

They both laughed, knowing full well the only thing wrong with Rosie was that she wanted to stay home with her aunt.

'Oh, Joan, you don't know what it meant t' me to wake up and know you were here.'

Joan shook her head. 'It cuts both ways, Martha. There has been times when I've been so lonely I've thought about chucking the job in and coming back to London.' Yet she knew they were both thinking the same thing.

What was there for her in London?

You count yer blessings, Martha wanted to say, because Joan had fallen on her feet when she got that job down in Kent. She would also have liked to add, Sufficient unto the day; let tomorrow take care of itself. Instead she playfully pushed her sister and said, 'Anyway, I've got the porridge all ready for Sid and the boys. I'm just going to rake the embers of the range. It never goes out, not this cold weather, but I'll get it built up and the fire roaring away by the time you're ready to come down.'

Rosie had won.

Her mother had had to agree. How long would it be before they set eyes on Joan again? Rosie sat back on her

108

heels and pushed a strand of hair out of her eyes. She was sitting on the rug in front of the fire and had been making toast for her mother, her aunt and herself.

'That'll be enough for now,' Martha said. 'Come and sit up at the table, 'cos as soon as we've had our breakfast, had a quick dust round an' made the beds, we can be off down the market an' the rest of the day will be all ours.'

Never had toast and marmalade tasted better, Joan was thinking, but she knew it was mostly the company. Just looking at her niece made her heart jump for joy. She really was a beauty. Rosie would break many a young man's heart before she was much older.

Between mouthfuls of hot toast, Rosie said, 'I'll come upstairs with you, Aunt Joan, 'cos if we make the beds together it won't take us long.'

'All right,' her mother agreed, 'but no playing about else by the time we get out all the best things will be gone off the stalls.'

'Do they still have a stall that sells remnants?' Joan asked.

'Now why did I know that you were going t' ask me that question?' Martha grinned. 'Still beavering away with yer needle, are you?'

'Oh, there's much more to it than that,' Joan told her, sounding really enthusiastic. 'Leave it for now, but when we sit down tonight I've got a whole lot to tell you.'

'You always were one for planning things on the quiet.' Glad to see the smile on her sister's face, Martha went on, 'You wouldn't believe the people what still knock on this door asking where you are 'cos they want something altered. One woman even wanted to know if you'd make her daughter's wedding dress and when I told her you didn't live here no more she asked if I'd do it. I ask yer. Me with a needle? I couldn't mend a hole if yer paid me a pound a stitch.' Then Martha added, 'Our Rosie ain't bad, though. I always said she looks like you, an' when it comes to needlework she takes after you for that an' all.'

Deep thoughts began to run through Joan's mind. She might never be able to put them into practice but it didn't cost anything to dream.

Even on a bitter cold day like today Joan loved the street market, and although Martha kept saying how much warmer it would be in the indoor market Joan and Rosie would not be persuaded.

'You go inside and do your bits of shopping, and then sit in the café and have a cup of coffee and Rose and I will come and find you later,' Joan said, patting her sister's shoulder kindly.

'I 'ate coffee and I need t' buy some fresh veg an' it's much cheaper out here on the stalls,' Martha grumbled, but she walked away, throwing over her shoulder the sharp words, 'I know you two. Don't take all day. I'll see yer in the café.'

The barrow boys were cheekily shouting their wares, each one trying to outdo the other. Paraffin lamps were lit as well as the gas jets above the stalls, relieving the gloom of the damp dark January day. Joan watched with pleasure as Rosie bent over the haberdashery stall, fingering soft ribbons and strands of velvet, exclaiming over the cards of buttons, so many varieties, from ordinary shirt buttons to coloured glass ones, and even silver and gold ones, in all shapes and sizes. There was braid to match. Oh, what she couldn't do with just ten per cent of this marvellous stock.

'There it is, Aunt Joan. It's the same lady and gent that you used to buy from. Look, over there. It's your material stall.'

Joan walked slowly towards the stall, savouring the sight of the bolts of cloth and remnants in every colour you could name laid out for buyers' inspection. Martin and Marjorie Goldsmith. Joan felt a surge of happiness. It had been ages since she bought material from them. As soon as Martin spotted her he came round from behind the stall. He looked just the same, tall and gangly, with his hair flying all over the place.

'Joan, me darling.' He grinned, kissing her cheek.

'Oh, Martin,' she gasped. 'It's so good to see you. How are you?'

'Doing very well.' He grinned again. 'And it looks as if you ain't doing too badly yerself.'

Marjorie had finished serving her customer and soon she too was kissing and hugging Joan. A lovely smart lady, was Marjorie, and she made every customer feel that their custom was important. A great dressmaker herself, she was always ready to offer advice, and Joan had brought many a problem to her when she had first started to sew for other people. 'I was sad to hear that you'd gone away into service, Joan,' she said now, still keeping her arm round Joan's shoulders.

'Needs must when the devil drives.' Joan smiled. 'But I'm on holiday for a week, staying with my sister Martha.'

Marjorie turned to Rosie. 'You used to come and tell me how your aunt was doing, but we haven't seen you for ages.' She looked back at Joan. 'My God, she's a beauty and no mistake. Make a wonderful model, she would.'

The kind words had Rosie blushing, but the very thought set Joan's mind working overtime. Plans. That's all she had at the moment, but if only!

Marjorie linked arms with Joan. 'You do know everyone round here is so proud of you,' she said. 'When we think of what you've been through and the fact that you literally lost everything and then had to go into service just t' put a roof over your head. It all seemed so unfair. We were all concerned for you and most of us still are.'

'Thanks, Marjorie. I don't know that I did the right thing, but at the time I hadn't any choice.'

111

'Martin and I had hoped you would come to us for help. We could have put many a sewing job your way. My main thought at the time was that there isn't a maternity stall here on the market. You know the kind of thing: cheap wrapround skirts and loose tops for mums-to-be, then maybe baby clothes and even pram covers.'

'That's the kind of thing I would love to do,' Joan confessed, 'but work was not the only problem. I had to find somewhere to live, somewhere with a rent that I could afford.'

'You could have gone on living with us,' Rosie chipped in. 'Me nor me mum wanted you to go away.'

'It wasn't fair to sponge off your mum and dad any longer,' said Joan regretfully as she turned swiftly to Rose and took her hand in hers.

Martin was busy measuring and cutting cloth and there were several customers waiting to be served. A middle-aged man, who sold ready-made dresses with his brother from a stall opposite the Goldsmiths', called, 'It's all right, Marge, you chat away with Joan. I'll give Martin a hand.'

'That's Jack Parker, isn't it? And his brother is Brian. They must have been on the market a few years by now,' Joan remarked thoughtfully.

'Yes, you're dead right, Joan. Thing is, stalls don't very often come up for rent, not on the open market at any rate. They get passed from one member of the family to another, hardly ever does a mother or father let one go.' Marjorie informed her. 'Still, I'll keep me eyes and ears open for both an opening and a decent flat, and I'll let your Martha know if anything comes up. You can always say no if you decide you've made the right decision, but I'll tell you this for nothing, love. Service wouldn't do for me. And with the talent you've got, well ... but keep on with your sewing and if we can help at any time you have only to ask. You know that, don't you? Never could understand why you upped and disappeared so quickly.'

'You always were so good to me.' Joan hugged her.

'You won't have heard, but Martin has his own warehouse now and we have a shop in Balham, so any time you need some cloth you know where to come.' Marjorie laughed. 'Got a gorgeous length of white grosgrain there. Make a lovely wedding dress.'

'Oh yeah.' Both Rosie and Joan laughed.

'Course, I'll find something smashing for your aunt to make up if you're thinking of being her bridesmaid,' Marjorie teased Rosie, looking slyly at Joan, who grinned.

'I've got one answer for you, my dear friend: with me it's a case of once bitten twice shy. But I could do with some remnants today. I've a sewing machine at my disposal where I work and making a few bits for myself for a change wouldn't come amiss.'

'Since you've mentioned it, Joan, I'd say that coat you're wearing ain't exactly keeping the cold out.' Marjorie turned to nod at her husband and silently mouthed a few words. Martin dived underneath the stall and came up with a bulky brown paper parcel which he held out to Joan.

'What is it?' Joan asked, reluctantly taking hold of the parcel.

'You tell her, Martin. I've got t' go now, luv, customers waiting, but I meant every word I said and you know I did. We're here when you need to talk.' With that Marjorie leaned over and kissed young Rosie first and then Joan, holding on to Joan's hand for a long minute. Which said far more than words to Joan.

'Martin . . .' Joan was lost for words. She was clutching the bulky parcel to her chest and finally she managed to say, 'Please let me pay you for this.'

Martin grinned. 'You'd buy a pig in a poke, would you? Don't be so daft. It was a special order that we had to buy in and that piece was surplus to requirements. We are not a penny out of pocket so you are more than welcome to it.'

'Martin,' Joan said shyly, 'I stopped believing in the tooth fairy years ago. But thanks. Thanks a million.'

'Do me one favour,' he asked as she and Rosie turned to go.

'Anything.'

'Don't be a stranger. Come and see us more often – and we want to see that material made up and you wearing it. That's part of the deal.'

Rosie's eyes were wide with excitement as they made their way to the café to meet Martha. 'Wonder what sort of stuff it is? What colour?' she kept saying, once she had related every detail of what had happened to her mother.

'Well, you are going to have to wait until we get home to get the answers to all your questions.' Joan held out a ten shilling note and said, 'Be a dear and fetch me a cup of tea and a Bath bun and anything you fancy for yourself.'

'Ooh, ta,' Rosie answered, lapsing into the kind of speech that was going on around her.

'Wait a moment,' Joan called, having glanced at her sister's empty cup. 'Fetch a fresh tea for your mum and make it two Bath buns.'

It was darts night down at the local pub for Sid and his sons. With dinner all over and the chenille tablecloth covering the wooden top of the table, Joan and Rosie sat with a pad of plain paper and a pencil in front of them.

'Don't be giving me any of that,' Martha said from the comfort of her armchair besides the fire. 'I couldn't make a sketch of a tom-cat, never mind a winter coat. But I have to say I've never seen a finer piece of cloth in all me days.'

The parcel had been undone and the oohs and ahhs had shown how much the contents were appreciated. The colour of the cloth that Martin had given to Joan was beige according to Martha, biscuit according to Rosie and camel according to Joan.

114

'Let's leave 'em to it,' Sid had bellowed as the argument hotted up.

The opinion that the fabric was a very soft pure wool was unanimous. Martha had it in her lap, letting her fingers run slowly over the surface. How kind some people could be. She prayed with all her strength that Joan would be able to make herself a really decent coat from this unexpected gift. God knows she deserves it, she thought as she looked at her sister and Rosie with their heads together. A lump came to her throat. Why had her sister experienced so much bad luck? It never came to those who deserved it. Why did she have to be so far away all the time? In order to make a living, was the only answer she could come up with.

Joan softly cursed under her breath as she and Rosie discarded another drawing. 'We both have a good idea of the coat I would like to make,' she said as she watched Rosie throw her pencil down, 'but we are never going to be able to make our own pattern, never mind put scissors into that cloth, until we are absolutely sure that we know what we are doing.'

'You can buy patterns for coats, can't yer?' Martha's deep growl made them both jump.

Rosie sorted through the pages of paper that they had cast aside until she found the one she was looking for. 'This is the one we agreed we both liked best, Aunt Joan, though each of us said we hadn't got it exactly right, didn't we?'

Joan took the drawing from Rosie's hand and studied it closely. It was one of Rosie's sketches. Wide collar, large revers, double breasted, two side pockets cut on the slant. 'No belt,' Joan murmured.

'I thought a half-belt at the back with two enormous buttons would look different,' Rosie said wearily.

'Oh, darling, it is cleverly drawn. It is along the lines of what I think is known as a reefer coat.' Joan raised her head to look at her niece and said swiftly, 'Oh, I am sorry, pet. You look tired to death. Let's clear all this away and leave it for tonight. I'll make us all a cup of cocoa. Is that all right, Martha?'

'For God's sake,' Martha moaned. 'You don't 'ave t' ask. You know where everything is an' you making us all a hot drink is the best idea you've 'ad tonight.'

Rosie had just finished straightening out each drawing and was putting all the coloured pencils they had been using into a wooden pencil box when Joan came in with the tray. When they each had their drink Joan glanced at her sister.

'Fancy a trip to Croydon tomorrow? I take it Grants is still there.'

'Course it is,' Martha said, looking thoughtful. 'Bit posh, though, and very expensive.'

'I'm only think of buying a pattern and maybe some sateen for the lining,' Joan said gloomily.

'A pattern I agree. You won't get a decent one anywhere else, but you ain't spending good money buying lining from Grants. Not unless you've come into a bloody fortune.' Martha finished on a laugh. 'Besides, you ain't going back for days yet. We can still take another trip to the market. Oh, and that reminds me, Mrs Bradshaw called in when you were upstairs before dinner, said she couldn't stay but if you could spare a few minutes she'd love to see you. I told her you'd probably pop over early in the morning.'

'Mrs Bradshaw, eh? Course I'll go and see her. She was very good to me. Especially when I had that job making lampshades and had to go to the factory two evenings a week. She used to come over and sit with Granny Baldwin – though sit is probably not the right word. Such a busy lady, Mrs Bradshaw, always on the go. Used to bring a pile of ironing over to my house to do rather than just sit and twiddle her thumbs.'

'Yeah, well, when you were brought up like we were you

learnt to keep busy. Remember what Dad used to say? The devil finds work for idle hands.'

Joan smiled at Martha. 'And whenever we got given a job to do, such as cleaning those long brass stair-rods, Mum used to put that wooden motto in the middle of the table.' Rosie looked on in amazement as her mother and her aunt fell about laughing, both saying in a sing-song tone of voice, *'If a job is worth doing it is worth doing well.'*

'I'm going to bed,' Rosie said, her own lips curling with laughter as she hugged each of them in turn. 'Good night, God bless.'

Chapter Twelve

JOAN RAPPED ON THE DOOR with her knuckles. If she were still living in this area she would slip her hand through the letter box and pull out the length of string to find the door key that was always fastened on to the end. It seemed a bit of a liberty to let herself into Mrs Bradshaw's house when it was such a long time since they had met. The front door opened and Joan got quite a shock. Mrs Bradshaw had aged so much, and her face had such an unhealthy drawn look, that for a second Joan did not recognise her.

'Ah, it's you, Joan dear. Please come in.' The old lady smiled and stepped back to let Joan come inside.

Joan felt uncomfortable as she sat in the homely kitchen that she remembered so well from the time when they had been good neighbours. Mrs Bradshaw seemed to be staring strangely at her, and when at last she spoke her voice was not at all steady.

'Oh, Joan, I've got something to tell you, something I think you should know, and yet I am not at all sure that it would be right to open up old wounds.'

'Mrs Bradshaw, whatever is it? You look done in.' Joan put out a hand and patted her knee, but her own heart was thumping with apprehension. Whatever could have happened to affect this kind lady so much? 'I'll make you a strong cup of tea,' she offered. Receiving no reply, she took herself out into the scullery, found the teapot, ladled in two heaped spoons of tea and took the pot back into the living room, where a large black kettle was singing away on the back of the range. Having poured the boiling water on to the tea leaves she set the pot to stand in the hearth and fetched a cup and saucer from the dresser. She looked around but couldn't see any milk, and then it dawned on her that the bottle was probably standing outside the back door. It was certainly cold enough out there to stop the milk from turning sour.

She was right. There was half a bottle of milk with an upturned earthenware pot covering its top on the back doorstep.

Mrs Bradshaw accepted the tea gratefully and as she sipped it a little colour gradually came back into her cheeks. At last she began to speak, shaking her head from side to side. 'As I said, I have something to tell you. It will come as a shock, and I'm sorry.'

Joan was well and truly bewildered by now. She turned to look at Mrs Bradshaw, a slight frown on her face. 'Whatever it is, I think you had better tell me and be done with it. Come on, get this thing that's worrying you off your chest. You know what they say: a trouble shared is a trouble halved.'

Mrs Bradshaw took another sip of her tea. 'It's about my granddaughter. You must remember Linda? My daughter died when she was born and she lived with me all her life 'cos her father married again within six months and his new wife couldn't be bothered with another woman's baby.' She paused and tried to catch her breath. Meanwhile Joan was completely at sea.

'I well remember Linda. I watched her growing up. There

119

was a time when she used to come round to my place quite a lot. Kind girl, was Linda; she used to sit and talk to Granny Baldwin. Weren't many youngsters who would give a sick old lady the time of day.'

Mrs Bradshaw muttered something, but Joan didn't catch her words.

'Anyway, what about Linda?' Joan prompted. 'Something must be wrong. You look worried to death. I can see you're not yourself. Linda moved away some time ago, didn't she?'

'Yes, she did.' Mrs Bradshaw kept her head down and would not meet Joan's eyes. 'Just over two years ago she came t' me an' told me she was pregnant. She was only sixteen. The shock of it nearly killed me, I can tell yer.' Now she had actually got to the point, there was no stopping her. 'I wasn't 'aving my good name dragged through the mud. Folk 'ave a rotten name for a baby born out of wedlock and what they call the mother doesn't bear thinking about. Bad enough if we could 'ave 'ad a shotgun wedding. But oh no, the father was a slimy git, he got off scot free. My Fred only just stopped short of blaming me. Said I should 'ave kept an eye on her, but I didn't know she was carrying on with a married fella. Anyway, give the girl what's due to 'er, she up an' left this house, more for my sake than anything else. She kept in touch. I 'ad a few letters. Apparently her and a mate both got a job and a flat and they did shift work bringing the baby up between them. Then it became a case of be sure yer sins will find you out. Her friend got herself married and moved out, and then my Linda met a bloke who wanted to marry her and take 'er back to where he came from. New Zealand, would you believe.'

Joan remained silent while Mrs Bradshaw nervously cleared her throat before continuing. 'Talk about history repeating itself. This fella was keen enough to have my Linda, the baby was another matter altogether. He wanted nothing

120

to do with the boy. Oh yeah. I didn't say, did I? It was a boy. He's about eighteen months old now.'

A white-faced Joan badly wanted to ask what all this had to do with her. A fearful expression had settled on her face. She could smell trouble brewing and to be honest she just wanted to get up and go. She couldn't bring herself to do it. This old lady had been kind to her in the past and more so to Granny Baldwin, yet fear was gripping her heart and she somehow knew she was going to be very sorry that she had walked into this house this morning.

'Better finish what I've started.' Mrs Bradshaw sighed. 'A month ago my Linda asked me to meet her on Victoria station and spend the afternoon with her. She told me she had put the child into care with a view to having it adopted and the very next day after we met she was off to New Zealand. Just like that. All cut and dried. Going to get married and live out there, so she said. Can't say I altogether blame 'er. Have to grab at what bit of 'appiness yer can get in this life. She'd done well in my opinion. At least she had tried to bring the child up on her own.'

Sitting there in the cosy living room Joan felt horrified, knowing she had to ask the vital question. Yet in her heart she already knew the answer, because there could be only one reason why Mrs Bradshaw was pouring the tale out to her now.

'So you've brought me here today to tell me who the father is? I am right, aren't I?'

Mrs Bradshaw really did look worried to death. Tears trickled down her cheeks and she began to cry. 'I loved my Linda from the day she was born. I was her mother in every sense of the word. What that bastard did to her wasn't right. She was only a slip of a girl.' She waved her hands at Joan as though trying to tell her to go.

'I'm sorry to see you so upset, and truly I do understand,

121

but please, Mrs Bradshaw, you asked me to come here this morning because you wanted to tell me something. Be honest. You haven't told me the main part, have you? You've only hinted, and I can't live with that. So please, find the courage and tell me who the man was who made your grand-daughter pregnant.'

'Your husband. Bloody Bill Baldwin.'

Trembling with anger, Joan went to the sobbing woman and held her in her arms. Somehow she had to find words that might comfort this grandmother, but it would be one of the hardest things that she had ever had to do. What she really wanted to do was get out of this house. But she breathed in deeply and spoke with as much sympathy as she could manage.

'I can only hope and pray that you might feel relieved, even find a little comfort in the fact that you have been able to tell me this terrible, shameful secret, which came about because of the wrong my husband did. From now on you have to believe that Linda will be settled and happy in her new life.'

Mrs Bradshaw dabbed at her eyes and managed to smile at Joan. 'I've tried to tell myself all that, but what it really means is I shall never see my granddaughter again. At my age I'm never going to visit New Zealand. Nor will I set eyes on the baby who is rightfully my great-grandson.'

Joan could find no answer to that.

The silence between them hung heavy until Mrs Bradshaw timidly asked, 'Did I do right to tell you?'

Joan had to sniff hard. Again she couldn't bring herself to voice the whole truth. 'If telling me has made you feel better, then I am pleased that I was able to listen.' Feeling that she couldn't just walk out and leave the old lady suffering as she was, she added reluctantly, 'Perhaps you'll come over to Martha's and have a cup of tea with us before I have to return to Kent.'

'I can see I've upset you, but if you really mean it, thanks very much, Joan. I'd love to.'

Joan covered the short distance back to her sister's house very slowly. Should she tell Martha? She had to tell someone. If she kept mulling over and over this turn of events she'd end up going out of her mind. Bill Baldwin! Even dead and buried he was still intruding, upsetting her life, to say nothing of the poor young girl he had made pregnant.

Why hadn't she noticed anything wrong at the time? She knew the answer to that question only too well. For one thing, he had never told her where he was going or when he would be back. And another reason was that she had learnt the hard way not to ask questions. She needed no reminding that all she had ever got for her trouble was not a straight answer, just a slap round the head to begin with. Should she have been daft enough to persist, a jolly good beating would have followed.

The business with Linda, however, was a terrible shock. She had always known her Bill was a gambler, an out and out liar, and someone with a reputation for being a lady's man. But a young girl! Hardly out of school!

To say the least, that must have been his dirtiest trick ever.

Martha took one look at her sister's face and cried, '*Joan!* Gawd almighty, what's 'appened? What's wrong?'

Joan lowered her eyes. 'Oh, Martha. I just don't know where to start.'

'Sit down, do, Joan. Before yer fall down. And a good place t' start is always at the beginning.' Martha took hold of Joan's hand and found it icy cold. 'Oh my God, girl, you're like an iceberg!' She began to chafe her hands between her own. 'What in the world is the matter with you?'

Joan was trying to tell her, but it was hard. Her teeth

were chattering so that speech was difficult and the words, if they came out at all, were disjointed. And now for the first time helpless tears began to trickle down her cheeks.

'What did Mrs Bradshaw say to you that seems to 'ave turned your world upside down?' Martha pushed Joan down into an armchair and then perched herself on the edge of the chair opposite her. 'Come on then, out with it,' she commanded.

Still Joan hesitated, but she knew she had to share the sad story. The question was how to do it. Yet she didn't feel that she should be held responsible for Bill's misdeeds. She fiddled with the wedding ring she still wore, avoiding her sister's gaze. Then she took the bull by the horns, lowered her voice and, speaking slowly, did her best to repeat word for word the tale Mrs Bradshaw had told her.

When she had finished, Martha was biting her bottom lip and her cheeks were bright red, but so far she hadn't said a word.

'I suppose I'll have to seek legal advice.'

Joan had spoken with such sadness that Martha got quickly to her feet and moved to stand looking down on her. 'You ain't gonna bother about no advice, Joan, legal or otherwise. All of what Nellie Bradshaw has told you 'appened over two years ago. I reckon her Linda was a great kid. She took it on the chin and now, after having done her best for the baby, she's decided to cut an' run. *Her* decision. *Her* choice. She's done what she thinks is best for her child an' now she's gonna make a new life for 'erself, an' I fer one say darn good luck to her.'

'But what about Mrs Bradshaw? She's ever so upset,' Joan stammered.

'Nellie Bradshaw should count 'er blessings. Things might 'ave turned out a whole lot different if at the time Linda found she was pregnant her grandparents had said sod the neighbours, ignored all the gossip and stuck by Linda and

124

let her keep the baby. Mind you, I ain't saying that would have been the right decision.'

Joan's face went bright red. It didn't bear thinking about. The entanglement that would have come about if two years ago Mr and Mrs Bradshaw had encouraged Linda to stay around and have the baby!

Martha gave her sister a wry grin. 'I can read your thoughts, yer know. I can tell exactly what's going through your mind. Would 'ave been a right old shemozzle, wouldn't it? I got ter say again, I admire that Linda.'

What Martha was also thinking was that it would have broken her sister's heart to see a young girl with a baby in her arms that had been fathered by her own husband. Best not voice those kinds of thoughts out loud, she scolded herself. Pulling the kettle near to the front of the range she said, 'It's on the point of boiling. We'll 'ave a cuppa an' I'll put a drop of the 'ard stuff in it. Do us both good.'

Soon they were both sipping the tea to which Martha had added a good drop of whisky, each busy with her own thoughts. Martha was the first to speak.

'It must 'ave took that young girl some courage to meet up with her grandma and tell 'er to her face that she's gonna live on the other side of the world. *And* to be honest enough t' tell her what arrangements she had made for the baby. There's some that would 'ave just gone off without saying a word an' Nellie wouldn't 'ave been any the wiser. No, say what yer like, that Linda's been a brave girl. Right from the start when she moved out, not leaving the mess on her gran's doorstep.'

Joan couldn't bring herself to believe how callous her sister was being. 'Martha, don't you care that little boy is my Bill's son?'

Martha assumed a measure of dignity. 'To be honest, Joan, no, I don't care. That child is better off without Bill Baldwin as his father. If I'm sorry at all it is because young

125

Linda's new boyfriend isn't willing to take him on. It would seem he asked Linda to make her choice and she has. She might live to regret it and she might not. But that's her business. You have to go along with it and leave it at that.'

Still Joan did not feel it was right. 'The little boy has been placed into care,' she protested.

'I'd bet my last tanner not for long.' Martha pressed her point. 'If he were ten or eleven I'd say he hadn't a chance in hell of being adopted, but a dear little boy, hardly more than a baby, there'll be couples lining up to give him a good home.'

'So I'm to sit back and do nothing.' This time Joan shouted at her sister.

'Actually,' Martha tried her best to soften her voice, 'that is exactly what you should do. Bill is dead. Nothing will alter that fact, and as I've already said, I reckon that Linda has sorted matters out very well, all things considered. After all, it's her life we're talking about. So it was up to her an' her alone to make the choice.'

Throughout the day Joan repeatedly told herself that Martha had given her a straight talking to. She almost came to believe that the suggestions she had offered were sound advice. One very sore point rankled, though, and it probably would for the rest of her life.

How she would loved to have had children. From the day she and Bill had been married it had been her dearest wish. Her arms ached when she thought of the three miscarriages she had suffered. But nearly's didn't count. She had never got to hold even one of her babies.

She would go to the ends of the earth to find this little boy if she thought she might be allowed to adopt him. To hold him in her arms. Be allowed to bring him up as her very own boy. Love him for always. However, common sense told her it would be as useless as banging her head against a brick wall. She was on her own. Adoption societies would be looking for two parents. Another point: she'd be considered too old. Anyway, what security could she offer a child? Where would she take him to live? How would she keep him fed and clothed? What education would she be able to offer him? Stop it. *Stop it!* Her head was going round and round, and the more she tried to convince herself that she should do something for her husband's son the more confused she became. At last she made herself acknowledge that she had to do what Martha had said she should do. Absolutely nothing.

All the same, she knew this was not the end of the matter. At the end of the day it would not be gone and forgotten. In the future there would be many a time when her mind would be full, wondering where that little boy was and whether he was happy. To think it could have been her and Bill's son. She must strive hard not to dwell on what she had been told, because the irony of it was enough to break her heart.

She closed her eyes, hating herself for the resentment she felt. If only things could have been different. If only . . . Best to let sleeping dogs lie.

Chapter Thirteen

THE DAYS THAT FOLLOWED went far too quickly. Martha and Joan had a day out on their own looking round the shops in Croydon. Of course their first stop had to be in Grants, where they had sat in armchairs and waded through endless pattern books. Spoilt for choice and undecided, they had been approached by a young lady dressed in the customary little black dress with a white collar, who asked politely, 'Would you two ladies like any help?'

Joan explained that she had been given a present of a length of cloth and was intending to make herself a winter coat. 'I was thinking of a double-breasted one with perhaps raglan sleeves.'

'I would be better able to advise on a pattern if Madam would say what type of cloth it is, and the colour would be helpful.'

'I've been told it is seventy per cent pure wool and thirty per cent cashmere.' Joan spoke hesitantly. 'And beige – or maybe you would call it camel.'

'Madam is not taking the material to a tailor?' The shop assistant sounded horrified. Joan realised that although the clothes she was wearing were neat and tidy they didn't send out the message that she could afford material made of such fine soft wool.

'It won't be the first coat I have made, nor yet the last I hope, but as the material was a present from a gentleman who owns a warehouse, I shall be extra careful when cutting the cloth.' Joan's answer was like an iron fist in a silk glove. The young lady's attitude changed immediately and she came as near to saying sorry as she could.

'We have a pattern for what is known as a reefing jacket. It can be made up to any length that Madam would wish.'

'That is kind of you. I would like to see it, if I may,' Joan said, smiling to herself, because she hadn't told the assistant that the gentleman also had a stall on the market. That bit of information she had thought it wise to keep to herself.

Martha smiled with pleasure and pride in Joan. She didn't know where her artistic talent sprang from but she knew from past experience that her sister's taste was always the best. She felt like telling this toffee-nosed shop girl that Joan was a natural genius when it came to sewing.

Joan knew instinctively that the pattern she was now looking at was exactly what she had been searching for. 'Thank you.' Joan looked up at the young lady, her blue eyes smiling sweetly as she said, 'That will be perfect.'

'If Madam would like to come this way I can show you a wide choice of linings and we could match up the sewing thread.'

'I'll just pay for the pattern, please,' said Joan as she rose from the comfortable chair that Grants provided for their customers.

Outside the shop the two sisters looked at each other and burst out laughing. Martha, still wobbling with merriment, said, 'Come on, let's find a café an' have a cup of tea.'

Joan went to the counter while Martha found two seats, and when Joan came back with two steaming teas and two plates that each held an enormous meat pie, Martha could not resist teasing Joan. 'I'll just pay for the pattern, please,' she mimicked. Then, in her own voice, she said, 'I noticed you didn't tell Miss Smarty-pants that Grants lining is three and eleven a yard and cotton is sixpence a reel, whereas on the market cotton is only tuppence a reel and lining starts off at a shilling a yard.'

'Course I didn't, yer daft ha'p'orth, but while I was waiting for my change I had the feeling that any minute now that's exactly what you were going to tell her.'

Martha let out a bellow of a laugh. 'I was sorely tempted, I'll tell yer. But you'd 'ave hit the roof and we both would 'ave got thrown out.'

'Eat your pie and shut up,' Joan pleaded. 'We'll go to the market and see Marjorie and Martin tomorrow. You can say what you like there without treading on anyone's toes.'

'What makes yer think I won't?' Martha was still giggling as she tried to drink her tea.

'Oh, Mum, please don't make me go to school today. I'll be leaving at Easter anyway.'

Rosie was pleading and Joan covered her mouth with her hand to hide her smile. She knew full well Rosie would win her mother over if she kept on long enough.

'It's not fair, Mum. You had Aunt Joan all to yourself yesterday when you went to Croydon. A few more days an' she'll be going back to Kent and how long before I'll get to see her again? I bet it will be ages and ages.' Rosie knew how to lay it on. Her beautiful big blue eyes were sparkling with tears.

'Oh, all right.' Martha gave in grudgingly. 'But we're going to the market first. Yer aunt needs to get a few things off Mr Goldsmith's stall.'

Rosie jumped up from the breakfast table, plonked a kiss on her mother's cheek, winked at her aunt and made a bolt for the door. Her voice was as sweet as honey as she called out, 'Shall I wear my Sunday coat and the new scarf that Aunt Joan bought for me?'

Both sisters shook with laughter. 'What would yer do with 'er?' Martha asked.

'Like you always do. Love her t' bits,' Joan answered, still laughing.

Joan was miles away as the three of them got off the tram and made their way to the lively market. She felt happy enough working at Mulborough House. True, when Christmas had passed she had sighed thankfully, relieved that it was all over. Even in a crowded room you could feel lonely if there was no one to call your own. These past days with her sister and her family had made her realise what she was truly missing. Her own home, and cheery companionship.

It would be almost February by the time she returned to Kent. The weather had not got any better; in fact they had announced on the wireless that all parts of Kent had suffered severe snow storms. That meant that even on her day off she would be unlikely to get outside the house. She had no friends or relations living locally whom she could go and visit. No, she said to herself, to be truthful I am not looking forward to going back to work.

'A bit quiet this morning, ain't yer, Joan?' Martha's expression was amused. 'You've got the feel of London again. Don't wanna go back t' be buried in the countryside, do yer?'

Joan shook her head. It was truly amazing how her sister could almost always read her thoughts.

They arrived at the Goldsmiths' stall and Martha related in detail to Martin and Marjorie what had taken place during her and Joan's visit to Grants. Jack and Brian Parker heard the laughter and walked across from their own stall. 'Can anyone join in?' Jack asked, smiling broadly.

131

Martha didn't need much persuasion to begin again at the beginning, exaggerating the details as it suited her until everybody was having a good old laugh.

'I'll cut you off enough lining now and throw in two reels of thread,' Martin said to Joan, 'though I think you should wait till you finish the coat before you decide how many buttons you are going to need.'

'You lot doing anything this afternoon?' Marjorie asked.

'Why? D'yer want us t' mind the stall for yer?' Martha giggled, staring at Martin.

'God forbid!' Martin cried. 'We'd have more customers demanding their money back tomorrow than we could deal with. Don't forget, Martha Brown, I've seen the way you slice a loaf of bread. What you would do let loose with a bolt of cloth and a pair of scissors don't bear thinking about.'

'Cheeky sod.' Martha grinned. 'You wait till you come to my 'ouse an' say you're 'ungry, I'll cut you a sandwich, you see if I don't.'

Marjorie butted in. 'If you lot have finished sparring I was going to suggest that you come home with me for the afternoon. It's not very busy here today. Martin can manage, can't you, love?'

'Do I have any choice in the matter?' He smirked.

'You do, actually. I could stay here with you all day and when we get home you'll get cheese on toast *or* I can sneak off now and have a really good dinner ready for you by the time you get home tonight.'

'Stewed steak and dumplings *and* the gravy thick with vegetables?'

'Yeah, all right then,' Marjorie agreed gleefully. To Martha, Joan and Rosie she said, 'Quick, jump in the van before he changes his mind.'

An excited gleam came to Joan's eyes as all four of them stood on the pavement in Balham outside a double-fronted shop which had a sign above it saying Goldsmith's Haberdashery. There were three people looking round inside the shop and two middle-aged ladies, both wearing long-sleeved black dresses, were serving. The first window was dressed to seem as if one were gazing into a lady's parlour. The backdrop had lace curtains in the centre, while a heavily embossed linen curtain was draped at each side, looped back and held by a silken rope from which hung long, heavy tassels.

Set out on various tables were bolts of cloth in all the beautiful colours of the rainbow. Cushions large and small were scattered on the floor, some plain, some braided, some with frilled edges, others with corner tassels. All could be colour-coordinated not only with the curtains but also with the lengths of material on display. There were also two amazingly beautiful standard lamps with huge lampshades so elaborately embroidered that Joan found herself longing to own one.

Moving across to stare into the second window even young Rosie let out a great 'Ah' on seeing the much lighter materials on show.

'Much more suitable for dressmaking,' Joan mumbled enviously to herself. There were a few rolls of suit-weight cloth, plus a great many bolts of both linen and cotton material, plain, patterned or floral. Again, it was no ordinary display, with a great variety of hats, gloves, shoes and handbags scattered loosely about, all compatible with the various shades of the draped cloth. Joan turned to Marjorie, her curiosity getting the better of her. 'Whatever gave you the idea of setting out such wonderful window displays?'

'It was Martin's idea in the first place, but who knows what made him think of it,' she answered with a shrug. 'All the backdrop framework – which is altered every now and again – is made for us by a man on the market, Jim Taylor.

I call him the bare wood man. Anyhow, it's freezing us all standing here. Come on upstairs and let's get into the warm.'

To Joan and Martha's surprise the flat above the shop was much larger and a great deal grander than they had expected. The kitchen was large and homely but the sitting room was something else, more like two rooms in one. A large sofa and several comfortable armchairs, a sideboard and two small occasional tables were set round a huge marble fireplace at one end of the room, while at the other stood the most beautiful mahogany table surrounded by six matching chairs. The carpet was attractively patterned and of a good quality. Within a very short time they had removed their coats and Marjorie was pushing a well-laden tea trolley into the room. The tea was hot and strong, the cakes absolutely delicious.

Joan couldn't take her eyes off Marjorie. Up until now she had mostly seen her behind the stall on the market, buttoned up to the neck in a heavy coat and wearing a scarf and a velvet hat. Even during the summer months she was never what Joan considered well dressed. Now she looked entirely different. She was wearing a sage green woollen dress which had a long straight skirt and long sleeves with wide cuffs decorated by a row of glittering buttons. The same ornamental buttons were sewn round the neck of the dress to form a collar. Joan was impressed. Marjorie looked immaculate. Before, her hair had been hidden; now the sheen of her wavy auburn hair was a joy to behold.

Rosie had found a jigsaw and was sitting on the floor quite happily finding pieces to fit the spaces. Martha thought she was in heaven. Big cosy armchair, feet up on a foot stool, nothing to do but glance through the glossy magazines that Marjorie had placed on the floor beside her. Weren't many lazy afternoons like this, not for her at least. Martha sighed contentedly.

For her part, Joan wanted to ask numerous questions and

Marjorie had detected as much. Apart from the fact that it was obvious that these two sisters loved each other dearly, there was no comparison. Martha had a heart of gold, was never discontented with her way of life, and her attitude was always take each day as it comes. Joan was intelligent besides being beautiful in a strange sort of way. She had the clearest of blue eyes, dark hair that had golden glints and a refined look about her even though she was not dressed as well as she might be. But my God, Marjorie was thinking, Joan Baldwin would pay for dressing. She could easily be a model, for she had a figure that most young women would die for. But she wasn't a young woman. Looking at her now and thinking of all the years she had known her, Marjorie came to the conclusion that Joan had never been given a chance. Worse than that, she had had a really rough deal.

'First question?'

Joan was startled. 'How do you know I wanted to ask questions? Everybody seems to be able to read my mind today.'

'Don't dilly-dally. Ask away.' Marjorie laughed. 'I won't be in the least offended.'

'Well . . .' Joan hesitated. 'The man you said made the backdrop for the window dressings, Jim Taylor, I think you said his name was.'

Marjorie looked surprised. 'That's not at all the kind of thing I thought you were going to ask me about. Why him?'

'Because you called him the bare wood man.'

'Oh, I see.' Now Marjorie threw back her head and laughed. 'I didn't mean he stood bare in the market.'

'I never thought you did,' Joan said, laughing at the thought, 'but I still can't fathom out how he came to be given that name.'

'Easy. He works with every different kind of wood he can lay his hands on. As a carpenter he ranks with the best but no matter what he makes, be it a plain pine shelf or a

135

mahogany table, he never gives it the finishing touches. He has a deal with a well-known firm that do the polishing and fix the handles. On his stall in the market he sells mostly cheap white wood things – clothes horses, stools, boxes of all shapes and sizes or anything you fancy he'll make to order. But tell me, Joan, why the sudden interest in Jim?'

'I did see a nicely shaped wooden stool in the market this morning. Didn't give it another thought until I saw the display in your shop downstairs.'

Marjorie frowned. 'I don't get the connection.'

'I don't know that I do exactly. But my thoughts were that maybe, only maybe mind, I might be able to teach myself to pad and cover the seat of a stool, kind of make it into a dressing-table stool, probably to match a pair of curtains or even a bedspread.'

Marjorie was suddenly intrigued, as she always was by new ideas. 'Jesus, gal, I'll have to get you talking to my Martin. You're wasted being a ruddy servant. You should have yer own shop. There's no limit to what you can do with a needle. I know that of old, and customers still ask after you. And as for the upholstery, you could get a book on that. Probably got several in the library.'

Joan was so surprised that Marjorie had taken her seriously that she was almost speechless. At last she found her voice. 'Oh yeah, I could reach for the stars but I'd never get them. Where would I get the money from to rent a shop, even if I found somewhere up here to live?'

'When are you going back to Kent?'

'Day after tomorrow.'

Marjorie glanced at her. 'Don't give up before you've even started. Take your time. Give a whole lot of thought to what we've talked about. You'd be more than halfway there as regards cloth and suchlike. Martin would see to all that for you, you know he would, and he'd give you credit till you got on your feet.'

Marjorie was talking so enthusiastically that Joan was halfway to believing it might all come about. Big ideas were rolling round in her head but still disbelief showed in her eyes. It would not be easy, Joan was well aware of that, but the seeds of ambition had been planted. Perhaps all she needed was determination. On the other hand, a great deal of dedication wouldn't come amiss either. That would only leave the question of how and where she was going to be able to come up with enough working capital to start her own commercial business. Her next thought brought her sharply down to earth with a bump. Suppose she did manage to convince a bank to lend her just enough money to start her off, where on earth would she find suitable premises?

'Lot to think about when you get back to Kent,' Marjorie said encouragingly. 'But you'll do it. I know you will. Just keep telling yourself, nothing ventured, nothing gained.'

Joan smiled at the dear friend who was going out of her way to help her, but she didn't answer her. She really didn't know what to say. Dreams come cheap. Reality was a different matter altogether.

Chapter Fourteen

JOAN'S THOUGHTFUL MOOD stayed with her for the rest of the afternoon and well into the evening. She was glad when their dinner was over and Bernie got out a pack of cards. Sid poured the drinks and they settled themselves round the table. Joan was grateful to Lenny and Bernie for staying at home this evening. They were only doing it because her holiday was almost over and they knew it might be some time before they all met up again.

'Listen, all of you,' she announced abruptly. 'There's something I would like to talk to you about.'

Martha looked at her sister closely, frowning. 'You sound serious, luv. I knew there was something wrong. You've been dead quiet ever since we left Marjorie's. If you don't tell us what's wrong 'ow the hell can we 'elp you?'

Joan hesitated, and cleared her throat. 'There's nothing wrong, honestly. It's just that Martin started the ball rolling by giving me that lovely material and then Marjorie came up with some ideas that got me thinking. She suggests that if I want to come back to live near all of you I should find an empty shop to rent, preferably one that has living quarters above it. She also said that she and Martin had spoken about me and that Martin was all for it, recommending I start up slowly at first, taking in sewing repair jobs, then progressing to making various things to sell.'

Sid's face turned red. 'I guessed you weren't all that 'appy, stuck away down there in Kent, and watching you these past few days all my fears 'ave been confirmed. I don't want you rushing into something you might be sorry for. Getting up to yer ears in debt. Don't be too 'asty. But if you're not 'appy then don't go back. I've told yer time an' time again, as long as Martha an' me 'ave a roof over our 'eads there will always be a 'ome here for you with us.'

'Please stay, Auntie. I know you don't want to go back,' Rosie pleaded tearfully.

'Oh, dear. None of you have understood what I was trying to say. I didn't mean to upset any of you. Of course I am going back to my job. I would never leave Mr and Mrs Hamilton in the lurch. What I will admit is that there are times when I feel really lonely. Though I know full well how lucky I was to be offered this job, and I really am treated very well, I'm not young and I have to say that the future worries me.'

'Good 'eavens, Joan, we wouldn't see you with nowhere to go.' Martha leant across the table and grasped her sister's hand.

Bernie, who was sitting next to her, put his arm round his aunt's shoulder and for a horrible moment he thought she was going to cry. 'Come on, Aunt Joan, buck up. You haven't finished telling us what it is you're thinking about doing, have you?'

'No, I haven't,' Joan said, looking thoughtful. 'I have loved being here and I do appreciate how you all care for me. It has made me realise just how much I do miss my family. All the same, I am going back to Mulborough House. It wouldn't be right not to. In the meantime,' she paused and looked at each of her dear ones in turn, 'I'd like you all to keep your eyes and ears open for a property that you think might be suitable, and if, and God knows it's a great big if, I can find enough money to start me off I would like to own my own business.'

There was a stunned silence, broken by a very excited Rosie. 'Cor, can I come and work for you, Auntie?'

Everyone laughed. Sid Brown found it especially funny. 'Well there you are, gal. Staff already pleading for a job. Just goes to show that yer niece has faith in yer.'

'Yes,' Joan said emotionally. She moved towards Rosie, who got to her feet straight away, and the two of them stood in front of the fire silently hugging each other tight. One middle-aged woman, and one young girl just starting out on the road of life, each of them letting her imagination run riot, building castles in the air.

The whole family had helped to persuade Joan to stay until the Sunday and take the midday train to Tunbridge Wells. Now, on this brilliantly sunny but bitterly cold February afternoon, she walked along the long drive that led to Mulborough House. She was lost in thought as she put her hand on the latch of the back door, but was suddenly startled back to the present by Kathleen O'Leary's voice as the cook came towards her with her arms outstretched.

'Ah, there ye are, me darling. Am I glad to see you.'

Joan went into Kathleen's arms, lowered her head, and kissed her affectionately on the cheek. She was unable to keep the worry out of her voice when she asked, 'Why, what's wrong?'

'Ah, Joan, I don't know where to start. I'll make us a pot of tea, you sit yerself down and while the kettle comes to the boil I'll begin at the beginning.'

Joan watched as the dumpy, lovable woman pulled the kettle to the front of the enormous range. Her hands were shaking and her head was nodding non-stop, and despite her words she seemed reluctant to begin her story. Joan pushed her attaché case across the floor with her foot until it rested against the wall out of the way, then returned to the table and laid out two cups and saucers. She wished to God Cook would tell her what had happened while she had been in London. She knew that sooner or later she would hear all the news, down to the very last detail, but not before Kathleen was good and ready. Yet having poured the boiling water on to the tea leaves the cook was stirring the tea round and round in the pot until Joan was on the point of asking her to stop. When at last the two of them were seated, each with a cup of tea in front of her, Joan could stand the silence no longer.

'Well, Kathleen, are you going to tell me what's been going on while I've been away? Because I don't have to be psychic to know that all is not well in this house at the moment, do I?' Joan demanded.

Kathleen looked upset. At last, she sighed and said, 'To start off Mr Hamilton had a stroke, only the day after you left. Mrs Hamilton wouldn't hear of him being taken into hospital so we've had nurses living in, day and night, an' by golly they want more waiting on than I should think the Queen herself does.'

Joan took her hand gently. 'I'm so sorry. How bad was the stroke, and how is Mr Hamilton now?'

'I haven't seen him, but the missus tells me he is in a very bad way. I gather all the right side of his body is affected, even his face. His mouth is so twisted he can hardly speak, and apparently his right arm is useless. When you go in to see him you should be prepared for quite a change in his appearance. He can only drink through a straw or a special feeding cup Mr Bruce brought down from London. I prepare special meals for him – have to mince or mash everything up – and the nurse feeds him, though she moans about the mess, says more food dribbles out than goes into him. Real

141

uppity those nurses are. Both the day and the night nurse think I'm here to wait on them.'

Joan could sense how worried and tired Kathleen was. She lifted her shoulders helplessly. 'This would have to happen when I was away. You must have had so much put on your shoulders.'

'You ain't heard the 'alf of it yet,' Cook said sharply.

'Well, whatever more there is to tell it can hardly be worse,' Joan said glumly.

'Can't it?' Cook looked at her reproachfully. 'Just listen to this. Miss Reid took a jug of coffee upstairs for the night nurse and was bringing that lazy beggar's dinner tray down when she tripped and fell from the top of the stairs to the bottom. We just couldn't move her. Had to send for the ambulance an' she's been in hospital ever since. Broke her hip, and her arm, would you believe.'

Joan sat back, placed her teacup down on its saucer and stared at her in astonishment.

'And before you ask if that's all, Mr Farrant's wife has been taken ill. Don't know what's wrong with her. Only know he comes up to the house each morning for about an hour and we don't see him again for the rest of the day.'

Joan could hardly believe that all these disasters had taken place in the short time that she had been away.

'Well, say something,' Cook demanded impatiently.

Joan shook her head sadly. 'I can't think of anything to say. So much worry for everyone.'

'You know what they say, everything comes in threes,' Cook said, leaning towards Joan and studying her face carefully. 'Worked out yet what this is going to mean for you, Joan?'

Those few words hit Joan almost as if lightning had struck. They had a far deeper meaning than Kathleen O'Leary could imagine. For, while Joan had thought that she had come to a decision regarding her future, she found that what

142

she had just heard had changed everything. Now she really would have to make a choice!

She took the cups and saucers to the sink, rinsed them under the running tap and set them upside down on the wooden draining board. Then, feeling very far from confident, she turned to face Cook. 'I'm going up to my room to change and put my uniform on, and then I suppose I'd better go and speak to Mrs Hamilton.'

'Madam will be lying down. She needs her afternoon rest. Miss Delia and Miss Fiona have been here for about four days but they left on Friday. Mr Bruce and his wife are both in the drawing room. I think it would be best for you to have a word with them. They seem very capable and I for one will be eternally grateful that they turned up so quickly when they got the news about his father.'

While Joan changed her clothes, her thoughts were going round in circles. She had come back to Mulborough House fully convinced that she was going to hand in a month's notice. So much had been offered to her. Wouldn't she be doing the right thing, branching out on her own? If everything worked out as planned she would not only be earning a living but once again have a home to call her own.

On the other hand, what if everything failed? She had made up her mind to put that thought to the back of her mind. At least she would have tried.

Martha had confessed that she had thought Joan's idea of opening a shop very foolish at first, but later, having listened to Marjorie, she said she was beginning to think it might turn out for the best. At least it would bring her sister back to London and she'd see a darn sight more of her.

Sid had been very supportive. 'Go for it, gal. In this life if you're given the chance to achieve something it's best t' grab it with both 'ands, 'cos opportunity don't knock twice. With Marjorie and Martin backing yer I'd say yer can't lose.'

The offers from Martin and Marjorie had been amazingly generous. They had even asked if she'd like to work on their stall in the market until a suitable property could be found. 'Your expertise in sewing would be invaluable, especially with some of our more dodgy customers,' Martin had said laughingly. He had also reassured her that he was more than pleased to do as Marjorie had suggested. 'Unlimited credit until yer on yer feet, my darling. I'd not lose a wink of sleep 'cos with you I know I'd be backing a winner.'

Where else would she find such support and so many friends?

Jack and Brian Parker had urged her to take up the offer, telling her she would be an asset to the market. And she'd had a long talk with Jim Taylor, the bare wood man. She smiled to herself, thinking of the name that Marjorie had given him. When she had told him about her idea for padding and upholstering a dressing stool, he had suggested he make her one with a curved surface. 'Much easier on the ladies' bums,' he had joked. Joan had felt he was a thoroughly nice, middle-aged man, and if Martin said he was honest and reliable she felt sure he was right.

All these plans! Come to nothing now, wouldn't they? Not that any of them had materialised yet, but there had been a chance. A slim one, perhaps, but at least it had given her hope that maybe she could go back and live with her own kind. Somewhere where she knew people, could knock on several doors and always be sure of a cuppa and a chat. And the thought of owning her own little business had been a great ambition. Now what? She knew what she would like to do but she hadn't the heart. It would be like deserting a sinking ship.

She did her best to walk briskly down the stairs and tap lightly on the door of the drawing room.

'Come in.' Bruce's voice sounded firm. His pleasant face

lightened as Joan walked into the room. Both he and Pamela walked towards her, hands outstretched. 'Very pleased to have you back,' Bruce said as they shook hands.

'I am so sorry to hear your father is ill,' Joan said politely.

'Thank you, Joan. Please come and sit down. My wife and I have something to ask you.' Joan remained silent.

Bruce took a deep breath and said hesitantly, 'We'd like to offer you the position of housekeeper here in my parents' house.'

Joan spoke without thinking. 'You must be mad! Me, housekeeper! I wouldn't have a clue about the household books – and a good many other things besides.'

Bruce regarded her intently. She was direct and honest, there was no doubt about that. Her spirit was refreshing and his apprehension about her ability was rapidly diminishing.

Pamela spoke up. 'I take it Mrs O'Leary has given you the facts of the predicament we find ourselves in?'

'Yes, Cook did outline what has happened, but I have only just arrived back and am not sure of all the details.'

Bruce nodded. 'Of course, we could call a domestic staff agency. I am sure there must be one in Tunbridge Wells. However, my mother is not herself, and does not want too many strangers in the house. She is finding it hard to cope with the nurses, who are an unavoidable necessity, whereas she is familiar with you. Fond of you, I'd say. And of course your wages would be increased considerably.'

Joan hesitated. 'I don't really know what to say.'

Conscious that she was wavering, Pamela spoke up again. 'Joan, we wouldn't expect you to do the impossible. My husband and I have to be back in London by Tuesday and on Thursday we are due to go to Italy. We cannot allow our business to slide. Competition is always so great. We would feel so much better if we knew Mother had you here with her. Say you will give the job a try, if only temporarily.'

Pamela Hamilton was a nice person, but she thought she could always get her own way. Both Fiona and Delia asked favours from time to time, but their approach was much softer. Still, Mr Bruce had said her wages would be increased, and young Mrs Hamilton had said it could be a temporary arrangement. She could save the extra money towards a deposit for when she found premises in London. But how long was temporary?

Pamela leaned forward and touched her arm gently. 'Your duties wouldn't be that much different from what you have been doing. You have made yourself useful in so many ways, and if you need help with the heavier tasks we can ask the gardener to let you have one of his lads for a couple of hours each day.'

Joan shivered as another thought struck her. 'Cook said Mr Farrant wasn't able to be in the house on a regular basis now. Is that right?'

Bruce and his wife exchanged regretful glances. 'That unfortunately is true,' Bruce admitted. 'We aren't exactly sure just how ill Mrs Farrant is.' He sighed heavily. 'It seems to be true that troubles never come singly.'

A heavy silence hung between them. Joan felt she had to get out of the room before she committed herself to something she might later regret. She stood up and said, 'Please may I have a short while to think about this? I also feel I shouldn't make a decision until after I have spoken to Mrs Hamilton.'

'Quite right, my dear,' Bruce hastily agreed. 'My mother will be able to put you more in the picture as to my father's health, and the extra work all this trouble will entail for you.'

Joan quietly closed the drawing room door behind her, leant her back against the solid wood and let all her breath out in one great gasp. Talk about being betwixt and between! Would she have come back to Mulborough House if she had known the confusion that would be facing her? However, it was too late to be asking herself such a question. She was here and she'd have to refrain from giving the family her answer until she'd had time to consider very carefully what she would be letting herself in for.

She went about her business, doing all the jobs she normally would have done. Tackling the dining room first she suddenly stopped short. How many should she set places for? Thank God for young Mabel, who came through the door beaming with pleasure and hugged her, telling her how glad she was that she was back.

'Only three places, Mr Bruce, Mrs Bruce and Mrs Hamilton.' Mabel told her, adding, 'Course, Madam would prefer to have her dinner on a tray and sit beside the poor master, but that day nurse terrifies her. She frightens the life out of me an' all. Still, as Mr Bruce keeps saying, it does his mother good to come downstairs and eat with them – not that she eats enough to keep a fly alive these days.'

'Thanks, Mabel.' Joan smiled. 'Can you tell me where Mrs Hamilton spends most of her time now?'

'I can tell you where she'd like t' be, day an' night, an' that's beside her husband, but the nurses won't hear of it. She stays in the small back sitting room staring out over the garden most of the time. She's only allowed to go in and see Mr Hamilton when the nurse says she may and even then she's not allowed to stay in the big bedroom for long. By the way, does she know you're back?'

'I'm not sure. I haven't seen her yet.'

'Well I'm just about to take her up a jug of cordial. Would it be all right if I tell her?'

Joan laughed. Mabel was like an excited child. Joan supposed that she must feel relieved there was someone else in the house now to take on some of the responsibility. Poor kid – she must have been run off her feet this last week.

'It would be fine, Mabel. Just let Mrs Hamilton know I

147

shall be waiting table for tonight's dinner and if she feels up to it I would like to have a chat with her this evening.'

'Oh, miss, she'll be over the moon. The times she's said to me that she'd feel happier when you came back.'

Joan had to keep a tight rein on her thoughts as she responded to Mrs Hamilton's greeting and watched as her son seated his mother at the head of the table.

She looked so fragile. The delicate features that had contributed so much to her beauty were now drawn and tired-looking. Her honey-coloured hair had turned almost white and her hazel eyes were filled with sadness. Joan watched her toy with each course, and as she removed each plate, the food hardly touched, she thought, I can't leave this woman. She offered me work and shelter when I had neither. I have to stay in this house for as long as she needs me.

It was eight o'clock before Joan tapped softly on the sitting room door and went in. She had always loved this room. It was small but neat, and not at all cluttered. The heavy blue velvet curtains at the window were drawn, but she well knew the glorious view of the gardens that lay beyond. The pieces of furniture that she had polished so regularly were dark mahogany.

Mrs Hamilton was sitting in one of two armchairs drawn up to a roaring fire. Gesturing to Joan to take the other, she said, 'I'm so happy to have you back, Joan.'

Joan felt she had to say, 'I am happy to be back, Mrs Hamilton.'

'You will stay even if you won't accept the position of housekeeper, won't you? Please say you will.'

The request was uttered so softly and so kindly that it brought a lump to Joan's throat. Then, speaking gravely, Mrs Hamilton gave Joan the precise details of the stroke her husband had suffered, and the consequences he was having to endure in the aftermath. Joan's blood ran cold as she listened. Mrs Hamilton's bearing and clothes were still immaculate, but by God she had aged. Joan shuddered, and her heart ached as she imagined the torment this poor woman must be going through as she watched her husband change from a normal man into a damaged invalid.

'Of course I will stay, and I will undertake as many of Miss Reid's duties as I can,' she said.

'I can't begin to thank you, Joan. My children lead such busy lives one cannot expect them to be here all the time. I shall see that not too much work is put on your shoulders.' Mrs Hamilton put out a slender hand and as Joan shook it gently Mrs Hamilton smiled and whispered, 'You won't regret your decision.'

Joan sighed as she stared into the fire. Beneath her breath she mumbled, 'I hope you're right. Believe me I do.'

Chapter Fifteen

JOAN FOUND SETTLING BACK into a much more harassed way of life at Mulborough House more difficult than she had imagined. To begin with she was on the go from morning till night, and try as she would, she could not get used to taking orders from the four nurses who between them looked after Mr Hamilton. Without Miss Reid and Mr Farrant the atmosphere was totally different. Cook kept saying that they must take it all in their stride. But there didn't seem to be any time for joking or laughing. Hardly any time for the odd cup of tea.

Each of the nurses was harsh and demanding. Rigid discipline reigned. The only member of staff allowed to enter the sick room was Joan. She hated the smell of the oil with which the nurses continually rubbed Mr Hamilton's withered limbs. Her heart did lift when she dusted near to the bed or changed his water carafe and he recognised her and managed a twisted smile. The bedroom was enormous, light and airy, but to the old gentleman lying there it was still a prison. Why didn't they get him out of bed? Let him sit in a chair near the window? Of all the rooms in the house this one had the most breathtaking view of the garden and the fields beyond. If he wasn't able to sit in a chair, surely they could at least have moved the bed nearer to the window.

Four months had slipped by since she had come back from London, months that had seen the coming of spring with all the buds on the trees bursting into new life, and great clumps of daffodils, jonquils and tulips making a glorious blaze of colour while the air was heavy with their scent. Soon it would be high summer, and Joan found herself once again longing for a week's holiday. Two of the nurses had left, but their replacements seemed to Joan to be just as hard-hearted as their predecessors had been. Miss Reid had never been fit enough to return to Mulborough House and Mrs Farrant had died. Mr Farrant had somewhat reluctantly resumed his duties but he was not the bright soul that he had been and Joan often wondered whether, if it wasn't for the fact that the cottage in the grounds in which he lived was owned by the Hamiltons, he would have returned at all.

Mrs Hamilton was a considerate employer, satisfied as long as the household was running smoothly and there were no problems she was expected to deal with personally. Mr Bruce and his wife came down every other weekend, but they only stayed the one night. Mr Bruce would spend at least a couple of hours each day with his father. Mrs Bruce just about managed to put her head round the door of the bedroom where the dear old man still lay.

Miss Fiona and Miss Delia came down from time to time, always unannounced and always with requests that Joan sew up a torn hem of a dress or secure loose buttons on their blouses. They breezed into their father's room but never stayed long. One good thing the two daughters always did was take their mother out for a nice long lunch. It was a treat that Mrs Hamilton always enjoyed, praising her girls for being so thoughtful. Joan kept her own thoughts to herself.

She never had a spare moment, and as for her sewing, let alone tackling the lovely material that Martin had so kindly given her, that had all been shelved. Maybe by next winter she would get round to making herself the gorgeous coat she had dreamed about. For she was still determined to better herself someday. She tried to reassure herself that her chance would come sometime. And when it did she would seize it with both hands. What scared her most was that she had overheard Mr Bruce telling his mother that sooner or later his father would have to be taken into a nursing home. And then what?

Her worst fears were realised when Mr Bruce came to the house on a weekday, bringing a solicitor with him. The two of them were closeted in Mr Hamilton's bedroom for some length of time. Later, as Mr Farrant opened the front door to let him out, the lawyer shook hands with Mr Bruce and said, 'I'll have the papers ready for your father's signature in three days' time.' When Joan related this piece of news to Kathleen, she folded her arms across her ample bosom, nodded her head wisely and gave her opinion.

'They're making sure that the old man's affairs are all in good order. Trust Mr Bruce to see everything is done legally and above board.'

'Well, isn't that better than leaving things to chance?' Joan asked.

'Better for Mr Bruce, I'd stake me life on that. After all, poor Mr Hamilton is in no state to make his own decisions, is he?'

Joan thought the best policy was to keep quiet. She nodded her head, but her thoughts were running along different lines. Mr Hamilton might be unable to do much for himself, but there was nothing wrong with his brain. His speech was by no means perfect, even after all this time, but Joan had not only got to know the old gentleman quite well but also become very fond of him, and there was no way anybody could convince her that he wasn't fully aware of what was going on around him.

As time passed the house began to feel different. The dining room was hardly used. Guests for dinner were a thing of the past. Occasionally Joan would stand in the huge room and daydream amid the two cabinets holding glittering crystal glasses and fine china, the thick soft Chinese carpets and the floor-length velvet curtains. Just looking at the sheer luxury of it all made her feel so sad.

John still collected and cleaned the silverware. There certainly weren't any boots for him to clean these days, though he was invaluable in so many other ways.

If some different arrangement were to be made for Mr Hamilton, his wife would not want to stay on in this large house, would she? She'd rattle around like a pea on a drum. And where would that leave me, Joan asked herself.

She had, just once, taken the bit between her teeth and asked Mr Bruce what would become of the staff if things turned out as she suspected they would. He had merely stared at her and Joan had burned with humiliation until he had finally said, 'We'll all have to wait and see.' In other words, the inevitable would happen sooner or later.

She still received long newsy letters from Rosie and short but more to the point notes from her sister Martha. She even had a letter from Marjorie telling her not to lose hope. Yet not one of them mentioned that they were still keen on her coming home or that they were still searching for a suitable property for her. She did her best to keep cheerful but she was only human and there were days when the thought of where she might end up in the future filled her with foreboding.

For the moment, she was content to remain at Mulborough House and do all she could to make life easier for Mrs Hamilton during this awful time. One thing that helped keep her going was her relationship with Kathleen O'Leary, which had developed from a working arrangement into friendship. A cuppa and a good old chat in the vast kitchen always boosted Joan's spirits. Nevertheless, constantly at the back of her mind was the hope that one day things might finally start going her way.

Whenever she thought about Martha and Sid and their lovely family she felt envious, and that in turn made her feel guilty. She'd had her chance. The fact that she had chosen to marry a man who had turned out to be no good was neither here nor there now. She had been grateful to have been given this job and she had done the best she could to be loyal to the family, but the thought persisted that she was letting life pass her by. Living in the country hadn't altered her allegiances. In her heart she was still a Londoner. A cockney born and bred.

Summer had come. The trees around Mulborough House were green, their branches covered with foliage, and heavily scented white and mauve lilac sprays dangled from the great bushes in the garden. Mr Hamilton's health had slightly improved. Only a night nurse was now in attendance, from eight in the evening until eight o'clock next morning, and this had made life a great deal pleasanter for both the inside and the outside staff. It had become a habit for Joan to sit with Mr Hamilton during the afternoon. Sometimes she would read to him. He showed an interest in passages from the daily newspaper, seeming to enjoy keeping up with day to day happenings. His speech had improved, though he found certain words difficult to pronounce and at times became so frustrated that the remaining words blurred and ran together. However, being a good listener, Joan had learned a lot about the early life of Edward Hamilton. He had been a captain in the army and had been awarded the Victoria Cross for 'bravery above and beyond the call of duty'. Over the weeks Joan had come to admire his patience and the fact that he never grumbled when God above knew he had enough cause to. He could manage to feed himself with his left hand provided the food was cut into small pieces for him, and with help he would leave his bed of a morning and sit in an armchair which Joan herself had positioned near to the big window in his room. She often wished that she could put him in a wheelchair and take him for a walk around the gardens, in the sunshine she felt would do him so much good. Time was passing quickly and soon autumn would be here.

It was the first of October. Joan was sitting quietly sewing beside Mr Hamilton who, propped up by four pillows, had dozed off.

The doorbell rang, echoing through the silent house. Knowing that Mrs Hamilton had been driven into Tunbridge Wells by Mr Farrant, to have her hair washed and set, Joan rose and went out on to the landing. She looked over the banisters but there was no sign of Cook or Mabel. The bell rang for a second time so she went quickly down the stairs. She opened the front door and the smile on her face faded. A young policeman was standing there, his helmet tucked beneath his arm.

'Good afternoon, miss,' he said respectfully. 'I'm sorry to be the bearer of bad news, but the station officer said you needed to be informed that Mrs Hamilton has been taken into hospital.'

'Oh my goodness.' She stared blankly at him, her lips trembling. Eventually she managed to ask, 'Can you tell me what has happened to her? Has she been involved in an accident?'

'Not that I'm aware of, miss. All I've been told is that

the lady was taken ill while in the hairdressers and the proprietor thought it best to call an ambulance.'

At that moment the family car turned into the drive and Joan and the police officer stood silently until the car was brought to a halt at the foot of the entrance steps and Mr Farrant got out from the driver's seat. When he came quickly up the steps carrying his cap, looking extremely upset, the policeman turned to face him, but before the young man was able to say anything Mr Farrant let him know that he was in charge of the situation.

'It's all right, constable, I know what has happened. I was hoping to arrive back here before our housekeeper became aware that our mistress has been taken into hospital.'

'In that case, sir, I'll leave the lady in your good hands.' The constable put his helmet on, touched the brim of it with two fingers and said, 'Good afternoon, sir, miss,' and ran down the steps.

Joan stepped back, watching Mr Farrant as he stepped inside and closed the front door. 'Thank God,' she murmured beneath her breath, at the same time heaving a sigh of relief. At least Mr Farrant could take over now. If he hadn't turned up she wouldn't have had the slightest idea of what she was supposed to do.

'Mr Hamilton was asleep when the door bell rang,' she told him, then quickly she added, 'I'll just pop up and see he's all right and then I'll come down and make us all a strong pot of tea.' She almost took the stairs two at a time, thanking her lucky stars that the butler was going to be the one to break the news to Cook and Mabel.

Mrs Hamilton hadn't been herself for some time. Only to be expected, really; it was a wonder she hadn't been struck down before this, what with all the worry and stress she'd had forced on her. But by golly, this was going to create a good many more problems! Still, the reins were in Mr Farrant's hands now. He was the one who would have to notify the Hamiltons' son and daughters, and they'd have the biggest decision of all to make.

What was going to happen to their parents?

It was ten o'clock that night before Mr Bruce and his two sisters arrived at the house. All three had travelled from London and gone straight to the hospital. Thankfully the news was not too bad. The doctors feared Mrs Hamilton had suffered a heart attack, no doubt brought on by months of worry. They had admitted her to the cardiac care unit, where a close watch would be kept on her for the next twenty-four hours, and then, if she was fit enough, several tests were to be carried out to determine what medication should be prescribed. For the time being, the heart specialist who had spoken to Bruce had said absolute rest was the best remedy.

Cook had plates of sandwiches all ready and for once everybody gathered in the kitchen, drinking hot cocoa. As Joan looked around it didn't seem strange to see the family sitting round the wooden-topped table. The fire was still alight, even though the night was warm, and the glow from the range made the big room seem very comforting. Bruce and his sisters seemed to be lost in contemplation. And who could blame them? It would take a wise man to sort this household out from now on.

Bruce was the first to rise. 'I am going up to see Father; better I tell him straight away. He must be wondering already why Mother hasn't been in to see him.'

Delia looked at Fiona and it was apparent what each was thinking: rather you than me.

Mr Farrant coughed. 'Excuse me, Mr Bruce, but might it not be a good idea if the night nurse gave Mr Hamilton a sleeping draught?'

Bruce looked tired and apprehensive as he said, 'I will mention it, thanks.' I expect Father is given one every night, he thought.

The lights were lowered and the fire was banked down, and as everyone prepared to go to bed Mr Farrant said he would stay in the house in case he was needed during the night.

It seemed to Joan that she had barely closed her eyes when she heard a tapping on her bedroom door and the voice of the night nurse calling urgently, 'Mrs Baldwin.' The nurse opened the door a crack, allowing the light from the landing to shine into Joan's room, and called again, 'Mrs Baldwin.'

Joan was shocked. She looked at the small clock that stood on her bedside table and saw that it was five minutes past three. She needed no telling that the nurse was the bearer of bad news. Why else would she be calling her in the early hours of the morning? She was out of her bed and across the room in seconds.

Poor woman, was Joan's first thought as she faced the nurse. She looked petrified, and when Joan put a hand on her shoulder she jumped nervously and she began to shake. Joan took hold of her firmly, attempting to calm her. 'Please, nurse, calm down and tell me what has happened.'

'It's serious, Mrs Baldwin,' she answered sadly. 'It's Mr Hamilton. I thought you were the best person to come to.'

'Had a bad turn, has he? I'll see about contacting the doctor straight away. He'll be here very . . .'

'I think he's died,' the nurse interrupted mournfully.

'Dead!' Joan took an involuntary step backward. She felt as if the world was falling round her ears. She could feel the colour draining from her face and her legs trembled. For a split second the two of them stood staring at each other as if they had lost the power of further speech.

Joan was the first to recover. She realised she must go and tell Mr Bruce, but at that moment the butler appeared at the top of the stairs. Joan stared at him, her face registering utter relief. Had he had a premonition that something was going to happen during the night when he had offered to stay in the house rather than returning to his own home? He was wearing his black trousers and black butler's coat, as if he had not got undressed. He leant on the upright post at the top of the stair rail and pushed his hand over his forehead in a futile gesture.

'It's the master, isn't it?' he said quietly. It was a statement rather than a question. He turned to the nurse. 'Is he dead?'

The nurse felt more composed now. She looked Mr Farrant straight in the eye and as calmly as she was able she said, 'Mr Hamilton spoke to me for a while after his son had told him that his wife was in hospital. He seemed agitated but he would not accept the sleeping pill I offered him. He merely asked me for a glass of water. Some time later I heard him coughing and went to his bedside. I managed to prop him higher on his pillows and then I sat beside him. Not long after that he turned a little blue and then I think . . .' She couldn't go on.

Mr Farrant noticed that Joan was shivering and suddenly he was very apologetic. 'I'm so sorry, Joan. Please get yourself dressed, or at least put your dressing gown on. I will see to everything that has to be done, and while we wait for the doctor I think hot tea and a good-sized brandy would be in order for each of us. So come downstairs when you're ready.'

The silence in the sun-filled kitchen was heavy, broken only by the soft crying of Kathleen O'Leary. John was holding Mabel's hand and Joan had her elbows on the table with her head resting in her cupped palms. After a while Mr Farrant emerged from his pantry and said bluntly, 'All this sorrow won't bring him back, you know, and if you want my opinion it is a happy release for the poor master. It was odds on that he was going to be placed in a nursing home sooner or later. If the mistress is going to be poorly it would have become a certainty. None of us would have wished that on him, would we?' He cleared his throat. 'Miss Fiona, Miss Delia and Mr Bruce are talking to Dr Simmons in the drawing room. I will tell you the arrangements as soon as I know them myself. Meanwhile, let's get a move on down here. For a start, one of you make a pot of strong tea for all of us, and would you, Joan, please lay a tray and take it into the drawing room. Better add a few savouries. I don't suppose any of them feel like eating but it won't hurt to offer.'

Joan nodded, and hurried to do as he had asked.

Mr Farrant spoke to Cook in a louder voice. 'Pull yourself together, Kathleen. Please, there's a lot to be done and everyone will be here for dinner tonight.'

Cook lifted her tear-stained face and wiped it with her overall. Her big bosom was still heaving, but her crying had stopped. Nodding her head, she pushed herself up out of the chair, picked up her massive white apron and tied it round her waist. 'Let me have a cup of tea and then I'll start on lunch and dinner. Not that I think anybody will want to eat much.' Turning to Mabel, she said, 'You can make a start on the vegetables,' and then to John she added, 'And you can go round the house and draw all the curtains. We must show proper respect for the dead.'

Joan laid a large doily on a silver tray, set four cups and saucers, milk jug and sugar basin, then followed Cook into the larder to discuss what eats she should take up for the doctor, Mr Bruce and his sisters. As she worked there were two questions running through her mind and it didn't take much imagination to know that one of them was also troubling Kathleen O'Leary.

With the master dead and the missus ill, where did that leave them? For each of them this was not only a job but the place where they lived and laid their heads down at night. For Kathleen it had been so for a good number of years and Joan felt immense pity for her. And what about Mr Hamilton. When told that his loving wife would not be coming in to say goodnight to him, had he felt lonely, perhaps even abandoned? Joan felt she could easily imagine his misery. And then to die alone. Without one member of his family at his side. It seemed so unfair.

Joan found herself crying softly for the loss of this decent man, and for Mrs Hamilton, who had not been given a chance to hold his hand as he died or even to say her goodbyes. She prayed that Mrs Hamilton might be comforted by many good memories of the life they had shared together.

Chapter Sixteen

THERE CERTAINLY WAS a lot to do and yet the days seemed long and the weeks dragged by. Joan was aware that all the staff were unsettled because they knew they would soon be leaving Mulborough House, but in her own case it couldn't come quickly enough. Not now.

Mr Hamilton's funeral had been a well attended and dignified affair. Mrs Hamilton was back living at home but rarely left the house. She looked like a lost sheep and no one could blame her for that. Mr Bruce had been more than fair. He had held a meeting in the dining room to which every member of the staff had been invited, from Mr Farrant down to the stable lads. The house and grounds were to be sold and it was his and his sisters' intention to take their mother to live in Kensington. The apartment they had bought for her would be near enough both to himself and to Delia and Fiona to enable them to visit her frequently. They intended to employ a companion for her, too.

Joan was flabbergasted. Poor Mrs Hamilton, to have to leave this beautiful house and the wonderful grounds that surrounded it, to go to London and live in an apartment.

Mr Bruce asked the staff to stay on until the sale of the

house was complete. He had many business matters to see to but he promised that all would be finalised before Christmas. He added that his father had remembered them in his will and left a token bequest to each member of his staff according to the length of time they had been in his employment.

Mrs Hamilton had made her choice of which articles and pieces of furniture she wanted to take with her. It had torn Joan apart to watch the sad lady run her fingers over several objects and murmur, 'Bruce will say this is far too big for the apartment.' What decisions! What memories she would be leaving behind!

Some curtains had been taken down and sent to the dry cleaners; others so heavy that only professionals would be able to remove them had been left hanging at the windows. Dust sheets now covered most of the furniture that was to be sold with the property. Joan had just finished wrapping several delicate pieces of bone china in tissue paper. The set was a twelve-piece tea service and because it was so exceptionally fine she found herself wondering if it had been a wedding present to the Hamiltons all those years ago. She put the lid on the box and leant her head against the window pane, closing her eyes. In a few weeks' time it would be Christmas again and this time she would be back in London herself. Was she sorry that she had come to work at Mulborough House? She could answer quite truthfully that she wasn't.

It had been an experience. Some days she had thought it not unlike the time when her mother had first put her into service, only then she had been a mere slip of a girl. Now she was a middle-aged woman. She was glad she was going to spend Christmas at Martha's, but what then? As Mr Bruce had said weeks ago, one had to wait and see. Well, since the death of Edward Hamilton she seemed to have done a lot of waiting.

She took Martha's last letter out of her pocket and read it again. Short and to the point, it reminded her that she would always have a home with her and Sid and how much all the family and the neighbours were looking forward to seeing her. She smiled to herself as she remembered that Rosie had informed her that she had a boyfriend and that he was dying to meet her Auntie Joan.

She was going to enjoy every minute of the Christmas holiday. But as soon as the holiday was over she wasn't going to waste much time. She had saved nearly all of her wages: there had never been very much to spend the money on. And she was to receive two hundred guineas from Mr Hamilton's estate. The amount seemed like a fortune to her. Probably it would be cold and icy as soon as January came in but that wouldn't bother her. She was determined to walk her feet off, read every property advertisement and visit every estate agency. Surely somewhere there was a small shop standing empty with a couple of rooms over the top. Who knows, if Sid would get her sewing machine out of the shed and Martha could spare the space, she would go to work like mad to make herself that long promised winter coat.

On 4 December Mr Farrant drove Joan to the railway station. She couldn't say she was sorry to go, because the atmosphere in Mulborough House had become very morbid, only Kathleen O'Leary suddenly becoming like a bird that had just been set free from its cage. A cousin of hers had written and invited her to return to Ireland and share her house with her.

'Sure and hasn't St Anthony turned up trumps for me,' she cried joyfully to Joan. Seeing the look of bewilderment on Joan's face she had enlightened her by saying, 'St Anthony is the patron saint of lost things. And wasn't I lost, and half out of me mind not knowing where it would be that I'd end up. And then there was Molly, owning a house but having no company. So St Anthony has set us both up proud.'

Joan tried hard not to laugh at Kathleen's reasoning but it didn't take a minute before the pair of them were laughing fit to bust. Their parting, however, had been a tearful one, each saying the other must come and visit, both knowing they would probably never meet again. But they promised to keep in touch by letter, because it had been grand working together, and they both knew they had formed a special kind of friendship.

To begin with, the house in Blackshaw Crescent felt cramped and inconvenient after Mulborough House. Here there was no countryside, the small terraced houses had shiny slate roofs and smoky chimneys, and try as she would Joan could not get used to having no running hot water. The shock hit hard when she remembered that the only lavatory was outside in the back yard. Martha still seemed to take all this in her stride. Both she and Sid had urged her to forget about looking for work.

'For God's sake give yerself a break. Just enjoy being with us for a change, instead of being at the beck an' call of rich folk all the time,' was Martha's advice.

'Time enough after Christmas for you to think about setting up yer own business if you're still of the same mind.' Sid smiled down at her.

'Thank you, both of you. You're so good to me,' Joan answered with a sob in her voice.

'Are you all right, Joan?' Martha poured her a cup of tea. 'You look as if you ain't 'ad a good night's sleep for ages.'

Joan sighed and leant forward in her chair, holding her hands out to the blazing fire. The gaslight was dim but it still showed up the deep hollows beneath her cheekbones, and Martha knew darn well that her sister had not been happy these last few months, stuck away down there in Kent.

'Tell yer what,' Martha said, doing her best to sound merry, 'tomorrow you can spend the whole morning in bed. By lunch time I'll have the big bath ready for you in front of the fire. Everyone will be out except us two, and you can have a good soak. Then we'll go down the market. I 'aven't told Martin and Marjorie that you've finished at that job. Be a nice surprise for them.'

Joan was so taken aback that she didn't know what to say, but she quickly found her voice. 'Why, thanks, Martha, that'll be great.' To herself she was thinking, I'd almost forgotten. I used to think nothing of having a bath in front of the fire in an old tin bath when I lived round the corner and I always used to get down on my knees to scrub Bill's back. Like living in two different worlds! Still, don't suppose it will take me long to get back into the old ways. It has to be a case of needs must when the devil drives.

The market was alive and doing great business. The buying and selling, especially at this time of year, went on from early morning until as late as ten at night, when huge paraffin flares would light up the stalls and kids would scavenge under them hoping to find pieces of fruit and vegetables that were still eatable. Each and every stall was decorated in the true Christmas spirit.

An excited gleam came to Martin's eyes as he spotted the two sisters. 'Marjorie, look! Joan is back.'

While Marjorie finished serving her customer Joan took the time to look over their stock. She was surprised at the variety and quality of the gifts on show, and even more so when she read several large printed cards stating which articles were hand-made. To think Marjorie had done all this. The very thought left her speechless.

When at last they had a spare moment Martin kissed Joan on each cheek and Marjorie put her arms round her and together they did a little dance, Marjorie chanting, 'Free at

166

last. Free at last.' Other stallholders were not going to be left out. Their greetings to Joan were loud and saucy but Joan gladly went along with this bawdy reception.

Nellie Rogers, the local flower seller, looked exactly the same, almost as if she hadn't moved since Joan's last visit. Her humpy shoulders were wound very tight in a black shawl, a flat battered old hat that hid her wispy hair was secured with a large hatpin, and her face was wrinkled and weather-beaten, for she plied her trade in all weathers.

''Allo, Joanie, gal. 'Ow are yer?' Nellie Rogers called, her voice sounding much stronger than one would have imagined. Joan walked the few steps to where the old lady sat, bent down and kissed her withered cheek.

'I'm very well, thank you, Nellie. But how about you, aren't you cold?'

'Nar, take more than this gusty wind t' kill me off.' She held up her hands, showing Joan her thick woollen mittens. 'See these? Great, ain't they? Me granddaughter made them for me at school, doing a darn sight better than I ever did. I couldn't learn t' knit t' save me life.'

'They are really nice,' Joan said admiringly, thinking how little it had taken to please the old lady. 'I'll see you later, Nellie.'

'All right, Joanie. I'll be 'ere any time yer feel like a chat.'

Martin chuckled as Joan came back to join her sister. 'Go on, Marge, take them both over t' the café an' get yerselves a big mug of tea, 'cos we're not going to take much money with you lot just standing around kissing an' hugging each other.'

It was Martha who said, 'Thanks, Martin. It's a long time since I've seen my sister look so 'appy.'

'Get on with yer. Her eyes are brimming with tears,' Martin teased her.

'Yeah, they are, an' you an' I know why. 'Cos she's back among her own kind an' she knows she can't do better than that.'

Martin came to the end of his stall and hugged her tight. 'You've missed her, 'aven't you, Martha?'

'Yeah I 'ave, an' you're all 'eart, Martin, letting Marge slip away to 'ave a cuppa with us.'

'Go on then, before I change me mind,' he said, giving her a frisky shove. And as the three of them pushed through the crowds he shouted after them, 'And don't forget to bring back a large tea for me.'

'Us an' all,' the two Parker brothers called. 'And you can give a hand on our stall any time you feel like it, Joanie dear.'

'In yer dreams,' Joan shouted back, and Martha slyly said to Marjorie, 'Ain't taken 'er long to realise where 'er roots lie, 'as it?'

The market café was large, warm and steamy, and furnished with numerous tables, each surrounded by six chairs. Reg and Hilda Kennedy were the proprietors, and had been for as long as Joan could remember. Hilda was behind the counter dressed in a long-sleeved black dress and a crisp white apron. She nodded her head and smiled broadly as the three of them came through the door. She couldn't return their wave because both hands were needed to hold the enormous teapot from which she was filling a line of six big mugs.

'You two sit down and catch up on the news,' Martha ordered Joan and Marjorie. 'I'll fetch the teas.'

Within minutes she returned with three large mugs on a tray. She handed one to each of them. 'That'll put 'airs on yer chest. Hilda is bringing over a plate of hot toast as soon as she gets a free minute.' She kicked her shopping bag under the table and struggled to get her backside down on to a chair.

It was Reg who brought the toast to the table. 'Haven't yer got any staff on today, Reg?' Marjorie sounded concerned.

'Neither of the sods turned up this morning,' said Reg. 'An' this time I ain't 'aving them back. Bleeding good riddance. I've stood all I'm gonna stand from that pair of saucy bitches. I was going to boot them out soon anyway, an' Hilda's already put the word out. We'll take on a couple of older women this time, more reliable types, I 'ope.'

'Would you like me to give you a hand, just for today?' Joan asked timidly.

Reg let out a roar of a laugh. 'Thanks, luv, but we'll get by. You just enjoy being back 'ome with yer sister.'

'He thinks your posh voice will frighten his customers away.' Martha grinned.

'You're taking the mickey out of me,' Joan said crossly. She sounded as if a deep melancholy had come over her and Martha realised that it was a long time since her sister had been amongst market folk.

'Course I'm not,' she cried, passing the bowl of sugar to her sister. 'It's worrying you that you ain't got a job, I know it is, but when we get 'ome you can tell me all your troubles, Joan. I've burdened you often enough with mine.'

Joan was well aware that her sister meant well, and what was more had hit the nail on the head. She was back where she had been when Bill had died. Living with Martha and Sid, with no home of her own, and although she had savings now, how long would they last?

Marjorie looked at her sympathetically. No two sisters had ever been closer and she understood the tension that lay beneath Joan's tetchiness. God knows she had been through the mill these last few years. Martha was a rough diamond, but Marjorie knew that beneath that rough exterior she had a heart that was bursting with love for her only sister and all she wanted was what was best for her. 'Get Christmas over, Joan, and we'll have you sorted in no time,' she declared.

Joan smiled, sorry she had snapped at her sister. She

sipped her tea and immediately muttered, 'Dear God.' It was sweet and hot, but that didn't account for the way it burnt her throat like blazes.

Martha had been watching Joan's face and she had to laugh. 'Reg put a drop of whisky in it, said to say welcome 'ome.' Marjorie started the ball rolling, leaning across the table and taking hold of Joan's hand. 'You can make as many plans as you like, but try and be patient. Nothing's going to happen this side of Christmas, is it? So why not make up your mind to enjoy the holiday?'

'You're right, Marjorie, and I've just decided, I intend to make a start on my coat.'

'Martha has kept us up on all the news. We know you haven't had any time to yourself, but leave the matter of your making that coat for the moment. Would you like a job for the next three weeks?'

Joan felt her cheeks redden, wondering if Marjorie thought she was short of money. 'You mean working for you, don't you?'

'Course I do. You'd be a godsend.'

'Marjorie, it is ever so kind of you but I couldn't, really I couldn't.'

''Cos you think it's charity we're offering. That's it, isn't it?' Marjorie said bluntly. Then, without giving Joan a minute to think of an answer, she went on, 'Well you're wrong. Dead wrong. What with the shop, the warehouse and the stall we're rushed off our feet. Don't get me wrong – I am not complaining. What we earn in the run-up to Christmas has to last a while. January and February half our customers won't have two pennies t' rub together. We do need another pair of hands and we need someone we can trust. We want to sell gifts, not give them away.'

Martha nudged her sister and they both burst out laughing.

At that moment Hilda came to the table bringing another

170

plate piled high with thick slices of toast that were dripping with butter. 'Get that down yer,' she said as she set the plate in the middle of the table. Turning to Joan, she put her arm round her shoulders and said, 'By Jesus, you need fattening up. Looks like they've been starving you down in Kent.'

Reg was going by carrying a tray loaded with dirty plates, but he stopped and grinned at Joan. 'You tell 'em, luv. Can't fatten a thoroughbred. An' another thing – I've aways found the nearer the bone the sweeter the meat.'

Martha was the nearest to him and she playfully swiped his arm. 'Saucy sod, ain't yer? Been at the bottle yerself, 'ave yer?'

'Sorry, Martha. Honest, darling, when I look at you I know just how lucky your Sid is, 'cos yer can't 'ave too much of a good thing.' And with that he went on out to the kitchen, the sound of his laughter bellowing back to them.

'That man will trip himself up one day,' Hilda said, wiping the tears of laughter from her eyes. 'He always believes in running with the hare and the hounds. That way he covers himself on all sides.'

Chapter Seventeen

FOR THE NEXT THREE WEEKS Joan really did live in a different world and she enjoyed every minute of it. Working on Martin's stall was a joy to her. And the thing that really put a smile on her face was that most mornings her young niece Rosie came to work with her. The fact that amazed her most was just how much Rosie had altered. Her skin, her hair and her eyes glowed with health. Her body had rounded out in all the right places. She had taken notice of what Joan had said about her speech and the way she now spoke really pleased her aunt. Her natural cockney tones had faded almost completely. But not quite. She could still hold her own with the costermongers if needs be.

Joan was anxious to do well on the stall and prove her worth to Martin and Marjorie. Besides, she liked the way the other stallholders treated her. They kept an eye on her, especially the Parker brothers, who were forever calling out, 'All right, Joanie? Say when yer want us to fetch yer a hot drink.'

Jim Taylor had also become a real friend, even though he was a quiet man, thin and serious-looking with glasses and not very much to say for himself, though he had a warm smile when he chose to show it and a good head of dark brown hair. He hadn't forgotten their previous conversations and one morning very early, before most of the stalls had their goods out on show, he had come to Joan with a charming dressing stool, its curved seat ideal for padding and covering. Joan had stared at it, delight shining in her eyes, her thoughts running wild.

'Oh, Jim, that must have taken you ages to make. I really want to buy it, and after Christmas perhaps I can see about upholstering it.' She spoke with such eagerness that Jim had to smile.

'Martin has told me a bit about your hopes for owning your own business and I've actually made three stools and a tea trolley,' he sheepishly told her. Before she could think of an answer he added quickly, 'I've used good wood and I can varnish the legs of the stool and do whatever you think best with the trolley, paint it or varnish it.'

Joan was taken aback. 'But Jim,' she stammered, 'I can't afford to buy all those pieces right now, although I would love to. For one thing, I don't have any storage space.'

'Please don't upset youself, Joan. I didn't mean you should buy any of my work. Martin suggested I made things for you on a sale or return agreement – that is, of course, if you think my work is good enough for you to put on display.'

Joan found herself smiling. 'I think we're both jumping the gun a bit here, Jim. I would be proud to put your work on show but I don't own a business yet, let alone have any suitable premises in mind.'

'Oh, you will,' Jim assured her. 'Meanwhile, I have two sheds besides the place I use as my workshop, so if you think of any other item you would like I would always be willing to have a go at making it for you, and then I could store it until you were ready.'

'Jim . . . I don't know what to say. I am grateful, and if and when I ever do get started up on my own I would appreciate your co-operation very much.'

'That will do me for now,' he said softly. 'If at any time you want to take a look at my workshop I'd be happy to show you. Would you like to keep the stool for now?'

Joan frowned. 'There's nothing I would like better, but I just don't have any room to store anything. I feel I am imposing on my sister and her husband as it is.'

'I'm sure they don't feel that way.' He smiled. 'Anyway, I'll hold on to it for the time being and we'll talk again after Christmas, shall we?'

'I shall look forward to it,' Joan told him. And she meant it.

The house was usually in an uproar of a weekend. Len and Bernie went to play football, Sid took himself off to the pub for a game of darts, and Martha caught up with her chores, sweeping and dusting and – weather permitting – getting all the men's working clothes washed and hung out on the line in the back yard.

The Saturday before Christmas, both Rosie and Joan were going like the clappers, selling boxes of initialled hanker-chiefs, embroidered pillow cases, gorgeous cushion covers and dozens of paper tablecloths that were adorned with Father Christmases, holly and golden bells. They must have sold more than fifty celluloid fairy dolls for the tops of folk's Christmas trees. At a shilling each, they were good value. Each doll had a pair of wings attached to her back and a tinsel-wrapped wand in one hand. They had almost sold out of red and gold candles. Paper chains and rolls of tinsel were unavailable now unless Martin turned up with a fresh supply.

The noise going on around them was almost deafening. The fruit and vegetable sellers, the butchers with their rows of poultry, the hot chestnut man, the lads selling clockwork toys, none of them suffered from lung disease, that was for sure. At one time Joan thought they were all endeavouring to outdo each other by seeing who could shout the loudest.

Never before had she been wished 'Happy Christmas' by so many folk. And Rosie wasn't shy at playing to the crowd. Looking as sweet and pretty as ever, she smiled at the lads as they winked at her.

Joan woke to the sound of bells pealing out from the church in the next road.

It was Christmas Day.

On the bottom of her narrow bed lay a full stocking. She hadn't heard anyone come into the room, but then the whole family including herself, plus more than half the street, had gone to the pub last night and they had all had a few drinks and sung carols and songs of yesteryear that brought tears to the older folk's eyes.

Crawling down to the end of her bed, she grabbed her stocking. Dear, dear, Martha! She had put in a tangerine, some nuts, a sugar mouse, a bar of Nestlé's chocolate and a brand-new shiny penny. What a start to what was going to be a wonderful day. Already the smells rising up the stairs from the kitchen below told her that the turkey and a half-leg of pork that Sid had brought home yesterday morning were slowly roasting in the oven, together with the gorgeous bowl of stuffing that Joan had watched her sister make last night before they went out. Joan laughed to herself. Good job she had. Martha wasn't in any state to make anything when they'd come home, and all she had had to drink was three glasses of port wine and lemonade.

Still, it never took much to make Martha merry. Bless her.

At two o'clock Martha said they could all come and sit up at the table. The boys had put planks of wood along what chairs they owned, placing cushions on top to make enough seating for ten people. There were the six of them, plus Ivy and George Martin who lived next door, and Nellie and Fred Bradshaw. Since having been told that Linda had

had her baby adopted and taken herself off to New Zealand, Joan had not felt at ease on the odd occasion that she had met Nellie Bradshaw, but today was Christmas and Martha had opened up her heart and invited them. A cracker and a paper hat lay by everyone's knife and fork. On an enormous china dish set at the head of the table the turkey lay browned and basted to a turn, ready for Sid to carve and just waiting to be eaten. Dishes containing every kind of vegetable, roast potatoes, stuffing and apple sauce and two jugs of gravy ran the length of the table, and in front of each person was a hot dinner plate on which had been placed two thick slices of roast pork and a glistening piece of crackling.

Sid held the bird steady with a long-handled fork and started to carve while Martha, grinning from ear to ear, loudly ordered, 'Come on, everyone get stuck in an' 'elp yerselves. We don't want our Christmas dinner going cold, do we?'

To say it was a jovial meal would be to put it mildly. The noise was at its height by the time Martha carried in the Christmas pudding, blue flames burning merrily on top thanks to the generous amount of brandy Sid had poured over the pudding and then set light to.

By five o'clock presents had been exchanged and opened. The inevitable cups of tea and hot mince pies appeared, and by half past six Lenny and Bernie had gone off to visit their girlfriends, taking Rosie with them as far as the corner of the street where Elsie Jones, a schoolmate of Rosie's, lived. The Jones family had five children, three of them girls, and it was only natural that Rosie should fancy being with her young friends for a couple of hours.

Ivy and George Martin followed them out of the front door and Sid watched until they were safely in their own house. They had both assured Martha that they had spent a marvellous day, but now they were tired, which was to be expected since both of them were turned eighty. Then Sid and Martha took themselves off to the kitchen to sort out drinks for everyone, leaving Joan alone with Nellie and Fred Bradshaw.

During the day Joan had got the feeling that everyone was skirting the subject of their granddaughter. After all, the two families had been neighbours for years, and Martha had been a tower of strength to Nellie when her daughter had died. The sudden silence in the room was unbearable and Joan decided to take the plunge. 'Does Linda write regularly?' she asked Nellie.

'She used to, luv, when she first went to New Zealand. We answered every letter straight away, didn't we, Fred?'

'Yeah, we did.' Nellie's husband never had much to say for himself but now he added, 'I always wrote a few lines on the bottom of Nellie's letters.'

Nellie gave a sad little sigh. 'The gap between Linda's letters got longer each time and now . . . well, August it was when we last 'eard from 'er. Not even a Christmas card this year.'

Their obvious sadness made Joan's heart ache and she said the first thing that came into her head. 'They do say no news is good news. I'm pretty sure you will hear from Linda again soon. After all, you were mother and father to her and she is not going to forget you just like that. If you think about it, you know she really loves you and she must have a good reason not to be writing.'

'I suppose so,' Nellie said reluctantly.

'You got to stop worrying over 'er,' said Fred, a trifle irritably. 'If she don't wanna write no more there ain't much we can do about it.'

At that moment Sid pushed the door to the front room open with his bottom. He was carrying a scuttle full of coal and in the crook of his other arm he had tucked half a dozen logs. 'Just been out to the coal shed,' he muttered. 'It's so damn cold out there it's enough to freeze yer t' death.' That said, he placed two logs on the glowing embers of the fire and then tipped the lid of the scuttle, allowing several great knobs of coal to settle on the top.

Martha followed him into the room carrying a tray which held several bottles and five glasses. 'Let's 'ope that on a night like this there aren't any poor devils who can't afford coal,' she said quietly.

Sid poured whisky into each glass and added a drop of ginger wine. Fred accepted his drink but said gruffly, 'We'd better get 'ome after we've drunk this.'

Nellie did her best to smile. 'Been a smashing day, an' we can't thank yer enough. It was ever so good of you to 'ave us both.'

'Our pleasure,' Martha assured them.

'I'll get your coats an' me own,' Sid insisted. 'I'll walk you round. Don't want yer slipping over, do we?'

'Well, this'll be a great end t' the day,' Nellie laughed. 'Two men, one on each arm, to take me 'ome. Maybe me luck will change with the new year.'

When they were alone the two sisters looked at each other. 'They had nowhere else to go, did they? They'd have had a rotten Christmas if it weren't for you and Sid,' said Joan very quietly.

'Oh, Christ, Joan, you're as big a mug as me,' Martha said. 'Come on, get on yer feet an' make us a cup of tea, I'm parched. That blooming whisky has dried me throat up.'

'I think maybe you deserve one,' Joan told her, thinking what a kind person her sister was. She smiled as she put the kettle on. It really had been a great day. And it had taught her one thing: there were hundreds of people far worse off than she was. At least she had a loving family.

Joan was very restless that night. She couldn't get the thought of Nellie Bradshaw's young granddaughter out of her mind. What on earth could have happened to Linda that would prevent her from keeping in contact with her grandparents? Her mother had died giving birth to her, and had it not been for them Linda could easily have grown up feeling she had been completely abandoned. But Nellie and Fred Bradshaw had done even more than was asked of them. They had loved that child. Had the fellow that Linda had gone off to New Zealand with ever married her? Was she happy? It must have torn at the young girl's heartstrings to put her baby into a home and sign adoption papers, then go off to the other side of the world, to live among people where she did not know a single soul. Joan herself had never had to give a living child away, but no one knew better than she did what it was like to carry a baby within your own body only to lose it before it had taken a breath.

Joan felt herself getting really agitated. Her own husband had been the father of Linda's child. It was his brutal treatment that had caused her own childlessness, yet he had been callous enough to get a young girl pregnant. If anyone had asked her at this moment whether she was sorry that her husband had died, the answer would have to be no. He didn't deserve to die the way he had. But then neither herself nor young Linda had deserved to be so ill treated by him.

She prayed silently that the Bradshaws might hear from Linda soon.

Chapter Eighteen

IT WAS A TYPICAL BOXING DAY. No one rose early and when Sid came back indoors from picking up the two quart bottles of milk off the doorstep he yelled loudly, 'It's too bloody cold for snow.'

'He's probably right for once,' Lenny remarked to his brother. 'That flipping wind bites right through yer. Just listen to it howling.'

'How would you know? You ain't been out, 'ave yer?'

'Only to the paper shop t' get some fags. I got twenty for you as well. Didn't think you'd be wanting 'alf an ounce of Old Holborn today.'

'Oh, thanks, Len. Are there any papers today?'

'Well if there are they're not in yet. Did yer want t' see if there was any racing on anywhere?'

'I did think you an' me might slope off somewhere after breakfast. Bound to 'ave 'alf the street popping in an' out t'day an' we don't wanna be sitting around listening to old wives' tales, do we?'

Lenny stared at Bernie and burst out laughing. 'Breakfast? You've got some 'opes. Mum an' Aunt Joan are out there getting the dinner ready.'

'But we always 'ave our dinner at night-time,' Bernie protested.

'Not on Christmas Day, nor on Boxing Day. Call it lunch if yer like, but you're getting it soon anyway.'

'But I'm starving now,' Bernie declared.

'In that case you shouldn't 'ave stayed out until the early hours of the morning an' then you might 'ave got up in time for a bit of breakfast.'

It was true. Martha had announced that she wasn't going to spend the whole day slaving over a hot stove. Joan had agreed with her. There were tons of cold vegetables left over from yesterday and Joan had tipped them all into a large mixing bowl, added two eggs, and mixed it all up. Now she began to pat portions of the mixture into shape and fry bubble and squeak. Martha had peeled a load of potatoes and already the big black saucepan was on the gas stove. She dipped her hand into the brown earthenware jar and came out with a half-handful of salt which she added to the now bubbling water, turned the gas down lower, placed the lid on the saucepan and said, 'I'll mash them later with plenty of butter and there are about four different jars of pickles and out in the shed there's salad, with plenty of beetroots. We can do some hard-boiled eggs if yer like but there's loads of turkey and pork so if they don't like it they can lump it today.' Joan was prevented from answering her sister by an excited call from Rosie, who was still upstairs.

'Mum, Mum, a car's just pulled up outside our house.'

Martha pretended not to have heard, and Joan looked at her suspiciously. There wasn't one person in a hundred who owned a car round these parts. 'You expecting anyone?'

'Not really,' Martha said, keeping her face turned away from Joan.

The boys had been quick to open the front door and the pleasure was plain in their voices as they both shouted, 'Mum, it's Marjorie and Martin.'

'Did you know they were coming?' Joan asked.

Martha just shook her head and moved past Joan to go and welcome her visitors, who wore beaming smiles and were loaded with fancily wrapped parcels. The fire was roaring halfway up the chimney, and Rosie took their coats upstairs to lay on one of the beds. Sid made sure that everyone had a drink in their hand before he proposed a toast. 'Good health and prosperity. Lovely to see you, Marge, an' you, Martin.'

'Plenty of grub t' go round, but it won't be ready just yet,' Martha told them. Again Joan gave her sister a funny look. It was as if she had been expecting Martin and Marjorie, yet she hadn't said a word to her.

Rosie dragged parcels from under the tree and handed them to the Goldsmiths and they in turn handed out a parcel to every member of the family. Finally, Martin offered a small, neatly wrapped package to Joan. Before she could take it, however, he drew his hand back. 'I forgot. This present was to go with the coat you were going to make for yourself, but you never got around to doing it, did you?'

Joan felt her face flush up. Martin made her feel ungrateful, and she stammered something about what a busy year she'd had and how she had worked every day on the stall with him since she had been home.

'Never mind, Joan.' He patted her shoulder. 'But what did you do with the material?'

Again Joan wished the floor would open up and swallow her. 'It's upstairs, underneath my bed.'

'Well, just pop up and fetch it down and we'll see if this present does tone in with the colour. Marjorie said it would.'

The silence in the room was awful and Joan felt like a naughty child. She felt even worse when she got down on her hands and knees, moved her old suitcase backwards and forwards but could find no sign of the brown paper parcel. She attempted to crawl beneath the bed but all she managed to do was bang her head twice. The parcel was not there.

The thought entered her head that she could climb out of the window and run away. She moved the short lace curtain to one side. It was a fair old way down to the pavement and the drainpipe looked very icy.

There was nothing else she could do. She had to go downstairs and ask Martha if she had put the parcel somewhere safe.

The door to the front room was firmly closed and she stood in the passageway and listened. She couldn't hear a sound. Slowly, she opened the door and the sight that met her eyes would stay with her for the rest of her life. It fair took her breath away and she didn't know whether to laugh or to burst into tears.

The whole family, including Martin, had joined hands and formed a circle. In the centre of the circle Marjorie was standing on a chair. Her right arm was held high. She was holding a wooden coat-hanger aloft and buttoned up on the hanger was the smartest double-breasted camel coat anyone could wish to see.

Joan's hands flew to cover her mouth, and that was the signal for Martin to help his wife step down and for the family to start cheering as he unbuttoned the coat and held it for Joan to try on. It fitted perfectly. Joan turned this way and that, turned up the collar, put her hands in the pockets and strutted up and down while everyone clapped their hands. With tears pricking the backs of her eyes she asked, 'How . . . when . . . who made it?'

Everyone in the room was laughing fit to bust. Rosie even more than her brothers. Joan turned to Martha and Sid first. 'You knew about this, didn't you?'

'Course we did,' Sid told her. 'The way you were going on, Martha said the moths would have eaten 'alf the cloth away before you got round to making it into a coat.'

'It were Marge's idea to have a tailor do it,' Martha admitted, 'and it were easy enough t' find the parcel, but I turned that little bedroom out at least 'alf a dozen times before I come across the place where you'd put the pattern. Time and time again I was on the verge of asking you what you'd done with it but that would have given the game away. Smashing Christmas present, ain't it?'

Joan was still wearing the coat but for the life of her she didn't know what to say. She accepted the handkerchief that her sister was laughingly holding out to her, brushed the tears away from her eyes and took a minute to calm herself down. Never before in her whole life had she been on the receiving end of such a lovely surprise. Then she flung her arms wide, gathering Marjorie and Martin together so that she could hug them both at the same time. 'How can I ever thank you?' she whispered.

'By wearing it often and keeping yourself warm,' Martin told her as Marjorie reached for the small package and said, 'You can open this one now.'

Slowly Joan tore open the pretty paper to find a pair of leather fur-lined gloves. She held them to her nose and sniffed at the luxurious smell of real leather. The rich deep brown colour would go well with the beige of the coat. Martha rounded the moment off for her by saying softly, 'Always remember, my luv, you're as rich as the number of friends you've got.'

Chapter Nineteen

TWO DAYS AFTER BOXING DAY the snow fell in bucketfuls, and it seemed as if it was never going to stop. By New Year's Eve deep mounds of the stuff had frozen and made the pavements treacherous to walk on. No one went out unless they had to, and beyond the windows all was frosty, white, silent and still. Rosie was anxious. If she didn't meet her friends that night to wish them all a happy new year it would turn out to be a very unlucky year. And the local publicans weren't too happy either. They took more money over the bar on New Year's Eve than at any other time of the year.

The thought of spending the evening stuck indoors drove Lenny and Bernie into action. 'Shut that damn door,' Sid shouted as the two of them made it down the back yard and into their father's old shed. It was about twenty minutes before they returned and it was hard to say which member of the family was the most staggered.

'What *do* you look like?' cried Martha.

Rosie was the only one who thought it funny. She stopped laughing only long enough to say, 'You're not going out like that! Are you?'

Lenny had on an old overcoat of his father's, what looked

like two woollen scarves round his neck, and a flat cap on his head. Bernie had found a pair of dungarees, covered in old paint, over which he had struggled into a padded mackintosh which was so large it must have at one time belonged to his mother and a woolly bobble hat that came well down over his ears. Each of them had dirty wellington boots on his feet and their hands were covered by very thick gardening gloves.

'We're just popping up t' the pub,' Len declared.

'They must 'ave come up with some kind of idea to get customers into the pub tonight. New Year's Eve without a sing-song an' a knees-up! The old regulars will go mad if they can't 'ave their do on this one night of the year,' Sid remarked.

'Well, yes, it would be sad for the old 'uns,' Martha said sympathetically, 'but I fail to see that you two dressing up like blooming tramps is going t' help a lot.'

'We'll see,' Lenny said, firmly walking up the passage and opening the front door.

'Give 'em credit,' said Sid, as he watched his two boys and four other young men knock on doors and call out, 'Are yer ready?' The six of them had already been round all the houses and explained that anyone who wanted to come to the New Year's Eve party which was being held in the local pub would be fetched and brought back home safely soon after the new year had been seen in. Horses and carts had been the answer.

The rag and bone man had generously offered his one cart and two horses. Dunnett's the coal merchants had offered two carts and horses, nobly doing their best to clear some of the coal dust from the carts and finding something to line the floor so that folk would not get their clothes too dirty. Several people had offered to lend blankets to wrap the passengers in, even though it would only be a short trip to the pub. Carrying the old folk from their houses across the slippery pavement and raising them up on to the carts had proved hilarious. Each time there was a new arrival in the bars, cheers from the customers rang out loud and clear. The landlord and his missus were of the opinion that where there's a will there's always a way. Cockney traders had brought their wives and young men their girlfriends, and the young mums and dads had brought their children because the landlord had set aside his own sitting room for them to play in. Parents took it in turn to stay with the kiddies and lemonade, Smith's crisps and arrowroot biscuits kept them happy as they showed off the toys they had received for Christmas.

After being cooped up indoors for days on end because of the weather, everyone was determined to enjoy the party. The drinks flowed freely, the music got louder and people had to shout to be heard above the din. Joan was amazed at the goings-on, especially when six women she did not know came into the bar. The older people present, herself included, looked at them curiously, taking in the different artificial shades of their coloured hair and the outrageously short skirts they were wearing. As for their jewellery, Joan had never seen the like: long dangling earrings, bangles, chokers, and rings on almost every finger. The married men heeded the warning looks their wives were giving out, but the young lads were eyeing them eagerly, asking what they would like to drink, though Martha said in a voice loud enough for her boys to hear, 'Underneath all that war paint they're probably as old as me.'

'You wish,' murmured Lenny, but made sure his mother hadn't heard.

'Bit cold fer them out there t'night,' Bernie offered by way of explanation, and his words made the penny drop for Joan.

'Are they what I think they are?' Joan had leant nearer

to Martha and whispered the question into her sister's ear.

'Are you dim or what?' Martha looked at her sister in disbelief. 'Suppose they've got t' earn their living in the only way they know. More than likely got 'alf a dozen kids between them an' I'd lay my money that they take bloody good care of 'em an' all. But for the next hour or so they're going to be in the warm an' 'ave a darn good time. You watch them. Two or three drinks an' they'll be goofy gigglers.'

It turned out that the newcomers actually made the night. The entertainment they put on was exceptional. One, wearing a very long curly wig and looking quite attractive, at least from a distance, turned out to have a beautiful voice. After at least four gins, she sang haunting songs about bonny Scotland, very fitting for New Year's Eve, and Joan felt sad for her, thinking that she was probably far away from her own kith and kin.

Five minutes before midnight the landlord was doing his best to quieten some of his customers down. He placed a wireless set on the counter and switched it on. The loud singing tailed off as they listened to the sound of Big Ben striking twelve. Everyone rose to their feet and formed three circles, crossing their arms and holding their neighbours' hands. It went without saying that the woman who looked like a tart but sang like a songbird led the singing of 'Auld Lang Syne'. As the last notes died away there were not many women who were dry-eyed.

Joan wondered what it was about New Year's Eve that made everyone so emotional. She was blinking quite hard herself when she looked up and saw her two nephews bearing down on her.

'Happy New Year, Aunt Joan!' They each hugged her warmly, and when they saw the tears in her eyes they both laughed.

'Now, none of that,' Len said, as he bent his head and kissed her cheek. 'It doesn't pay to look back. It's 1929 and

I predict that you are going to become a very good business woman before this new year is out.'

If only Lenny's prediction were to come true, Joan was thinking as her brother-in-law helped her into her coat. Any effort would be worthwhile if she could achieve that.

Chapter Twenty

JANUARY WAS A HORRIBLE MONTH, full of cold dreary days which were dark by four o'clock, and long, long evenings. Joan did her best to keep herself occupied but she wished she had something permanent to do. She made several trips to the library and took out books on upholstery. One such book was of great value because the illustrations showed step by step exactly how to set about tackling small objects.

There were days of indecision when the family argued as to where, how, and when Joan should start looking for premises that would not only be suitable for business but also provide her with living accommodation. Her two nephews were of the opinion that she should go upmarket. 'Go where the money is and some of it is sure to rub off on you,' said Lenny in his outspoken way. His father disagreed.

'She's got to learn t' walk before she can run. Besides, poor folk need alterations to their clothes, sometimes curtains made an' such like, don't they?'

'Who said she was only going to do needlework?' Martha was quick to add her twopennyworth. 'According to Marjorie she's hoping to get our Joan set up in a variety of other things.'

'Now, now, Rosie laughed. 'No squabbling. Auntie Joan knows what she's doing, she's just feeling a bit down because things aren't happening quick enough.'

A wise head on young shoulders, had Rosie! Sid Brown had never been a great talker but that was not to say that he didn't do a great deal of thinking. He looked steadily at his sister-in-law and said quietly, 'Why don't yer get on t' Martin, ask him if you can spend a few days in his Balham shop? I'm sure you could make yerself useful in a good many ways. You could also look and learn. See the difference in customers, for one thing. Some like to be waited on hand, foot and finger, others just want to browse and take their time before they part with their cash. I bet Monday is a quiet day, though as things stand at the moment I suppose most days are quiet when you're in trade.'

'Sid, that's a marvellous idea,' replied Joan gratefully. 'But don't you think it would be a bit cheeky to ask Martin?'

'Well, it's up to you,' replied Sid placidly. 'But did I ever guide you wrong? It's something you need to do, get a bit of experience. I promise you, luv, you'll find a great deal of difference working in a shop rather than on a stall in the market. And, who knows, you might even find a rich backer. Martin will show you the ropes and probably take you to a few warehouses with him, teach you to be selective about what stock you buy.'

'You might even find a rich husband out there,' Len said cheekily.

'Oh, shut up!' cried Joan, blushing madly.

Eventually everyone agreed that Joan should stop dithering and go for it. Bernie set out a pack of cards and they began to play. So, by the end of the evening, Joan had stopped wavering and promised she would get in touch with Martin in the morning.

*　　*　　*

Marjorie and Martin had been all for it and Joan now worked four days a week at the Balham shop. The job kept her occupied from nine in the morning until six on Mondays and Tuesdays, and on Fridays and Saturdays she stayed until seven. She enjoyed the work, and had done so since the first day. Her way of life had changed, and so had her image. Early every morning she washed herself from head to toe, set her hair, put on the smart black dress she had made for herself and her new camel coat, and set off to catch the tram with a smile on her face. It gave her great satisfaction to know that she was working and learning, preparing the way for when she would become her own boss. It was strange how different she felt. Her timid approach to life, even the feeling that she would end up a complete failure, seemed to have entirely disappeared. For a whole month now Martin had employed her and had insisted on giving her a weekly wage. Even after she had paid Martha for her keep she still had money over.

During her lunch hour she wandered around the big stores because it was warm in there and there were so many nice things to look at, but she seldom bought anything unless it was a small gift for her sister or for young Rosie. She had not touched the money she had saved while she had been at Mulborough House, or the sum she had inherited from Mr Hamilton. The thriftiness of a lifetime was still with her.

Martha was thrilled with the change in her sister and one Wednesday when they were out together she suddenly remarked, 'I wonder why you are so much shorter than me?'

Joan smiled. 'I guess God patted me on the head when I was born.'

'Well, if that's the case he must have dragged me up by my hair,' Martha replied huffily, scrutinising her sister closely. 'I must say, you look a lot taller than you used to. You are walking more upright now. Before, you used to wander around with your shoulders hunched and you tended to lean forward all the time.'

'I'm glad you approve of the change in me,' said Joan with a gentle smile.

'Oh, I do. I hated it when you were always so down-trodden. You led such a rotten life one way an' another. Bill was never a good 'usband and you took on the job of caring for his mother right up until the day she died. You were always so sad when you lost yer babies and in the end you lost yer 'ome as well. I'd say you were about due for some luck, and I pray that good times will come for you before too long.'

'Thank you, Martha. You've always been there for me, and even though what you say is true, you have only to look around you to see that there are a good many folk who have been forced to lead lives far worse than mine has been.'

'True,' Martha said thoughtfully, then grinned. 'I'll tell yer something else while I'm about it. You're much more relaxed these days an' you look a good ten years younger.'

'I think you've flattered me enough for one day.' Joan chuckled. 'Come on, we'll go into the ABC and I'll buy us a pot of tea and we'll have a buttered bun.'

'Does it 'ave t' be the ABC?' Martha grumbled. 'The complicated self-service system drives me mad. Can't we go to the café in the market?'

'No, we are going to have a nice change. You can sit yourself down and I shall line up and carry the tray.'

'Oh, all right.' Martha sighed, giving in gracefully. 'I was only thinking of you really. It costs less up the market an' you're gonna need every penny when you find a place of yer own.'

'I know you were, Martha,' said Joan, kissing her. 'Nobody ever had a better sister than you, but I do wish you wouldn't worry quite so much over me. I'm doing fine, thanks mainly to you and Sid, and the future for me is looking good. The bad part of my life is all over now.'

As they walked towards the ABC they met Nellie and Fred Bradshaw. Martha asked if they were both all right.

'Not too bad. Jogging along,' replied Fred with a deep sigh.

'Have you had any news of Linda yet?' Joan asked.

Nellie shrugged and said sadly, 'Not a word.'

Joan hugged her affectionately. 'Would you both like to come and have a cup of tea with us? We're going into the ABC.'

Nellie gave her husband a doubtful look and he quickly said, 'No, thanks all the same, Joan, but we're on our way to the market. We always have a cuppa in there, don't we, gal?'

'Yeah, we do. It's cheaper down there.'

Martha was grinning cockily and Joan only just stopped herself from saying that it would be her treat. Martha saved the day by saying, 'Come on. We'll all go to the market café, and since Joan is a working gal now she's going to pay today.'

If it were possible, Joan loved her sister even more than usual at that moment. For such a big, rough and ready woman she certainly knew how to be tactful. Martha's care for others ensured that she was always mindful of their feelings.

It was true what folk said. Martha Brown had a heart of gold!

Chapter Twenty-one

QUITE BY CHANCE, Marjorie Goldsmith was up very early. At seven o'clock she decided to take a run up to Brixton, watch the market stallholders setting out their gear. You were never too old to learn new tricks and it paid to keep abreast of what was for sale. Actually, she was missing Martin. He had been gone three days now, touring the cotton warehouses in Manchester, and it seemed much longer.

It was as she walked back to where she had parked her car that Marjorie saw it. *The shop!* The shop that just might be suitable for Joan Baldwin. It was on the opposite of the road, near the Brixton Empress.

Marjorie stopped dead in her tracks, staring across at it in utter disbelief. It was the end one of six that fronted on to the high street. The other five shops looked fairly prosperous. This vacant one was filthy. The large window had been whitewashed, but by the look of it now, that must have been ages ago. She walked briskly across the road, stood well back on the edge of the pavement and stared upwards. Yes! She screamed the word inside her head. Above the shop were two sets of windows facing the road still hung with greyish-looking torn lace curtains.

The name plate had been removed from the front, but there was no sign to say that the premises were 'To Let' nor any indication as to where one might contact the landlord. However, Marjorie was not deterred. She was prepared to go to any lengths to find out why such premises had been left to go to the dogs. And where better to start than in the local pubs?

Marjorie was very familiar with Brixton but she did not know it as well as Martin did. She knew how much he liked the Prince of Wales and remembered what good times they had enjoyed there in their younger days. It was a massive pub, a Free House, at the corner of Brixton Road and Atlantic Avenue. More than once she and Martin had been invited to a party there. The first occasion had been a family wedding where the reception had been held upstairs and as Marjorie recalled that day she found herself laughing out loud as she walked.

Besides several bars and function rooms downstairs, 'the Prince' boasted more than 20 rooms upstairs and the *kitchen*! well, one guest had remarked that one of the three ovens was large enough to roast a cow!

That pub had been in the hands of the same family for donkey's years, according to the tales that folk had to tell about the place. The present landlord and his wife, Les and Annie Jackson, had been there for as long as Marjorie could remember. She made a spur of the moment decision. If anyone would know about the empty property she'd just spotted she felt sure Les Jackson would. Besides, her tummy was rumbling. She hadn't had any breakfast yet, and the Prince was known for the good homemade food it served. That was one of the main reasons Martin liked to go there.

Marjorie wondered if the district would be suitable for Joan. She couldn't see why not. Brixton was a district of south-west London, in the borough of Lambeth, about four miles from the city. It was a friendly place. Like most it had its poorer areas, but there were also plenty of good-quality detached houses. Lambeth Town Hall had always been known as a showpiece, and the Empress Theatre put on some marvellous old time musical shows. Marjorie chuckled as she remembered her parents making her and her brothers climb up all the stairs to The Gallery, known as The Gods, because the tickets to sit up there were only a tanner and it was half price for the kids. The place used to get packed on Friday and Saturday nights.

Having made her decision, Marjorie hadn't too far to walk. The Prince of Wales stood right opposite the Town Hall and as it came into view she couldn't help thinking what enormous, grand, old-fashioned buildings both the pub and the Town Hall were. She looked at her watch. Shame. It was still barely nine o'clock, and none of the bars would be open until eleven. However, luck was still with her. The Prince of Wales was getting a delivery.

Two, big wooden doors had been folded back, one to the left and one to the right, to lie flat on the pavement, and the draymen were rolling barrels of beer deep into the cellar below street level by means of a wide wooden plank which they used as a slide.

'Mind where yer going, darling.' A burly, bald-headed man wearing a heavy leather apron grinned at Marjorie as she approached. She stepped off the pavement and into the road, and walked past the cart, which still held several barrels, enjoying the sight of the great dray horses nibbling from their nosebags. She slowed her pace, and as she approached the door marked in gold lettering 'Saloon Bar' she heard the sound of bolts being drawn back. A tall, very sturdily built youngish man appeared. He was fair-haired, almost pure blond, with large blue eyes. He was in his shirt sleeves and his handsome face broke into a smile as he saw Marjorie standing there.

'Well, this is a surprise. Been out on the tiles all night, have you, Marjorie darling?' he joked.

Marjorie stared up at him, surprised to see Jeffrey Harper. Yet she had to smile as he came towards her, took hold of both her hands and gently kissed her on each cheek. Jeff was still running true to form.

'Is Martin with you?' he asked. When she shook her head, he pretended to look hurt. 'Nevertheless, my darling, you will sweeten my morning by coming inside and having breakfast with me and Mark.'

Marjorie stood still, her mind in a whirl. Breakfast sounded good, but what on earth was Jeffrey Harper doing there? She watched as he signed the drayman's waybill, and slipped a folded note to each of them. ''Bye,' he called, 'nice meeting you.' Then, his arm round Marjorie's shoulders, he led her into the pub.

Inside were three women cleaners, each wearing a floral wraparound overall. Two had their hair tied up in headscarves, while the other one wore a man's flat cap on her head. One was washing tabletops, another was cleaning the massive mirror which hung over the bar, and the third was on her hands and knees polishing the brass foot rail that ran the full length of the long counter. Behind the bar two brawny barmen were bottling up the shelves. In the distance she could hear the hum of what might be a Goblin cleaner, and the thought of the wage bill that Les Jackson must have to fork out every week had her cringing.

'What the hell are you doing here?' cried Marjorie at last, as Jeff walked her towards the staircase. 'Don't tell me Les has given you the job of manager. I wouldn't have thought working in a pub was your cup of tea.'

'As if, sweetie. Can you see me working seven days a week?' Jeff swiped the air with his hand as if to indicate that Marjorie had taken leave of her senses. 'One of Les's customers offered him the use of a flat he owns in Barcelona and poor old Annie needed a break. Come to that they both did. So Mark and I said we'd step into the breach, kind-hearted souls that we are.'

'Bet that gave some of the customers a bit of a surprise.' Marjorie could hardly contain her laughter. She had known Jeff and all his family since she was a young girl. He really was a lovely man, but a publican he was not and never would be. She'd lay a pound to a penny there would be a lot more young ladies using this pub while Jeff and his companion were here, but they'd be wasting their time. Although he would treat them really nicely and certainly admire their clothes if they were well dressed, he wasn't into affairs with girls.

She and Martin had known Jeff Harper and Mark Townsend for a very long time and counted them as their friends. As to their lifestyle, her and Martin's thoughts on the subject had always been live and let live. They weren't young lads; they were well into their forties, although from the smart way they dressed and the way they kept themselves so fit they could easily be taken for much younger.

'Come on, let's go upstairs,' Jeff said, leading the way.

Mark had been watching from the window and he greeted Marjorie warmly. 'It's great to see you, Marjorie,' he said, and hardly pausing for breath he added, 'You'll eat with us? Scrambled eggs and smoked salmon sound all right? Jeff will make us loads of toast.'

'More than all right,' Marjorie said politely, inwardly wondering how all this had come about.

It would be an understatement to say that she enjoyed her meal. Everything was perfect. Even the coffee was beyond reproach: served black by Jeff as Mark hovered waiting to add a measure of Irish whiskey and pour cream slowly over the back of a silver spoon to complete the concoction. The companionship of the two good-looking fellows was remarkable and Marjorie felt totally at ease as they chatted about friends the three of them had in common. Jeff's pure blond head, his handsome face and kind-looking eyes made her think, what a waste! Then in her next breath she was saying to herself, 'As long as they are happy, it's their lives, bless them.'

Suddenly Jeff looked serious and turning to face Marjorie he asked, 'Why don't you tell us the real reason why you are wandering the streets of this district so early in the morning?' he said. 'Can we help in any way?'

Marjorie felt her cheeks flush. Not knowing quite where to start, she looked round the room. She almost grimaced as her eyes took in the over-stuffed furniture – not that it wasn't good furniture, she thought. There was just too much of it. And in her mind's eye she pictured the glorious flat where these two men lived on the other side of the river. She and Martin had been invited to an evening do at their place and she remembered how everything had seemed so smart yet so simple. She recalled thinking at the time that money talked in all kinds of voices and that neither Mark nor Jeff gave the impression of being short of a bob or two.

'Why am I here? To be honest, it began this morning merely as a whim to get out and about, mainly because I was missing Martin and was fed up with my own company. But now . . .' Marjorie paused for a second and then took the plunge. 'I have an irresistible temptation to tell you about a lady who has, so far, had a rough deal from life. I would give a great deal to be able to give her a helping hand.'

'Is it money she needs?' Mark asked quietly.

Marjorie's eyebrows shot up. 'Oh no,' she answered sharply, 'I'm not on the scrounge. If anything, all I would like from you two is information. The lady in question is strong-willed and does her best to stand on her own two feet. Given the chance she would seize it with both hands, because life has taught her that opportunity does not come knocking on the same door twice in a lifetime.'

It was a very thoughtful Jeff that got up from the table to fetch fresh coffee for each of them, and as he passed Mark he placed his hand on Mark's shoulder using a certain amount of pressure. Mark knew it was a signal.

'Marjorie,' he spoke softly, 'Why don't you tell us the lady's name and just what you have in mind for her?'

Marjorie remained thoughtful as she watched Jeff refill their cups.

'Begin at the beginning, tell us how you came to know so much about this lady,' urged Mark encouragingly. 'And are we allowed to know her name?'

'All right. All right.' Marjorie grinned nervously but she decided to take a gamble and started the story of Joan Baldwin right from the early days when Joan had been unfortunate enough to be married to a right loser. She was downright in her speech, as she related how Joan had worked two jobs and still cared for Granny Baldwin right up until the day she had died. How Joan had carried three babies and lost them all because of the way Baldwin had bashed her about.

By now, both men were seething with rage as they listened to Marjorie.

Then smiles came to Jeff and Mark's faces as she related how Joan's brother-in-law and his two sons had given Joan's husband a right seeing to and forced him to take a job as nightwatchman in a Wandsworth Brewery. After a short pause she gave them an account of the fire in the stables and consequently the many interviews with the police. With her husband and her mother-in-law both dead, Marjorie went on to explain how Joan had lost her home and owned nothing but what she stood up in. However, Marjorie was quick to assure them, Joan had not lain down and bemoaned the fact that nothing good ever came her way. The Labour Exchange had found her a job in service. It was a good job, and Joan had proved her worth. The only trouble was that it was miles away in Kent, she knew no one in the area and often did not take her day off because she knew of nowhere she could pop in and be made welcome.

Marjorie paused and then thoughtfully muttered, 'I suppose it was really a case of once a Londoner always a Londoner.'

They looked from one to the other and all three burst out laughing, which eased the tension for a while.

Marjorie carried on, telling the men how Joan had been working for Martin and herself on the stalls over Christmas and that at present she did four days a week in their Balham shop.

'Hang on a minute, Marge, I think you've jumped the gun a bit here.' Mark said cheerfully. 'If she's working in a household down in Kent how come she's been working for you?'

Marjorie's smile was sad as she said, 'Yeah, I've missed out quite a lot, haven't I? But I don't want to take up too much more of your time.'

The two men grinned. 'Handsome bleeders we are, decorative, not the run of the mill. Our motto is never do what you pay your employees to do for you,' Mark joked, 'so go on, finish what you were saying and then maybe we'll get to the point as to why you are here so early in the morning.'

'Not that we're not thrilled to see you,' Jeff hastened to add.

Marjorie sighed, it all sounded so unbelievable in the cold light of day, but she carried on. 'Last year when Joan got leave from this Mulborough House, Martin remarked at how sad she looked and Joan admitted she was lonely, she missed her neighbours and her family. Martin and I persuaded her to give her employers a month's notice when she returned and we promised that we would help set her up in a little business of her own. Any premises we did come across had to have living accommodation over the shop because more than anything Joan wanted a home of her own.

'Sadly, as always, it must have seemed to Joan, that fate was still not on her side. She never did hand her notice in because the household was in uproar when she got back. The master had suffered a stroke and her mistress was very ill. Never one to desert a sinking ship, Joan stayed on another year until the master died. She did inherit a small legacy, from Mr Hamilton, he was her employer, plus she had saved almost all of her wages, and since her return she has been living with her sister and brother-in-law. They have two sons and a young daughter. They really are a nice family and I'm sure they love Joan dearly, they do their utmost to make her feel welcome but she feels as if she's intruding too much now because the house is very small and cramped.

'Martin, myself, and all of her friends have been looking for suitable premises for her. We've none of us had any luck until this morning when I saw this shop. An empty shop! With what looked liked spacious living quarters up above it. It was filthy, mind, but nothing that a bucket of soapy water and some elbow grease couldn't cure.' Marjorie had spoken these two last sentences with great emphasis and her eyes were half closed as if she could already visualise Joan's dream coming true.

'At last!' Mark punched Jeff playfully. 'We have finally got to the crunch of the matter.'

Jeff winked back at him before saying, 'In a nutshell, Marjorie, you want to rent or buy the property, even though you haven't set foot inside the door yet.'

'Well, I suppose we do have to give the premises the once-over first, always providing we can find the owner, but other than that, Jeff, you've got it in one.'

'Who's we?' Mark asked, smiling.

'Daft question,' Jeff rebuked him. 'Marjorie needs our

help, and isn't it ironic that we two know all there is to know about that shop?'

'I was only joking,' Mark hastened to assure her. 'And I do think it's a marvellous case of us all being in the right place at the right time.'

'Really?' Marjorie's voice was full of disbelief. 'How long has the place been empty? And why has nobody rented it? Can you get in touch with the owner?'

'Whoa, hold your horses, Marge.' Mark took a snow-white handkerchief out of his pocket and made an exaggerated show of wiping his brow. 'Slow down and we'll answer your questions one at a time.'

Jeff leant forward and took one of Marjorie's hands and held it between both of his own. His lovely blue eyes, full of emotion, were staring straight at her. 'We know all there is to know about that shop and the gent who owns the whole caboodle and if your friend doesn't end up as the new tenant then I promise you, Marge, it won't be for the want of us trying.'

Marjorie sank back in her chair and silently sent up a prayer of thanks. The two men got up slowly from their seats and Jeff said, 'We're just going down to the bar. Make yourself comfortable, Marge. We won't be long.' When they had left, Marjorie let out a long drawn-out sigh. If only everything would turn out as easy as Mark and Jeff seemed to think.

Within the hour Marjorie was in a taxi with Jeff and Mark. There was no conversation between them until the cab drew to a halt outside a tall house set back from the embankment on the other side of Albert Bridge and fronted by massive iron gates which automatically opened as the taxi driver sounded his horn. Marjorie's nerves were jangling and she swallowed deeply as she walked up the steps to the front door. They were obviously expected because the door was open and standing in the hall was an immaculately dressed grey-haired man who was very tall with a military bearing.

'Come in.' It was an order rather than an invitation. He stepped aside and allowed them to pass and then followed them down the hall and into the sitting room.

'How about a drink?' he asked gruffly. 'Tea, coffee, whisky?'

Marjorie shook her head. 'No thank you, nothing for me.'

Jeff and Mark both said, 'Scotch will be fine.'

'Forgot yer manners, 'ave yer? I thought better of you two than that. No drinks until you have introduced the lady.' The man smiled but it didn't reach his eyes. Jeff crossed the room quickly.

'Marjorie, this is Edward Tyler, a big businessman in our manor.' Then, turning to their host, he said, 'Teddy, this is Marjorie Goldsmith. I know you have met her husband Martin on many an occasion, but . . .'

'I've never had the pleasure,' Teddy Tyler cut in. 'No one could forget having met this beautiful young lady.' He bent low, took her hand and brushed his lips lightly over the back of it.

Marjorie was always elegantly dressed but the brown suit she was wearing today was far more expensive than most of her other outfits. The beige colouring of her neat blouse matched up well and the two colours suited her. Her shoulder-length dark hair gleamed like spun silk. Her high heels made her seem taller than she was and she looked closer to forty than her real age of fifty-three.

'Very pleased to meet you, Mr Tyler,' Marjorie said, feeling intimidated by this tall, strange man.

Edward straightened up to his full height. 'I'm aware that this is our first contact, but I hope you will find it in your heart to call me Teddy. I loathe the name Edward.' He grinned widely, walked over to a drinks table and poured two measures of whisky. 'Help yourselves to soda,' he said as he handed Jeffrey and Mark their drinks. He then took a bottle of white wine from an ice bucket, poured some into a tall, slender glass and offered it to Marjorie. 'Relax,' he said. 'Nothing like a glass of wine to give you a bit of Dutch courage when you're seeking to do a business deal.'

'Thank you.' Marjorie suddenly felt more at ease with this unusual man. She took a sip and found the wine to be excellent. It was certainly not a cheap bottle of plonk. She sipped it appreciatively.

Suddenly Teddy Tyler became businesslike. 'The lads here have given me the gist of why you want to rent the Brixton shop. They told me on the blower that your Martin is away. Can't it wait till he gets back?'

'Is there a reason not to do business with a woman?' Marjorie said, sounding far more confident than she actually felt.

'Ooh, you answer a question with a question. Right Londoner's trick. Born within the sound of Bow Bells, were you?'

'Well, in North London,' said Marjorie, 'a place known as the Nile.'

'I know it well,' he said. 'Used to play around there when I was a boy. I was born in Ludgate, you know, Whitechapel Road area. Don't know about you, but we used to play out in the streets till it was dark, and there wasn't much we wouldn't 'ave done to earn a penny.'

While this bit of banter was going on, Jeff and Mark had made themselves comfortable and behind Teddy's back they both gave Marjorie the thumbs-up sign.

'Ever 'eard of Jimmy Erlock?' Teddy flung the question at her.

'Can't say that I have,' Marjorie answered seriously.

'You ain't missed much. Nasty piece of work. He was the last tenant of the Brixton shop. I did a deal with him in good faith but he used my premises to set up a scam and no one gets away with tucking me up.' He turned to the two men. 'Top yer drinks up, lads,' he ordered, and let out a great belly laugh. 'Jimmy Erlock is getting free board and lodging at the moment, compliments of His Majesty.'

Both the lads laughed but it was Jeff who said, 'Anything been heard of his bird?'

'No, but I'm in no hurry. Remember how she was always going on about sex and violence? Especially when she'd had too much to drink.'

Jeff nodded. 'Bit of a simpleton, we both thought.'

'Not too silly to have scarpered with most of the dosh.' Mark's remark touched a sore point with Teddy and he turned and glared at him.

'Yeah well, let's hope she's making the most of it 'cos it's only lent. When my lads do catch up with her, and they will, she'll be screaming about violence all right.'

Having listened to the men talking Marjorie was feeling a bit apprehensive and she decided she'd rather have Teddy Tyler as a friend than an enemy. Teddy gave her a kind but critical stare. 'You're convinced this Mrs Baldwin is on the level? Deserving of your 'elp?'

'Definitely. One hundred per cent, Mr Tyler.'

Teddy was looking very thoughtful. 'Known her long, 'ave you?'

Marjorie nodded. 'Yes, since she was a young girl. Why?'

'Just wondered,' Teddy replied. He walked over to the window to avoid the necessity of explaining himself, or being accused of going soft. Although he had only been given a sketchy outline of Joan Baldwin's circumstances, he found himself fully understanding her frustration at having no home of her own. If Martin Goldsmith's wife thought so much of her he felt she must be worth helping. He turned from the window and said quietly to Marjorie, 'I've a proposition to put to you. Your friend can have the shop in Brixton high street and the rooms above, rent free for three months, in return for cleaning the place up from top to bottom.'

'She'll jump at the chance, Mr Tyler, I just know she will.'

'In that case the lads can 'ave the keys and take yer to see over the place. But I'll set up the long-term details with Martin when he gets back. Right?'

Marjorie was tongue-tied. She just nodded her head and smiled happily and stammered, 'Thanks, Mr Tyler.'

'I don't want no thanks, but could yer try an' remember I'm Teddy to me friends. Edward makes me flesh crawl and Mr Tyler is a bit stuffed shirt. I keep that for those that owe me.'

'Sorry, Teddy,' Marjorie said sheepishly.

Jeff and Mark drained their glasses and got to their feet, and Mark caught the bunch of keys that Teddy threw at them.

Marjorie was thinking she could come to like this old man and she was so happy that at last she might be able to tell Joan she was to be given a new start in life.

Teddy held out his hand and Marjorie shook it gratefully. 'If you do come to an agreement with Martin, I promise you, Teddy, Mrs Baldwin will be a good tenant.'

Teddy Tyler looked into her eyes and said flatly, 'If she isn't, Marjorie, you will be the first to know.'

Chapter Twenty-two

IT WAS WEDNESDAY MORNING and Joan was having a lie-in. Outside it was still a cold winter's day and the windows were frosted up. The men had all gone to work and Rosie to the office job she had got in the paper mills. It didn't seem possible that Rosie would soon be sixteen. Snuggling deeper down in the bed Joan smiled because she knew that very soon now Martha would come upstairs bringing her a cup of tea. Suddenly the sound of the door knocker going rat-a-tat-tat made her sit up straight. When she heard Martha open the front door and scream 'Oh my Gawd, it's a blinking telegram' she flung back the bedclothes and ran to the top of the stairs. Telegrams always meant bad news – at least to people in this area they did.

Martha leant against the wall, her chest heaving. Having read the typed words on the front of the envelope she sighed and looked up at Joan. 'It's addressed to you, luv.' She didn't hand it up to her sister, instead she said thoughtfully, 'Go and put your dressing gown on and come downstairs. I was just about to make a fresh pot of tea. You can read your telegram down 'ere in the warm – I've got a roaring fire going.'

Martha knew she was talking too much but her thoughts were all for her sister. What if it were really bad news? She didn't want her falling down the stairs. Who the ruddy hell would be sending Joan a telegram anyway? She looked up and saw that Joan had gone back into her bedroom and she was half tempted to slit the envelope open and read the message for herself. However, she didn't let her curiosity get the better of her, but went into the warm kitchen, laid the yellow envelope down on the table and busied herself by lifting the big black kettle off the hob and pouring the boiling water over the tea leaves she had spooned into the large brown teapot. Bad news or good news they still needed a good strong cup of tea. Seeing the telegram boy standing on her doorstep and his red bicycle propped up against her front gate had half frightened the life out of her.

She heard Joan coming down the stairs, and as the kitchen door opened Martha forced herself to smile. Nodding to where she had placed the telegram she said, 'Sit yerself down, luv, before you open that.'

Joan did as she was told and for a minute she sat bolt upright in the chair and clutched the arms. 'I can't think of a single soul who would want to get in touch with me by sending a telegram,' she cried, her eyes flaring with apprehension.

Conscious of her sister's feelings, Martha picked up the envelope and said gently, 'It won't take you a minute to find out.' Thrusting it towards Joan she urged, 'Go on, open the ruddy thing. The suspense is killing me.'

Joan took a deep breath to steady herself, took the telegram from Martha and slit the flap open with her thumbnail. In no time at all Joan's face lit up. 'It's all right, it's all right,' she cried, her voice rising to a shriek.

'Then for Christ's sake put me out of my bloody misery and read the damn thing to me, or at least tell me who it's from.' Martha had been so afraid that it was some sort of bad news that by now her temper was smouldering.

'It's from Marjorie,' Joan said, and grinning from ear to ear she silently reread the short message, hardly able to take it in. 'Get a cab. Come to shop. Good news. Marjorie.'

Joan read the message aloud this time, then jumped to her feet, crossed the room and threw her arms round her sister.

Martha was moved to tears as they hugged each other tightly. 'Wasn't it only the other day that I said you were about due for some good luck,' she murmured when at last they separated. 'Sit yer down and I'll pour the tea out. I don't care what you say, you are not leaving this house until you've got some food inside you.'

'Oh, Martha, I am so excited. What do you think Marjorie means by good news?'

'Oh, 'ere we go. Supposing this that an' the other ain't gonna get you anywhere. Just drink yer tea and then while you're getting washed and dressed I'll cook yer a bit of breakfast an' then you can be off.'

The two sisters sat facing each other as they sipped at the strong, scalding tea. They weren't talking for the simple reason they were both lost in thought. Whatever the good news turned out to be, Martha was truly thrilled. For more years than she cared to remember Joan had been the main worry of her life. She knew for a fact that Joan wouldn't rest until she had got herself regular work and, more to the point, her own place to live. She was well aware that her sister's main aim in life was to be independent. She was also sure that never again would she allow a man to treat her in the awful way that bleeding Bill Baldwin had. She might even end up being well off, because she'd succeed no matter what she took on.

But at what cost? Martha asked herself. Look at her now. She's as thin as a rake. I thought her idea of having a shop was really daft when she first started going on about it, but now I am beginning to think it might be the best thing that could happen to her. But only if it puts a roof over her head.

Joan had finished drinking her cup of tea, yet she stayed perfectly still. Her heart was beating rapidly and a tingling excitement surged through her veins. For the life of her she couldn't put into words the way she was feeling. Suddenly she sprang to her feet. 'I'm going to have a wash and get dressed,' she cried.

'All right.' Martha laughed. 'And while you're getting ready I'll cook you that breakfast.'

'All right, Martha. Thanks, dear, but please don't do me a huge fry-up. May I just have some toast?'

'With a boiled egg and some soldiers?' Martha kept a straight face as she teased her sister.

Joan could give tit-for-tat when the occasion arose and she saucily answered, 'I'm not very keen on soldiers. Please may I have ladies' fingers and gentlemen's thumbs?'

'I'll 'ave less of yer cheek,' said Martha, swiping Joan with the tea cloth she had in her hand. 'You'll eat what I set in front of you.' Joan was still laughing to herself as she walked slowly up the stairs.

Martha cut two thick slices of bread and took the toasting fork down from where it hung on a nail in the wall beside the cooking range. While she prepared the light breakfast for her sister, she murmured, 'Please, let this turn out to be the break that Joan has been waiting for. Dear God, you know she deserves a chance if anyone ever did.'

As Joan stepped into the taxi there was a look of resolve on her face. She leant back against the soft leather and looked down at herself. The beige skirt in strong, twilled fabric and the long hound's-tooth check jacket in brown and white were the best she'd ever made. Martin had given her the two remnants and while she was sewing them she had kept telling herself how lucky she was. They weren't for some lady, they were for herself. She had debated as to whether or not she would wear a hat today; finally decided against. Instead she had wound her long, soft brown hair into a French pleat and had pinned a few strands of hair into curls and set them just above her forehead, which made her look at least a little taller than she was.

It seemed to take ages for the taxi to reach Balham. Finally the cab drew to a halt outside Goldsmith's Haberdashery and Marjorie and Martin were rushing from the shop to greet her. While Martin paid the cab driver Marjorie wrapped her arms round Joan and whispered in her ear, 'I think I have found just the place for you.'

These few hurried words set Joan's heart beating rapidly and a tingling excitement surged through her veins.

'Break it up, you two.' Martin laughed. Joan went to him and he lovingly kissed her cheek.

'What are we standing about outside on the pavement for?' he asked. 'Take Joan upstairs, Marjorie. The side door is open and I'll be up myself in about ten minutes.'

A few minutes later, as Joan walked into Marjorie's beautifully furnished front room, she got a surprise. Standing in the middle of the room was a tall man. Marjorie quickly made the introductions. 'Joan, this is Mr Edward Tyler, the owner of the property we are going to take you to view. Teddy, this is our good friend Joan Baldwin.'

Mr Tyler was, without doubt, impressive. Easily over six foot tall, he was large, but not fat. There was a lot of heavy muscle in the shoulders of his immaculate dark suit. Thick, grey wavy hair spilled over the collar of his jacket.

'Pleased to meet you, Mr Tyler,' Joan said, holding out her hand.

He shook it, immediately thinking how cold it felt through the thin gloves she was wearing. 'Bit on the small side, aren't you?' he remarked, then added, 'And before we go any

213

further, as I told Marjorie, I'm Teddy to my friends, I loathe the name Edward and Mr Tyler is useful only for business and those that owe me.' His accent was pure London, powerful and positive.

'Yes, I am small,' Joan answered, 'but my mother always insisted that good things come in small parcels.' The minute the words left her mouth she wished she hadn't been so flippant.

'Well, Miss Baldwin, I've heard quite a bit about you and I understand you would like to rent a shop from me, is that right?'

Joan was saved from answering straight away because Marjorie came back into the room carrying a tray which held four cups of coffee. Martin joined them at the same time, and straight off he said, 'Why on earth are you standing up? For goodness' sake sit yourselves down and be comfortable.'

Joan sipped her hot coffee gratefully. She felt a bit intimidated by this big man. Mr Tyler seemed to suddenly sense just how ill at ease Joan was and in a much softer voice he turned to her and said, 'Miss Baldwin, you haven't answered my question.'

Just as quietly she replied, 'Yes, I would like to rent a shop and start up my own business, but shall we start again? I am Mrs Baldwin, not Miss. However, since you asked me to call you Teddy, you may call me Joan.'

He actually laughed, a great belly laugh. 'Well, Joan, that gets us off on a better footing. What experience do you have of retailing?'

The question surprised Joan and she wondered why he wanted to know. It wasn't as if he was interviewing her for a job. However, the last thing she wanted to do was rub him up the wrong way. So she said, 'I have a great deal of experience of working for myself. For many years I have been doing dressmaking, alterations and curtain-making.

Whilst I was in service I made two ball gowns and a silk two-piece suit for the ladies of the house. If only I had the space I feel I could build up a trade with good, steady customers. Besides, I have Martin and Marjorie to guide me. They won't let me buy shoddy stock and when it comes to material Martin is an expert.'

'Oh,' said Teddy, dumbfounded. He shook his head. 'Got it all worked out, 'ave you? You think yer could earn a living and pay a rent just by doing needlework?' He sounded unimpressed.

'More coffee, anyone?' Marjorie asked cheerfully, feeling things were getting a bit tense. Martin also thought that Teddy was being a bit forceful. He wanted to say why the hell don't you give us the keys and let us take Joan to see the place. But one didn't argue with Teddy Taylor.

Joan grabbed the moment to drive her point home. 'Not just needlework. I do have other things in mind.'

''Ave yer now. Such as?'

Joan sighed. 'Well, I can't decide until I know how big the premises are. And then there is the living accommodation. I can't afford to rent if I can't live there.'

'Oh, you could live there all right. I've been told you're a lady on yer own. Well, the living quarters are good. There are two big rooms in the front, a very large kitchen, a flush toilet but no bathroom. Oh, an' there's a huge cellar for storage.'

Martin had had enough. 'For God's sake, Teddy, you aren't offering her bloody Buckingham Palace. From what Marjorie has told me it's you that's getting a good deal if she's got to clean it from top to bottom.'

Teddy was taken aback and it showed. He glanced at Marjorie. 'Did you think it was that bad?'

'Disgusting would be an apt description,' Marjorie quietly informed him. 'Mark and Jeff considered you'd need to put an army of cleaners in there. But I really don't know why we're sitting around like this. Why the hell don't you just give me the keys and let me take Joan to see the place? After all, it's her decision.'

Martin glanced at the clock. It was ten minutes to eleven. 'Come on, Teddy. Pubs will be open by the time we get there. Let's leave the girls to it. They can catch up with us later and we'll all have a bit of lunch.'

Teddy didn't say a word. He stood up, shrugged himself into his black overcoat and took a small bunch of keys from the pocket and handed them to Marjorie. Martin kissed Joan first, then his wife. 'Make it the Prince, shall we? About one o'clock?'

Teddy Tyler merely nodded at the two women as he followed Martin out of the room. Marjorie and Joan heard Martin whistling as he went downstairs and they each breathed a sigh of relief.

'Come on,' Marjorie said, 'put your jacket on. My car is just round the corner. Let's go and see what you're letting yourself in for.'

Chapter Twenty-three

Marjorie parked her car in the road behind the shop and Joan couldn't get out quickly enough, keen to see not only the inside of the shop but the living accommodation. The very thought of having her own home had her quivering with excitement. They walked side by side for a few yards until Marjorie stopped and pushed open a gate and they went into an untidy, neglected back yard, past a water tap, a coal shed and what appeared to be a washhouse. Then, selecting a key from the bunch that Teddy Tyler had given her, Marjorie turned the key in the lock and they went through into what might have once been a downstairs kitchen. There was an iron stove with a flat top on one side and an oven on the other. Joan thought that it must have been many a long day since that stove had seen any blacklead. There was also a shallow brown sink fixed beneath a small window so dirty one couldn't possibly see out of it.

'Would you like to go through to the shop first or go upstairs?' asked Marjorie. Smiling, she added, 'You'll probably have a fit whichever way we start.'

'No doubt,' said Joan, 'but then I'm not expecting anything special.'

Marjorie shrugged. 'Come on then, follow me.'

They went down a narrow corridor and into a large shop at the far end, and although it was in a filthy state it made Joan's heart sing. Double fronted, it had two huge windows with a door in the centre leading out into the main road. The premises had at some time been an estate agent's and was still partly furnished as an office, but by God the whole place smelt awful, there was rubbish and litter all over the floor and Joan could have written her name in the dust.

'I did try to prepare you.' Marjorie sighed. 'If you think this front shop is awful wait until you see the side room, and the upstairs looks as if the last occupants lived like pigs. And as to the cellar, the Lord only knows for what purpose they used that.'

'This room is not so bad,' Joan exclaimed, looking at the shelves that were fixed along the full length of one wall and held an array of books and papers. There were also several tin boxes, all bearing labels. A wall safe was set into the far corner, its wide-open door showing that it was completely empty.

Marjorie sighed once again as they both stared at that empty space. 'In some ways I can't help feeling sorry for Jimmy Erlock. He's inside. Teddy's lost a lot of money on the place, I gather, but he's more upset that the man he trusted did the dirty on him.' When Joan made no answer Marjorie went on almost as if she were talking to herself. 'That Rita Thomas is something else. Beautiful, mind you, and always dressed as if she's just stepped out of a bandbox, but selfish, pompous and vain are only a few of the words I can think of to describe her. Oh, I've thought of one more. Greedy. Oh yes, very greedy. And if I told you the whole truth about her you'd have every right to ask, "Why is it that only dogs are called bitches?"'

Joan was still looking around with interest. On the other side of the large room there was a long, narrow trestle-type table which would be very useful if and when she came to laying out patterns and cutting cloth. Also, a drawing board had been set up and pinned to it lay a map of the local district.

'Stop daydreaming,' Marjorie ordered, pointing a finger to a grubby-looking door. 'Through there is a small kitchenette, a washroom and a toilet. Downstairs is an enormous basement and most importantly, the flooring and the walls show no signs of dampness. I'm not sure about lighting – we'd have to get someone in to check on that but Jeff and Mark and I thought it might make a great workshop. Room down there for several people to work without getting in each other's way.'

Joan gasped. 'Getting a bit ahead of yourself, aren't you, Marjorie? According to you I shall have staff working here with me and yet I haven't taken the place yet. Who knows if I'll even be able to afford the rent.'

'Oh, don't be such a pessimist. If you want this place you've got three months free of rent. I know it will take a lot of elbow grease to get the premises looking shipshape, but try looking on the bright side. Three months is a long time – it will give you breathing space. Do you want to go upstairs or have you given up on the idea?'

'Of course I haven't given up, but the way you talk about me going into business seems hopelessly optimistic.'

'Oh, you're impossible. Have some faith in yourself, girl. Anyway, before we start another discussion, let's go and take a look at the living quarters. I know it's in a terrible state but for all that the accommodation is really good. Ever so spacious.'

Joan couldn't help smiling. Marjorie was such a good friend, and her bubbling enthusiasm so great it was impossible not to be carried along with it. Suddenly they both stood still. They could hear footsteps coming along the passageway. Then the door opened and Martin was standing there.

'Well, well, well,' Marjorie said, and from the happy look on her face one would never have guessed that these two people had been married for more than thirty years. As Joan watched Martin hug his wife she couldn't help thinking what a pity it was that this loving couple had never been blessed with children of their own. Though she was aware they had quite a few nieces and nephews whom they saw quite regularly. They certainly made a handsome couple. Martin also had a good head of thick dark hair and he was quite a few inches taller than Marjorie even though she was wearing high heels. Marjorie's shining auburn shoulder-length hair, and big, dark brown eyes made her attractive but she was also an expert when it came to make-up, her natural unblemished skin had been given a matt porcelain powdering, her lips lightly outlined with a dark red lipstick. The expensive black suit she was wearing and her manicured, red-nailed hands had her looking years younger than she really was.

He let go of his wife and kissed Joan on the cheek. 'Teddy couldn't stay, so I decided not to hang around in the Prince. All set up for business, are we?'

'We haven't been here very long,' Marjorie answered. 'We were just about to go upstairs.' She winked at her husband and nodded towards Joan. 'I rather fancy this is going to be the deciding factor.'

'Make or break, eh?' Martin wagged a finger at Joan. 'Nothing ventured, nothing gained.'

Joan was smiling nervously. 'I don't care how dirty the rooms are, I can soon sort that out. As long as it gives me a place to call my own home and I can afford to pay the rent I will be more than happy.' Her words were honestly said and with spirit.

'Well, view the rooms first and then we'll talk about finances later,' Martin said encouragingly.

At the top of the stairs Marjorie and Martin hung back, thinking it best to let Joan inspect the rooms on her own.

She stepped past them into what appeared a very narrow hallway and pushed open a door that was already ajar. Then she gasped in surprise. Never had she imagined any of the rooms would be as big as this one was. She walked around it, smiling, her eyes roaming from side to side. Her imagination had never led her to even think the accommodation might be anything like this. The main feature of the room was the fireplace, it was huge and Joan thought how lovely it would be to sit there if a log fire was burning in the open grate. She was quick to notice that the surround was probably made of marble. The mantelshelf had a velvet cover with a deep fringed edging. She thought the colour might be a rich dark green but there was no way she could be sure because from end to end it was thick with dust and in places cobwebs joined it to the wall. There were two big armchairs set one each side of the large fireplace, neither of which was any good, both being tattered and torn, with the springs showing through the seats. A few other pieces of furniture had been left behind, most of which would also have to be taken to the council dump. The carpet was rotten, so threadbare that in places she could see the floorboards showing through. Against the far wall there was a huge sofa which might have been bright red at one time but now, like the rest of the room, it had seen better days. However, although faded, it did not appear to have been badly treated and already Joan was imagining how good it would look if she set to and made a loose cover for it. Slowly, she walked to the window. She lifted the dirty lace curtain and felt it crumble between her fingers. She was surprised to find that she was now looking down on to the main road and that the area appeared to be thriving.

Martin's voice made her jump. 'Are you going to stay in here all day or would you like to see the other rooms?'

Joan smiled broadly. 'It's remarkable, it really is.'

'The walls and ceiling are filthy. Take some getting off

will all this old embossed wallpaper,' Martin told her wisely.

'Oh, I'd get Martha's boys and their mates up here. They'd soon scrape these walls.'

Martin threw back his head and let out a big belly laugh and to his wife he called, 'Our Joan has it all worked out. She's going to be the queen and get all her slaves working to make this place fit to be her palace.'

Joan was just as thrilled with the next room. It was almost identical, except the fireplace was much smaller. There were only two items of furniture left in here, one a marble-topped washstand on top of which stood a huge china bowl and a large jug to match. She itched to get the china into hot soapy water, for she suspected that beneath the dirt lay a charming floral design which, years ago, had probably been hand painted. The other piece was a coiled-spring double bed. It held no mattress. A tall, brass head rail with knobs at each end adorned the top of the bedstead, and a shorter version was placed at the tail end. The floor was just bare boards, and they were certainly in need of a jolly good scrub.

The third room was smaller and completely empty. A quick glance through the bare window told her this back bedroom looked down on to the grubby back yard, but already she was telling herself that she would soon have that area ablaze with colour by planting up lots of pots and dotting them about as soon as the spring plants were available.

The kitchen was an unbelievable mess. The sink was so badly stained it smelt rotten, and the wooden draining board was covered in what at some time might have been vegetables, now rotting and slimy. More than half the floor space seemed to be cluttered up with broken china. At one point Joan smiled broadly. She was gazing at a black, cast-iron *gas* stove, which even had a grill beneath the four burners. What a wonder! A closer look showed that the stove was thick with grease and as she pulled the grill pan out

222

she wrinkled her nose in disgust. That at least would have to go straight into the dustbin. How on earth could anybody leave a place as lovely as this in such an awful mess, Joan thought, seething with annoyance.

'Oh, Marjorie, Martin, I never in my wildest dreams imagined the living quarters would be anything like this.' She was blinking tears away, yet she smiled as she said, 'What a great size the rooms are. And when I've finished with it you won't know this kitchen.'

The indoor toilet was the jewel in the crown. To flush it there hung a knotted piece of rope for one to pull. Already Joan's mind had jumped to the day when she would visit an ironmonger's and choose a chain, perhaps with a shiny white enamel handle to dangle from the end. Martin and Marjorie watched the different expressions flit across her face and softly Marjorie murmured, 'Poor Joan. She has so much charm and talent, yet the whole of her life has been dogged by tragedy and sadness.'

Martin suddenly looked very thoughtful. 'You're right, my love. Joan deserves a successful future and we can help her with that.' He grinned, and almost as an afterthought he added, 'let's hope Mr Right might pop up along the way and that she'll find someone to really love and care for her.'

'Eeh ... you're still an old softie, Martin Goldsmith. Didn't know you had it in you to be a match-maker,' Marjorie said smiling.

Back downstairs, Martin insisted that he take them both to a nearby café and that no one should speak about their plans until they had a pot of tea in front of them and the meal of their choice was being prepared.

Marjorie said she would be mother and Joan drank her cup of tea gratefully while they waited for the homemade steak and kidney pie that Martin had assured them would be extremely good. She was thinking of her dear sister Martha and her good husband Sid. If things did work out well for herself she was going to make sure that she repaid those two for all the kindness they had shown her. Rosie was almost certainly going to come and work for her. The travelling distance wasn't too far: a tube train from Colliers Wood to Stockwell and a penny tram ride would bring her almost to the shop. As she ate her pie her mind was jumping miles ahead. That back room would make a lovely bedroom and she was sure Martha would let Rosie stay with her sometimes. Oh, she would make it look so pretty. Rosie would be over the moon with it.

Everything had been so much better at Martha's house since Sid was back working full time and both Lenny and Bernie were doing well, but she still felt that they hadn't much space in their little house at the best of times and it would be so good for her to be able to get out from under their feet. Not that she wouldn't be a constant visitor. Martha's Sunday dinners were always great.

When they had eaten their fill, which included apple dumplings and custard, and Marjorie had poured them all a second cup of tea, it was Martin who leant back in his chair and said, 'Come on then, Joan, talk away. Are you impressed enough with what's on offer or do you think it is a no go?'

Joan hesitated. 'Surely you both know how much I would like to have that place. But I will feel a whole lot better when Mr Tyler tells me what the rent is going to be.'

'Are you really that worried?' Marjorie asked, frowning deeply.

'Of course I am,' Joan answered crossly, which was unusual for her. 'I know Mr Tyler is allowing me three months free of rent but I think the situation should be on a solid basis before I commit myself.' Seeing the look that passed between her friends she hastened to explain. 'Supposing I scrub and clean the place, which I am more than willing to do, and pay my nephews and their mates to scrape walls. Even if I only give the place a clean coat of whitewash for now, it will still cost me money, and what if when it's all done Mr Tyler quotes a rent that is more than I can afford?'

'It won't be like that,' Martin promised. 'I will have a chat with Teddy, and whatever we work out we'll make sure he does the deal with you all fair and square and above board.

'And we'll come to the solicitors with you,' Marjorie added.

Martin was thinking hard. 'Joan, would you like to tell us what your financial situation is? It's not that I want to be nosy, but it will help us to help you more if we know your circumstances from the beginning. Do you mind?'

'Not in the least,' Joan was quick to assure him. Looking from one to the other she said, 'I thought I was nicely placed when I left Mulborough House, but now with so much to do and stock to buy I am not so sure. While I was working I hardly spent a penny, especially when I was helping to look after Mr Hamilton, because I never left the house for weeks. So I have quite a bit of money saved, and also the two hundred guineas which Mr Hamilton left me in his will.'

The silence that followed her statement was hard for Joan to bear and she spoke again. 'This is quite a posh area, isn't it? All the other businesses seem to be doing well and Mr Tyler has already lost money on those premises, so he's not going to let them go for a song, is he?'

Marjorie looked across at her husband and nodded her head, which meant nothing to Joan but to Martin it was a signal. He leant forward and patted Joan's hand. 'Just you listen to me. With your ability and organisational skills you'll be earning in no time. Meanwhile, Marjorie and myself would like to invest in your new business, that is, if you will have us.'

Joan lifted her head and glanced at Martin apprehensively. Then she asked, 'Why are you both being so good to me? If you had just offered to continue to employ me on your market stall I would have been grateful, though where I would live would be a problem.'

Marjorie gave her a puzzled smile. 'I don't know what you're on about. We struck oil finding those premises. You deserve your own business. You don't want to be stuck out on the market in all weathers. Think about the living accommodation you've just looked at and then tell me you don't want it.'

'Oh, Marjorie, I know I would simply love to live and work there. But . . .'

'No buts,' Martin cut in. Then, smiling gently he said, 'I'll set up another meeting with Teddy. Let him know that Marjorie and myself will be standing as guarantors.' Then, smiling again he said, 'The hardest thing you have to do is come up with a catchy name for your new business and stop worrying about finance. You'll be fine. Given time you'll end up really rich.'

'I'd like to think so,' Joan answered. But it was said without conviction.

Chapter Twenty-four

TEDDY TYLER'S VOICE was full of barely suppressed irritation as he pointed a finger at Joan and said, 'For God's sake look a bit more cheerful, woman!'

Joan was sitting on the settee in the Goldsmiths' front room with Marjorie beside her. Inwardly Joan was trembling, but not Marjorie. She purposely allowed her skirt to wriggle up to just above her knees, crossed her legs, and swung one foot from the ankle. Her long legs, pure silk stockings and high-heeled black court shoes were enough to catch Teddy's eye. He grinned, and Marjorie realised that he looked smug. Smug and very sure of himself.

'Lay off her, Teddy. I've told you Martin won't be long. He's bringing the cash, then everything will be sorted. I'll get you a drink,' Marjorie offered quickly.

'Best idea you've had this morning,' Teddy replied, his features relaxing as he watched Marjorie pour brandy into one of their cut-glass goblets.

Joan felt she owed so much to Martin. He had been slowly teaching her the ropes over the last three months, taking her to factories and warehouses, until now, the first week in May, she was finally feeling more confident of all the different aspects of the business. After today, when money changed hands, she would be the tenant of the premises, now to be known as 'Distinctive Designs'. The tenancy agreement had been drawn up for a period of five years.

God, it seemed a lifetime!

When it had come to the signing of the lease Joan had prayed that she would be able to work up enough business to last that long.

There had been a great deal of argument over the finding of a name for Joan's shop. In the end it had been Jim Taylor, the bare wood man, who had come up with the idea of naming the premises 'Distinctive Designs'. Martha had immediately begun to refer to the business as D&D and the shortened version had quickly caught on.

As the days and weeks had rushed busily by and the date set for the opening of her shop had grown closer, life for Joan had grown more and more hectic. There had been no time to brood on whether or not she was doing the right thing or to speculate about the future and Joan was thankful for that. Every member of her family had helped in various ways and friends she never even knew she had, mainly stallholders from the market, had thrown their weight in and offered whatever assistance they could.

Bernie, Lenny and four of their mates had given up their evenings and weekends to decorate the place throughout. Mind you, all six young men had become damn good customers of the Prince of Wales! Somehow Martin had acquired three fairly good sewing machines, Teddy Tyler had set a glazier on to put two windows into the walls of the part of the basement that was not entirely underground, and electricity was working now through the whole of the building. Joan had sewn until her fingers were sore, yet she still enjoyed listening to the burring of the machines and nothing pleased her more at the end of the day than to neatly fold and lay embroidered articles between sheets of tissue paper or to place all the finished garments on coat-hangers. More often than not she was too tired to think of what tomorrow might bring.

Martin had also sent two of his own needle-women over to help Joan, and for the time being he was paying their wages.

Upstairs was nothing short of a transformation. The whole place smelt of paint and both walls and ceilings were now pure white. Sid had told his boys the place looked like a ruddy hospital, but that did not deter Joan. Time enough for expensive wallpaper and carpets when she was earning money. She would be glad, though, when she could afford to have lino or cheap carpet on the stairs. The bare boards irritated her.

Today she would officially take up residence. For the past two weeks she had been camping out in the big front bedroom. If it weren't for the fact that she couldn't help worrying whether or not she was going to be able to make a success of this great venture she would gladly admit it was exciting to be setting up a new home. Martha and herself had visited several second-hand furniture shops and had, or so they had thought at the time, bought quite a few useful items at bargain prices, which they'd agreed would make the place homely, at least for the time being.

It was in the middle of a Sunday afternoon that Jim Taylor had turned up, driving a large van. When Joan went downstairs to answer the ring of the doorbell, Jim had opened the double doors at the back of the van and invited her to jump up and inspect the contents.

'Anything that takes your fancy, just name it and it's yours.' He beamed at her. Joan had a job to believe what she was seeing. A complete home and more was tidily stacked from front to back of the vehicle.

'I couldn't possible accept any of this wonderful furniture,

Jim. Where on earth has it come from? It looks as if the bailiffs have raided someone's home. All these cardboard boxes look to me to be full of cooking utensils.'

'Joan, it is nothing as bad as that, I promise you,' Jim answered quietly. 'There's a mate I do a lot of work with and his grandmother has been taken into an old folk's home. Sad really, because her daughter had been caring for her, but unfortunately the daughter has died first. My mate, Doug Morgan, had to empty the house out quickly because he couldn't afford to go on paying the rent. He offered me a business deal. I thought I'd be a fool not to take it up.'

'Oh, Jim! It's wonderful. The rooms upstairs are so big I thought it would be donkey's years before I would be able to furnish them all.' Suddenly she pulled a face. 'I'm jumping the gun a bit here, aren't I? You haven't told me how much any of this will cost me.'

'Oh, huh.' He wagged a finger at her. 'There's no question of you not being able to afford it. Just let me help you sort out what you can use and the rest I know full well I can sell on and I won't be a penny out of pocket.'

'I couldn't accept things without paying a penny.' Joan sounded outraged.

Jim let out a long sigh, then said as though by way of an explanation, 'I've done Doug many a favour and he's done the same for me. He did get one dealer in, who offered to clear the house for forty pounds. The cheek of the man – he would have stood to make a small fortune. If you must know, we settled on sixty-five pounds.'

Joan stood silent for a minute or two, weighing up in her mind how useful several of these items would be to her. It was the chance of a lifetime, but she wouldn't accept charity. She wasn't sure how Jim was placed financially, but in any case she wouldn't want him to be out of pocket because of her. She looked the length of the van again, her mind working busily. In fact it had already turned a few somersaults.

There was a single bed and a pretty little dressing table which would go beautifully in the small room she already thought of as Rosie's room. And an old-fashioned dining room table and chairs which she would dearly love to own. 'I can manage forty pounds,' she murmured, naming the items she had been thinking about.

'There is a single wardrobe tucked away at the back that goes with that single set,' Jim told her, smiling broadly. He guessed she had her niece Rosie in mind and it made him feel happy to think that the young girl might come to stay with her aunt from time to time. 'I'll take thirty pounds and throw in the contents all those cardboard boxes. It would be a job to get rid of the odd assortments of junk, but I will make money on those larger pieces of furniture, don't you worry.'

She glanced gratefully at him, knowing full well those boxes did not contain junk. 'You know, Jim, looking back, ever since I got married my life has been a bit complicated. Now suddenly even strangers are going out of their way to help me, and as for friends – they seem to be going to the ends of the earth to make sure that I have a decent place to live. I'll never be able to thank all of you.' They were smiling at each other now. 'You have surprised me today, Jim.'

'Oh Joan, not as much as you have surprised me on many an occasion, not nearly as much. Anyway, I'll garage the van at my place tonight and Doug and I will come back tomorrow and unload all the items you select.'

Suddenly, without stopping to think, she asked, 'Do you have to go now? What about coming upstairs and having Sunday tea with me?'

Jim didn't hesitate. 'No, I don't have to rush off and yes I would like that. I *would* like that.'

Joan gave him the Sunday newspaper to read and saw him settled on the big sofa, which she thankfully reflected looked rather good since she had made a jade green cover for it and four cushions, which she had covered in beige linen and piped the edges with strips of the jade green material. It was about twenty minutes before she came back from the kitchen carrying a heavy tray. Jim was on his feet in an instant, took the tray from her and looked around for a table on which to place it. Of course there wasn't one.

'Sorry. We'll have to put it down on the floor.' Joan felt really embarrassed, and explained hastily, 'I haven't eaten in this room yet. I've been eating in the kitchen.'

Jim badly wanted her to relax. 'We'll manage. Tomorrow you'll have your dining room set, and there is a small nest of coffee tables that will be handy for in here. Or there is always that tea trolley I made for you ages ago.'

Joan's voice was subdued as she said, 'I know I keep saying it but it's true. I'll never be able to thank you enough.'

They sat side by side and ate egg and cress sandwiches, and Joan got down on the floor to pour them each a cup of tea and to cut into portions a coffee and walnut cake she had bought the previous day from Fuller's.

'Tell me about your friend Doug. Does he know that you are letting me have some of his gran's furniture?'

'Oh yes, he does. He's a good man. We've known each other since our schooldays. He's good with his hands, does similar work to what I do. He's an intelligent fellow when you get to know him. Most likely he won't open his mouth when he first meets you tomorrow but once he gets used to you he'll be fine.'

Joan leant over and placed her empty teacup on the saucer. Then, raising her head, she stared intently at him and said, 'It's going to be a different life for me, Jim. Quite a new life.'

He held back from saying, 'For me too,' for he might have said it too eagerly. Not only did he need company to fill the great hole of loneliness he had felt in the years since his wife had gone off with another man, but in a strange way he knew he needed her, her in particular, and had done ever since Marjorie and Martin Goldsmith had introduced her to him. He couldn't help the way he felt, even knowing that the very thought was ridiculous and far-fetched.

Joan Baldwin had an outgoing personality, was small and beautiful, and her long soft golden-brown hair that she mostly wore twisted up into a bun had him longing to release it from the pins that held it in place and run his fingers through the long silky strands. If she gave him any thought at all she probably considered him to be quiet and serious, and the fact that he wore glasses didn't help. However, he had proved he could be useful to her and perhaps there would be many more opportunities when he could be of help to her.

But regarding anything more than that, he was well aware, he stood no chance. Still, having Joan as a friend was a bonus.

Chapter Twenty-five

JOAN PUSHED OPEN the back gate and smiled broadly. What a transformation!

The yard looked entirely different. There was no longer a mass of dirt and decay and no sign of the empty beer bottles and other debris that had been strewn around on her first visit. In one corner rotting refuse had been piled high; now in that same corner stood a wooden tub filled with compost and planted with high green plants at the back and a variety of brightly coloured flowers at the front. All round the edges were trailing petunias. In addition, several large stone pots had been scattered around and each one planted with a flowering shrub.

This was all down to Martha, bless her. Martha loved gardening. An image of herself and her sister sitting out here drinking a cup of tea on a nice sunny day came to Joan's mind. Then she shook her head, and laughingly reminded herself she'd have to find the time first. Her days were going to be really busy from now on. She spent another few minutes admiring her sister's handiwork, but now the time had come.

She had chosen to come here on her own today and yet

as she turned the key in the lock and stepped into what was now her own home *and* business she really felt lonely. So much had happened so fast, she had never dreamed she would feel the way she felt at this moment. All the same, she smiled. Here she was on her own facing the future and the results, whatever they might be, of her first major decision. She freely admitted to herself she was feeling very far from confident.

Where should she go first? Along the corridor and into the shop, or upstairs? Business first, she decided.

Joan stood in the middle of the floor and surveyed her own and Martin and Marjorie's handiwork with a great deal of satisfaction. Without a doubt everything looked wonderful, and had been well worth the hard work and long hours. She was longing to pull the cord and raise the blinds, but she had to resist the temptation. Tomorrow was to be the official opening.

If everybody that had promised to attend the opening were to turn up, well, what the outcome would be she had no idea.

Under Martin's watchful eye Marjorie and she had created special displays in both windows. They had taken notice of every word of advice he had given and the results were fantastic. Easter had come and gone so they had lost the chance to have small yellow chicks as a theme. However, the coming weekend was to be the Whitsuntide bank holiday and they had agreed to go for springtime.

Her keen eyes took in every item that was laid out in the left-hand window. One wax female model held centre position, wearing a flimsy ankle-length dress in the palest shade of green. The white silk lining was faintly visible. The waist sash was also white, and the wig that had been placed on the head of the model was shoulder length and pale blonde. One arm hung to the side while the other hand was positioned to hold a pretty wicker basket filled with moss

235

into which had been bedded several primulas, all one colour, a deep rich golden yellow. On the model's feet were sea green strappy sandals.

There was muslin draped along one wall. Three summery hats, three raffia handbags and three pairs of crocheted gloves were secured to the muslin with gay red ribbon. Laid out across the floor to the front of the display was a simple but very elegant navy blue silk dress. To the side had been placed a scarf and a pair of plain court shoes, both the exact same shade of deep old rose.

'Perfect,' Joan murmured as she walked to the other side of the shop. This window was entirely different. Joan, assisted by Martin's two employees, had spent endless hours making not only useful things for the home but decorative cushion covers, table runners, chair-backs and tablecloths. On the floor, bolts of cloth had been set out in a ring, making a colourful clock face. Textures varied, as did prices: some extremely cheap, others for the more wealthy ladies who could afford to indulge their taste. The original shelves which ran along one side wall had come in handy. Joan had made elaborate covers for them, finishing them off with dangling gold tassels, and then spread along them everything in the haberdashery line that one would need to do home dressmaking.

Jim had made two small wooden wheelbarrows and painted them green. It had been Marjorie's idea to fill them with fresh fruit. This had been done with much laughter and teasing as a pineapple and two grapefruit were placed in the bottom, apples, oranges and pears followed while jars of crystallised fruit and bunches of grapes were added until each wheelbarrow was filled to overflowing.

Martin had insisted that she bought a great deal of stock, and she was hoping and praying that they might do a brisk business in the first few days. Rosie had pleaded to be given a job straight away but both her mother and her aunt had insisted she remain where she was until Joan saw just how much trade the shop was going to attract. However, because Rosie had really implored, they had given in and told her she could take one day off and come to the opening of Distinctive Designs.

Joan gave the shop a final glance, her eyes lighting up at the difference they had made to this place. Between them they had made two sample pairs of curtains, one expensive, one much cheaper. Each set had been draped to great advantage. The more costly pair was tied back with contrasting silk cords, beneath a very full eight-inch frill. For the cheaper pair Jim had made a plain wooden pelmet board which the girls had padded and covered with the same material as the curtains, sewing a fringe along this valance. The idea for this pair of curtains had started out to be cheap and cheerful, and the end product was simple but very striking.

Along the two back walls Jim had made and fixed innumerable shelves which soared up to the ceiling. These now held bolts of cloth in every colour of the rainbow. There was even wall to wall carpet throughout the whole of the double-fronted shop which Bernie had insisted was surplus to requirements when some of his mates were fitting out one of the big London stores. When Joan had made it clear that she distrusted what Bernie was telling her because the asking price was so low, Bernie had been quick to say, 'Never look a gift horse in the mouth.'

His father told Joan it had probably fallen off the back of a lorry and Bernie's mates had picked it up from the middle of the road to prevent it causing an accident. Martha's comment had been, 'And if you believe that then you'll believe that some men can walk on water.'

Joan took the stairs slowly. The treads were still only bare boards, and she reminded herself yet again that she had to walk before she could run.

She stood in the doorway of the front room, placed her arms crossways around her body and hugged herself. Just looking at what was part of her new home gave her so much pleasure. As the transformation had taken place there had been times when she was afraid to go to sleep in case she woke up and found it to be all a dream. She was particularly pleased with the big old sofa which had been left behind. Self praise is no recommendation, she smiled to herself, but she knew very well that no matter what anyone else's opinion might be she had made a darn good job of covering it.

There was an armchair placed near to the open fireplace, which Jim had taken off the van and said was a present from him. Nearby stood the nest of coffee tables he had included in her purchase. The mahogany dining table and six chairs at the far end of the room almost took her breath away. She had polished that table top until she could see her face in it. She had many folk to be grateful to, but none more than Jim Taylor. As Martha said, 'Jim's a good man. Help anybody, he would, providing they were worthy like.'

Joan walked out on to the landing. Everywhere was spotlessly clean. The small bedroom was neatly furnished with the pieces she had got from Jim. The single mattress, like the double flock one for the iron bedstead which had been left in the larger of the two bedrooms, was brand new, and Martha had added the finishing touches by giving her a chair and two rugs, one for each side of the bed. They had already worked it out that if Sid and Martha wanted to come up for the weekend, she, herself, could easily sleep on the huge settee and Sid and Martha could have her double bedroom.

Suddenly Joan laughed out loud and the happy sound rang out loudly in the high-ceilinged flat. She was thinking back to when Martha had told her that Bon Marché, Brixton's largest department store, was having a white sale. The two of them had joined the queue at eight o'clock even though the store did not open until nine. They had brought a flask of tea with them and Martha had nipped across the road to the fantastic Yiddish bakery and bought hot bagels and pretzels. Then, rushing from counter to counter, they had spent thirty shillings! Joan had felt very proud as she had made up the two beds with new sheets and pulled snow white pillow cases on to plump new pillows.

As she looked now she vowed that the minute she got some spare time she was going to make a really pretty bedspread for Rosie's bed. She knew time would be precious. If things went well every minute would have to be made to count. She would work all the hours that God sent, seven days a week if necessary, to make a success of the opportunity that had been given to her.

Tomorrow was going to be her big day. She felt quite sure people would come. Martin had placed a large advertisement in the local paper inviting folk to look round and partake of free refreshments. But would they turn up just out of curiosity or would most of them become customers?

She hoped against hope for the latter. For there were only two routes open to her: survive or go bust!

Chapter Twenty-six

JOAN WAS AT A LOSS for words. Distinctive Designs had been open for almost three hours and still folk were coming in. She watched as Martha smoothed the fresh white cloth on the table which had been set up in the far corner of the shop. Martha must have spent hours baking all the little titbits. Marjorie had borrowed the small side plates, cups and saucers from the local café and Rosie was doing a good job of making tea and coffee. Part of one shelf had been cleared and now held wine glasses and bottles. Martin was offering wine to the commercial travellers who had called in, insisting that a little hospitality didn't cost much but paid enormous dividends.

The biggest surprise was that Teddy Tyler himself had turned up and with him were Jeffrey Harper and Mark Townsend. Jeff and Mark were immaculately dressed in dark double-breasted suits and were going out of their way to be charming to the ladies.

'Joan, do you have a moment?' Jeff smiled at her and she saw a hint of a saucy wink. 'I'd like to introduce you to Mrs Johnson. She and her husband own the local newsagent's.'

'I am so pleased to meet you, Mrs Baldwin. The way this

property has been improved will do so much good for the neighbourhood,' Mrs Johnson gushed as she accepted a glass of wine from Martin.

'Thank you, Mrs Johnson,' Joan answered. 'The place had been run down but hopefully things will run smoothly from now on and I shall be over to make a regular order for my paper and magazines to be delivered.'

Mrs Johnson's eyes roved over the shelves behind Joan. 'You certainly have a wide choice of material. Marion James, the wife of our local butcher, told me that she came in earlier and one of the girls you have serving behind the counter told her you are going to stock paper patterns and will make up dresses or even suits to order.'

'That's quite true. There will be three fittings for each garment, to be sure that at every stage we have the right cut and the right fit. We have a workroom downstairs and as soon as the workmen are free we hope to have a fitting room installed.'

A few minutes later, Jeff's face showed concern as he said, 'Joan, this is Mrs Bates. She would like to ask you a question.'

The lady was extremely large yet she seemed timid. Her face was pleasant and Joan couldn't have said why but she felt sorry for her. 'How can I help you?' she asked, smiling to put the woman at ease.

'Oh, please, don't bother. You are busy enough without me troubling you.'

'It's no trouble, Mrs Bates,' Joan assured her.

'If you don't mind I really wanted to ask if you were thinking of doing alterations. The ready made clothes I buy never seem to fit properly.'

Do I do alterations! Joan's mind jumped back to the days when she had sat at Granny Baldwin's bedside and shortened skirts, turned worn-out collars on men's shirts and put new pockets in many a pair of old trousers. The payment had never been more than a bob or two. She shook her head to clear it, then, smiling brightly, she said, 'We would be more than happy to oblige. Come in any time, Mrs Bates, and we'll discuss the best way to alter whatever garment you don't feel comfortable in.'

Another buxom woman was having a right old laugh with Teddy Tyler, and although they had each been given a cup of coffee by Rosie Joan would have bet a pound to a penny that Teddy had well laced their cups with brandy from the hip flask that he always carried.

'Joan, this is Molly Worsfold, the landlady of the public house known as the Beehive.' Teddy's voice as he made the introduction was full of joviality.

Joan's first thought was, well, that's not hard to believe, because the lady looked every inch the part. She was small in height, had a big bosom and bottle-blonde hair, and was wearing a brilliant red suit, sheer black silk stockings, and black patent court shoes with four-inch heels. Her nails were painted the same colour as her suit and her lipstick also was an exact match.

''Allo, darlin'.' Molly grinned. 'Gonna work for yer living, aren't yer? Wouldn't catch me within a mile of a sewing machine. I like t' mix business with pleasure, an' yer can't get much more pleasure than a load of blokes coming in to see yer every night all wanting to buy yer drinks.'

Teddy let out a great belly laugh. 'And you ain't ever been known t' say no, 'ave yer, petal?'

Joan wasn't sorry when it was six o'clock and time to close the shop. She had certainly had a far better day than she had expected. They hadn't sold much in what she now referred to as the made to measure half of the shop, but there had been a great number of enquiries from ladies who liked the idea of having a dress for a special occasion made to order in material of their own choosing. The haberdashery side, however, had exceeded all expectations. They had sold all but two of the embroidered cushion covers and a great many table runners and chair-backs. Trade had also been brisk in small items such as needles, reels of cotton and silk thread, buttons, tape and elastic.

As Joan walked into her sitting room, followed by Mark and Jeff, her sister handed her a steaming cup of tea. 'Here. For Christ's sake sit yerself down and drink that. You've been on yer pins the whole day long,' Martha said, sounding really concerned. Mark suggested that they all had a drink and relaxed for a while, and about eight o'clock he and Jeff would take them out for a meal.

'May I come too?' Rosie asked.

'Of course you can,' both men answered straight away and Jeff added, 'You've been a proper little gem today, keeping the drinks flowing and doing the washing up.'

'Hang on a minute,' Martha said sternly. 'Your father is coming t' take us home about seven and we said we'd get fish an' chips for our supper.' Everyone saw the funny side of Martha's objections and they had a hard job to smother their smiles.

'Give over, Martha,' said Joan. 'Even your Sid won't say no to a decent meal out for a change. He can have fish an' chips any day of the week.'

'Oh no he can't, Joan, you know full well I cook him a decent dinner every night. Very rarely do we 'ave fish an' chips 'cos they ain't cheap. A tuppenny and a pennyworth ain't enough for my Sid.'

'All the more reason for Sid to join us,' Jeff said. 'Anyway we'll ask him as soon as he gets here.'

It was almost half-past seven before Sid arrived and nobody was more surprised than his wife at the way he was dressed. Introductions were made, because this was the first time that he had set eyes on Mark and Jeff. They both shook hands with him and Mark explained that they were planning to take them all out for a meal. 'Is that all right with you, Sid?'

'Yes, mate, fine, just so long as it ain't in one of those posh places where all the money is spent on the furnishings and when yer dinner comes there's not much on the plate. Good job I went 'ome and washed and changed before coming 'ere, wasn't it?'

Jeff grinned. 'You do look well turned out, Sid. I like the whistle.'

Martha piped up. 'He only wears it for funerals and weddings.'

Rosie stared first at her father and then at Jeff, a very puzzled look on her face. 'What whistle? Dad's not wearing any whistle.'

Even Joan looked a little confused but Martha looked at Mark and Jeff and the three of them roared with laughter. Sid glanced down at himself before he self-consciously smiled at his wife. It was Martha who calmed down enough to say, 'You can see my sister has only rubbed shoulders with the nobs. And as for my Rosie, she ain't ever lived in the East End.'

'What's that got to do with it?' Rosie asked crossly.

Jeff straightened his face and very gently explained to Rosie that Mark had been using cockney rhyming slang. 'It goes like this, Rosie: "whistle" short for "whistle an' flute", meaning suit.'

'Oh,' she muttered, still looking bewildered. 'Are there any more such sayings?'

'Hundreds,' he told her. 'More than Mark and I know.'

'Tell me a few more,' she pleaded.

'OK, how about "china" meaning "china plate", mate or friend. "Cat" meaning "cat and mouse", house; "lean" meaning "lean and lurch", church . . . and so on. Once you get the idea, much of the rhyming slang can be worked out by using your common sense.'

'Ever been in the Prince of Wales, Sid?' asked Mark, while Rosie thought over what Jeff had said.

'Yeah, a few times when me an' Martha 'ave come up to Brixton to go to the Empress.'

'Have you ever had a meal there?'

'No. Can't say that we 'ave.'

'Well, Les and Annie Jackson serve up some of the greatest grub this side of the Thames. How about we all go there?'

'What d'you think, Martha?' Sid asked doubtfully.

Both Mark and Jeff could see that this kind-hearted working man was thinking about the cost of the meal, and they quickly did their best to put him at ease. Jeff spoke first. 'It's a very special day for Joan, and we've already promised Martin and Marjorie to bring her to the Prince as a kind of celebration.'

'It was Marjorie's idea to ask Joan's family to join us 'cos you've all done your bit to help her. I wouldn't be a bit surprised, Sid, to see your two boys and their mates there. After all, those young men not only decorated this place from top to bottom, they've become damn good customers at the pub, so Les tells us,' Mark added.

That settled the matter.

They had a great meal and a great night.

Once back at Joan's flat, Martha looked at the large clock on the wall. It was a quarter to one in the morning. 'Before we all go to bed, can I make a drink for anyone? Tea? Coffee?' she asked.

Joan smiled, 'Coffee would be great.'

Sid plonked himself down beside Joan on the settee. 'You've done a blinder today, gal,' he said, patting her knee. 'Nothing can stop you now.'

Joan grinned. 'Bit early off the mark for congratulations, wouldn't you say Sid?'

'Course not. You're up and running. No stopping you now, luv.'

Joan was dead tired but so happy. She leant towards him, resting her head on his shoulder and said, 'Let's hope so, Sid. Let's hope so.'

Chapter Twenty-seven

JULY 1930

THE PAST TWELVE MONTHS had been a real eye-opener for Joan.

She had made a few mistakes but she had also learnt a lot. Looking back, she knew darn well that with Marjorie and Martin Goldsmith as her backers she could hardly have gone wrong. Martin had taken her to Lancashire and Yorkshire to visit warehouses where she had seen such a huge variety of beautiful woven material that she had found herself gasping with envy. She hadn't known such mills and warehouses existed. With so much cloth to choose from it had been hard for Joan to decide which would be the most suitable for her type of work, and the best value for money. But with Martin on hand to negotiate on her behalf she was able to secure deals that meant she could make outfits for her customers at very competitive prices.

During these visits she had also become aware that in the north of England poverty was an even bigger problem than it was in the south. It was on a day when Martin had taken her to Jarrow that she had been shocked by the slum housing and the ragged children. According to Martin, it was a case of one half of the world not knowing how the other half lived.

'There had been a time,' he said, 'when the river port of Durham, on the Tyne, only four miles away, had two chief industries, shipbuilding and iron smelting. It had been a slap in the face to those hard-working independent men when their shipyards closed. There had been offers of help for even the poorest family but those proud men had said very bluntly that they didn't want charity, they wanted work.'

She also owed a debt of gratitude to Jim Taylor and to a lesser degree to his mate Doug Morgan. She had learnt that Jim played his cards very close to his chest. It had taken a while before she had discovered that he was employed by several auction rooms on a freelance basis. Jim never boasted. It was only by chance that she had come to know that he was an expert restorer and had done work for several well-known cabinet makers from time to time. On one occasion she had asked him why he still had a stall on the market and sold white wood furniture.

'Even folk who are not so well off need useful items in their homes,' had been his cagey answer. But then he had opened up and told her he liked meeting folk and appreciated the good fellowship and comradeship that existed between the stallholders. She had got the impression that his short spells on the market were probably the only bit of socialising that he did.

Over a period of time she had learnt quite a bit about this quiet man.

He was forty-nine years old, five years older than herself, and he didn't want to be fully employed by anyone. He liked being freelance where work was concerned. Since his wife had gone off with a younger man he'd never wanted a permanent arrangement. As there had been no children from the marriage he felt he had no one to answer to and so had become a free man in every sense of the term.

Joan and Jim had come to a mutually satisfactory

agreement. When it suited him, Jim would work downstairs in a partitioned-off part of the basement of Distinctive Designs, making useful items for selling on the market but also slowly and painstakingly restoring damaged and neglected items of antique furniture to their former beauty.

It had taken time for Jim to pluck up enough courage to ask Joan if she would like to accompany him to an auction sale. She had been very eager, and now whenever a large sale was taking place it had become accepted that they would go together. He taught her what to look for in various articles and how to assess their value. To his surprise, she quickly became an expert bidder, often getting valuable pieces that at first sight looked worthless for knock-down prices. On the other hand she was clever enough not to let herself be drawn in above her head. She was always quick to withdraw from the bidding if she felt the offers were going too high. House sales were her favourite. She loved to see how the upper classes lived.

She was now in a position to leave her premises in safe hands when she needed to visit warehouses with Martin or attend auctions with Jim, due to the fact that she was able to employ two loyal shop assistants: her niece Rosie, now seventeen, and Josephine Pattison, affectionately known as Jody, who was twenty years old. Despite the age gap the two young ladies had soon discovered that they had much in common, although they were as different as chalk from cheese in looks. They had liked each other on sight.

Rosie was small and dainty, with white-blonde hair, pale skin and wide blue eyes, still as pretty as any picture and still loved t' bits by her Auntie Joan. Jody was the reverse, tall and slender with shoulder-length thick dark hair that bounced as she moved her head. They both loved clothes and always wanted to stay after work if Joan declared that she was going to spend the evening drawing designs for costumes which would then be made up in her workroom where she employed three full-time machinists. Such garments were always advertised as being exclusive to Distinctive Designs.

Luck had also been on Joan's side the day that Mark Townsend had introduced her to Freda Preston, a tall, slim, extremely smart lady with threads of grey in her brown hair, sixty-one years old but wearing her age so well she could have passed anywhere for fifty.

Freda had worked as what was known as a selective buyer for a very well established fashion house in the West End of London. Customers would let the store know when they needed an outfit for a particular occasion and most would ask that Mrs Preston, personally, be allowed to bring a selection of appropriate garments out to their private residence. Extremely competent at measuring and fitting each individual, she had gained the reputation of having the ability to produce the desired result. Nevertheless, the store said they had to dispense with her services as soon as she reached the age of sixty.

Freda had been married, but after only five years of wedded bliss her husband had died of consumption at the age of thirty-one. Never having remarried, Freda had made her job her life. She had very much enjoyed visiting the homes of those she referred to as *well off*. Joan had listened spellbound to the tales that Freda had to tell.

At the time of their first meeting Joan felt they had hit it off from the word go. She had never taken to any other woman so quickly, or liked her so much, as Freda Preston. There was one fact of which she was sure: Freda was a lonely lady. Joan had explained that her establishment was very small, and nothing they made or sold could compare with the merchandise that Freda's old firm handled. 'Besides,' she had added, 'even if I could afford to pay you a suitable wage you would be dealing with a very different kind of clientele. This is Brixton, remember?'

The elegant lady had burst out laughing, and what she said next had Joan staring open-mouthed.

'God love yer, Mrs Baldwin, I was born just round the corner from 'ere an' I still live there. I can leave my posh voice behind whenever it suits me. For one thing, luv, how d'you think Mark Townsend came to recommend me to you? I'll tell yer. 'Cos Mark and Jeff have been good friends to me over the years and I often have a drink with them in the Prince of Wales. They know I'm not hard up – I get a pension from my old firm and I've savings. Some of my customers were very generous to me, though I never let on because we were not supposed to accept gratuities. Still, as I always maintained, the money was given voluntarily and what the bosses didn't know they didn't have to worry about. To be honest, I'd come here four or five days a week for next to nothing. It's company I need more than money, and to be able to keep in touch with the rag trade would be a bonus.'

'In that case,' Joan had said, with enthusiasm, 'let's start by calling each other by our Christian names. Then I think it's time you met the other members of my staff and gave our lowly premises the once-over.'

From the day Freda had joined Distinctive Designs Joan knew she had never made a better decision. To have an older member of staff to keep the shop and the workroom running smoothly meant that Joan herself could spend more time travelling with Martin and attending auction rooms with Jim. In fact, there were days when Joan worried because things were going *too* well. Over the months the business had slowly but surely changed from what had started out as a little business, which would provide her with a much-needed income and a roof over her head, into a small but thriving fashion establishment. However, Joan made sure that the haberdashery side of the shop – her bread and butter trade as she referred to it in her own head – was

251

never neglected. The stock varied considerably depending mostly on what she and Jim managed to buy at auction sales, and sometimes she was utterly amazed by what Jim could do with what some would regard as an old relic. His better objects were used as part of the window displays and a discreet notice would be placed stating that such artefacts were for sale. They always carried a good supply of the everyday requirements needed by housewives who were interested in knitting, sewing and embroidery. In addition, they were careful to cater for the needs of the poorer families and word soon got around that although the new shop had a posh side there was always a bargain to be had.

Joan saw to it that not a scrap of material was wasted. When a machinist happened to be having a quiet day Joan encouraged her to run up such items as workaday dresses, petticoats, nightdresses, blouses, aprons, and even clothes-peg bags, using pieces of material that were surplus from other jobs and so could be sold quite cheaply.

Martha had laughed her head off when two huge cardboard cartons had been delivered to the shop on a day when she was there. 'Where the 'ell 'ave they come from?' she asked, staring at them, her curiosity getting the better of her.

'Manchester,' Joan told her. 'You can open them up if you like,' she added, hiding a smile with her handkerchief by pretending to blow her nose.

Martha needed no second bidding, and looked round for something to cut the string.

'Don't you dare use those,' Joan screamed. 'They are my precious cutting scissors; they cost a fortune. Fetch a small knife from the kitchen.'

Martha did as she was told and soon had the string cut on both cartons. As she delved into the contents thrifty Joan carefully wound the long lengths of string into a ball to be saved and used again some other time.

'Socks! 'Undreds of pairs of bloody socks! What the 'ell d'you think you're going to do with them, for Christ's sake? You'll never sell them.'

'I will, yer know,' Joan insisted, lapsing into her sister's vocabulary. 'A girl in the warehouse office made a mistake and duplicated the order. Mr Morrison's such a nice man he didn't go mad even when he found out that the manufacturers wouldn't take the second lot back. He offered them to me for just what they cost him.'

'Who is this bloke?' asked Martha.

'The owner of a warehouse where Martin does a lot of business, but in the short time that I have been dealing with him he's become a friend.'

'Oh, come off it, luv. How many times have I 'eard folk say there ain't no friends when it comes to business?'

'Martha, don't be so cynical. There's an exception to every rule.'

Not being used to being chastised, Martha remained silent for a moment. Then, holding several pairs of white cotton ankle socks in her hand, she said thoughtfully, 'I must admit, they look jolly good quality, and the coloured tops on these little girls' ankle socks are ever so pretty. I'll give yer the benefit of the doubt and we'll wait an' see, shall we?' Martha suggested.

'Yes, we'll see. By the way, do you know what the going rate for socks of this quality is, on the market?'

'Fivepence or sixpence a pair, I'd say.'

'Well, I've done my sums and I could sell them for half that price and still double what I've laid out.'

'Crikey. Pity you ain't got any little girls of your own, ain't it?'

'Yes, it is,' Joan answered sadly. For a moment there had been an embarrassed silence in the shop, as they both thought about the children Joan might have had if her husband hadn't bashed her about so much when she was

253

pregnant. Martha had held her arms open and without a word being said by either of them had held her sister and comforted her. After a few minutes, Martha reminded her of the person who was still the apple of her eye.

'No matter what else,' she said, 'you know you'll always 'ave a share in Rosie. And there's another thing you don't need no telling: there ain't much my two boys wouldn't do fer you. Them an' their father would go to the end of the earth fer you.'

'Yes, I know.' Joan smiled again as she added, 'I just don't know what I'd do without you or your family.'

That memory had lingered. As each day passed she counted her blessings. Her family, her friends and the fact that her business was a success. On top of all that she also had a very comfortable home of her own now.

One way and another she was doing just fine.

Chapter Twenty-eight

IT HAD BECOME a regular habit for Joan's sister and brother-in-law to come up to Brixton almost every Saturday night. It had started because for one thing young Rosie was living with her aunt now, only going home on her days off, so naturally Sid and Martha frequently came to Brixton to visit. Another reason was that Joan and Martha loved to go to a show at the Empress while Sid and his sons had taken a shine to the Prince of Wales. They all declared they liked the pub so much because of the food that Les and Annie Jackson served. In their opinion it could not be beaten near or far. Another point, probably of even more importance to them, was that Les kept a good cellar. The pipes were cleaned regularly and the glasses shone, thereby assuring that Les served a jolly good pint.

Rosie and Jody would do their own thing as long as they said where they were going and promised not to be home too late. More often than not, with her parents' permission, Jody stayed the night, sharing Rosie's bedroom. Martha and Joan would go to the first house at the Empress, which started at seven o'clock and finished at nine, and then make their way to the Prince of Wales where they would meet up with Sid, and nine times out of ten Lenny, Bernie and several of their mates would be there. Some evenings the goings-on in the pub would be so entertaining that Martha, having laughed till she cried, would wipe the tears from her eyes and remark to her sister, 'I don't know why we bother going t' the Empress. There's more real life drama going on in this 'ere pub than any bugger could put on a stage.'

'You're dead right,' Joan would agree, digging her fork into a huge plate of steaming shepherd's pie, golden brown on top because Annie made sure her cook always grated a load of strong cheese on to the top of each plateful and shoved it under a really hot grill.

Les Jackson had always been a good landlord. He knew his customers and they knew him. He was a hard man but tolerant and fair in so far as he knew what most of his regulars got up to, but as long as they did not overstep the mark and jeopardise his licence his motto was live and let live. Most would say that he was a big fish in a little pond and they would be right, but if he overheard such a statement he would always say, 'Yeah, but the difference is that me and my Annie own this little pond! This 'appen's t' be a Free 'Ouse. My missus and meself don't work fer some big brewery, we work for ourselves.'

Joan, and indeed all of her family, had begun to look forward to Saturday nights which now were almost always spent in the Prince of Wales. Many colourful characters came into the pub and if Les knew them and knew their behaviour would be tolerable to his other customers then they were more than welcome. If some of the street ladies were vulgar prostitutes touting for business then their feet didn't touch the ground as either he or one of his barmen showed them the door. Given aggravation, Les could be as hard as the next man, and ultimately people respected him for it.

However, there was one exception to Les's rule. 'Lulu', known fondly as a 'tart with a heart'.

It was said you could set your watch by her. She would come in every day at noon, order an orange juice for herself and collect a bag of stale bread from Annie Jackson, then with great regularity, come rain or shine, she would walk to the small grassed area outside Brixton Library where she would sit and feed the birds. She would reappear in the pub at ten o'clock most evenings, half an hour before Les called time, and buy herself a whisky and dry ginger. The only time she deviated from this routine was on a Saturday night when the pub stayed open until eleven o'clock. Then Lulu would have two whiskies, but Mark and Jeff, and occasionally Les, were the only men she ever allowed to buy her a drink.

The first time that Joan's two nephews set eyes on Lulu was a Saturday night that Joan would never forget if she lived to be a hundred. The Prince was packed to the gills. Men were standing three or four deep at the bar and there were three barmen, besides Les himself, serving as fast as they could pull a pint. One of the reasons the pub was so busy was because it had been well advertised that several bouts of wrestling would be taking place that evening in Vassall Road, and the Prince of Wales, being the nearest public house to the hall where the events were taking place, was reaping the benefits. Both organisers and wrestlers had met in the pub at lunch time, for a meeting ground and to partake of some jolly good pub grub. By the looks of it they and a good many more men had decided it wasn't a bad place in which to pass the remaining hours of Saturday night.

Joan, Martha and Freda Preston were sitting on a long padded bench set up against the far wall, well away from the bar. Standing huddled in a bunch nearby were Sid Brown and his two sons, Lenny and Bernie, each with a pint glass in his hand. Within the last few minutes Jeff Harper and Mark Townsend had approached the three ladies and placed

257

a drink for each of them down on the table in front of them before joining their men nearby.

On the stroke of ten the double doors to the saloon bar swung open and Lulu walked in, dressed up to the nines. There wasn't a man in the pub who did not have his eyes glued on her. Conversations had ceased and eyes were bulging.

Jeff was the first to move and as Joan watched the customers stand aside to make a path for him she could not help but admire him. That he was not interested in ladies was a well known fact but there wasn't a man in the place who would face either him or Mark and question their morality. Their height was extraordinary, and one look at their broad shoulders, wide chests and hands that when clenched were as big as any you would ever see, would soon have you agreeing that you would rather have these two men as friends rather than as enemies. Besides, in Joan's eyes, they were not only real gentlemen, they were good friends.

Lulu had only moved a few paces from the door. Jeff offered her his arm and together they walked towards where Joan and Martha were sitting. Freda hunched up to make room for Lulu to sit down and Mark said, 'I'll fetch you a drink, Lulu.'

'Thank you, Mark,' she replied quietly.

It was all very civilised and very good-mannered. No more and no less. Sid and his boys looked at each other but their tongues could not form the words to describe what they were feeling.

Jeff, having rejoined them, grinned broadly. 'Something else, our Lulu, isn't she?' he asked.

Lenny, eyes still popping, said, 'You can say that again.'

Bernie was more outspoken. 'Blimey, I've seen some dames in me time but by God she leaves them all standing. She looks as if she's been poured into that dress!'

Freda, Martha and Joan would have agreed with him one hundred per cent.

From top to toe Lulu looked flawless. Her hair had been cut, coloured and arranged by a specialist, her face made up by an expert. The dress she wore was made from the finest cream-coloured lace interwoven with gold lamé threads and was lined with pure silk. The length of the dress was such that it reached to her ankles, allowing her gold strappy high-heeled shoes to peep from below. The *top* of this gorgeous dress, however, was extremely low cut!

Loosely draped round her shoulders was a stole the like of which Joan had never set eyes on before, and she had helped dress many a rich lady in her time. This one was entirely woven from gold and silver lamé threads.

Even Freda remarked that she could not recall having seen such an outfit before. She murmured beneath her breath, 'She's one hell of a lady, always has been. Easy to tell she works from home.'

Joan just about caught Freda's comment, but the implication of her words was lost on her. However, both Mark and Jeff had heard and they both grinned and leaning towards Joan, Mark whispered, 'You should see her flat!'

That was when the penny had dropped for Joan.

Chapter Twenty-nine

THE TELEPHONE WAS RINGING as Joan came downstairs into the shop. As usual, its demanding tone made her jump. She felt she would never get used to this new-fangled instrument that Martin had insisted she have installed. Marjorie was the one who had persuaded her, by saying it was a necessary evil of the modern times.

'Good morning, Distinctive Designs,' she said into the mouthpiece.

'Joan, I'm not going to be able to make it this morning, I'm afraid. You'll have to keep our appointment with Eric Roussel without me.'

'Oh no, Martin,' Joan gasped, gripping the phone very tightly. 'I've never even met the man and you've gone on and on about how important and rich he is.'

'So he is, and that's the reason you have to go. He won't bite.' She could hear Martin laughing at the other end of the line and that made her cross.

'How will I recognise him?'

'You know we were to meet him at the Strand Palace Hotel, so just take a cab and ask for him at the reception desk. I am going to ring him now and make my apologies.

I'll tell him you will be alone and he will be watching out for you.'

'Do I have to go? Can't you postpone the meeting until another day?'

'Now you are being silly, Joan. Eric has been a good friend to me over the years and he's only in London for a few days. You'll like him. Just look for a middle-aged, well-dressed man, listen to what he has to say but whatever you do don't sign anything. Oh, and remember Eric is a true socialite. See you tomorrow. Have a good lunch.' The line went dead and Joan stood there feeling an odd sense of adventure. It was only later, when she went upstairs to change, that she panicked.

Lunch with a stranger! A middle-aged businessman, Martin had said, and in a West End hotel! What should she wear? She shook her head and said aloud, 'I won't go.' But she knew she had to. Martin had done so much for her, it wasn't much for him to ask of her. She opened the wardrobe door, and flicked through the clothes that were hanging there. The last few days had been warm and sunny, showing that summer was well into its stride. She didn't want to wear a dress that looked too summery. Definitely a suit, she decided; after all, it was a business meeting. Not black: too hot. Finally she chose a beige linen suit, a dark brown blouse and a pair of brown court shoes with a beige toe-cap.

Eric Roussel stood to the front of the foyer of the Strand Palace Hotel, looking extremely smart and very cool in a silver grey suit with which he was wearing a crisp white shirt and a navy blue tie. Outside all the hustle and bustle of London was going on and taxis were drawing up to the entrance of the hotel every few minutes. The minute one slowed down and he spotted the single lady occupant he knew at once it was Joan Baldwin. In a trice he was out there, beating the doorman, he had the cab door open and was assisting Joan to step down on to the pavement. 'Excuse me just one moment,' he murmured, and turned to pay the cab driver the fare to which he added a generous tip. Turning back to Joan, he took her elbow but he did not speak again until they were inside the entrance hall of the hotel. Then he let go his hold on her, held out his hand and said, 'Eric Roussel. I feel I know you rather well. Both Martin and his wife have told me so much about you.'

Joan felt the colour rush to her cheeks. 'Joan Baldwin, pleased to meet you,' she whispered.

'Oh my goodness, have I blotted my copy-book already?' Eric hastily did his best to make amends. 'I assure you our friends have told me nothing but good about you. Shall we start again?' Not waiting for her reply he said, 'I'm Eric and you are Joan and we've plenty of time before lunch to get acquainted over a drink, so shall we make our way to the bar?'

Joan had to smile as she nodded her head. She had already decided that Eric Roussel was a real gentleman, courteous and kind. Look at the way he had rushed out to meet her, paid her cab fare, was opening the door to the bar. He was older than she had expected, late fifties or even early sixties she imagined, but everything about him suggested a man of taste. He wasn't over-tall, about five foot ten. His face was attractive and tanned. In fact he didn't look English. His silver grey hair had been styled very short which added to his clean-cut appearance.

'What would you like to drink?' he asked as soon as they were seated.

Joan hesitated. She wasn't used to drinking alcohol at midday.

'How about white wine? Nice and cool and not too heavy before we eat.'

'That would be nice,' Joan answered shyly. She watched as he summoned a waiter and gave his order, naming the exact bottle of wine he preferred, and again Joan came to the conclusion that his world spun round smart hotels and good restaurants.

'Cheers,' they said as they touched glasses. He smiled down at her. He had already noted how softly spoken she was. Now he had time to study her and found she was small but beautiful in a really unassuming way. She didn't use thick layers of paint and powder, just enough to give her complexion a truly natural look. He was thinking that her thick golden-brown hair must be quite long because she had put it up in an intricate style and he couldn't help but wonder what it would look like hanging down over her shoulders. She also had the most beautiful clear blue eyes.

Joan could feel that he was studying her and she lowered her eyes and sipped her wine. It was very pleasant. After a few more sips she felt easier.

'Tell me about your business,' he said. 'Martin tells me you're making a great success of it.'

She smiled at him. 'I've had a great deal of help from Marjorie and Martin and they tell me you import a wonderful variety of cloth from many different countries.'

'Yes, I do. My main supply, though, comes from Italy.' He went on making small talk, telling her how he had started in the business. He found himself wondering what had driven such an obviously intelligent woman, who spoke so well, to work on a market stall before Martin Goldsmith had helped to set her up in a business of her own.

The restaurant of the Strand Palace Hotel was vast and as a waiter pulled out a chair and helped Joan to be seated she felt very intimidated. There were a great many businessmen lunching there, but at the next table was a family with three teenaged children and that took the edge off Joan's fear – until she was presented with the menu, which was so huge she could only stare in bewilderment.

'Shall I order for you? Melon to start with and roast beef to follow, perhaps?'

'That would be very nice, thank you, Mr Roussel.'

'I thought we had decided on Christian names. You can't call me Mr Roussel all the time if we are to be friends. If I tell you a bit about myself maybe you will find it easier to call me Eric.'

'All right.' She smiled.

'I was born in Malta, so naturally I am a Roman Catholic. I shall be sixty this year, which I am sure makes me old enough to be your father.'

'Now you are flattering me,' said Joan.

He ignored that remark and continued. 'You could say I am jack of all trades but master of none. I went to a church school on the island of Gozo, did very well according to the priests, but I never thought of getting a proper job or joining any of the professions, which is what my parents would have preferred. I came to London, studied art, even found a job in an art gallery. Then my father died and left a lot of money so my mother and my sister and myself were well taken care of. So you see I've never had to face up to the real world. I could lead my life as I saw fit.'

'Did you get married?' something prompted Joan to ask.

'No,' he said thoughtfully. 'I have to admit I love the companionship of beautiful women, but I also love to travel. I've never felt the urge to settle down in one place for any length of time.'

They had finished their melon, and as the waiter carved their roast beef at the table the wine waiter was pouring a little red wine for Eric to sample. He took a minute, then nodded his approval. The waiter wiped the neck of the bottle with a white cloth before filling Joan's glass. She had never tasted red wine before. Mr Farrant used to drink it when she had worked at Mulborough House, but she herself had never fancied it.

'Does your sister have a family?' she asked.

'Yes, she does. She married quite young and has five children.'

'Well, that must be a blessing for you, especially at holiday times and most of all at Christmas.'

'I hardly ever hear from them, let alone see them,' he answered jovially, but Joan couldn't help wondering whether it was all bravado. She put her hand over the top of her glass to prevent him from refilling it and watched as he refilled his own. 'Your turn now,' he said.

If she hadn't already drunk both white and red wine, Joan might not have been able to tell a virtual stranger as much of her life story as she did. She started by telling him how she had come to work on the market stall for Martin and Marjorie, then suddenly she had gone back in time and all her bottled-up feelings came pouring out. Her disastrous marriage, the jobs she had taken on to enable herself to look after Granny Baldwin. The three times she had been pregnant and the beatings that had been the cause of her losing her babies. How wonderful her sister Martha, her husband Sid and their two sons Lenny and Bernie had been to her, and how these three men had given her Bill a jolly good hiding and made sure that he had got himself a job.

'Whoa, whoa. Take a deep breath and I insist that you have at least half a glass of wine before you go on.' His concern for her was real. How could anyone pick themselves up time and time again when their life had been so cruel?

Joan did slowly sip her wine before she told Eric how Bill's death had come about. She didn't leave out the fact that he had bravely brought three of the horses through the fire to safety.

Then she related the story of her going into service because she had nowhere to live. The benefits weren't left out. The dress-making for Miss Fiona and Miss Delia. The legacy that Mr Hamilton had left to her in his will. Then

265

last but by no means least, how Marjorie had found her premises which had great living accommodation up above.

As she described her landlord, Teddy Tyler, Eric Roussel was smiling broadly. 'I think we'd better retire to the lounge and have some strong coffee, don't you?' he finally said.

It was late afternoon before Eric looked at his wristwatch. They hadn't even mentioned business but he didn't give a toss about that. He had never before met such a regular normal woman whom he really felt was a genuine, honest, sweet lady. There weren't many of them about, as he knew to his cost.

He stood up, held out both his hands and lifted her to her feet. 'Joan,' he said quietly, 'it *has* been a pleasure to meet you. I'll give Martin a ring tonight, set up another meeting with him. But look,' he stammered, 'may we stay friends? Would you come to the theatre with me one evening?'

'Are you asking me just to be polite?' Joan asked in her own straightforward way.

'I never say or promise anything that I don't mean. I really would like us to meet again.'

'In that case, I would very much like to.'

'So we part as friends, even if we didn't get down to discussing any business, yes?'

'Certainly. One can never have too many friends,' Joan replied.

'Does a friend get a kiss, then?' He smiled.

For a moment Joan hung back. Suddenly she found herself acutely aware of Eric Roussel as a man, not just someone Martin had asked her to have a business lunch with.

He looked at her serious face, leant forward and gently placed his lips on hers.

'Thank you for lunch,' she stammered.

It seemed natural then for his arms to go round her and

266

for her to respond to his hug. That they were two very different people from two very different worlds didn't seem to matter one iota.

Just two people, meeting for the first time and finding that they liked each other.

Chapter Thirty

THERE WASN'T MUCH THAT Martha Brown missed. Not when it concerned her sister's well-being. What Joan had just told her had her worried and her voice was raised as she said, 'You had lunch with this foreign bloke, on yer own, and after that one meeting he wants to take you out to dinner and to the theatre afterwards? What did yer say his name was?'

'Eric Roussel, and he's not that much of a foreigner. He was born in Malta.'

Martha threw back her head and let out a great belly laugh. It was ages since her sister had found the time to come and visit her. It was usually the other way round. Now they were sitting opposite each other in her kitchen drinking a cup of strong tea, and she couldn't believe that her sister who was normally so sensible was acting so foolishly.

'Course he's foreign if he weren't born in this country. My Sid always says 'alf the Mafia live in Malta an' the other 'alf live in Sicily.'

Now it was Joan's turn to laugh. 'Since when was Sid an authority on the Mafia? I've never even heard him mention such a thing.'

Martha grinned. 'Don't suppose he knows sod all about them really. It's just that his dad died when him and his brothers and sisters were all small and he left behind a load of gambling debts. His poor old mum had a helluva job convincing them bookies that he'd left her stony broke. My Sid always declared that the bookmakers that pestered the life out of his mother were part an' parcel of the Mafia.'

Joan giggled at her sister's reasoning. 'Martin has known Mr Roussel for years. They do a great deal of business with each other and I'm quite sure it does not involve gambling or bookmaking. Besides, I liked him. He was a real gentleman.' Joan stated firmly.

'How can yer tell? You've only met him the once.' Martha looked carefully at her sister. She had certainly altered a helluva lot since she had opened her own business. These days she was an entirely different person compared with how she used to look and act when she lived just round the corner and was married to that brute of a bloke Bill Baldwin. In those days she was frightened to open her mouth for fear of getting a bashing. And as for her clothes, if it weren't for the fact that she was damn good with a needle she would have been walking about in rags. Today her clothes were fashionable, her skin was clear and her brown hair gleamed like a polished chestnut when the light caught it. And she wasn't that old. Forty-four was a good age for a woman to find the right man if he still had plenty of life left in him.

'How old was this Maltese bloke then? And is he married?' she was bold enough to ask.

'He's sixty and no, he's never been married. Though why you want to know all about him beats me.'

'Hmm. You've only got his word for both those statements when yer come to think about it.'

'It wasn't a pack of lies he told me,' Joan insisted. 'I believed him.'

'That still doesn't alter the fact that he's sixteen years older than you are.'

'What difference does that make? I only met him because Martin asked me to. We had a very nice lunch and that was that. Now please may I have another cup of tea and may we change the subject?'

Martha had a sly smile on her face as she got to her feet, picked up the teapot and made for the scullery to make a fresh brew. As she tipped the cold tea leaves down the sink she was saying to herself, she's smitten with this fellow! She can say what she likes but the truth is staring me in the face. 'Let's hope t' God that he sees you all right,' she said, coming back into the kitchen and setting a fresh jug of milk down on the table.

'Hold on a minute.' Joan didn't know whether to laugh or lose her temper. 'You're reading far too much into this. It's not the way you think.'

Martha grinned. 'If you say so. Of course if he were married that would be an entirely different kettle of fish. But if Martin vouches for him I suppose it's all right. Let him take you out an' about if you're so sure he's on the up an' up. Grab the chance while you can. God knows you deserve it.'

'Martha, will you stop it,' Joan pleaded. 'I don't for one moment think he meant it when he said he'd like to take me out one evening. He was just being polite, that's all.'

'By the sound of him, he's well off, footloose and fancy-free. So why don't yer start thinking about what a good time he could give you? You like him, you said he's good-looking, well mannered and easy to talk to. What more do you want?'

Joan thought hard for a moment. Her sister had just put a very difficult question to her. She thought she knew exactly what she wanted out of life, but to put it into words that Martha would understand was beyond her. She actually would like to have what her sister had. A good steady husband, the security of knowing that she was loved day in and day out. And above all else, children of her own.

Now she was being envious, she chided herself. Nobody had everything in this life. Not so long ago she had been praying for a roof over her head and a way to earn her living without having to go back into service. Now she had both, thanks to her many friends. I'm happy enough, she insisted to herself, though in her heart she felt it would be nice to have a man in her life.

Martin had told her that he had met up with Eric Roussel and that they had done a deal which if all went well would be very profitable for both of them. He had also added the fact that Eric had been very impressed with Joan and had sent her his good wishes.

In Brixton the shops had Wednesday half-day closing while in Wandsworth they closed half day on a Thursday, which meant the shops there were open when Joan had time off. Quite often she took advantage of this as she had today. It was almost five o'clock when she staggered up the stairs with bags of shopping, put the bags down, put her key into the lock, turned it and pushed the door shut behind her with one foot.

As she staggered down the hallway, Rosie appeared from the kitchen. 'Oh, Auntie, you're absolutely loaded. Here, let me take some of those bags. I've got the kettle on. You go into the front room and sit yourself down and I'll bring you in a cup of tea straight away.'

Joan passed the bags over and heaved a sigh of relief, then she lifted her hands and cupped her niece's face. 'You're a little treasure,' she said.

Rosie laughed. 'I've laid the table and I've made a salad. It's far too hot to eat anything else, isn't it?'

'Oh, Rosie, what would I do without you?'

'Drink your tea and stop being so daft,' Rosie ordered.

271

'I've put some new potatoes on to boil – they won't be long – and we've got tinned salmon and grated cheese to have with the salad. By the way, a letter came for you by the second post. I've put it up there, behind the clock. It looks personal, nothing to do with the business I wouldn't think.'

Joan drained her cup, stood up and looked behind her. Rosie was such a good girl. She had set the dining table so prettily, even put two roses into a slender vase and placed them in the centre of the table. She turned and walked to the fireplace, took down her letter, slit it open, glanced at the signature and felt the colour rush to her cheeks.

It was a short note written on thick hotel paper from Manchester.

Dear Joan,

I will be back in London for the August bank holiday weekend. I will ring you on the Saturday morning. Hope you don't have anything planned for the Sunday and Monday.

Eric

Thursday and Friday dragged by and every time the telephone rang on Saturday morning it took all Joan's courage to pick up the receiver. Finally she heard his voice say, 'Joan?'

'Yes,' was all she managed to say.

'How early can you meet me tomorrow?' he asked, then not waiting for an answer he suggested, 'How about ten thirty at the Strand Palace again. We can have coffee and decide where you would like to have lunch and plan the rest of the day.'

Joan could not believe her ears. He sounded so masterful. 'All right,' she stammered.

As the taxi approached the hotel Joan again had butterflies

in her stomach and her heart was banging against her ribs. It was the liveried doorman this time who opened the cab door and she paid the taxi driver herself. She had to take a deep breath before she could face walking through the big doors.

Eric had said he would be waiting in reception, but at first she couldn't see him. When she did spot him she breathed out. He came quickly towards her, smiling, then caught hold of her hands and kissed her cheek.

'It's so good to see you again. I've thought about you a lot.' He could tell that she was flustered and said quickly, 'Come and have coffee.' Taking hold of her hand, he led her towards the lounge.

He looked very distinguished in his dark suit and striped tie. His face still had that healthy tanned look and she dropped her eyes so that he wouldn't think she was staring at him.

'You look very smart,' he told her as they sat down. 'Nice and cool. This August has turned out to be a scorcher, hasn't it?'

'It has indeed.' She smiled, thankful that she had chosen to wear a navy blue linen suit, the jacket being edged with white.

Over coffee, Eric told her a little about the deal he had struck with Martin.

'Seems I am to benefit too.' Joan smiled. 'Martin said you had a few bales of winter-weight cloth that he selected for me – ideal for skirts, apparently.'

Eric reached across the table and put his hand over hers. 'I am so pleased your business is doing so well. What about the living accommodation? Are you sure you are comfortable?'

'It couldn't be better,' she said, and went on to describe how her nephews and their mates had decorated the flat throughout and how Jim Taylor and his mate Doug had provided her with some really good furniture. 'It really is a nice home, and more so since my young niece, Rosie, has moved in with me.'

'Well, good for you. I wish you continued success, you really are a determined lady.'

Later he took her to a really lovely restaurant in Knightsbridge and over a leisurely meal he told her about all the countries he'd been to. 'My visits usually turn out to be quite profitable.' He laughed. 'Keeps me in the way I have become accustomed to and keeps the bank manager happy.'

Joan studied his face as he was speaking. She noticed the way he hesitated sometimes and didn't say what he had been going to. Was he wary of her knowing too much about him? He was a clear-cut example of a prosperous businessman, everything about him was immaculate, and yet there was a tiny feeling in her head that warned her he was overdoing the good life just a bit. Martha's words about him being older and the fact that she had no way of knowing if he were telling her the truth about his prosperity were niggling her. Was he laying it on a bit thick?

When they had finished their meal, Eric ordered two brandies to come with their coffee. 'Promise me something, Joan,' he suddenly said. 'That you won't make your business your whole life. Try not to do that. I know how it will be for you if you aren't careful.' He spoke gently. 'If you will let me I can show you how to have fun, even be irresponsible at times. It would do you a world of good.'

'What's wrong with being independent, earning one's own living?' she asked.

'Nothing at all.' He squeezed her hand. 'But you know the old saying, all work and no play. Tell you what, tomorrow I'll pick you up in my car and we'll head for the coast. None of the popular resorts, they'll all be too crowded with it being a bank holiday. I shall think of a nice quiet spot. What do you say?' Despite her age, Eric was thinking that Joan looked like a frightened rabbit. She had never really lived. 'Come on,' he urged, 'be daring.'

Joan could hardly believe what he was saying. A whole day in his company! She thought she ought to say no, but she liked the idea of a car ride and a day by the sea. She hesitated.

'I'll pick you up at your place about eight o'clock, get an early start. We'll have a lovely day and I'll bring you home safely in the evening.' Joan was torn two ways. She stirred her coffee and took a gulp of her brandy to cover her confusion, before saying, 'Thank you, Eric. I would love to spend the day with you.'

There was no need for Martha to know, she decided. It would only be a one-off. Besides, what the eye doesn't see, the heart doesn't grieve over. As Eric had said, it was about time she learned to live a little.

Chapter Thirty-one

JOAN WRIGGLED BACK COMFORTABLY in the front passenger seat of Eric's car. It couldn't have been a better day. There wasn't a cloud in the sky and the sun was already shining brightly even though it was only nine-thirty. There were green fields on either side of the road they were travelling and in every field a great number of sheep were grazing.

'Where are we?' she asked.

'We're into Kent.' Eric smiled faintly. 'We are actually crossing the Romney Marshes. We'll stop in Romney village and have coffee, then we'll go on to Greatstone where there is a beautiful long stretch of sandy beach.'

Joan turned her head towards him. Today he was much more casually dressed, in fawn trousers, a dark brown open-necked shirt and a beige pullover with a V-neckline. On his feet he still wore brown lace-up shoes of the finest leather. For the first time she noticed that despite his tanned skin his eyes were an astonishingly light and clear blue.

'What are you thinking about?' she asked.

'About today, how I have you all to myself and what to show you first. Have you ever been in this part of the world before?'

'No, I haven't. I was in service, as you know, in Tunbridge Wells but I never got to go out and about much because I didn't have friends or relatives in the area to visit.'

Eric parked the car and they found tearooms that served coffee and hot doughnuts. They looked at each other and laughed and Eric said to the elderly waitress, 'Who could possibly resist such a tempting offer?'

The coffee was served with thick fresh cream and the doughnuts were so warm and sugary that they found themselves not only thoroughly enjoying this unexpected treat but licking their fingers into the bargain.

Back in the car they drove down one very long road and came to the beach. There were folk walking their dogs, children running in and out of the sea, and adults either sitting in deckchairs or lounging on the grass. Greatstone not only boasted the most wonderful sands but acres of grass verge which was sprinkled with every type of wild flower it was possible to imagine. The beach was so long and so wide that it did not appear even remotely crowded.

Eric had come prepared. He had brought swimming trunks with him and changed in the back of the car. Joan walked to the sea edge with him, removed her sandals and stepped into the warm shallow water.

'I won't be long,' he called as she watched him wade in to deeper water. She was finding it hard to believe that all this was actually happening to her. Bank holiday Monday would usually be spent with Martha and Sid on Tooting Bec Common or Ravensbury Park, and the day would more than likely have finished up with them having a drink in the nearest pub. Now she was looking at Eric's tanned back, his broad shoulders and strong arms. Suddenly he dived beneath the waves and arm over arm he struck out, swimming strongly against the tide. She continued to paddle, walking up and down, kicking at the waves as they swept over her ankles.

Eric was out of sight now. Joan walked back up across the wide beach to the car, fetched two towels which Eric had told her she would find in the boot, and spread them out on the grass. Some time passed before she saw him striding towards her, droplets of salt water glistening on his tanned body.

'That was great,' he shouted, as Joan flung him the larger of the two towels which he straight away wrapped round his middle, using the smaller towel to rub his limbs and to dry his mass of grey hair.

'Right,' he called later when he emerged fully dressed from the rear of the car. 'Now we're going to Dungeness.'

'Why, what's there?' Joan was eager to know.

Eric laughed loudly. 'Well, there's a lighthouse and a coastguard station and the whole area is a haven for wild birds, but the main reason we are going there is because I am very hungry and there is a very old pub there which serves the freshest fish you've ever eaten.'

'With chips?' Joan playfully asked.

'Oh, Joan, promise me you are not going to demand chips.'

'I'll do my best not to, but the idea is very tempting,' Joan said, smiling affectionately as she handed him a comb because his towel-dried hair was sticking up all over his head.

Dungeness turned out to be like nothing Joan had ever seen before. The first word that came to her mind was ramshackle.

One side appeared to be efficient and very well managed, with both the lighthouse and the coastguard station standing out on the sky-line as the tide swept along easily and swiftly, forming a white foam as it lapped the sand.

The other side of the bay was totally different.

The homes, they could hardly be called houses, for in the main they were wooden contraptions, were so badly constructed and disorganised that Joan wondered if people

278

really did live in them. However, long lines of washing blowing in the breeze proved that family life really existed in this quaint place. There were fishing boats everywhere, some bobbing out to sea, others drawn up on to the beach. Several men were sitting in groups repairing their nets. As Joan looked round she was glad that Eric had persuaded her to come, for it was a perfect day, with a nice cool breeze that smelt salty. Besides it was good to see how the other half lived.

Just five minutes' walk and they came to a long, low wooden building that Eric told her was the one and only public house the area had, and that it was suitably named the Pilot. Joan was smiling even before they actually reached it, for she could see and hear that the atmosphere was jovial as a bank holiday should be. It was also a sight to behold.

A whole row of hanging baskets decorated the front of the Pilot, each packed tight with pink and purple fuchsias which dangled down like miniature ballerinas. The place was very busy. Apart from the fishermen leaning up against the bar in what Eric said was known as the snug, there was a long wide bar with many tables, the far wall of which was mainly glass so that diners could look straight out over the glorious sandy beach to the sea beyond whilst eating their meal.

Eric ordered a lager for himself and Joan chose to have a sweet sherry. They had to wait twenty minutes before a table was available, but it was well worth the wait. The menu itself was enormous, bristling with the names of fish that Joan had never heard of. The choice of shellfish included oysters, scallops, mussels, prawns, cockles, whelks and even winkles and shrimps.

After much deliberation they both settled for a grilled Dover sole, new potatoes and asparagus tips. When the food came Joan couldn't stop herself from letting out a gasp of surprise. Their meal was served on platters that were so large they would have held a roast turkey! The new potatoes were well buttered and sprinkled with freshly chopped parsley, and wedges of lemon lined the big fish. There were crusty rolls in a basket, a dish of butter and a jug of a creamy sauce so delicious that Joan felt she would die to have the recipe and be able to make it at home. Eric beamed at Joan's reaction as he watched her take her first forkful of a perfect Dover sole.

They rounded off their meal with ice cream, followed by coffee, and then walked slowly back to the car, holding hands.

The next place they visited was Rye, with its cobbled hilly streets. Joan was much more at ease with Eric now, but though she admired everything about him she was finding him baffling – especially when, just after nine o'clock that night, he drew the car to a halt outside Distinctive Designs.

'Thank you, Eric, for a truly lovely day,' she said, leaning towards him meaning to kiss his cheek. He turned his head away, got out of the car and came round to her side to hold the door open for her.

'My pleasure,' he told her. Then he did brush her cheek with his lips but so lightly she scarcely felt it. 'I will be in touch soon,' he called as he got back into the car.

As she put the key in the lock of her side door she was telling herself to be grateful for having been taken out for the whole day and for having been given such a wonderful time. But instead she felt like crying. Why hadn't Eric kissed her properly? Had he tired of her already or had he discovered that he didn't find her attractive?

August had given way to September. The weather was holding well and autumn still seemed a long way away. Life was good, the business was doing well, and Joan had decided to have a sale, reducing the price of nearly all the summer items they still had in stock to make way for the winter designs. It had been a great success. The cloth that Martin had ordered from Eric had arrived and it was excellent, even better than she had anticipated. Already her machinists were busy making up samples using the sketches that she herself had drawn.

Socially, though, her days seemed humdrum. August bank holiday had given her a glimpse of another life, allowing her to realise there was a big world out there and all work and no play did not have to be the way one lived. Yet from that day to this she had not heard a word from Eric Roussel, except when Martin mentioned him during the course of business. Actions speak louder than words and Joan had drawn the conclusion that Eric had not enjoyed her company.

One evening she felt so low that she stripped off her grey suit, and stood for a moment in front of the wardrobe mirror wearing only her underwear, looking herself over from top to toe. She was forty-four, but her body was still as good as when she had been thirty. Her breasts were firm, her waist was slim, she had curvy hips and really good-shaped legs. She sighed. She knew she was doing well, but there was no trace of smugness in her face and certainly no one special person in her life, she admitted sadly.

The family still came over on a Saturday evening and they always had a jolly good time at the Prince of Wales. Recently Jim Taylor and his mate Doug Morgan had joined the party. It was good to end the week together. The women talked non-stop about anything and everything and the men didn't do so badly either. There was no getting away from it, Les and Annie Jackson ran a lively pub and the food they provided continued to be really good. Martha and Sid were thrilled that Lenny had found himself a young lady, Janet Marshal, and they had decided to get married early in the new year. It seemed natural that they had already asked Les if they could book their wedding reception at the Prince, so that was something for them all to look forward to.

Joan felt a little guilty when she thought about Jim Taylor. He was always there when she needed to talk, and when it came to the day-to-day repairs of the building he took a lot of responsibility off her shoulders. She had built up a trade in smart ready-to-wear clothes which sold at affordable prices. She also had a list of better-off customers who regularly asked her to design and make an outfit when they needed to look good for a special occasion. However, the small items that Jim secured at house sales also brought in a good income and the antiques he renovated so lovingly were always a good talking point when used as part of a window display. For some time now she had been thinking of a way in which she could show him her appreciation. And when he suggested that she accompany him to a very large house sale that was to be held in Richmond she thought it would be a golden opportunity to talk to him.

It was only nine o'clock when they arrived in Richmond and the sale did not start until ten. Jim had visited the salerooms two days ago and bought a programme on which he had marked off several items that would be of interest to them both. With an hour to spare Jim took her to a small restaurant near the river. He was more smartly dressed than she had expected, in a lightweight suit and a tie. They agreed that a fried breakfast and some hot toast would go down very well. When Joan watched Jim glance up at the young waitress and almost plead, 'Would it be possible for us to have a pot of tea right now, please? I'm parched,' that everyday saying endeared him to her because she felt exactly the same way.

They each had the devil of a job securing the items that Jim had marked off on their programme, and three they had to let go because the bidding was so brisk. On the other hand, there were four additional articles that caught Joan's eye and she managed to bid successfully for all of them.

The sale wasn't over and when it was there would be a long queue of folk waiting to pay for their purchases. 'Let's go and sit in Richmond Park,' Jim suggested. Joan was all for it. The air in the saleroom had become hot and stuffy.

'There was once a royal residence in Richmond Park,' Jim remarked, doing his best to make conversation as they walked along by the River Thames, because he thought Joan was miles away. When she made no answer, he added, 'It is still crown property.'

Joan shook her head. 'I'm sorry, Jim. Do you mind if we sit down?'

'Not at all,' he said straight away, pointing to a vacant bench beneath a sprawling leafy tree.

It was now or never, Joan decided once they were seated. 'I have a proposal to put to you, Jim,' she said.

'Really?' Jim sounded surprised. 'What do you have in mind?'

'You and me becoming partners.' She saw his face stiffen and hurried on. 'Please, Jim, don't dismiss the idea out of hand. This isn't a sudden suggestion. I have given the matter a great deal of thought. You do so much for me, give most of your time to making sure that my business runs smoothly. I think we've reached the point when sharing the load legally would be more fitting.'

'*No.*' He reached out and took her hand between both of his. 'I can't thank you enough for the offer, but it is your business, you've worked your socks off to make a go of it and for the first time in your life you are an independent lady.'

Joan slid along the bench to be a little closer to him. 'I am not going to take no for an answer. If it weren't for you starting me off, even furnishing my flat, I probably would never have got the business up and running.'

'You're being too generous with your praise,' he said gently, wondering what would be the outcome if he agreed.

'I am not,' she declared. 'If you would only agree I wouldn't have half the headaches.'

Jim's face wore a guarded expression. 'I'll think about it.'

Joan's face broke into a wide grin. 'I'm not asking you to put any money into the business. I don't want an investor, I just want us to carry on as we are but on a much firmer footing. We could go together to a solicitor and have him draw up an agreement.'

'I've said I will think about it.' He smiled sheepishly at her.

Joan flung her arms around him and hugged him.

She would never know how much he wanted to respond in the same manner. Instead he said, 'We'd better go and make arrangements for our purchases to be delivered and then get back to the shop before Freda begins to think she's the one in charge.'

He would dearly love to become Joan's partner, in more ways than one. However, he knew only too well that what she was offering was a purely business deal and before he made a decision on that he would have a great deal of soul-searching to do.

Chapter Thirty-two

FREDA PRESTON WAS the last of the staff to leave. She pulled up the collar of her coat and opened her umbrella. 'Filthy rotten night,' she said. 'Like me, I don't suppose you'll be going out tonight.'

'No, cosy night in, put my feet up,' Joan answered. 'I do miss Rosie.'

'I expect you do. It seems such a shame that the weather has turned so bad just when you'd given her a week's holiday. Anyway, see you in the morning. Good night, Joan.'

'Good night, Freda. Glad you haven't got far to go.'

Joan stood in the open doorway of the shop for a few minutes watching the rain lashing down. Then she stepped back, shot the three bolts on the front door and pushed the latches up on the two Yale locks.

It was well over two months since Eric Roussel had taken her out for the day and she had not heard a word from him in all that time. These last few days the weather had been as miserable as she'd felt, strong winds and heavy rain warning that winter was almost here.

'Lovely,' she muttered sarcastically. Such a lot to look forward to, short gloomy days, dark evenings. Sundays

285

visiting Martha and Sid or staying home on her own hugging the fire and doing endless sewing, while continually thinking of Eric. Maybe he preferred younger women? Did he think she wasn't sophisticated enough for him? However many excuses she thought of, it didn't make her feel any the less rejected. It was a shame, really, because during that day something amazing had happened. When Eric had held her hand it had been like a sudden charge of electricity passing between them, taking her totally by surprise. At the time an uncanny instinct had told her that the attraction was the same for him as it was for her. How wrong she must have been!

In the short time she had known him he had held out a dream to her. Companionship at the very least. Someone to share her old age with. Marjorie and Martin had lunched with him two days after their trip into Kent and they had told her that Eric hadn't stopped talking about her. 'Really smitten with you, is Eric,' was how Marjorie had put it. If that were true then he had a funny way of showing it.

One minute she was sad because he had held so much hope out to her, the next she was angry and bitter. As she walked down the passage towards the stairs she was giving herself a good talking to. *You've got far more here than you ever thought was possible, a well-established business, good friends. You don't need a man in your life, certainly not like the one you were daft enough to marry when you were only a slip of a girl.*

Yes, that was true, and over the years since Bill's death while she had concentrated on earning her own living the fact that there hadn't been a man in her life hadn't worried her too much. At times it had actually been a relief. Then Eric Roussel had come along and altered her whole way of thinking. He had shown her there was more to life than just work, in fact, he had started her dreaming of maybe living a more interesting life.

The days passed quickly enough though. They were busy in the shop, a fact that Joan thanked God for every day, for she had never imagined that running her own business would bring so many bills through her letter box. Teddy Tyler had raised the rent, the electricity bill had arrived and as sure as eggs were eggs the gas and phone bills wouldn't be far behind. Jim hadn't yet taken her up on her offer of a partnership, but had quietly told her that he was still giving the matter a lot of thought. Joan half smiled to herself. Jim was not a man who would rush blindly into anything.

With only herself to cater for she couldn't be bothered to cook a dinner. Cheese on toast, she decided.

Her foot was only on the first tread of the stairs when she heard an urgent rapping on the front door of the shop. She hesitated. She made it a rule never to open the door after dark to anyone when she was alone in the building. No, she was going to ignore whoever it was, she decided, and although the rapping continued she carried on up to her living quarters, closing the door at the top of the stairs very firmly. She went into the kitchen, half filled the kettle, placed it on the stove and lit the gas ring beneath it, then set about laying a tray ready for her evening meal. She had decided that for once she would be lazy, take the tray into the lounge, put some records on the radiogram and eat her meal off the tray balanced on her lap.

She was just pouring boiling water on to the tea leaves she had spooned into the pot when the telephone rang. She picked up the receiver, but before she had time to even say hello an oh so familiar voice said, 'Oh, Joan dear, please come down and open the door. I'm getting soaked to the skin.'

'Eric!' she shrieked. 'Go to the side door.' She banged the phone down, all trace of tiredness now vanished, and her feet scarcely touched the treads as she flew down the

287

stairs. She fumbled to unlock the door but at last she had it open and Eric was standing there. He must have run all the way back from the phone box on the corner. He held open his arms and Joan flung hers round him.

'What a lovely surprise. I'd begun to think I would never see you again.'

He didn't answer, just held her close. She could feel how wet his thick overcoat was.

'Never mind explanations now. Come on upstairs and let's get that wet coat off you.'

Over a cup of tea, which Joan had laced with whisky, he gave her a number of plausible reasons as to why he hadn't been in touch before now, none of which Joan felt she could wholeheartedly believe. His face looked thinner and his skin did not have that healthy glow. She was almost sure that he had lost quite a bit of weight.

'What is it, Eric?' she asked anxiously. Just the sound of his voice had brought back happy memories of the short times she had spent with him, but he was acting very strangely.

'You seem as glad to see me as I am to see you, and yet you are not being straight with me.' She said, wanting so much to be reassured.

'You wouldn't like it if I were to tell you the truth.'

'Try me. We are at least friends, aren't we?'

'I've been in prison,' he blurted out.

Joan was lost for words. There was much she wanted to ask, but all she could do was stare at him.

'I got three months and I've served two.' The silence hung heavy between them until Eric asked, 'Why have you got tears in your eyes? Not feeling sorry for me, are you?'

'No, it's because I'm so pleased to see you again and I want to know what you've been up to,' she said, with a funny smile. Then very quickly she asked, 'Am I allowed to hug you?'

Eric carefully laid his cup and saucer down on a side table and got to his feet. She felt his arms go round her waist and her head was soon nestling against his shoulder. They stayed locked together for some time until Eric led her to the sofa and they sat down side by side.

'You know, you are something else,' Eric told her, smiling broadly. 'You haven't even asked why the police picked me up or why I was given a prison sentence.'

'You'll tell me in your own good time,' she answered with confidence. 'Meanwhile you can make that fire up while I get us something to eat and then we can talk as much as we like.'

Joan changed her mind and laid the table. She still did cheese on toast but with more pleasure as it was now for two. While it was under the grill she quickly chopped up a large salad, tossing it into a glass bowl she sprinkled in olive oil and spooned mayonnaise into a dish and potato salad from a tin into another dish. It was a bit of a scratch meal but the best she could manage, not having had any warning that she might be having a visitor.

There was no deep conversation while they were eating. Eric was certainly not at ease. There was sweat on his brow and several times Joan watched as he wiped the palms of his hands on his napkin. They finished eating and Joan got up and cleared the table. Minutes later she was back with a tray that held a pot of coffee, two cups and saucers and a jug of cream. Tucked beneath her arm was a bottle of brandy. She left the coffee to steep and poured two generous measures of brandy into cut-glass goblets. 'I shouldn't,' Eric protested as she handed one to him. 'My car is parked round the corner and I have to drive back to my hotel.'

'If you drove here how come your coat was so wet?'

'Because I was walking up and down outside waiting until your staff had left before I could screw up enough courage to come in and face you.'

'You don't have to drive anywhere tonight if you don't want to,' she told him quietly.

He gave a low whistle.

She knew exactly what he meant. She was being far too trusting. Asking for trouble, actually, but she had come this far and she did not want to turn back. Naturally she wanted to know why he had been in prison. Truth to tell there was a whole lot more she would have liked to know about Eric Roussel, but she was throwing caution to the wind. She hadn't felt like this since she was about sixteen years old and that was a very long time ago. Almost a waste of a lifetime.

'I want you to stay, Eric.' Her voice was low.

He pulled her closer to his side, slid an arm along her shoulders and, lowering his head, placed his lips over hers.

Joan felt her insides turn to jelly. His kisses became stronger and his tongue flicked in and out of her mouth. His non-committal attitude towards her had gone. He was no longer treating her as if she would break, and certainly not as a mere friend.

'Oh, Joan,' he finally gasped, 'I've dreamt of kissing you like that every day for the past two months. In fact I've wanted to do that from the first moment I met you.'

She raised her eyebrows. 'Then why didn't you?'

'Because you were . . .' Joan could sense him searching for a word and wondered what he would come up with. 'Unworldly,' he finally said. 'I didn't want to take advantage of you, mostly because I am so much older than you are.'

'Unworldly? That's a funny word to use.'

'It is entirely appropriate where you are concerned, Joan. You haven't even asked me why I was sent to prison. You know nothing about me and yet you trust me.'

Joan smiled. 'It was my good friends Marjorie and Martin who first sent me to meet you on my own, and if you were their friend that was good enough for me.'

Eric sighed heavily. 'The Goldsmiths and I have known each other for many years and we do a great deal of business together, one way and another, but it is a wise man who treads carefully during any business transaction.'

Joan felt her heart sink. 'You wouldn't do the dirty on Martin, would you?'

Then to her amazement Eric actually grinned and winked at her saucily. 'I'd not pass up the chance to get one over on him if he were daft enough to let me.'

Joan moved back along the sofa and sat up straight. Doubts had crept into her mind. 'Eric, perhaps you had better tell me why the police arrested you.'

They sat for a while in silence before Eric said, 'You're a funny one, Joan, and no mistake. You invite me to stay the night with you and then suddenly you decide you had better find out why I was sent to prison.'

Joan saw his point and started to giggle. Eric chuckled with her and soon they were both helpless with laughter. When they calmed down Eric stretched his hand across the space between them and took hold of Joan's. Squeezing it tightly, he said, 'I owed a fellow a lot of money and the bank returned the cheque I gave him marked "insufficient funds".'

'When you wrote the cheque weren't you aware that you didn't have the means to cover it?' Her voice sounded sceptical.

'I don't expect you to believe me, the judge didn't, but the answer is I should have had ample funds in my account.' He took a gulp of his brandy. He needed a stiff drink in order to convince Joan that he was telling her the truth and to let her know what he intended to do. The thought that if things did not go right for him he might well end up back in prison, and for a very much longer time, had his heart hammering against his ribs.

'I have to go home to Malta,' he said bluntly. 'I need to see a few men who have made the mistake of double-crossing

291

me. I sent their goods in good faith and they accepted them, but they have been slow to pay and consequently it was like a rack of dominoes. One falls they all fall. Only this time it was me that fell the hardest. It has never happened before and I shall make damn sure it never ever happens again.' As he looked at Joan he saw only her lovely trusting face. 'I'm sorry . . .' His voice trailed off. He felt so bad he could not meet her eyes.

'Will you be able to sort it out?' Her voice sounded small and hurt.

He laughed bitterly. 'Oh, yes.' The two words held a great deal of confidence. Suddenly he sat up straight, looking at Joan. He thought she looked frightened. It was then that an idea came to him and he wasn't going to take no for an answer. 'Come home with me, Joan. It will only be for a short time, and we could go at the weekend.' He looked really pleased with himself as he added, 'Please, Joan, say you will come. I can see about our tickets tomorrow.'

Joan's face was full of concern and her hands were fluttering.

'You all right, love?' Eric asked quickly.

She gave him a small smile. 'No, actually I'm confused. You asked me to go home with you. Where exactly is home?'

Eric was stunned. 'I've told you I come from Malta. You'll be made so welcome. My father is dead but my mother and all my family will love to meet you. It will give you a chance to meet my family and see something of the island at the same time.'

Thoughts were flying round in her head. How badly she wanted to say yes, let's go. She had never in her whole life been offered such an opportunity and yet all she was asking herself was, what am I going to do? Her mind was racing from one question to another. 'I can't just walk off and leave the shop.' Her voice was shocked.

'Why not?' Eric was now full of good cheer. 'You've plenty

of good staff, and friends who will keep an eye on them. We need only stay in Malta a few days as long as two of the days are when the banks are open. My accounts both here in England and in Malta need to be replenished and believe you me, Joan, they will be. I unconditionally promise you that our journey will be well worth while.'

Joan found herself believing him. His enthusiasm was infectious. 'How would we get there?'

Eric smothered his laughter. 'It is some years since I went home so I'll have to check the travel arrangements but I'm pretty sure that P&O have not gone broke. I think we can safely assume that they are still running their liners.'

'But I've never been on a ship before.'

'Well, you'll have a couple of days to think about getting your sea legs,' he teased her.

Much later Joan asked, 'Shall we go to bed?' Her voice was childlike.

He put his arms round her, moved her long hair to one side and kissed her neck several times. 'You are amazing! And I love you, Joan. More than you think.'

She smiled at him. She hoped that what he said was true because she was about to commit herself to something from which there would be no turning back.

Chapter Thirty-three

ERIC WAS STILL SOUND ASLEEP, lying on his stomach, his head resting on one curled-up arm.

Joan was also still in bed but wide awake, sitting up beside him, staring at his brown body, broad back, firm buttocks and slender legs. She was actually finding it hard to believe that last night had really happened. The longing had started within her the minute he ran his fingers over her bare flesh. Never in her wildest dreams had she thought that lovemaking could take place with such sensitivity. Eric had been so gentle from the first moment that their lips met. Starting with her forehead he had gently kissed her body from top to toe. Then he parted her legs and his kisses were growing stronger.

No longer was she able to lie still and passively let him do anything he wanted to. She realised that her own feelings had been pent up for far too long, mainly because sex in her mind had always been associated with brutality. Bill hadn't known how to treat a woman with care. According to him she was his wife and there for him to use whenever he felt the need. He had never been interested in satisfying her.

As Eric had kissed her again and again, Joan had felt her own emotion matching his. Suddenly her body was arching up towards him and within seconds wanting had become fierce desire.

A long time after that, when they were lying contented, he with his right hand cupping her breast, he had murmured, 'Oh, Joan, my darling, you make me feel really young again.'

Their ages were immaterial now.

Time to wake him up. Bending over him, she put her lips to his ear and whispered, 'Good morning, my darling.'

Eric opened his eyes, turned over to lie on his back, put his arms round and held her tightly, his face burrowing into her neck. 'Are you all right, Joan? I watched you for ages last night before I fell asleep, wondering if you would have any regrets when you woke up.'

'Oh, Eric, I'm . . .' She hesitated, searching for the right words, because it had become very important to let him know exactly how she was feeling. 'I had no idea lovemaking could be so meaningful. For me it was like being loved for the very first time in my life.'

'So, my love, are you going to come to Malta with me?'

A silence fell between them. He was waiting for her reply.

She wriggled out of his arms and sat up. 'It's a big decision, Eric,' she said at last.

'I know. You must have time to think about it. How would it be if we got ourselves washed and dressed, had something to eat and talked the matter over in a bit more detail?'

To Joan's utter surprise he insisted on beating up eggs and chopping up some ham and then made two light fluffy omelettes while she made a pot of coffee and some toast and laid the table. They ate their breakfast in the kitchen, and afterwards Eric said it was time he went because he had a number of things to do and Joan had to think about opening the shop.

They stood in the open doorway and Eric kissed her gently on each cheek. She still hadn't given him a straight answer as to whether or nor she would travel to Malta with him.

Suddenly Eric said, 'I may not be able to get back here tonight but I will phone you sometime during the day.'

Joan, who had been feeling on top of the world, watched him walk away, a well-dressed, efficient man-about-town, briefcase in one hand, car keys in the other, and found herself trembling with panic. Was that the last she was going to see of him?

The day seemed endless. Twice Freda asked if there was something troubling her. The telephone only rang a few times and Joan asked Jody to take the calls. Her instinct told her it would not be Eric on the end of the line.

Two days went by without a word from him and Joan asked herself how she could have been such a fool. The evenings were long and she was thankful that Rosie was not here to see the state she had worked herself up into. Nevertheless, with time to consider her actions, she came to the conclusion that she wasn't sorry she had allowed Eric to spend the night with her. Everyone was entitled to some joy in their life and for those few hours she had felt loved and wanted. She smiled ruefully as she murmured to herself, 'At least I have been given a glimpse of what life could be like.'

As the third day drew to a close Freda drew Joan to one side. 'I want to talk to you and I'm going to make sure that you listen to every word I say. Understood?'

Joan looked at Freda Preston and knew that she wasn't going to be able to give any excuses. She sighed and said, 'Well, let's go through to the back room.'

They didn't sit down but stood facing each other. The older woman came straight to the point. 'You can tell me to mind my own business but it won't do you a scrap of good because I'm gonna talk straight. Something has happened and it has knocked you for six. My guess would normally be a man was at the root of the trouble but you never go out anywhere socially except to the Prince on a Saturday night. There's plenty of men there who think you're a really nice lady but you never give any one of them the time of day. A few months ago your sister Martha and I thought you were finally going to live a little when you had a few meals and a couple of days out with that foreign bloke who Martin deals with on and off, but as he's not been around we presumed that had fizzled out.'

Joan had thought of herself as too old to cry, and certainly too old to fall in love, but by now her eyes were brimming with tears.

'Right, here's what we are going to do,' Freda said forcefully. 'We will close the shop on the dot of six, go upstairs and freshen ourselves up, and then you and I are going to the Prince of Wales. We'll have a meal, and a few drinks, and if they loosen your tongue you'll find I'm a good listener. If not, at least we'll drown your sorrows together.'

As Annie Jackson placed a loaded dinner plate in front of Joan, and another one in front of Freda, she said, 'There's treacle pud or spotted dick for afters when you're ready.'

Joan looked at her plate. Toad in the hole, Brussels sprouts, carrots, mashed swede and at least five roast potatoes. 'Good God,' she said, 'I'll never get through half of this.'

'Take a good swig from your glass of lager and I'll call Les to bring us a bottle of wine. That will help wash it down,' Freda said, signalling to Les to come over to where they were sitting.

Les grinned broadly at the pair of them as Freda asked him for a bottle of wine. 'Oh yeah! And who let you two out on the loose tonight? Special occasion, is it, gals?'

'More like drowning our sorrows,' Freda said mournfully, taking the mickey out of Joan. 'Drastic measures are needed sometimes, yer know.'

'Well get stuck into that plateful an' I'll be back in a few minutes.' Les was shaking his head as he walked back to the bar. He'd send Annie over with the bottle; she'd be the one to find out what was wrong with Joan. Obviously something was, because she had a face like a wet weekend and that wasn't like the Joan they all knew and loved. On the other hand, he decided, if Annie sat down with those two he wouldn't get another stroke of work out of her tonight.

Joan and Freda managed to clear their plates despite the fact that Joan had said it was far too much. 'Can't manage a pudding though, can we?' Freda asked as she filled their wine glasses for the third time.

'Oh, no!' Joan muttered, patting her tummy. 'I couldn't eat another morsel.'

There had been a lot of cheering every now and again, coming from the very end of the long bar where a darts match was in progress. Suddenly there was complete silence and both Freda and Joan turned their heads to see what was going on. Four Salvation Army girls, working in pairs, were going round the bars rattling their tins and selling copies of their paper, *War Cry*, to raise funds to enable the Army to continue its good work.

'Some of those "Ally Looya Lassies" are strikingly pretty,' Freda remarked as she and Joan fished in their purses for coppers to put in their tins. Joan fully agreed. These four wore dark cloaks which had stand-up collars embroidered with the initials SA in gold thread. From beneath their black Victorian bonnets peeped their lovely curly hair and the big bows of black ribbon which were sewn on to the left hand sides of the bonnets helped to make the girls look very young and vulnerable.

'How brave they are to go into public houses, some of which must be very rough,' Joan remarked.

'Yes, you've got a point there, but even the roughest of men respect them. God help a man who so much as laid a finger on any one of those lassies. No matter whether you believe in their religion or not they do some marvellous work, especially amongst the poor.' That was quite a speech coming from Freda.

Joan smiled, for the first time since they had sat down. 'It always amazes me how happy every member of the Salvation Army always seems to be. When I was in service in Kent their band used to march past the gates every Sunday morning and even Cook would start singing the well known hymns they played.'

Freda straightened herself up and looked Joan straight in the eye. 'Well, are you still going to keep your troubles to yourself? I promise I am not a gossip. Whatever you choose to tell me would go no further and who knows, I might even be able to help.'

Joan felt the need to talk to someone and the wine had certainly loosened her tongue as Freda had said it would. From their first meeting, Joan had been impressed by Freda. When it suited her to influence a client she could be quite snobbish, but most of the time she was a very down-to-earth kind of person. A good worker and a good friend to Martha as well as herself. Saturdays when they all went out together Freda had bothered to show both sisters how to use make-up effectively and she had persuaded Martha to have her hair cut into a smart but easy to manage style.

'All right.' She heaved a sigh. 'I suppose sooner or later you will find out anyway.' She proceeded to tell Freda how successful her outings with Eric Roussel had been and how disappointed she was when he hadn't turned up for over two months.

'And now?' Freda prompted.

'He came to visit me three days ago. Remember when I saw you off and it was raining cats and dogs? Well, he was outside then.'

Freda didn't need a picture drawn for her. She grinned and shook her head. Joan felt the colour rising in her cheeks but then the thought came to her that she was a grown woman, not a silly lovesick teenager. She returned Freda's look and they both laughed.

'All right.' Joan grinned. 'So I let him stay the night.'

'Good for you, Joan. You've no one to answer to and if he's halfway as dishy as you make out then you did right.'

Joan felt a bit guilty. She hadn't told Freda that Eric had been in prison or that there was something devious about him that she couldn't quite put out of her mind.

'When was he supposed to be seeing you again?' Freda felt compelled to ask.

'He said maybe he wouldn't be able to get back that same day but that he would phone me.'

'Hmm, and he hasn't or you wouldn't have been walking about looking like a lost sheep.'

In for a penny in for a pound, Joan decided. She blurted out, 'Eric said he was going to make arrangements for me to travel home with him. I told him I wouldn't be able to leave the shop and he said I had a gem in you and from what I had told him about you he thought you were more than capable of running the business. He also said that Martin and Marjorie would keep an eye on the place.'

'Hey, hang on a minute! Couldn't get a word out of you for days and now you're running on like a steam train. When he said travel home with him, where exactly was he talking about?'

'Malta,' Joan told her. 'Apparently he still has quite a big family living there but he hasn't been home for years.'

'Did you say you would go?' Freda was all ears by now.

Joan dodged the question. 'Not exactly.'

300

Freda rested her elbows on the table, cupped her hands round her face and said, 'I don't believe you! I just wish I were your age an' a bloke asked me to go abroad with him. I'd have been up to the travel agent's with him before the office opened.'

She had spoken so loudly that everyone near them stopped talking and looked at her. 'Don't be ridiculous,' Joan said huffily.

'You can't turn an offer like that down,' Freda went on, undeterred. 'I've lived a long time and I've come to know that it's best to grab any gift that comes your way 'cos you get no second chances. Sometimes of course it's risky, but taking a risk just adds to the spice of life. You'd be mad not to go. Wish he'd ask me.' She gave another roar of laughter.

I didn't say I definitely wouldn't go. Joan kept this snippet of information to herself. For all she knew she might never set eyes on Eric again and she didn't want to be made a laughing stock.

They were both a little unsteady on their feet as they made to put their arms into the sleeves of their coats. Les came across to them, smiling broadly. 'This is one time when I really wish that Jeff and Mark had been in the bar tonight. They could each have taken one of you home. Still, I've called a cab and he can drop Joan off first as she's nearest and then see you to your front door, Freda.'

'No need,' Freda declared haughtily. 'We are quite capable of getting ourselves home.'

'You think so, do yer? Well for once, ladies, you're doing as I tell you,' Les said, grabbing an arm of each of them. 'Got yer handbags, 'ave yer?' He propelled them through the open doors to where the cab was already waiting at the kerbside. Kissing them each in turn, he helped settle them both on the back seat and then had a few words with the cab driver, who let out a belly laugh and said, 'OK, Les, they'll be all right with me. I'll see yer later.'

It was only when Joan opened her front door that a feeling of melancholy came over her. The flat felt so empty. And for all she had opened up her heart to Freda she was still no wiser as to when or even *if* she would see Eric again.

The thought that she might not did not do much for her self-esteem.

Chapter Thirty-four

IT WAS SIX THIRTY by the time Joan had cashed up and filled in the ledgers, one for each side of the business. She had just reached the foot of the stairs when there was a knocking on the side door. Slowly she turned and made her way back through the dark shop. If you had any sense at all, she was saying to herself, you would ignore the knocking and not open the door. Every instinct told her Eric was standing on the other side and it would only lead to more heartache if she were to let him in again. Hadn't he proved beyond any doubt that he was not to be trusted?

She ignored her warning thoughts, and opened the door.

'Oh, Eric.' For a ridiculous moment, Joan felt a bit weepy, but instead she took a deep breath, put her arms round him and hugged him tightly. He stepped inside and Joan closed the door and before she could protest he was kissing her, long lingering kisses that melted her heart.

'May we leave explanations until later?' he pleaded when at last he let go his hold on her. 'At a guess I would say you need reassuring and cheering up. Well, I'm back, and with a whole lot of good news, so let's celebrate. How long will it take you to get ready? We'll go to any restaurant or hotel of your choosing and have a slap-up meal, a bottle of bubbly, and drink to our holiday in Malta.'

'You've made all the arrangements?' Joan sounded flabbergasted.

'Of course. Didn't I say I would?'

It was almost ten thirty. Not being familiar with fancy restaurants Joan had left the choice to Eric. She had tried to persuade him to stay in and talk to her. There were still a lot of unanswered questions where Eric was concerned and she felt she would never get open and honest answers while having a meal in a public place. He would have none of it. They had much to celebrate, he insisted.

Joan changed into what she called her glad rags and went along with his wishes, but she did so reluctantly, and it was just as bad as she had feared, with too many people talking loudly and much noisy laughter. Not the right place in which to make important decisions. It had been a very good meal but now she was tired. She found herself staring at Eric, her hands clamped round her coffee cup, while he tossed down another brandy.

'Now,' he said as he set his glass down, 'have you decided if you are coming home with me? Yes or no.'

Joan leaned back in her chair and smiled. 'When we get home and you give me the full details as to how and when you suggest we are going to travel to Malta, then I'll decide.'

It was dark and very cold when Eric parked the car and they walked the few remaining yards to the shop. Once upstairs he stayed silent for a moment. 'Shall we leave all the details until the morning?' he asked finally. 'Let's go to bed.'

'I think so.' Joan wished she could tell him that she felt she couldn't trust him, but her pride wouldn't let her. Much as she wanted him to hold her and make love to her again she felt irritated that he hadn't bothered to tell her why he hadn't even telephoned.

'You only think so?' He smiled, the lines on his tanned face seeming deeper than she remembered. 'Let's make tonight something special.' He took her in his arms, and as his lips met hers all the longing came flooding back and her doubts were wiped away. Much later, as she lay content in the curve of his arm, she felt she would have to agree. It had been very special.

Eric was as good as his word. He had made good use of the days that he had stayed away. He had used his contacts, his keen mind and his powers of organisation to make sure that they travelled to Malta in the utmost comfort possible. As he explained the journey, step by step, Joan began to see how Eric Roussel had become so successful. He had the ability to motivate others. Whether his intentions and actions were always completely honest remained to be seen.

He teased Joan unmercifully by making her wait until they had eaten breakfast before laying out two Malta guidebooks and some pamphlets for her to look at. Eric had marked the relevant pages and Joan smiled as she studied them. There were two P&O steamers to choose from, the Peninsular or the Oriental line. The advertisement stated that an all-sea route leaving London every other Friday and arriving every other Sunday was a nine-day trip, first-class fare from twenty pounds, second class from fourteen pounds. P&O also ran a service across the English Channel and down to Marseilles, from where one travelled on by mail boat to Malta. That journey only took three and a half days, first-class fare from eighteen pounds and sixteen shillings, second class from twelve pounds and sixteen shillings. Or there was an all-sea route going by the Commonwealth line. This was a six-day trip, one class only, a return fare costing eighteen pounds, but that ship only made the journey once a month.

Joan looked up, both surprise and joy showing on her

face. 'You said you've already bought the tickets, so please, Eric, which way are we travelling and when are we supposed to be going?'

'No suppose about it, my darling,' he said, producing a large paper wallet from the inside pocket of his jacket. 'We are going on a nine-day, first-class cruise.'

'Oh, Eric!' Joan was stunned. Doubt, fright and excitement were all mixed up in her mind. Should she be going off to a place that she had hardly ever heard of before? With a fellow she hardly knew? She began to argue with herself. *You know him well enough to have spent practically two whole nights making love with him.* Besides, on the plus side, he was introduced to her by Martin and Marjorie Goldsmith and you couldn't find two more reliable people than them.

But nine days to get there! How long would they stay in Malta? Then another nine days for the return journey. God almighty! She'd be away the best part of a month! How could she leave her business for that long? Then there was her sister Martha. What in heaven's name would she have to say about all of this?

Then another thought struck her. Eric had said his term in prison had been because he had written cheques without sufficient cash in the bank to meet them. If that were so, where on earth had he found the cash that he was flashing around now? Their meal at the restaurant had cost a pretty penny, which Eric had paid in cash. Then there was these first-class tickets, and he had not given her any real explanation of why he needed to go to Malta so badly. Was she mad to be even considering going with him?

Eric watched the different emotions flicker across Joan's face and he could have made a very good guess at what she was thinking, but he was used to getting his own way and this time wasn't going to be any different. There wasn't any problem that he couldn't iron out, given time. The length of the trip, nine days, had set him a problem to begin with, but he had found a way to turn that to his advantage. A few phone calls and a few owed favours called in would help to give him the advantage of surprise when he did arrive in Valletta. Then he certainly meant to repay those who had sought to cross him. He would live to have his day!

'What about my business, Eric? It's taken me all my life to get as far as I have. I've worked hard to get it up to standard.'

'Joan, that is one of the reasons why you deserve a break. Have you never thought that it was about time you began to have some fun?'

Every member of Joan's staff and each member of her family urged her to take the break that was being offered her.

In the end she convinced herself that she would regret it for ever more if she didn't grab this once in a lifetime offer. But settling business matters, and sorting out what clothes to take, was more traumatic than she had even dreamed it would be. There was so much for her to do.

Eric was very understanding. He booked them into an hotel in London the day before they were due to board the P&O liner, and held her in his arms for most of the night. When she awoke and realised that this was the day when she was setting out on the high seas to a destination unknown to her, and to whatever else was anybody's guess, she was suddenly filled with a wonderful sense of well-being and vitality, and it was at that moment that she made a resolution. She was leaving all her cares and worries behind her. She was going cruising in the Mediterranean. Who would have thought that she, Joan Baldwin, would be travelling on a P&O liner, first class at that!

She took her time to have a bath and dress in what was an entirely brand new outfit.

At the sight of her Eric let out a long, low whistle of

admiration, which gave her an exhilarating sensation of carefree happiness.

They were welcomed aboard by two extremely smart uniformed officers. A young sailor, dressed from head to toe in white, showed them to their outside state room and informed them that their luggage would be delivered quite soon. Joan's eyes nearly popped out of her head. This was luxury personified. Their cabin had everything that one could wish for and more. And that was only the beginning.

'One does not dress for dinner, not on the first evening,' Eric informed her. Then he went into the bathroom and came back holding out a large white box tied with silver ribbons. Even to Joan the name of the firm which was printed on the lid was familiar. Swears & Wells, dealers in quality furs.

'You will have to wait until tomorrow to wear it, my darling, but open the box and give me a private showing now, please,' he implored her.

Joan did as he bid and as she removed the lid she exclaimed, 'Good gracious!' Gently she lifted a honey-coloured fur stole from the layers of tissue paper, held it up to her face and buried her cheeks in its softness.

Eric took the stole from her and lovingly draped it round her shoulders. She absolutely loved it, but the thought of how much money this gorgeous fur must have cost him frightened her half to death. Thank God she had brought two new long evening dresses as well as the three she had made herself.

Before the second day was over Joan was telling herself that this had to be the best thing that had ever happened to her in her entire life. Eric was there to hold her hand, pay attention to her all day, and then be there in the same bed with her for the whole night long.

She could not begin to describe the ship. To her it was a floating palace. The passengers had freedom of movement and could indulge in all kinds of sport, most of which Eric excelled in. There was a theatre, a hairdressing salon and shops which sold exquisite gifts. Eric's opinion was that the cuisine served on the liner was equal to that of a really first-class hotel. By the time the steamer docked at Malta, Joan wholeheartedly believed that her trip in the Mediterranean had given her the holiday of a lifetime and left her with a sensation of carefree happiness. Yet as they took their leave of the captain and stepped on to the long gangplank, she couldn't stop herself from wondering.

What next?

Chapter Thirty-five

'GOOD TO SEE YOU, Emmanuel.'

Three men greeted Eric, each in turn hugging him and patting his back. They were identically dressed in black suits, crisp white shirts, and black ties. All of them were dark-skinned, but while two had a good head of dark hair, the third man was completely bald. Joan guessed that each was in his late thirties or early forties. All much younger than Eric.

Eric introduced them, stating only their Christian names. 'Nicholas, Gerard and Anthony, this is Madam Joan Baldwin.' Each in turn lifted her right hand and lightly brushed the back of it with his lips, and then the five of them got into a very large black car that looked to Joan as if it had taken a bit of a battering at some time.

She felt most uncomfortable. Eric, who had suddenly become Emmanuel, got into the front seat beside Nicholas, who was the driver, while she was squeezed between the bald-headed Anthony and the good-looking Gerard, who informed her he was the brother of Nicholas. The conversation between the men was non-stop yet Joan was unable to understand one word because none of them, including Eric, was speaking in English. She was puzzled, because while they had been standing on the quayside they had spoken in English.

Soon Eric rested his arm on the top of his seat and turned his head to face her. Smiling, he said, 'We are lucky indeed. We are being allowed the use of a property at Spinola Bay for the duration of our stay.'

For all Joan knew he might just as well have said Timbuctoo but she was relieved to hear that they would not be staying with a Maltese family. At least, she gathered as much from the little that Eric had said.

In less than thirty minutes they had passed through the town and a couple of villages, and the car was slowing down as they approached a narrow road that held a bar, two or three shops with goods displayed out on the pavement under shady blinds, and what looked like a small restaurant. Set back from the street was a church and to the side of it Joan could see an ancient graveyard.

At the end of the road Joan caught a glimpse of a small harbour and a rocky beach. There were few people about, and when she remarked on this fact Gerard replied, 'It's siesta time. You'll get used to it.'

Moments later the car turned off to the right down an old country lane as Eric said, 'This is Spinola Bay.'

Joan was pleasantly surprised as the car turned into a paved courtyard and Nicholas turned the engine off. As she got out of the car, she was looking at what seemed to be a very old stone cottage such as a farm labourer might have been allocated in England.

She felt ridiculously excited. This holiday was turning out to be quite an adventure. She had never in her wildest dreams even thought that something like this might happen to her. Especially at her age! When she had opened Distinctive Designs she had been amazed and relieved that at last she had her own home and a means of earning her own living. She had thanked her lucky stars, thinking she had reached the top of the tree, and had been thoroughly content.

Well, mostly. At times when she was alone she did still feel lonely because everyone else of her age seemed to have children, or at least a partner.

Then Eric Roussel had come into her life, and now here she was, having crossed the Mediterranean, contemplating a holiday in this stone house with Eric, who had suddenly become Emmanuel!

She went inside the house, loosened the buttons on her coat and hung it on a hook behind the door. There were two very large rooms, one apparently a family kitchen with a huge fireplace in which a fire was laid, an oven set in the wall, a deep sink and a wooden draining board. An enormous dresser covered almost the whole of one wall and there appeared to be a plentiful supply of china. Copper-bottomed pans hung from a bar which stretched across the ceiling. The centre of this room was taken up by a large table, the top of which was covered by a heavily fringed chenille tablecloth, surrounded by six high-backed chairs.

To the back of the house was a sitting room, sparsely furnished but comfortable. Three small windows set into the far wall looked out over farmland, though no animals or buildings were in sight. At each end of this room a huge lantern-type lamp had been placed, so Joan assumed that there was no electricity. She hoped that at least there might be running water.

She decided that she would wait until the three men had gone before she explored the upstairs. She hadn't long to wait. While their luggage was carried in, the men continued to talk non-stop, all the time making frantic gestures with their hands to emphasise what they were saying. Joan had the feeling that tempers were becoming a little frayed and she was right because suddenly Eric thumped the table with his fist and very loudly and aggressively spat out a whole string of words.

Joan's face turned scarlet. Whatever had she let herself in for? Tears of frustration burned at the back of her eyes and she stood staring at Eric while she wondered what to do. He ignored her. Anthony, the bald-headed one, opened a wooden door which was set into the stone wall and took out a bottle of Scotch whisky and four glasses. Having poured generous measures he handed the glasses round. The men raised their glasses high and in unison they loudly proposed a toast. Whom or what they were toasting Joan had no idea. Although she would have refused a drink of whisky if it had been offered she was a bit piqued at being totally disregarded.

In one gulp the drink was swallowed, the glasses placed down on the table and all three men in turn shook Eric's hand. To Joan they merely nodded. Eric went outside with them, and as she didn't hear the car start up Joan went up the stone steps that led to the first floor. Going straight to the window of the room that looked out over the front of the house, she found she could look over the strip of lace curtain and down to where the men were standing around the car in the courtyard. She was in time to see Nicholas open the driver's door, reach down, and pull out a leather briefcase from beneath the seat. He placed the case on the bonnet of the car, snapped open the lock and took out a sheaf of papers and a bulky manilla envelope, both of which he offered to Eric. Eric grinned broadly, and said something which was obviously amusing because all three men laughed heartily.

Before accepting the papers and the envelope Eric slapped Nicholas on the back and then shook his hand. Then stepping back a few paces he watched as the three men got into the car. Joan noticed that as the car moved off it was still Nicholas who was driving, while Gerard and Anthony were sitting together in the back.

Hurriedly, Joan went from the front bedroom into the back room. She couldn't for the life of her have said why but she knew it wouldn't have done for Eric to find out that she had been looking down on him from above.

The bedrooms were identical, each furnished with a large double bed which had brass rails at the head and foot. Both beds were made up ready for use, covered by a pure white lacy bedspread, and placed at the head of each bed were four large white cotton-covered pillows. Each pillow case had an edging of the most beautiful heavy lace that Joan had ever seen, and each strip of lace was at least four inches wide. Later she was to learn that lace-making was one of the main industries on the island.

Everything smelt sweetly clean. A rug was placed on the stone floor on either side of both beds. Two very ornate but shabby armchairs, a pine chest of drawers and a marble-topped washstand on which was placed a large jug and bowl completed the furnishing of both rooms. Each washbowl and jug was decorated with a bright floral design, and beside each washstand was a free-standing wooden clothes horse, from which hung a large white fluffy towel and a huckaback hand towel. There go my hopes for running water in the house, at least upstairs, Joan said to herself. After the luxury of the P&O liner it was only natural that she felt a bit let down.

Eric was calling her and as she came downstairs she was taken aback to see a quantity of provisions laid out on the table.

'Where on earth have they come from?' She sounded as surprised as she felt. There was fresh milk, a very unusual-shaped loaf of bread, several lovely brown eggs, a whole cheese, a dish of butter and a great deal of assorted salad including the biggest ripe tomatoes she had ever seen.

Laughing, Eric took hold of her hand and led her through a back door into what appeared to be half garden and half courtyard. The stone-paved area was shaded by a huge awning beneath which stood many large earthen pots, each with its own heavy lid.

'This is where all perishable goods are kept. A cooling space. Every house has one.' Then, pointing a finger, he said, 'Look up.' On top of the end of the far brick wall were pumpkins, marrows and tomato vines. 'Summer is over now but there is still enough produce to last a few more weeks,' he told her as they went back inside the house.

After a refreshing salad and a glass of cool creamy milk, Eric carried their cases up the stairs. He placed his belongings in the back bedroom and Joan's in the front, yet he smiled at her in such a saucy way as he told her he was going to hang his clothes up that she needed no reminding that come night time they would be using only one of the double beds. A warm glow of anticipation came over her as she thought of what might lie ahead that evening.

'If you've finished unpacking, would you like to go for a walk?' Eric called to her from the back bedroom.

'Yes, that would be nice,' she answered. 'I won't be a few minutes.' She had changed from her suit into a linen dress that had a jacket to match, and her shoes for a pair of sandals. Eric had told her that with Christmas not too far away the evenings would be drawing in, but the weather would stay warm for a few more weeks yet. If today was anything to go by he was right. The ship had docked in brilliant sunshine and it was still quite warm.

As they left the house they were holding hands, a fact that had Joan smiling to herself. There were open fields on each side as they wandered down the lane. What few houses they did pass had a lot of character about them. All were made of stone, and had small windows with shutters, and open courtyards. Some even had external staircases leading up to a garden terrace.

When they reached the bay, Eric gave a happy shout.

'Couldn't have timed it better,' he called, dragging her down the beach to stand at the edge of the sea, where the waves were breaking against the rocky beach sending salty spray up into the air. Joan sniffed. The air was fantastic.

Although they had been at sea for nine days, it hadn't felt like this. With luxury all around, it hadn't seemed like the real world. She slipped her sandals off and ventured into the water, wriggling her toes and murmuring, 'Free! No customers, deliveries, or accounts to deal with. I still can't take in how all this has come about!' Just then three seagulls swooped low and she laughed, thinking to herself, yes, I am as free as you are, at least for the time being.

'Look.' Eric excitedly pointed a finger. 'It's years since even I have seen this.'

Not too far from the shore several fishing boats had anchored. Men wearing rubber aprons, knee-high boots and waterproof leggings were leaning over the sides of their vessels hauling in their nets. 'Looks like they've had a good catch,' Eric remarked as loads of fish were tipped into boxes, some left to lie on the deck while others were hand-lifted from cradle-like pots and tipped into big water containers. 'That last lot will be going on to St Julian's Bay. Crabs and lobsters for the restaurants and a couple of hotels. Tomorrow we'll go into St Julian's for our evening meal. Would you like that, Joan?'

'Very much so, please.' She smiled.

'I thought tonight we can just laze around, or maybe wander down to the local taverna.' He grinned broadly. 'Might as well let the locals get a good look at you because there isn't a man or woman in the village who hasn't heard already that you have arrived.'

It was nine thirty before they walked down the main street. It was dark, but there were two street lights and doors were open, and old people were sitting on chairs placed along the outside walls. Eric held the beaded curtain up out

316

of the way to enable Joan to enter through the doorway of what looked to her very much like a homely café, because all the tables had red-checked linen tablecloths. She sat herself down on a chair at the nearest table. Eric did not follow suit. He remained standing just inside the doorway, and as Joan gazed at him, his appearance tonight seemed suddenly to be totally out of place. Very smart. Black suit, white silk shirt, open at the neck to reveal a heavy gold cross and chain, gold watch on his wrist and three heavy gold rings on the fingers of his right hand.

Joan was no fool. Eric had planned this. As she watched she had to smother the urge to laugh. There were three other woman besides herself, but the majority of the customers were men. She had sensed the masculine interest, seen the glances and the heads turn her way as she had sat down, but now it was as if Eric was on a stage and playing to the crowds. Seconds ticked by and the silence was not broken until at the back of the tavern a door opened and a gorgeous-looking man came forward leading a tall, white-haired, elderly gentleman. Joan thought the younger man to be about forty and quite the best-looking fellow she had ever seen.

The older man squinted his eyes, took two more steps towards Eric and then flung his arms wide. Eric went into them and the two men stood holding on to each other and rocking on the spot, one saying, 'Oh, my dear Emmanuel. Manny, my boy,' and Eric saying, 'Isidore, Isidore, we have left it too long.'

When at last they broke free and came to sit at the table with Joan she could see that each man had tears sparkling in his eyes. Introductions were made, and the younger man, whose name was Stephan, went away and came back with a bottle of red wine which he deftly opened. 'Do you wish to taste it, Grandfather?' he asked.

The elderly gentleman shook his head. Four glasses were

filled, and the bottle was placed on the table. When the three men raised their glasses to their lips Joan did the same and found the wine to be delicious. Eric and Isidore began to speak in low tones and the language was not English, and Joan was more than pleased when Stephan asked, 'Would you like to come and sit with my cousin and her husband? We can leave these two to catch up on old times.'

Stephan introduced his cousin as Anastasia, but quickly added, 'We mostly call her Anna, and her husband is good old plain John.'

John jumped to his feet and gently shook Joan's hand before playfully punching Stephan's shoulder. 'Joan and John are good solid names given to saints in years gone by,' he said knowledgeably.

'If you say so.' Stephan grinned.

Joan was thankful that all three of them were speaking to her in English. She learnt that this couple lived on Gozo, and were here to visit members of the family who were too frail to come to their home. 'I will ask that Emmanuel bring you to meet our family,' Anna said, sounding sincere. 'We don't often see friends from England and you would be sure of a welcome.'

Stephan looked thoughtful. 'I don't know what Emmanuel's plans are but a visit to Gozo for all of us is long overdue. We'll see if we can persuade Grandfather to come with us.'

Anna clapped her hands, tossed her sleek black hair over one shoulder and smiled at Joan. 'I shall look forward to it, as will John. You'll see. The visit will happen.' Anna's big dark brown eyes and well-tanned skin made her beautiful, and she was a lovely person. In fact Joan was thinking she was the kind of young woman she could easily be friends with.

It was after midnight, and four empty wine bottles stood on the table at which Joan had been sitting with her new-found friends, when Eric placed his hand on her shoulder.

'Hello,' she giggled. 'Where have you been?'

'I know where you are going,' Eric said, grinning widely. 'You've obviously found you like Isidore's stock of wine.'

Joan made to rise, but sat down again quickly with a bump.

With Stephan on one side and Eric on the other, they slowly walked Joan the few yards down the lane to where they were staying. All the while Joan was protesting, 'You didn't give me time to say goodnight to Anna an' John.'

'You will see them again tomorrow,' Eric repeatedly assured her.

'Shall I give you a hand to get Joan upstairs?' Stephan asked as he held her upright while Eric opened the front door.

'I'm sure I can manage,' Eric said as he took her weight from Stephan and placed her bodily across his shoulder. Her hair was loose, her head pointing downwards and her legs were dangling across Eric's chest, held secure by his strong arms.

Stephan went on his way, whistling to himself, while Eric negotiated the stone stairs with care. In the front bedroom he laid Joan across the foot of the bed, removed her sandals, and undid the two top buttons of her dress. She must have taken the jacket off and it had been left behind in the taverna. He folded the lace bedspread back and then half pushed and half pulled Joan's body until she was lying between the sheets, her head resting on two pillows. She was out like a light. Dead to the world.

For a long time he stood smiling down at her, then shaking his head he went slowly into the back bedroom where he undressed and got into bed. His last wakeful thought was, this night had not gone according to plan!

Next morning Joan woke up with the mother of all headaches. She too cast her mind back to the previous evening. She should have acted a lot more wisely than she had done. She had drunk far too much wine and as far as she could tell Eric must have slept on his own in the other bedroom. 'Oh well!' she sighed sleepily, as she closed her eyes again. Too late now to think about how differently the night had turned out from what she had been anticipating.

Chapter Thirty-six

JOAN OPENED ONE EYE to see Eric standing there fully dressed, washed and shaved. She tried to raise her head from the pillow but failed miserably.

He was smiling as he set down a small tray which held a steaming cup of tea. Placing one arm beneath her shoulder blades he dragged all four pillows into a heap and helped to prop her up against them. 'Good morning, my darling. I won't bother to ask how you are feeling.' He grinned. Then he handed her a glass that held a small amount of colourless liquid. 'Here, drink this, and then you may have your tea.'

Gingerly she took the glass from his hand and sniffed the contents. 'Ugh, it smells terrible,' she moaned.

'I know it does, and it won't taste good either, but you *will* drink it.'

Joan squinted up at him, gaining the impression that she had better do as he said. She tightened her hold on the glass, tossed the liquid to the back of her throat and shuddered as she swallowed. It tasted utterly foul. She grabbed the cup that Eric was holding out to her and gratefully took a gulp, not caring that the tea was hot. Then she took another before she sighed and said, 'Oh, thank you. That's much better.'

Eric sat on the edge of the bed and waited until she had drained the cup. 'Did you have a good time last night?' he asked finally.

Joan thought for a minute before forming an answer. 'Yes, yes I did. That is, what I remember of it. I liked Anna – she was such a nice person. It wasn't until I made to stand up that everything went wrong. I am sorry.'

Eric soothed her tangled hair away from her face. 'I am to blame for the state you were in and it is me that should be apologising to you.'

'How did you work that out?' Joan muttered. Her tongue felt as if it was made of dried cotton wool.

'You were given too much wine to drink. I should have warned Stephan that you were not used to it. I met Isidore and we stayed longer than we had intended.'

'Please, may I have another cup of tea?' Joan begged.

'Of course, my darling, and then I will bring you up two pitchers of hot water so that you may get washed and dressed. I am so sorry that the accommodation does not run to a bathroom. There is a shower rigged up in the outside courtyard but the supply of water is only cold.'

Joan shivered. 'I'll manage,' she said, longing for him to go so that she could at least use the chamber pot and then clean her teeth.

Whatever the foul drink was that Eric had given her, the effect it had had on Joan was like a shot in the arm. Her head had cleared in no time.

They had skipped breakfast but over lunch they talked of all manner of things including their proposed visit to Gozo, which Eric promised would take place at the weekend. Joan drank three glasses of clear water and when she emerged from the kitchen, after clearing the meal away and washing up their plates and dishes, she found Eric waiting for her, already dressed in his overcoat and looking very different from yesterday. Today his image was more businesslike and the fact that he was impatiently leaning against the doorframe, with his hands resting on the bone handle of a very posh walking stick, was very puzzling. She had never known him to use a stick before. She didn't even know that he owned one. Come to think of it, there was a lot she didn't know about Eric Roussel.

'Let's be off then, and I promise we shall have a slap-up meal tonight.'

'You'll have to give me a few minutes, till I finish dressing and change my shoes.'

'Get a move on then. It is imperative that I meet up with a couple of men and I am late already. No, wait. I've had a better idea. I can't be doing without a car for the length of our stay. You stay, take your time, I'll get off, attend to my business and while I'm in the city I'll hire a car and come back for you later. Stephan will drive me in now.' He crossed the room, gave her a quick kiss, and then was out of the door like a bat out of hell.

It was after five o'clock before he came back, driving a dark saloon car, the first decent vehicle that Joan had seen since she set foot on the island. He offered no explanation as to where he had been and Joan did not ask. He did seem immensely pleased with himself as he set a bottle of Scotch on the table and threw his arms round Joan's neck, kissing her on both cheeks.

'Oh, my darling, I have everything sorted out. I am taking you out tonight and we are really going to celebrate.'

Eric was humming to himself as he drove and as they passed a sign which pointed the way to St Julian's Bay Joan felt compelled to ask, 'Weren't we supposed to be going to St Julian's tonight?'

'How observant you are.' Eric laughed. 'We were indeed, but during the course of a business meeting this morning I met some friends, one of whom owns a restaurant up in the north part of the island, and we, my darling, are invited to dine there tonight.'

'Eric,' Joan said cautiously, 'may I ask you a question?'

'Of course. Fire away.'

'How is it you know so many people and have so many friends here when you told me that you haven't been back to Malta for years? And just where are we going now?'

Eric took his eyes off the road for a second and smiled at her. 'That, my darling, is two questions. First, I was born here, and what I said was, I have not *lived* here since I was a lad. That's not to say I haven't made flying visits from time to time. When one is in business it pays to keep in contact with one's business partners and to strike without warning never does any harm. Can't let it be thought that I am getting too old to cope. My motto is, the older you are the wiser you are, and during this visit I promise you there are some fellows who are going to be brought up sharply to my way of thinking. I have already settled my account with two men who thought they could outwit me.'

'Hmm.' Joan was busy with her own thoughts. Eric's mind was like a deep well. Hard to get to the bottom of. 'You still haven't told me where we are going.'

'We are heading for the north of the island, to a place called Marfa. Wait till you see it. I guarantee you will remember this visit for the rest of your life.'

Eric was right.

The building itself was not much to write home about but the setting was what Joan could only describe as paradise. They were high up and the whole area seemed to be planted with exotic trees, shrubs and wild flowers, while the scented air was bracing. They were seated at a table which was set outside the café in what appeared to be a built-on annexe. Three walls were of plain wood, the fourth was sheer glass. It was a glorious evening, with the sound of waves breaking on the beach far below and the flimsy curtains stirring at the open window.

'It's a pity it has got dark so early,' Eric said. 'If we have time I must bring you back here during the day, because looking out across the water from up here one can see the islands of Comino and Gozo.'

Not only was the eating of the meal a delight, but the preparing and the cooking of the food was a joy to watch. Out on the hillside great flares were lit and in a deep hole that had cemented sides a fire was kindled. Iron grids were laid crossways over the top once the embers were red and glowing. Healthy, tanned young men skinned and filleted huge flat fish which they brushed with melted butter and sprinkled with a variety of mixed herbs and then grilled to perfection. The fish was served with tiny boiled potatoes, dishes of pasta, rice and salad, and hot crusty bread. Also placed on the table was a tray that held six round china dishes, each one containing a different delicious-tasting homemade sauce. Several different kinds of wine were liberally poured, but Joan had learnt her lesson last night.

She suddenly smiled to herself as her thoughts flew back to England and her sister Martha. In the Prince of Wales she had often sailed near the wind but never had she been so drunk that she couldn't remember how she had got home and into her bed. The last thing she remembered about last night was trying to stand up and failing miserably. She smiled again, hearing in her head Martha's voice loud and clear saying, 'You were as pissed as a pudding!'

With the first course over, glasses were refilled, and the taste of the sweet that followed had Joan smacking her lips: big succulent strawberries surrounded by brandy-flavoured ice cream.

'Strawberries, at this time of the year?' she exclaimed to Eric. 'And I have never tasted such sweet ones.'

'This is Malta,' he reminded her. 'Here everything is different.'

'You can say that again,' Joan said as she looked towards the inside of the café. It was by now almost ten o'clock at night but scores of people were still dining and gorgeous, healthy-looking children sat with their parents or on the floor. Nearly every child had a mop of thick curly hair and their skin was in the main the lovely colour of milk chocolate.

It was one o'clock in the morning when they finally left Marfa. For the last hour they had drunk nothing but very strong black coffee. The farewells they received were affectionate and warm, every man in sight hugging Eric and giving him what seemed the obligatory pats on the back.

It really was a lovely night, or early morning, the sky dark but twinkling with more stars than Joan remembered having seen before. Eric drove slowly and Joan had the window on the passenger side of the car wound down. Coming down from the hills she could at times hear the sea lapping against the shore. She had been wined and dined to perfection, and this evening she was well aware of where she was and what she was doing as she snuggled up against Eric's shoulder.

Only one bedroom was occupied that night and Joan's last thought before she fell asleep was that Eric was like no other man who had been in her life. Would his lovemaking, his wealth and his wisdom be enough to sustain their future together? One little point still niggled at the back of her mind as she lay naked in the crook of his arm.

There was still an awful lot that she did not know about Eric Roussel.

Chapter Thirty-seven

IT WAS WITH A horrible sinking feeling in the pit of her stomach that Joan watched from the bedroom window as a big black car drove into the courtyard, and it did not make her feel any better to see two men whom, at first glance, she would describe as thugs get out of the car and stride towards the house.

There definitely was something sinister about both of them. Tall and heavily built, they had very broad shoulders, their arms rippled with muscles and their hands were enormous. Unusually for Maltese men, they wore no jackets, and their shirt sleeves were rolled up to beyond their elbows.

Joan came quietly down the stairs in time to see one of the men pass an envelope to Eric. His fingers were trembling slightly as he unfolded the single sheet of paper he had withdrawn from the envelope. Then, having read the words, he exploded with rage. His cheeks turned blood red as he thumped his fist on the table top, and he screamed what Joan feared had to be a whole string of offensive words at the two messengers. He looked furious when he glanced up and saw Joan standing on the bottom step of the stone staircase.

'Put your coat on and go for a walk,' he shouted.

Joan had no option but to do as he said. It was not a suggestion, it was an order. The silence hung heavy in the room as she took down her coat from the hook behind the door. Without waiting to put it on, she walked out of the house, hearing the door being slammed behind her as she walked away.

In the lane she hesitated. To say the least, she was frightened. No, that word did not describe her feelings. She was terrified! Should she turn left and go to the taverna? Maybe tell Stephan that she felt something was wrong? Or should she turn right and head for Spinola Bay?

Better to mind your own business. Eric is more than capable of taking care of himself. Normally that would be the case, but this morning she was not so sure. If those two men calling on Eric were friendly then she would hate to be around when his enemies made an appearance.

Sighing heavily, she decided her best course was to take a walk, give herself time to calm down. At the moment her heart was still beating nineteen to the dozen and her stomach was churning. She walked slowly towards the bay, her mind playing tricks all the time. Eric had been well pleased with himself when he came back from Valletta yesterday and on the way to Marfa last night he had said that he had settled his account with two men. From his choice of words, she had judged the outcome to have been to Eric's benefit. But now what?

There was no one in the cove with the exception of one fisherman sitting on the rocks. Joan stood watching him for a while as his fingers weaved in and out repairing his nets with an instrument that looked like a cross between a knitting needle and a crochet hook. Looking up and seeing Joan, he called a cheery greeting and beckoned her over. By the time she reached his side he had laid aside the nets and was slicing into a fat juicy melon. He patted the rock beside him and gestured for Joan to sit beside him. She did so gladly and accepted a huge slice of his melon. He fished in a bag that lay at his feet, brought out a small bundle of white cloth and tore off a wide strip. 'Napkin,' he said, laughing loudly, and Joan laughed with him as she held the piece of cloth beneath her chin to catch the juice that was running from the ripe fruit. How kind and generous these local people were.

This man had a wrinkled weather-beaten face, though he was not that old; about the same age as herself, she guessed. Both his trousers and his thick, heavy, navy blue jersey had seen better days, yet he was as happy as a lark. The ordinary Maltese folk certainly seemed to live an entirely different life from Londoners. The other men, always dressed in black suits, whom Eric associated with were a different breed entirely from her companion, who was now offering to roll her a cigarette.

Soon the fisherman took up his nets again and Joan watched with admiration as his knobbly fingers flew in and out. It wasn't long before he was joined by another man, similar in size and dress to himself. The two men spoke a few words and they seemed to be in agreement, for they turned to Joan, smiling broadly and making gestures with their hands towards a boat that lay bobbing at the edge of the sea. Joan frowned. It took a couple of minutes before it dawned on her that they were inviting her to join them on a boat trip.

'Please, miss, you enjoy,' the second man said, and then as if it had only just dawned on him he pointed to his mate, saying. 'He Tamara,' then stabbing his own chest with his forefinger added, 'me Zack.' Then he pointed to the sky. 'Nice day, you enjoy.'

Joan repeated each of their names, smiled, and holding out her hand said, 'My name is Joan.'

'Please, Joan, you come,' said Tamara.

A trip out to sea with two men she didn't know from Adam? On the other hand it was certainly an attractive proposition. Joan suddenly laughed aloud, stood up and said, 'Why not?'

The two men grinned at each other and began to walk towards the boat. Joan followed and smiled in appreciation as Zack placed a cushion on the bare seat of the boat and Tamara steadied her as she climbed aboard. She was thinking that it was a godsend meeting these fishermen this morning. Her head had been full of dreadful thoughts as she had left Eric in the house with those two brutes. But if she had gone against Eric's orders and stayed, what could she have done? She hadn't got the slightest idea as to what they had come to the house for. Eric had certainly not been pleased to see them!

She hadn't been able to understand a word they were rattling on about, but it didn't take much deduction to realise that the argument that was raging when she left had hardly been a friendly one. No, she had done the right thing. She was well out of it.

The purr of the boat's engine was reassuring and the further out to sea they got the easier Joan began to feel. The sight of the sparkling, brilliant sea for as far as she could see went a long way towards calming her feelings. When Zack cut the engine and the two men prepared to haul their lobster pots aboard, he motioned to Joan to stand up and lift up the top of the seat on which she was sitting. She did so, and smiled. At her feet was a deep cupboard which held a few thick china mugs and two thermos flasks which must have stood the battering of time for they bore the marks of a few dents. She needed no further instructions.

Setting three mugs in a line, she unscrewed the cap of one flask and found it to contain boiling hot strong black coffee. Delving further into the cupboard, she wasn't in the least surprised to find a jar of sugar and a bottle, which had a spring-like buckled top, containing a thick yellow creamy liquid that Tamara later told her was goat's milk. Whatever, the brew they eventually sat slowly sipping as the boat rocked gently was one of the best drinks of coffee that Joan had ever tasted.

The companionable atmosphere was to Joan like no other that she had ever experienced. It was as if she had known these two middle-aged men all her life and that they had always been friends. When they were back at the bay and she was being half lifted from the boat by their four strong arms she was almost reluctant to leave them. Three times she paused as she walked up the beach and turned to wave at her new friends, who were still standing watching her.

It had been a unique experience. To others, the telling might sound like just an ordinary boat trip out with two fishermen to bring in their lobster pots. To Joan it had been a delightful change. A soothing time that she would remember for the rest of her life.

Now she had to go back. To what? Her thoughts shied away from forming an answer to that question.

She lingered in the courtyard, unable to believe her ears. The sounds of revelry coming from inside the house were enough to give anyone the impression that a party was going on. Gingerly, she opened the door and the sight that met her eyes amazed her. There were at least a half a dozen men, all holding glasses in their hands. But there was no sign of the two men who had been with Eric when she had left. Whatever had transpired, there was no mistaking the overall happiness. Never could Joan remember being so pleased to see anyone as when Anna broke free from the back of the room and came smiling towards her.

'Where ever have you been?' Anna asked, as she hugged Joan tightly. 'Manny has been afraid for you.'

331

Joan looked to where Eric was standing, surrounded by men and looking extremely pleased with himself. As yet he hadn't even noticed that she was back.

Anna steered Joan into the back sitting room, closing the door behind the two of them. 'You deserve an explanation,' she said. 'You must have been frightened this morning, but you should have come straight down to us, not wandered off on your own.'

Joan didn't know what to say. She still hadn't the slightest idea of what was going on.

'Nothing happens on the island that Isidore does not get to know about, and Stephan and some other relatives were ready for Emmanuel's visitors this morning.' Anna was quick to reassure her. 'All is well now. So smile, Joan, and try to remember that Manny has more friends than enemies. There is not a village on Malta where the inhabitants do not have great respect for the Roussel family.'

If her speech was supposed to make Joan feel better and clear the air it hadn't worked. It hadn't been an explanation that Joan could understand, but she knew by now that it was not her place to ask questions.

'Only one more day and the whole family is off to Gozo,' Anna said breezily. 'Once there you will meet Manny's closest family and we shall all have a great time. But come now and have a drink. There is plenty to eat and much to celebrate.'

To say that Joan was bewildered would be putting it mildly. However, she put on a brave face and followed Anna.

The minute Eric saw her he set down his drink and reached out his hands. 'Come here.'

Joan went to him. He pulled her straight into his arms and kissed her, very gently and tenderly. It was a while before he drew away from her and stood smiling down into her clear blue eyes. 'I almost wish,' he told her, 'that I hadn't promised we would go and eat with Isidore this evening.'

'We'll still have the whole night to ourselves,' she told him.

The answering squeeze that he gave her wiped away all of her misgivings. At least for the moment.

That night it was cold as Joan climbed in between the linen sheets, and she tucked her feet up into the bottom of her satin nightdress.

Eric came and flung the bedclothes off her, laughing as he did so. 'You won't be cold for long, that much I promise you.'

She was freezing, but his touch was warm and she snuggled up close to his body. They were together now and she felt safe. Her face was pressed into his bare shoulder, his fingers twined in her long hair and they kissed liked young lovers who had only recently met.

Tonight was different again. There were no problems. England was far away; this was their time with nobody to disapprove. Eric was the only person in the world that she wanted to be with.

Much, much later she lay on her side, Eric's arms still holding her close. 'Oh, Eric . . .' It was a whisper, because she wasn't capable of putting into words what she was feeling.

Eric smiled and said, 'I love you.' He kissed the top of her head. 'I love you,' he repeated. 'I think I've been in love with you since the first moment I set eyes on you, when you were terrified because Martin had sent you to have lunch with me on your own. You feared I might turn out to be an ogre, didn't you?'

'Well, I didn't know what to expect.'

'And I let you down so many times by not turning up. Why did you let me come back into your life each time?'

Joan answered without thinking. 'I couldn't get you out of my mind. And looking back I don't think I tried very hard. I only knew that everything about my life changed when you walked through the door.'

'And, my darling, do you still feel the same way?'

'Oh, Eric, how could I not? Look what you've done for me! Taken me places, shown me a whole different life. Before now I could never have imagined that I would do the things that I have with you. My previous life was dull and dreary compared to what it is now.'

'I like the bit about doing things with me.'

'Now you're teasing me rotten.' But she laughed as she said the words.

'Well, if you make us each a nice cup of coffee we might be able to start all over again and the rest of the night might even turn out to be better than it has been so far.'

'Oh, Eric.' She sighed, but it was a happy sigh. 'I never knew. I never even guessed that lovemaking could be . . .' She couldn't go on.

'You are a wonderful lady, Joan. Until now you haven't really done anything with your life except look after other people. In future you must keep reminding yourself each and every day that you will not just *get by*, or just *exist*. Life is for living and we should all of us live it to the full.'

What Eric was saying was exciting but a little bit scary, and she felt compelled to ask, 'Don't you ever give a thought to tomorrow?'

'Tomorrow may never come, sweetheart.' He grinned. 'I've told you things can get even better. Who knows?'

Joan looked into his twinkling eyes and she began to laugh and that was when he tried to kiss her. But her mouth was wide open, laughing with sheer joy. So he took her into his arms and words were no longer necessary.

Chapter Thirty-eight

WHAT A HAPPY GATHERING.

Judging by the number of people, half the residents of Malta must have relatives living on the tiny island of Gozo, Joan was thinking to herself as she watched several small craft ferry their way along the quayside. All around her were families; young children, their parents, grandparents and even great grand-parents. The waterfront seemed to be humming with the same excited expectancy that she was feeling. She could hear a hubbub of voices as people formed orderly queues to board one of the boats. It was Sunday morning: blue skies and weak sunshine, a typical autumn morning. Joan felt like a child going on a Sunday school outing. She was excited at the thought of crossing the water to visit another island and at the same time a little fearful at the thought of meeting Eric's family.

Three horse-drawn carriages had brought Eric, herself and the rest of the relations and friends down to the dock. Stephan, Eric and John were helping the older folk along the quayside and assisting them to board one of the largest boats. Anna was standing beside Joan, waiting until everyone else was safely settled. Suddenly Anna asked, 'Joan, is something bothering you?'

'No, not really.'

'What do you mean, not really? Either there is something wrong or there isn't, but the look on your face tells me you're a bit bewildered.'

Joan gave a small sigh. 'To tell you the truth, Anna, I am, but I don't think I should be talking about it.'

'Don't be silly. Is it something one of my aunts said or did?'

'No, honestly. Besides, it isn't only your family – it's almost everyone who is stepping into the boats.'

Anna looked mystified, so Joan told her what she had seen.

'Adults and even children all touch their foreheads and then their chests. Left to right, making the sign of the cross. Some are even fingering small gold medals hanging round their necks, while their lips are moving all the while as if they are praying.'

'They are praying. To St Christopher, the patron saint of travellers. The medallions they are wearing are figures of St Christopher.'

'What? You mean they are afraid of crossing this stretch of water?'

'Not exactly. Most folk do it when they travel no matter by what means. Everyone wants a safe journey.'

'Oh, I see,' said Joan, not sure that she really did.

John held his arms out and lifted Anna down into the boat and Eric did the same for Joan. She let out a great sigh of pleasure as the mooring rope was freed and they set out on their short crossing.

A small edition of an ancient coach was waiting for the family when they arrived at the landing stage. The driver was treated as an old friend by all the men, who put their arms round him, kissed his weather-beaten cheeks and patted his back. Not at all the way the men acted towards one another in England. The arrival of the women he totally ignored. Joan thought she wouldn't care to guess his age but she couldn't help but notice that his clothes hung on him as though he had shrunk.

On the bus Eric came to sit beside her. He was looking exceptionally smart this morning, as though he had been dressed by an expensive tailor, and smelling good too. As they drove along, he held her hand between both of his. They did not talk, as Joan was too busy looking at the countryside. Her first impression of Gozo was that it was even greener, quieter and more unspoilt than Malta was. They passed a couple of picturesque fishing villages, clusters of stone-built houses and a fair number of churches. Then the coach began to climb and Eric explained that his family all lived in a farmhouse on the outskirts of the village of Xaghra. Joan did her best to repeat the name, but although Eric slowly spelt it out for her she was unable to get her tongue round such a difficult word.

'Never mind,' Eric sympathised. 'Enough for you to know that it is on high ground, a very rural area, breathtaking scenery, but a slow way of life.'

He was right. The driver brought the coach to a halt and Joan got her first glimpse of country folk living on a small island. It was like stepping into another world.

There were about five or six houses set almost into a semicircle yet leaving plenty of space between each rustic building. The large open courtyard in which they stood also boasted a watermill which actually worked, and Joan was fascinated as she watched the wooden paddles being driven by the clear sparkling water. There seemed to be animals of every description roaming over the cobbles, yet there was still a feeling of peacefulness, almost as if time did not exist in this place.

'Come,' Eric said. 'Meet my mother and the rest of the ladies.'

The elderly female members of the family sat together in

a line, their backs ramrod straight against the stone wall. Each was dressed in black, with a beautiful lace mantilla draped over her grey hair. All of them were working. And what an art! Knitting needles flew as some produced chunky jerseys from thick oily wool, the type that fishermen wore. Others were making lace, bringing forth articles so exquisite they resembled cobwebs. As Eric and Joan approached the work was dropped on to their chairs and they all got to their feet, crying, 'He's come. He's come. It really is our Manny.'

They rushed to put their arms about him to the extent that he was almost smothered. Younger women ran to join the throng, every one of them eager to embrace him. Joan stood to one side, feeling left out.

Finally Eric broke free, took Joan's hand and began to introduce her. 'This is my mother, Nadia Roussel. Isidore whom you have met is her brother-in-law.'

The elegant but frail little lady was smiling sweetly at Joan. Joan almost felt she should curtsey, but instead she held out her hand and said, 'I am very pleased to meet you, Madam Roussel.'

'I am more than pleased that my son has brought you to join our party.'

Party? By now Joan had got the jitters. Was it some special occasion? Should she have brought a present? She hadn't time for more reflections, Eric was taking her along the line, names running off his tongue: Bianca, Chloe, Fiona, Ingrid. Two maiden aunts had come to swell the family, and even more cousins, though it appeared that Nadia was the only one who spoke any English. Suddenly Anna was at her elbow, speaking to her relatives in their own language. Whatever she said to them it must have been something nice, for all the ladies were smiling and nodding their heads in approval.

'Halfway there,' Anna laughed. 'Now you get to meet the men.' Leaving Eric surrounded by the women, she took Joan by the elbow and led her across the courtyard to where a bar had been set up. All talking and laughter ceased as the two young women approached. The men moved sideways to make a pathway for them and at once Joan could see that two large wicker chairs had been placed at one end of the bar. Isidore was seated in one, and the other was occupied by someone who was introduced to Joan as Theodore. She needed no telling that they were related because they were as alike as two peas in a pod.

Isidore smilingly kissed the back of her hand and in perfect English asked if she had enjoyed her short trip over to Gozo. This was a bit of a shock, because in the taverna she had been under the impression that he did not speak English. She would have to watch her step, she warned herself.

Theodore got to his feet and he, too, gallantly took her hand and kissed it, saying, 'Welcome to the home of the Kramer and Roussel families.' Then he looked towards the group of men and issued a curt order in his own language. It seemed it was to be left to Anna to make the introductions this time. Dark, swarthy-looking young men, older men who had the same grace and elegance as oozed from Eric. 'Claude, Boris, Luke, John my husband you already know and Stephan my cousin, Marcus, Ezra.'

Joan's jaw ached with smiling and she almost pleaded with Anna to stop, but she was saved the embarrassment. Several young women were clapping their hands and pointing to where several trestle tables had been joined and set up as one very long table. It was time to eat. As if from nowhere, hordes of laughing children appeared and were seated at a table of their own which ran parallel to that where their parents would be eating.

Joan could not remember having seen so much food laid out at any one time. Dishes lined the table from one end to the other, and every morsel looked superb. Good food was taken very seriously in Malta and it would appear to be no different on this wonderful little island where time seemed to stand still.

Before they started to eat, while the wine was being poured, Eric disappeared for a few minutes and came back bearing a sack of gaily wrapped presents. He knew each child by name. They were beautiful children, beautifully dressed and well mannered. A chubby little girl aged about four tore the wrapping off her present and found a doll which she immediately cradled in her arms, murmuring, 'Thank you, Uncle Manny.' The young boy sitting next to her, obviously her brother but slightly older, had received a clockwork lorry and the expression on his face as he wound the key was a joy to watch. No child had been forgotten, and all of them were agog with excitement as boys set out toy soldiers and girls discovered all kinds of pretty things according to their age. Joan couldn't fathom Eric. He was so kind and thoughtful most of the time, but remembering the morning when those two thugs had come to Spinola Bay she knew only too well that there was a darker side to him.

Everyone was in a happy mood. Men came up from the village to play for them. Some had fiddles, one even had a banjo, another an accordion, and as the music started Nadia gave the order and everyone began to eat.

Between courses local girls danced for them. Then the band changed their instruments and began to play waltzes. Eric roared with laughter as couples got to their feet and attempted to dance on the flagstones of the courtyard, but Stephan wiped the smile from Eric's face when he came and asked Joan if she would dance with him. Tall and slim, light on his feet, Stephan was the perfect partner. Joan hadn't danced in years and yet with Stephan's arm around her, his hand in the small of her back, she never put a foot wrong. It felt as if she was gliding in time to the music. Stephan lowered his head and deliberately let their cheeks touch, and every now and again he would murmur in her ear, 'Good to be able to show old Manny just how lucky he is. He's too old to be able to move like this.'

'I bet you wouldn't say that to his face,' she teased.

Stephan wouldn't let her go when the tune ended, but kept her out in the open ready for the next dance. She felt like a young girl when finally, holding hands and stifling their laughter, they made their way back to the table. To her utter surprise Eric had stood up, and as she reached his side, to her great embarrassment, he took her in his arms and kissed her long and lovingly.

She couldn't meet the look in Stephan's eyes as he thanked her for dancing with him and turned and walked over to the bar. They both knew that Eric's kiss had been his way of staking his claim to her. It made her feel extremely special, but at the same time she knew that every eye had been on her. She mustn't drink any more wine, she told herself, she was getting too cocksure of herself. But then, when in her life had two men paid her so much attention in one day? Or even *one* man, come to that!

No sooner was she seated than Eric took off his jacket, unknotted his tie, loosened it and undid the top button of his shirt. Then he pulled her to her feet and laughingly said, 'My turn now.' He made hand signals to the musicians, and the couples who were already dancing stopped and formed a circle. The music changed to catchy tunes, the beat now loud and fast, but that was all right because Joan and Eric had their arms round each other and were moving as one. Every now and then Eric would kiss her on the lips, whispering outrageous suggestions as their friends and relations clapped their hands and egged Eric on. Joan knew why he was entering into the spirit of it all. He was determined to show that anything Stephan could do he could do better, even if he were a good few years older.

The breeze had strengthened and several older folk

proposed that they cleared the tables and go into the house. However, Nadia Roussel had other ideas. She called Anna and Eric to her side and issued instructions. Eric stayed by his mother, talking softly to her, while Anna came back over to where Joan was sitting.

'Aunt Nadia says you cannot visit Gozo without going into at least one of our churches. There are two nearby. They are entirely different, yet both are beautiful in their own way. Manny is going to ask Joseph, the coach driver, to take those of us who wish to go to visit both churches. Would you care to come with us, Joan?'

Joan didn't hesitate. 'Of course. It would be a privilege.'

'Well, let's go inside and freshen ourselves up first, shall we?'

As the coach came to a halt the men got off first, and as Eric handed Joan down he looked very serious. She felt something was wrong.

Eric nodded to where three of the older men and Stephan were standing apart. 'Bit of business to attend to,' he said vaguely. 'If we're not back by the time you have visited both churches we'll meet up again at the farmhouse.' He planted a hasty kiss on her cheek and moved away, leaving only four women besides Anna and Joan to go viewing.

The church they were standing outside looked to be very old and desperately in need of repair and yet it somehow gave off a graceful appearance, mainly because the structure was tall and narrow. Near to the top of the stonework there were four round empty spaces, one on each side of the building. Joan thought they might at one time have held the face of a clock. Similar to London's Big Ben. Not that the spire of this church was anywhere near as impressive as London's world famous clock.

As one of the aunts pushed open the door to the church, Anna held Joan back and from her bag she produced two black mantillas. 'We cannot enter unless we cover our heads,' she explained as she demonstrated how Joan should twist one into shape to cover her hair.

The outside of the church had given Joan the impression of an ordinary place of worship for a working-class farming community. She couldn't have been more wrong. One look at the beautiful interior had her gasping in surprise.

The sun had gone down, but the stained glass windows shone with so many colours that Joan was transfixed. The women dipped their fingers into a bowl of holy water and made the sign of the cross on their foreheads, Anna also performed this act on Joan, then they toured the small interior of the church walking in single file.

Above the altar was a mighty display of Christ's crucifixion but dominating the whole scene was the figure of the Virgin Mary. Her facial beauty and the glorious simple robes in which she was adorned was enough to bring tears to Joan's eyes. But that was *not* what amazed her. If someone had related to her the sight she was now looking at she knew she would have found it hard to believe. Pinned to the robes of the Virgin Mary were many treasury notes in several different currencies and dominations. That was not all. There was also jewellery in different shapes and forms, including wedding rings. Anna had to nudge her to move on, so spellbound was Joan by this unusual sight.

The second church they visited, only a short walk away, was beyond description. In London this church would be referred to as a cathedral. It was on a par with St Paul's with its golden dome which was a landmark wherever one was in London. This was indeed a rich Catholic church. Its beauty beyond belief.

Joseph took them back to the farmhouse, where a hot meal of braised kidneys and rice was waiting for them. Although Joan didn't think her stomach would hold much more food she had to admit to Anna that she had thoroughly enjoyed the unusual meal. It was now getting dark and the men had still not returned. Joan could only tell that the older women were getting anxious by the tone of their voices and the agitated glances they kept casting at each other. Anna translated some of the comments for her, but she knew full well she wasn't being told the whole story. Even Anna herself was showing signs of becoming uneasy.

When at last the men did return there was a rush to get everyone on to the coach. Anna explained to Joan that they would miss the last boat if they did not leave immediately. Hurried, affectionate goodbyes were said, and Anna explained that the women were urging Joan to come back and spend Christmas with them. Joan smiled, but gave non-committal answers. She had had a lovely time, but Christmas was for families, and Martha and Sid would never forgive her if she were not sitting at their dinner table on that one day of the year.

They were in the boat before Joan noticed that Eric was clutching a small leather attaché case. Its corners were reinforced with steel studs, and besides the main lock there was a heavy padlocked chain which ran beneath the handle and round the whole of the case. He never once released his hold on that handle, not even when they were back in Malta and he stood on the quay to assist her to climb up beside him. The horse-drawn carriages were waiting for them, and Eric and Joan were the first to get off. Joan hugged Anna lovingly, and Eric promised to bring her down to the taverna the next day. Then, arm in arm, they turned off down into the lane that would take them to what had almost become home to Joan. The attaché case was still held fast in Eric's right hand and he swung it jauntily as they walked. Joan would be lying to herself if she said she didn't wonder what the case contained. On the other hand, she was wise enough to understand that what she didn't know she couldn't worry about.

Once in bed, safe and content in Eric's arms, Joan found her thoughts were mixed. Despite her anxieties regarding Eric, there was no denying that she was living, and thoroughly enjoying herself, in a totally different world. She needed no reminder that soon it had to come to an end and she would have to return to reality. However, today had been an absolutely wonderful day, and now she had even more memories to add to her fast growing list.

Chapter Thirty-nine

Next morning Joan woke to find that she was in bed on her own. Eric usually made a great play of waking her up, sometimes by bringing her a cup of tea but mostly by kissing her and indulging in love play. He must have crept out of bed today, because she hadn't heard a sound.

Hastily she washed, using the jug of cold water from the washstand, thinking she would get Eric to carry hot water upstairs for her later in the day. Then she dressed and did her hair. Halfway down the staircase she hesitated. There was no hand rail or side to these stone steps and she could see right down into the main living room.

Eric was sitting at the table, on which was the leather case he had brought back from Gozo. The lid of the case was up and the contents were visible. Stacked neatly in piles were wads of notes. A few of these bundles of money were lying on the table beside the open case.

Joan lowered her head, and forced herself to cough as she came slowly down the rest of the stairs. She sensed, rather than saw, Eric gather up the bundles of notes, and it wasn't until she heard the lock click, confirming that Eric had closed the case, that she gaily called out, 'My, you're an early bird this morning.'

Treading the last steps slowly she could see that the case had been removed from the table. Thank God for that. At least she hadn't embarrassed him. On the contrary, Eric was full of the joys of spring as he came forward and kissed her good morning. 'Scrambled eggs OK by you, darling?' he asked.

'Lovely. I'll make the toast and coffee.' Joan could hear the tremor in her voice and tried to control it. That was no small amount of money that Eric had in that case. They ate their breakfast, each making small talk, but it wouldn't have taken someone with a crystal ball to realise that both of them were edgy.

As Joan began to clear the table Eric looked pointedly at his watch. 'I have to go into Valletta this morning and book our passage back to London. We'll travel Khedivial mail line this time. It only takes three to four days.'

'Sudden decision, isn't it?' He had taken Joan by surprise.

Eric sighed heavily. It was unusual to see him so straight-faced. 'Needs must when the devil drives. The quicker I'm back in London the safer I shall feel.'

Joan jumped on that word. 'Safer? Are you in trouble, Eric? Why do you not feel safe here?'

Eric laughed, but it was a hollow sound. 'Slip of the tongue, Joan. I didn't mean personal safety, only that I have a business deal going on and I don't want to lose it.' He was talking for the sake of talking, Joan thought, but better that she kept her own counsel. They had had a marvellous time and now it was time to go home.

'All right.' Making a great effort, she smiled. 'I'll do our packing while you are out.'

Eric shrugged himself into his coat, pulled the case out from beneath the table, and kissed her goodbye. As soon as she was alone, Joan sat down again. She didn't need to be told that whatever Eric was dabbling in, he was up to his ears in trouble.

'Oh well,' she muttered as she went upstairs to pack. 'Good times don't last for ever.'

How right she was.

They spent their last evening at the taverna. Joan and Anna sat together at the back of the large room. A huge round table was littered with food, glasses and bottles, and the double swing doors were propped open wide to cope with the cigar smoke. Joan had never seen Eric look so happy, and for that she was grateful.

Isidore was silently watching everyone with a wary eye and finally he asked a question. 'So what's going to happen, Manny, when you get back to London?'

Eric shot Joan a warning look before saying, 'I'll settle everything. Those entitled to it will get their share of the profits.' He had tried hard to speak in a jocular way, but Joan had heard the seriousness in his voice. It sobered her up immediately.

'Will you deal with the main business and be back here for Christmas?' Isidore sounded stern.

'I can't honestly answer that question,' Manny said. 'I will do my best, but I have no idea where everyone is or what the situation is at that end.'

There were quite a few men in the taverna tonight whom Joan had never seen before. They were all watching closely.

'All right, Manny.' Isidore stared at him, his old eyes never wavering. 'If you can't make it by Christmas, so be it, but New Year's Eve is the deadline.'

Joan felt very sorry for Eric. He knew he had the eyes of everyone in the room on him. 'I'll do the best I can, Isidore, you know that.'

The old man shook his head sadly. 'Manny, my boy, this

time you had better make quite sure that your best is good enough.'

There was a quiet discussion going on amongst the men until Stephan broke away and came to tell Joan that he and John were going to walk her home because Manny had some papers to sign for Isidore.

Joan felt sorrow right down to the pit of her stomach as she said goodbye to Anna. There was so much going on on this island it would take a month of Sundays for her to understand it all, and she wasn't at all sure that Anna didn't feel exactly the same way. It was a sad and lingering farewell, for they had become such good friends.

John and Stephan saw her safely into the house, then each in turn caught her fingers and raised them to their lips. So gallant. 'God go with you,' they called out as they closed the front door behind them.

Joan lay in bed listening for Eric's footsteps. Somehow tonight she didn't feel safe in this house on her own. She shook up her pillows in an attempt to get comfortable. She wondered what Eric was doing and tried not to care. It really was none of her business. She closed her eyes tightly and tried to stop her mind from imagining all sorts of horrors. Instead, she began to wonder what it would be like to be back home.

What had been happening while she had been away? Had Jody stayed over with Rosie? Had Freda kept an eye on them both and on the rest of the staff? Had Martha and Sid been over to the Prince of Wales and were Jeff and Mark still about?

It didn't work. She still couldn't sleep.

In spite of the good time Eric had shown her she wouldn't be sorry to set foot on that mail boat tomorrow. To be able see London and her family and friends again suddenly seemed a very attractive idea.

⋆   ⋆   ⋆

The return journey was nowhere near as romantic as their outward voyage had been. For one thing, the mail boat wasn't half as luxurious as the P&O liner had been and in future if anyone were to tell her that surroundings didn't make any difference she would certainly set them straight on that point.

Eric was still attentive to her but at times she wished she were able to read his mind. She was aware that his thoughts were often a long way away.

In what seemed like no time at all they were steering into London Docks, and that was where Joan got her biggest shock.

The stewards carried their luggage down the gangway and saluted Eric as he generously tipped each man. There was no sign of the leather attaché case, and Joan could only conclude that Eric had packed it inside of one of his large suitcases, amongst his clothes.

'Darling, I'll put you in a taxi. You'll be all right the other end. There will be plenty of folk to help you with your luggage.' Then he walked off and left her standing there surrounded by their luggage.

Joan was absolutely stunned. He hadn't given her a moment even to ask why he wasn't coming to Brixton with her. Was he dumping her?

It was only a couple of minutes before Eric was back with two black cabs. He was a passenger in the first one, and both drivers got out with him and began to pick up their suitcases.

Eric hastily drew her into his arms, kissed her long and hard, then let her go. 'I'll take the first cab. I have given the second driver your address, and I've paid him and tipped him well so you'll be all right.'

Joan had to bite her tongue to stop herself from saying, 'Bloody generous to the last,' but he sensed she wasn't too pleased.

'I will be in touch, my darling,' he whispered, 'but I do have quite a few things to do.' With that, he jumped into the back of the first cab, leant out of the window, waved and blew her a kiss.

Joan stood stock still. She was absolutely astounded.

But it was no good standing there like some stuffed dummy. Joan stared after the now disappearing Eric and muttered, 'Well, I won't hold my breath.'

The driver had finished loading her luggage and turning to her he said, 'Brixton is it then, ma'am?'

'Yes, please.' Joan settled back in her seat. Already everything appeared so different from Malta. For one thing, the weather was drab, and it was very cold. The driver seemed to be holding the middle of the road, hurtling towards the oncoming traffic. Just when Joan was bracing herself for the inevitable crash, the driver jerked to the left and slid past a lorry with only inches to spare. She let her head fall back against the upholstery and closed her eyes for a moment.

London! So familiar, and yet Joan found herself making comparisons. The pace of life was so much faster. The peace and quiet of Malta seemed a whole world away.

Already the area was teeming with life. Pedestrians jostled between the traffic to cross the road and one could almost have walked on people's heads, the pavements were so crowded. Everybody was in a hurry. Horns honked, bicycle bells rang continually, barrow boys shouted their wares: the noise was dreadful. Joan was relieved when the driver drew the cab to a halt outside her premises. She stepped down and stood on the pavement and looked upward to the sign *Distinctive Designs*, and found that mingled with her relief to be home was a real feeling of pride.

The cab driver tipped his cap to her and drove off, leaving her standing on the pavement surrounded by her luggage.

The windows were her first priority. The one on the left-hand side was crowded with as many goods as possible. Joan gazed critically at an array of bolts of cloth, all in lovely autumn shades. Paper patterns were laid in a semicircle on the floor. A whole row of fine wool jumpers and cardigans was accompanied by balls of wool, knitting patterns and knitting needles. Two very heavy jumpers, one in the palest shade of blue and the other one cream, were attractively laid out on a chair, one spread across the seat and the other draped over the back. That was good thinking, anticipating the coming winter. Finally, near the front of the window, someone had arranged a dazzling selection of reels of sewing thread and row upon row of cards of buttons, ribbons and tape, all giving encouragement to women who liked to knit and sew.

Joan moved along to look at the second window and found herself gasping with surprise. This display would catch any fashionable lady's imagination. There were only two models, one wearing a winter white coat with a huge dark fur collar and a small hat made out of the same fur. Gloves, high-heeled shoes and handbag were all of the finest, softest leather. *Since when did we sell shoes?* Was one question she was asking herself. Then she remembered that Freda Preston was well known and trusted in the trade. She had more than likely begged Jones's, the exclusive shoe shop, to loan her the shoes when planning the display.

Her eyes roamed quickly to the second model, placed slightly to the fore on the other side of the window. It was certainly aimed at the business type of woman. The outfit looked fantastic: the long black skirt in pure wool was slim and elegant, while the tight-waisted jacket had a velvet collar. Several leather handbags and pairs of gloves were arranged in sets on the carpet. The only other item on show was a magnificent carved mahogany writing desk on which had been placed a tall slender vase holding just one white rose and a spray of green fern.

One thought hammered inside Joan's head. *Jim Taylor*. No one else could have restored that desk to all its original beauty. To think that in her days on the market stall he was only referred to as the bare wood man!

For the umpteenth time, she thanked God for the staff who worked for her. Each and every one of them was loyal, capable of coming up with original ideas, never afraid to try something new.

She was just about to pick up some of her luggage when the main entrance door flew open and Rosie, screaming with delight, threw herself at her. Before Joan could catch her breath she was surrounded by Jody, Freda and even one or two of her machinists. For a moment she was overcome by the feeling of coming home, the slightly guilty pleasure of having been missed and now the thrill of actually being wanted.

Freda took charge. 'Calm down, everyone. Each of you pick up a bag or a case and let's get Joan inside. We're making a right show of ourselves out here on the pavement.' Everyone laughed but they immediately did as Freda had ordered.

Joan stood in the middle of the shop and gazed round in delight. The whole place had an inviting look, laid out in such a way that you could feast your eyes on all the colours of the rainbow. The display of drapery and such like was overwhelming. Moving over to what, in her mind, she still referred to as the posh side of the shop she couldn't help but notice that the floor was covered by a Chinese carpet which looked both beautiful and expensive. The soft thickness of the pile and the brilliant vibrant colours were a joy to behold.

She hadn't uttered a word, yet although the words were spoken softly from behind her, she clearly heard them. 'Gorgeous, isn't it?'

She spoke his name even before she turned round to face him. 'Jim!' Automatically she opened her arms, and so did he, and the two stood silently in a tight embrace. To an onlooker it could easily have appeared that these were two lovers who had been parted for a very long time.

Freda broke the silence. 'Come on, girls, back to work. You'll have a chance to talk to Joan later on.'

Recalled to a sense of his surroundings, Jim Taylor kept his eyes lowered as he picked up two cases and said, 'You go on upstairs, Joan, and put the kettle on. Bet you're gasping for a cup of tea. I'll bring your luggage up.'

'I can take some, otherwise you will have to make two journeys,' Joan protested.

Jim laughed. 'Get yerself away. Have you forgotten that I'm Superman?'

Joan still lingered. Jim Taylor looked different. He had put a bit of weight on and it suited him. His dark hair had been cut in a much better style and he was no longer wearing those awful steel-rimmed glasses. The new pair had a tortoiseshell frame which broadened his face and gave him a distinguished look.

'I can see you like the carpet,' he said softly.

'Yes I do, Jim, very much. Must have cost a bomb, though.'

'Now, Joan, you know me better than that. I picked it up in a house sale. At first sight it was a bit of a mess, but I took a chance. It took ages to clean and five days to dry out. Only laid it down the day before yesterday, after Freda had done the window.'

'Ah, the window. It looks great, but where on earth did that beautiful desk come from? I'll lay a pound to a penny it wasn't in that condition when you acquired it.'

'You don't remember us bidding for that? Even the auctioneer remarked that this piece was in a really bad state and would need a great deal of restoration. But because it was of such an early period I knew it would be worth the labour. It's a collector's piece now, and besides, it savours of bygone times, don't you think?'

'I do indeed. You have excelled yourself. But, Jim, I have to ask you something . . .' She hesitated.

'Well out with it then, because we can't stand here talking all morning. You should get yourself upstairs, get settled in.'

'All right.' Joan dropped her voice. 'It's just that on the other side of the shop I noticed there are still quite a few articles made by you for sale. Small things that when we were on the market you used to call white wood goods.'

'So?'

'Well, why do you bother now when we are doing so well with other things?'

It was a moment or two before he answered. When he did, he looked into Joan's eyes and spoke quietly. 'To remind me not to get above myself, and more importantly to remember that it is your business.'

'Oh, Jim!' Joan felt a lump rise in her throat. Some time ago she had suggested that he become her partner, but then Eric had swept her off her feet and she had disregarded the feelings of this kind man who from the very beginning had always been there for her. However, this was not the time nor the place for her to raise the subject, so she put on a smile and said, 'Thank you. Now I am going to take your advice and go upstairs and put the kettle on.'

Rosie was serving a customer as Joan made for the stairs but she called out, 'It's great to have you home, Aunt Joan.'

Joan smiled and continued up the stairs. In her front room, everything was sparklingly clean. The dining table was covered with the plush chenille cloth and a huge potted azalea had been placed in a glass bowl and set in the centre of the table. The brass fire irons were shining brightly in the

355

hearth. A fire had been laid in the grate, needing only a match to set it burning.

She sighed happily to herself. It was great to be home.

Chapter Forty

JOAN COULD SCARCELY BELIEVE that she had been home for five days, they had sped by so quickly. Now it was Saturday and every member of her staff, herself included, had been on the go from the moment they had opened the shop doors at nine o'clock. Everything and everybody seemed geared up for Christmas.

Tonight Martha and Sid and their two sons were coming over and all of them were to meet up in the Prince of Wales. As the day wore on Joan had to scold herself for feeling that she would much rather spend the evening indoors by the fire with her feet up. She knew it wasn't possible. This was such a friendly, caring community, and folk had gone out of their way to help her in so many ways. Besides, she hadn't seen any member of her family since she had been back, with the exception of Rosie.

Come to that she hadn't set eyes on Eric, nor heard a word from him, although to be honest she wasn't altogether surprised. Eric would turn up again when it suited him. He played things so close to his chest that it was a wonder he knew himself whether he was coming or going half the time.

Rosie was an absolute darling. She had sat on the rug in front of the fire every evening after they had eaten their meal, her back leaning against her aunt's legs, and asked question after question, really interested in hearing about Malta. Joan had stared into the flames and relived some of the days she had spent there. She hadn't found the words to describe to Rosie, the calmness, the beauty and the slow pace at which life was lived on the island but she had done her best. Rosie thought the story of how her aunt had put to sea with two fishermen she had never set eyes on before an absolute gem.

'Mum's got something to tell you,' she had blurted out last night.

'Oh, and what's that? Nice or nasty?'

'Mum made me promise not to tell you, but you'll be very surprised.' Rosie grinned impishly. 'She said we're all going to eat at the pub tomorrow night and that's when she's going to tell you.'

Several times during the day Joan had looked up to see Rosie gazing at her, and she couldn't help wondering what it was that her niece and her sister knew and as yet she did not.

That evening at seven o'clock, Joan was being hugged tightly by both Annie and Les Jackson, while several of the customers were shouting, 'Welcome home, Joan.'

'You'd think I'd been away for months instead of a couple of weeks,' Joan murmured as she found herself staring at a table laid for twelve people. After so many enthusiastic greetings she was flustered as she took her seat and looked at all the smiling faces. Rosie, Freda and Jim, Martha and Sid with Lenny and Bernie. Lenny had brought his fiancée, Janet Marshal, while Bernie had a gorgeous-looking girlfriend with him whom he introduced by merely saying, 'Aunt Joan, this is Linda.' And of course a celebration meal

358

at the Prince would not be complete without those two dear gentlemen, Jeff and Mark.

When the first course of thick vegetable soup served with hunks of crusty bread had been eaten and the plates cleared away, there was no shortage of conversation while they waited for the main course. Jeff and Mark started the men off on the topic of football, while Rosie was engrossed in telling Freda that she and Jody would be going to Tooting Bec Common tomorrow hoping to find some holly that had plenty of red berries. They also intended to gather some long strands of dark green ivy from the wall that ran the length of the avenue, because Joan had promised that come Monday morning they could start to decorate the shop.

Martha was sitting on Joan's right-hand side. Leaning nearer, she whispered to her sister, 'What d'yer make of our Bernie's girlfriend?'

'She's lovely,' Joan answered, looking down the length of the table to where her two nephews and their girlfriends were sitting. 'How long has Bernie been taking her out?'

'Your guess is as good as mine. He's only been bringing her to our house for about the last six weeks.'

'Rosie said you had something to tell me. Is this it? Bernie and his lady friend?'

'Our Rosie's mouth will get her into trouble one of these days.' Martha grinned. 'Sid always said she had eyes and ears out the back of her 'ead. While you were away Rosie popped over to see us on her 'alf-day and she listened in to me an' her dad having a conversation that 'ad nothing t' do with 'er. Still, it will be common knowledge soon. I'll tell you the whole story later on.' For the moment Joan had to be content with that because the main course was being placed in front of everybody.

It was well turned nine by the time all twelve of them left the dining area and retreated to the saloon bar.

Everything here was much the same as Joan remembered it. The Ally Looya Lassies were still wandering amongst the crowd selling copies of *War Cry*. The men managed to find an empty table and gathered enough chairs to allow the women to sit down. Martha looked across to where her husband was leaning against the bar, with both his sons and Mark and Jeff.

'Funny, ain't it?' Martha remarked.

'What is?' Joan looked puzzled.

'To see my old man out with our boys is great, but the fact that he would stand up to anyone and state that Mark and Jeff were two of his best mates, even part of our family if yer like, still wants some getting used to.'

'Why, Martha? Are you saying because Mark and Jeff live together men like your Sid shouldn't give them the time of day?'

'Course not, love. Didn't mean nothing of the sort. Sorry if it came out all wrong. But be 'onest, luv, before you opened your shop 'ere in Brixton, you wouldn't have seen that lot socialising, now would yer?'

Joan could hardly stifle her laughter, and to make matters worse, dead on the stroke of ten, the double doors swung open and there, in all her finery, stood Lulu.

Seeing Joan, she made a beeline for their table, said good evening to Freda, Janet and Rosie and nodded her head towards Linda, before embracing Joan and telling her it seemed that she had been away for ages.

'That young lady is Linda, my Bernie's friend,' Martha explained, and Lulu held out her hand and said graciously, 'I'm very pleased to meet you, Linda.'

Joan felt uncomfortable. Martha and even Bernie only referred to the girl as Linda, no surname. That in itself wasn't strange, but the fact that Martha had said she would tell her the whole story later was puzzling.

Jeff and Mark came over with refill drinks for the women

and a fresh double whisky and a bottle of ginger ale for Lulu. Placing all the glasses down on the table, the two men in turn bent low and placed a kiss on Lulu's cheek. Joan felt very tempted to say to her sister, how about that, then? Before I lived in Brixton you would have huffed and puffed at such goings-on. Instead she reminded herself that it was a big world and everyone must live their life as they saw fit.

Les Jackson called time dead on eleven, but by the time all the goodbyes were said and they had walked home, seeing Freda safely inside her house on the way, it was closer to midnight. The youngsters went their own way, but Sid and Martha decided to stay the night with Joan and Rosie.

On Sunday morning Sid did the honours by bringing a cup of tea to Martha in bed and to Joan where she was snuggled on the big old sofa in the living room. They agreed to let Rosie sleep late, as she was up early all the other days of the week. It was a companionable breakfast, Martha and Joan settling for toast and marmalade but Sid asking for his normal Sunday morning fry-up.

'And make it two eggs, please,' he called to Joan.

The morning was great. Sid took himself off to buy shellfish for their tea – or so he said, but as the shrimps, winkles and prawns were sold from a stall set up on the forecourt of the Prince of Wales it was a dead cert that he would be having a pint or two. The sisters didn't mind one bit. By the time Jody arrived to go to the common, Rosie was up and dressed and the girls left with a warning ringing in their ears that dinner would be on the table by half-past two. Most women had found from experience that there was no point in being ready any earlier because the pubs didn't close until two.

Martha was peeling the parsnips while Joan did the

sprouts. A nice rib of beef on the bone was slowly roasting in the oven and a huge bowl of batter, into which Martha had beaten four eggs, sat on the draining board. 'Before I start on the carrots, d'you fancy a cuppa?' Joan asked.

'Yeah, why not? By the way, how many are you expecting for dinner?'

'Don't know exactly. Freda and Jim were only too pleased to accept – well, it's natural, isn't it? They both live on their own. Doesn't matter if we do too much veg. Rosie and I can always have bubble and squeak tomorrow.'

'Are Jeff an' Mark coming?'

'Well, if they meet up with your Sid he's bound to bring them back with him. I never mind them coming, though. They are so generous in so many ways.'

'Sit down and take the weight off yer feet,' Martha ordered as Joan set two steaming cups of tea down on the table.

Joan did as she was told. She took a couple of sips of her tea, set the cup back down on the saucer, looked Martha straight in the eye and said, 'Don't you think it's about time you brought me up to date with what is going on with your Bernie and that new girlfriend of his?'

'I thought you might have worked it out for yourself by now.' Martha looked serious.

'Well, I haven't, so why all the mystery?'

'Doesn't the name Linda ring any bells?'

Joan thought hard for a moment and then she felt the colour drain from her cheeks. No! It couldn't be! But she still had to ask. 'The only Linda I've ever known was Nellie Bradshaw's granddaughter.'

'You've hit the nail right on the head.' Martha knew she didn't have to say any more.

'She really is Linda Bradshaw?'

Martha sighed. 'Well, what her real surname is now no one knows. Nellie Bradshaw brought her up and she took her gran's name right from the day that her mother died and her father rejected her.'

'How come I never recognised her?' Joan murmured thoughtfully.

'None of us did first off,' Martha reassured her. 'She's certainly altered her looks and dyed her hair, and she can't have been much more than a slip of a girl when she used to come round to your place and sit with Granny Baldwin.'

Joan was well and truly upset by now. She looked at her sister and there was a plea in her voice as she asked, 'Has there been any mention of the little boy?'

'Not that me or my Sid have heard, an' Bernie hasn't brought the subject up. Suppose he must remember what 'appened, but my Sid warned me not to poke me nose in or to ask any questions.'

'I dare say he's right. Your Sid usually is. From what I recall Linda tried hard to bring that baby up by herself in the beginning. Then she met a fella who wanted to marry her but the baby was another matter altogether. I think the man came from New Zealand. He's supposed to have told Linda that if she'd put the baby up for adoption he would take her home with him and that they would get married out there.

'Sounds all cut an' dried but I'd bet my last shilling things didn't work out so well for Linda. She wouldn't be back in London if life in New Zealand had been good. Is she staying with her grandparents?'

Martha crossed her arms over her chest and heaved her bosom up. 'So our Bernie said.'

'How old is she?'

'I should think you'd know better than me. About the same age as our Bernie, I would guess.'

'All I know is she was sixteen when she found out she was pregnant and she disappeared soon after to save her grandparents having to face the shame. That's a few years ago.'

'Did you know about it at the time?' Martha asked quietly.

'No, I didn't.' Joan sighed heavily, she hated the past being dragged up again. She took a deep breath before she raised her head and looked at her sister. 'Two years had gone by before Nellie Bradshaw felt she wanted me to know that her grandaughter had had a baby and that my husband had been the father of that child. If you work it out, my Bill was dead and buried before Linda left the neighbourhood so I suppose at the time they didn't see any point in bringing it all out in the open.'

'I remember now. You were working down in Kent, had worked all over the Christmas, and that Mrs Hamilton had let you come home for the New Year. You were staying with Sid and me when Nellie Bradshaw asked to see you. Christ, it gives me the shivers still to this day the way you looked when you came back and said she'd told you about your Bill making 'er Linda pregnant.'

'Could we please change the subject,' Joan begged. 'What good will it do raking over the coals after all this time?'

'No good whatsoever, I shouldn't think, but the truth is the girl has turned up again like a bad penny.' Martha leant across the table and took her sister's hand between both of her own. 'Seems t' me it's nobody's business except my Bernie's. If Linda has told him, well, he's a grown man and she's not a slip of a girl any longer so they can make their own decisions.'

In spite of wanting to change the subject Joan heard herself saying, 'Can't help wondering what became of the little boy.'

'Well stop wondering, luv. Be best all round if everybody were to let sleeping dogs lie.'

Joan was well aware that that was good advice, but . . .

Martha struggled to her feet. 'Come on, let's get a move on. The vegetables won't cook themselves.'

Joan did as she was bid, but her mind was telling her that none of them had heard the end of this story.

Not by a long chalk they hadn't.

Chapter Forty-one

IT WAS CHRISTMAS EVE, and the run-up had been exciting. Folk had money in their pockets because almost every pub in England ran a weekly money club which paid out two weeks before 25th December. Even so, the trade they were doing in Distinctive Designs was unbelievable and everything was going well until the moment when Joan looked up and saw Eric Roussel standing at the back of the shop. In one hand he was clutching a dozen red roses and in the other was the largest box of chocolates she had ever seen. His grin, as he watched her, spread from ear to ear. Joan told herself she wouldn't be human if she didn't feel a flash of excitement.

But today of all days, his turning up was a nightmare!

Still, she had to admit he looked superb. His taste in clothes was extraordinary, even if it was a little daring. His navy blue overcoat had a velvet collar of rich burgundy. Unbuttoned, it allowed the observer a glimpse of his dark grey single-breasted suit, worn with a crisp white shirt as always, complemented today by a silk tie the exact shade of burgundy as the collar of his overcoat. His iron-grey hair had been smoothed back, probably with brilliantine, because it had a habit of curling round his ears and Eric did not take kindly to being teased because of his curly hair. Handsome, clean cut and smart, he certainly stood out in any crowd.

Joan finished serving her customer, wished her a Merry Christmas and gave her a prettily wrapped parcel which contained a tablet of Yardley's lavender toilet soap.

'Oh, thank you, Mrs Baldwin, how kind of you,' the customer murmured.

'Just a little show of appreciation to our customers.' Joan beamed in reply. Then, coming round from behind the counter, she walked to where Eric stood, still smiling. 'Not today, Eric, please,' she whispered. 'You can see how busy we are.'

Eric lowered his head until his face was level with her own. 'Ten minutes, please, my darling?'

'No. I cannot spare the time.' Joan was trying to sound cross but really she was thinking how romantic he was. Unreliable but certainly romantic.

'Sorry, but it is extremely important. I cannot move from here until you have listened to what I have to say.'

'No, Eric. Go away,' Joan said as firmly as she could. But by the time she had again taken up her station behind the counter, Eric had placed the flowers and chocolates on a shelf and was lighting a small cigar. Oh no, Joan thought to herself. Those cigars had such a strong smell.

Eric took the cigar from his mouth and held up the five fingers of his other hand, mouthing, 'Five, I promise.'

His air of assurance didn't help. Sighing heavily, she called to Jody, 'I am going upstairs for ten minutes.' She knew whatever he had to say wouldn't be said in five. Eric picked up the roses and the chocolates, winked at Jody, and followed Joan towards the stairs.

Inside her front room they stood facing each other and suddenly they were both laughing. Joan tried to string words together but before she could get them out she was in Eric's arms and his lips were gently kissing hers. 'Oh, darling, I have missed you,' he whispered softly.

She almost said, me too, but stopped short and changed it to, 'Not enough to pick up the telephone.'

'To hear your voice and not to be able to reach out and touch you would have been too much to bear,' he murmured, his lips against her ear.

Reluctantly, Joan wriggled free from his arms. 'You really lay it on with a trowel. Now honestly, Eric, glad as I am to see you, today is *not* a good time.'

'All right.' He held up both hands in a gesture of surrender. 'I'll say what I have to say as quickly as possible.' His hand delved into his inside pocket and drew out two envelopes. 'All arranged and paid for, and as promised we shall see the New Year in together in Malta.'

You could have knocked Joan down with a feather. She didn't believe she was hearing right.

Her face did not leave Eric in any doubt. She would need some convincing before she agreed to go with him. So, smooth talker that he was, he vowed he would persuade her. 'Joan, my love, you will have all of the Christmas holiday period with your family. I do so want to see the New Year in with mine.'

'Nobody is stopping you. Go for Christmas and stay on.' Joan's short and sweet solution did not please Eric at all.

'We told my family we would be back for the New Year.'

'No, *you* told them. I did not promise anything.'

'Joan, my dear, you should be there. I want you there. It will only be a short visit and I promise there will be no business taking up my time. Last time, I admit, there were several matters that required my attention. Places I just had to go to. But this time it will be different, this time will be for *us*.' Judging by the softer look on Joan's face he thought she might be wavering, so he pressed home his advantage.

'Please come with me, Joan. We will stay at a first-class hotel, and have great celebrations with all of my family. It will be a joyous time that would not be the same if you weren't with me.'

Changing tack again, he took Joan into his arms, kissed the top of her head, then her forehead, then the tip of her nose, and finally placed his lips hard over hers. He was getting reckless, allowing himself to fondle her breasts, which were still high and firm. He could feel her gently rounded thighs and still flat stomach as he held her in his arms. When he did loosen his hold he was asking himself why he had ever let her go. Why hadn't he left her in Malta? Come to London, settled his affairs and then gone back to her.

It was astonishing how much this woman had affected him. He had made such plans since he had met Joan. To lose her now did not bear thinking about. One last try, he decided.

'Surely, my darling, after all we have come to mean to each other I deserve to have you to myself for this short time?'

Joan sighed softly. His hands running over her body had brought back to life the memory of the nights she had lain in bed with this handsome man. No one had ever said such sweet things to her. She hadn't known that lovemaking could be as thrilling for a woman as it was for a man. Eric had shown her a whole new way of life. Treated her as if she was someone very special. She raised her head until she could look directly into his eyes. If she were to refuse him now she might never get another chance. Could she refuse him?

Eric knew she was wavering but he was an old hand at this game. He sighed heavily before saying, 'I understand, Joan. I have taken too much for granted. Of course you want to see the New Year in with your own folk, but I had to try. Better go now and let you get back to your business, busiest day of the year and all that.' He kissed her gently. 'Happy Christmas, my darling. I shall be thinking of you every minute.' Pulling his gloves from the pocket of his overcoat, he turned to go.

'Eric.' Joan put out a hand and touched his arm. 'I am really sorry. It isn't that I don't want to come with you, but you have sprung this on me. You've given me no time to make arrangements. You say we would only stay a short time, but with the journey both ways I doubt we would be back in time for the January sales.'

Inwardly Eric was smiling, but he sighed again, softly this time. 'I'm not only thoughtless, I am selfish. Let me ask you to do one thing. During the day, will you give the matter some thought? Talk it over with your staff if you get the chance – or even ask them to stay behind for a few minutes after you close the shop. Ask them if they think they could cope again without you. I'll phone you, but not until about nine o'clock, and if you still feel you have to turn me down . . .' He shrugged his shoulders, turned again, and this time he left her.

Joan was thankful that for the rest of the day she didn't have much time to dwell on Eric's plans. The thought of returning to that lovely island and being with him again, this time staying in a real hotel, was never far from her mind, but customers came non-stop. The atmosphere was festive. Each one received a small gift and the regulars were offered a hot mince pie and a glass of sherry.

It was six thirty by the time the shop had closed and Martha and Sid had arrived – because where else would all of them spend the evening of Christmas Eve if not in the Prince of Wales? Not that they would be getting there until about nine thirty, but Les had applied for an extension of his licence which allowed him to remain open until midnight.

The team that Joan employed as machinists were so good.

She only had to give them sketches, explain in detail such points as seam length and trimmings and her women got on with the job. They had not worked today or yesterday. Joan had given them their wages plus a bonus two days ago, together with a present from her to each of them. She knew she could rely on them to help Freda at the start of the January sales should she decide to go with Eric.

For the rest of the staff, a few friends and her family she had arranged a small party in her flat upstairs. She stood in the middle of her front room and looked around her with a smile of satisfaction. Eric had not even remarked on the decorations, though Rosie and Jody had done a good job, with no small amount of help from Jim Taylor. Everything looked beautiful, she decided. And the food, which had been sent in by the local delicatessen, looked marvellous.

Martin and Marjorie Goldsmith arrived hot on the heels of Martha and Sid, bringing Teddy Tyler with them. He still looked and acted larger than life and still would not answer to the name of Edward. Jim had asked if his work mate Doug Morgan might be invited and Joan had not hesitated, well aware that she owed quite a lot in her lovely home to the generosity of Doug. A ring at the bell sent Jim down to open the door and she heard the voices of two of her favourite friends, Jeff and Mark. Since Lenny and Bernie had other plans – although they would be in the Prince with Janet and Linda at about half-past ten – the party was therefore complete.

When everyone's plate was full, Joan paused in offering food and stood for a moment staring into the fire. She had a problem. She had put it to the back of her mind all day but now she had to deal with it. She badly wanted to discuss Eric and his plans with her sister and her husband, but also with Freda because if – and it was still only an *if*, she told herself – she were to take up Eric's offer it would mean asking Freda if she would mind taking charge of the business

371

and the staff once again. She also felt that were she to ask Freda she would have to be truthful and warn her that she wouldn't be here for the start of the January sales, which were a great opportunity to clear out old stock and make way for the spring collection. But how could she get those three people on their own?

It was Jim, without knowing it, who came to her rescue. 'Listen up, folks,' he called, then having waited a few minutes to get everyone's attention he said, 'Taxi cabs are at a premium tonight. I've done the best I can and got two for eight o'clock, but I couldn't book another until nine thirty. Sorry to split the party up, but . . .'

'No, no, Jim, don't apologise. We should have booked cabs days ago,' Joan interrupted him. 'Sort out how many you can take. I'll stay behind; it'll give me a chance to tidy up.'

The gods were on Joan's side. 'I'll stay with you,' Martha offered.

'I better stay as well,' Sid said, 'otherwise I'll only 'ave Martha on at me the whole 'oliday about how I went off an' left 'er.'

'Won't hurt me to stay here awhile either, put me feet up,' Freda said.

'I have to be off anyway,' Teddy announced. 'I've a lady friend I promised to see at eight o'clock.'

'Running true to form, eh, Teddy?' Marjorie teased him.

Martin was doing a head count. 'I make that thirteen of us here, minus Teddy leaves twelve, four have offered to stay behind and wait for the later cab, that leaves eight. What do you reckon, Jim, eight of us all right in two cabs?'

'Fine, if everyone is happy.'

Joan was not only happy, she was really relieved.

It was an uncanny silence that reigned while the three women covered what food was left, carried china out into the kitchen and picked up bits and pieces from the floor.

Sid busied himself with the dirty glasses, putting tops on wine and spirit bottles, and throwing away the empty beer bottles. Martha knew her sister too well not to be aware that there was something bothering her, and after a while she just blurted out, 'Right, that's about it. Come on, let's all sit down an' Joan can tell us what is on her mind.' She stared straight at her sister and added, 'If you tell me there's nothing going on in that 'ead of yours I'll eat my ruddy hat.'

'All right, all right.' Joan smiled. 'Eric came to see me this morning.'

Freda laughed. 'I didn't need any telling it was down to him. I saw you both go upstairs and then come down. You weren't up there long.'

Joan looked to her brother-in-law for help. There had always been a close bond between them. Even when she was married to Bill Baldwin, Sid had always known when things got out of hand and he and his two boys had always rushed to help her. It was no different now. 'Come on, luv, get it off yer chest,' he ordered.

So, as accurately as she could remember, Joan set out the facts of what Eric had said. She had hardly finished speaking before Martha was loudly offering advice.

'For Christ's sake stop dithering an' make up yer mind. Go with the bloke. He treated yer all right last time, didn't he?'

Joan nodded her head.

'Well, answer me this. How many times has Lady Luck knocked on your door, Joan? I know you and Eric are not man and wife, but according to my Sid you never will be 'cos that man ain't the marrying kind.'

Joan turned her head to glance at Sid, who looked sheepishly down at his feet. They must have been discussing me quite a lot, Joan thought, and that surprised her. Martha and Sid never interfered. For one thing, Sid never had a lot to say, really. Over the years she had come to believe they were a wise and well-matched couple.

'Sid, why do you say Eric is not the type to get married?' she asked quietly.

'Oh my Gawd, do you really have to ask that question?' Sid sounded dismayed. 'How old is he? Fifteen, sixteen years older than you are. OK, he sounds a nice enough fella and from all accounts he's worn bloody well but you're not going t' tell me you're the first woman in his life.' Shaking his head, Sid muttered, 'Not by any means.'

'I'm not that daft,' Joan retorted, sounding unusually angry. 'Anyone only has to look at him to tell he's a lady's man, probably always has been, but he treats me well.'

'It's your life,' Sid answered abruptly. Then he half smiled. 'I'll always be here to soften the blow, you know that.'

Joan felt sorry for having snapped at Sid. As he said, no matter what, she could always rely on his being there for her.

'Opportunities such as this hardly ever come along. Certainly not twice, take it from me.' Freda brought herself quietly into the conversation. Receiving no answer, she felt it was all right to carry on. 'Just watching the two of you it is easy to tell that Eric adores you, Joan. I'll give you my advice, even though you haven't asked for it. Go back to Malta, see the New Year in. You work so hard. Live a little for a change.'

'Damned good advice,' Martha muttered.

'But Freda, it would mean I wouldn't be back for the January sales. It doesn't seem fair to go off again and leave everything to you.'

'Did I do so badly last time?'

'No, of course you didn't. You managed extremely well.'

'And you paid me a good bonus. Now listen, Joan, things between you and me cut both ways. I love to work, especially doing something for which I have been well trained. Up west, the big stores don't want to know me any more. I'm too old. I was grateful when you took me on and I still am.

374

You treat me as if I were family and that means a lot when one lives on one's own.'

'There you are then, one problem solved.' Martha couldn't keep quiet any longer. 'Joan, grab at the chance, go back to Malta, but just don't look at that man through rose-coloured glasses. From what you've told us I'd bet that underneath all that gloss and charm he's as deep as the ocean. In the short time that you've known him, luv, how many times 'as he disappeared? Not turned up when he promised he would? And more to the point, what does he get up to?'

'I know all that,' Joan admitted. 'But . . .'

'I know, luv, you've never been treated so well in yer life. He makes yer feel good and there's nothing wrong with that. Gawd above knows there ain't been a lot of spoiling in your life. Work from the day you left school – before that, even, because you were only seven when our dad died. I remember when our mum used t' take you with 'er up to the big 'ouses and if she were doing the washing you 'ad to turn the 'andle of the mangle while Mum fed the sheets an' things through the rollers. Eric has come late in yer life, 'cos let's face it, you ain't no spring chicken yerself, so that's all the more reason you should grab every minute of 'appiness he offers you.'

'Even if you really got to know Eric, you wouldn't like him, would you, Martha?' Joan shot the question to her sister.

Martha hesitated. 'Probably be hard not to, but . . .'

'Go on, please.'

'You want it straight?'

'Course I do, Martha. Don't I always come to you with my problems?'

'Right. Well, there has t' be another side to that man.'

'You think so?'

'Yes, I do. So do you, Sid, don't you?'

'Have t' say yes, Joan. I don't think you've scratched the surface of that man. I'd go so far as to say he's more than likely been involved in more dodgy deals than you, my girl, 'ave 'ad hot dinners.' That was a long speech for Sid.

Suddenly, Joan burst out laughing. In no time at all, all four of them were holding their sides. When they'd settled down, Joan spoke again.

'Sid, both you and my sister are something else. One minute you're telling me to live life to the full with Eric, and in the next breath you're telling me he is more than likely an out and out scoundrel.'

Martha grinned widely. 'Joan, remember there was a time when you said you envied me, married to a safe, secure, reliable man like my Sid. Well, my luv, I'm only human and while I do know how lucky I am and I wouldn't change Sid and our family for the world, that doesn't stop me from envying you some days. What woman wouldn't? This Eric, be what he may, 'as given you a great time: sea voyages, a chance to visit a foreign country. I'm telling you, luv, make the most of it while it lasts.' To herself Martha was saying, as sure as eggs are eggs it won't last, but that was all the more reason why her sister should go back to Malta. See the New Year in with gusto. At least when the bubble did burst she'd have some good memories to look back on.

Sid had had enough. He got to his feet. 'Nearly time that cab was 'ere. We're wasting good drinking time sitting around here.'

When the phone rang everybody looked at Joan and grinned as she left the room to answer it. She was only gone a short while. All three pairs of eyes were on her as she came back and stood in the doorway.

Eyebrows raised, it was Sid who asked the vital question. 'Well, are you going with him or not?'

Joan felt like a small child as she said, 'Yes, I am going

to Malta on the day after Boxing Day. Eric is picking me up here at three o'clock in the afternoon.'

'Good, that's settled at last,' Sid blustered, and grinned at his wife.

Martha, standing well behind her sister, held up two fingers which were tightly crossed. Freda, smiling, nodded her agreement. To her way of thinking Joan was doing the right thing, at least she hoped that was true anyway.

Chapter Forty-two

AT SEVEN THIRTY on Boxing Day morning Joan came downstairs in Martha's house to find her sister already unlocking the front door to bring the milk in. They smiled at each other as they went through to the kitchen, where Joan opened the window a chink to let the fresh air in and the smell of food and drink out. 'Some Christmas, eh?' she groaned, putting her hand to her forehead.

'One to remember I'd say.' Martha grinned. 'And the weather is running true to form. It always seems to save the worst until Christmas Day has come an' gone.'

'It looks great out there,' Joan said, 'though I think snow would have been better than this heavy frost. Look at the icicles hanging from the gutters of the houses opposite.'

'Too cold for snow, though it won't be many days off. You put the kettle on, Joan, an' I'll get the fire going. You an' me will 'ave a cup of tea on our own before we disturb the others.' Martha suddenly stopped talking and gave her sister a queer look.

'Something wrong?' Joan asked.

'Only that I haven't got a clue who slept in this house last night.'

378

Joan laughed. 'Well, I can tell you that neither Lenny nor Bernie did. They went off with their lady friends.'

'Well, folk were in an' out of here all day yesterday and during the evening I thought the walls of my front room were going to burst. I do remember you going out to the scullery with Linda Bradshaw and when you came back you were a lot quieter all of a sudden. Did she say anything to upset you?'

Joan shivered, glad that her sister was down on her knees holding a lighted quill to the newspaper and wood that she had arranged on top of the ashes in the grate.

'Well did she?' Martha turned her head to look up at Joan as she repeated the question.

'Not really,' Joan muttered.

'Oh for Christ's sake, Joan, either she did or she didn't.'

'Well, if you must know she asked me to pop over this morning and have a word with her and her grandma.'

'But her grandparents were both 'ere last night. Why didn't they say whatever it was they wanted to say to you then?'

'Suppose they didn't think it was the right time. Anyway, I couldn't have heard what they were saying. Most of the time we were all singing.'

'That were Jim Taylor's fault. As soon as one carol was finished he led us all into another one. Gotta say, though, Jim's got a ruddy good voice and it wasn't the beer egging him on because he didn't drink 'alf as much as my lads did.'

'I think a good time was had by one and all. But now, sister dear, are you going to stay on your knees all day, 'cos if you are all I can say is you are not as badly in need of this cup of tea as I am.' With that, Joan plumped herself down at the table and gratefully began to sip from one of the teacups she had filled from the big brown pot. It took a while for Martha to get back on her feet.

'Too much Christmas pudding,' she moaned.

'Washed down with too many glasses of port, you mean.'

'Hey you, you didn't do so badly yourself.'

'No, nobody did. Thanks to you, Martha, a lot of people had a great Christmas. Jim said it were the best Christmas he had spent since his wife walked out on him.'

'It wasn't all down t' me by a long chalk. We all did our bit. Anyway, are you going to go over to see Nellie Bradshaw?'

'Doesn't seem like I've got much choice. But it won't be for a while yet; got to get my head clear first.'

'How about a nice fry-up?'

'Oh, Martha, don't be so wicked.' Joan made a horrible face. 'Piece of dry toast is about all I'll be able to manage.'

'You and everyone else right now, but come midday an' they'll all be here for cold turkey, ham, bubble an' squeak and pickles. You'll see.' Martha drained her cup and pushing it towards her sister said, 'Be a dear an' pour me another one.' She went to the range and opened the vent to stop the heat from going up the chimney before putting another shovelful of coal on to the glowing embers. 'There. That's all set for the time being and for once in my life I'm gonna put me feet up and have a lazy day.'

By ten thirty Joan was getting edgy. Better go and get it over and done with, she told herself. In the passageway, she took her thick coat down from its peg and pulled it on, then slung a woollen scarf round her neck, tugged her velour hat down tight over her ears and stepped into her ankle-length boots. She went back into the kitchen and picked up the pair of fur-lined gloves that Rosie had bought her for Christmas. Sid, Martha and Freda were in the front room, where Sid had got a log fire roaring away. She popped her head round the door. 'Won't be too long. 'Bye.'

Making sure that she had closed the front door tight Joan walked down the front path and into the cold, frosty biting wind of the December morning. All the time, as she walked, she couldn't help but wonder just what it was that Linda and her grandmother had to say to her. She was in no doubt that the one subject she had fought so hard to erase from her memory would be the main topic of the conversation. No doubt whatsoever.

Nellie Bradshaw opened the front door in answer to her knock. 'Come in, Joan, you're more than welcome. Everyone had a great time over at your sister's house last night, didn't they? Found it slippery walking round here, did you? Ice everywhere, isn't there? Would you like some hot ginger wine or a glass of port or maybe just a cup of tea and a piece of me Christmas cake? I did make it myself.'

God! The woman hardly stopped talking long enough to draw breath.

'Please, Mrs Bradshaw, I don't need anything. I'm fine. Is Linda in?'

'Yes.' She seemed to have run out of steam at last.

'Well, please may we get down to what it is you want to talk to me about?'

'All right.' The old lady sighed heavily and led the way into her front room.

Not much had changed since Joan was last here. Everything was spotlessly clean, there were antimacassars in place on the back of each armchair, family photographs stood on the sideboard and the brass fire irons had been polished until they shone.

Linda had her legs curled up under her as she sat on the sofa, but as soon as Joan walked into the room she came to her feet. 'Hello, Mrs Baldwin. I hope you didn't mind me asking you to call round here, did you?'

'Rather depends on what you want to talk to me about, Linda,' Joan answered, sitting down in the chair that Mrs Bradshaw had drawn up opposite the sofa.

When all three of them were settled, Linda's grandmother

said, 'Well, if she has as much to say to you as she has to her grandfather and myself, you won't be here for long, Joan.'

'Gran, I'm sorry, I really am. You and Pops have made me so welcome since I've been back and I know it's quite a few months now and I still haven't told you where I've been or what I've done. To begin with I didn't seem able to get up the nerve to spill it all out, and then I met Bernie and after he'd taken me out a few times I realised that he was Mrs Baldwin's nephew. I couldn't face meeting her or Bernie's mother at first. I thought it would be bound to cause trouble, be like opening up a can of old worms.'

Joan was intrigued. 'Why did you want me to be present when you spoke to your gran?'

'I thought I owed you that much. Bit late in the day, I know, but better we talked head on than you heard a load of the rumours that have naturally been flying around amongst the neighbours since I turned up.'

'All right.' Her gran spoke up. 'Whatever you have to say, Linda, won't alter my feelings for you one little bit. It was an answer to my prayers when you walked through that door. I'd almost come to accept the fact that I would die before I set eyes on you again.'

Linda was on her feet like a shot, kneeling down in front of her gran, clutching hold of both of her hands. 'You were the one person I never wanted to hurt. The only reason I went away was because Pops was laying the blame on you for me being pregnant. That and all the shame, it wasn't fair. Besides, you had done your duty and more. When my mother died giving birth to me you took me on. I've always thought of you as my mother, not as my gran. I couldn't ask you to take on my illegitimate baby and start all over again.'

The silence was heavy, each of them reluctant to break it. Joan was first. 'I still can't work out why you want me to be here,' she said, looking Linda straight in the face.

Linda sighed, got up from the floor and sat on the sofa again. 'I want to apologise, Mrs Baldwin. For ever having listened to the smooth talking that your husband was capable of dishing out. For using make-up as soon as I was out of this house. For wearing tarty clothes so as to catch Bill's eye. He was a very good-looking man, a man of the world to a starry-eyed fourteen-year-old girl, 'cos that was what I was when he first started buying me sweets and taking me to the pictures. He even took me to see the dog racing, which made me feel really grown up.' She hesitated. 'I know I'm making feeble excuses. The truth is I have met Bernie, about the only straight guy I've had anything to do with in my life, and things started to get serious between us before I found out that he was related to you. He has to be told that my baby was fathered by your husband. That is not something I feel proud about. I've done nothing but put off the day when it will all have to be brought out into the open.'

Nellie Bradshaw was wiping a tear from her eye as she turned to her granddaughter. 'Linda, do you remember the day you asked me to meet you in London?'

'Course I do, Gran. That's when I told you I had put my baby up for adoption and was going to New Zealand.'

'To be married, you said.'

'Yes, I know. Wish I had known then what I know now.'

'Can't put old heads on young shoulders. Have you heard enough, Joan? Do you want to get going? It is still Christmas.' Nellie sighed.

'No, I'm all right for a bit.' Turning to Linda, Joan asked, 'Would you like to tell us a bit about what happened to you?'

'I'll tell you the bare bones and that is all. No good comes of raking up things I can't alter. I gave birth to a little boy, set up home with a friend, and between us we did our best. Got ourselves shift work so that someone was there with him all the time. Even had him christened. Called him David. Fine until Penny, my friend, met her fella, got married, and I was on my own again.'

A lump of coal moved in the fire sending out a few sparks, which made them all jump. They laughed, but it was a weak kind of laughter.

'Then I met a lovely young man, Tony. He offered me everything. New life in New Zealand. Marriage as soon as we got there. Only one fly in the ointment. Just as my father's new wife refused to take on me, Tony said he wanted nothing to do with another man's son.' Linda closed her eyes and choked back the lump that had risen in her throat. 'I made a decision. A bad one, as it turned out, but God knows I've paid for it. It wasn't until we arrived in New Zealand that I realised Tony wasn't prepared to share his life totally with any one person, and I don't think he ever will be. I was too young and naive to realise it at the time.'

There was a long pause before Linda started to talk again and when she did, emotions between the two that were listening were running high.

She went on to tell them about the guilt she felt for having abandoned her baby. How Tony was in danger of becoming an alcoholic and when drunk became very violent towards her. She knew no one in New Zealand, had no one to seek advice from. Quietly she admitted she herself had declined into bitterness and alcoholism. 'My life would have been finished if a Catholic priest hadn't found me slumped in a doorway. He got me into a home, found people to help me dry out and finally paid my fare home.'

There was a long silence, broken only by the soft crying of Nellie Bradshaw. Eventually, she dried her eyes and said, 'Linda, love, perhaps it would have been better if you hadn't told Joan any of this.'

'Gran, I had been back in this country for five months before I contacted you. I got myself a bed-sitting room and

384

found myself a good job, the same one I am still holding down today. The truth is I longed to see you and Pops. I was so lonely. And then you both welcomed me with open arms and neither of you asked any questions.'

'So why tell us now?' Joan felt compelled to ask.

Linda gave a wry smile. 'I met your Bernie and that wasn't on the cards.' She paused. 'I couldn't just go on seeing him without him knowing. Someday, someone might find out and tell him, and then . . . who knows.'

'Telling us won't make any difference,' her gran said. 'What's done's done, I suppose, and it was all a long time ago.'

'Linda, you're thinking of telling Bernie yourself, aren't you?' Joan asked quietly.

'I didn't want to, but if I want to go on seeing him I have to. I will tell Bernie the whole story, but, Mrs Baldwin, I think it would be better if his mother told him about the baby being fathered by your husband.'

For a moment Joan looked very uncomfortable, then she had second thoughts. Hearing the truth from his mother would give Bernie time to digest the terrible facts, allow him to let off steam or not according to how he took the news. 'All right,' she said finally. 'I can't promise that our Martha will agree, but if she does she'll tell it fair and square. There's nobody more straightforward than my sister.'

Boxing Day, or what was left of it after everyone had eaten their fill, was every bit as festive as Christmas Day had been. It was getting on for midnight before Joan got a chance to have a word on the quiet with Martha. Having listened to what her sister had to tell her, Martha simply said, 'I'll sleep on it.' And for the time being Joan had to be content with that.

She kissed her sister good night and wearily climbed the stairs to go to bed. She had just reached the top landing when she suddenly realised that it was tomorrow that she was supposed to be going back to Malta with Eric. Oh well, she'd just have to get up early, get home and get a case packed. I'll take a cab, she promised herself. Her last thought as she scrambled into bed was that her life had suddenly taken an interesting turn. She certainly could no longer describe it as humdrum.

Chapter Forty-three

JOAN HEARD THE HONK of the cab's horn just as she looked at the clock. It still wanted five minutes to three o'clock. Eric was eager today. She ran lightly down the stairs, opened the door and practically fell into Eric's arms.

He held her close and asked, 'Are you looking forward to returning to Malta?'

'Oh yes, I am, Eric. It will be lovely for us both to be able to see the New Year in with your family.'

He held her at arm's length and looked lovingly at her small face. 'I am not having the family wanting to take you here there and everywhere. This is going to be just as I promised, *our* time.' He smiled reassuringly and kissed her before asking, 'And where is your luggage?'

'I've only packed one suitcase, it's at the top of the stairs.'

'All right, you get into the cab and I'll run up and get it. Give me your keys and I'll lock the front door.'

Joan was bubbling with excitement. Then, just as she was about to step into the taxi, she happened to look at the back of the cab and to her amazement saw that two huge cabin trunks were secured to the rack. How much luggage did one require for a short stay? She couldn't say why, but her immediate thought was, Eric isn't going to come back, he's planning to stay in Malta!

'Come on, slowcoach, we don't want the ship sailing without us, do we?' Eric had come up behind her and was almost lifting her into the taxi. 'Shift along,' he said laughingly, as he first handed her case to the driver and then planted himself beside her on the long, leather-covered seat. The cab had hardly drawn away from the kerbside before Eric had her in his arms. Joan responded immediately. It felt wonderful to be held by him again. He smelt as if he had come straight from the barber's, and the soft touch of his cashmere overcoat was heavenly as she buried her face into his shoulder. What a marvellous opportunity it was, to be taken again to that lovely island. How could she have hesitated for a moment over whether or not she should accept Eric's invitation?

He suddenly grinned and winked at her. 'My darling, we are going to have the time of our lives, you'll see. Nothing but the best on this trip.'

'Have you come into a fortune then, Eric?'

'Not exactly,' he answered, still grinning, 'but I have been thinking, what's the point of having money if you don't get any pleasure from it? So I'm aiming to spend it. That's what it's for.' He placed his lips softly over hers and when he lifted his head he spoke seriously. 'I aim to buy you everything your heart desires, Joan. You have become an inspiration in my life, like a really fresh breeze blowing away the cobwebs.'

Joan regarded him soberly. Mostly when she thought of money it was in terms of the necessities of life. Having at times not known where her next shilling was going to come from she was cautious. Like most women she enjoyed having nice clothes to wear, good food and enough heat in the house, but above all those things came the bills. The bills and the rent always had to come first.

'Joan dear, don't look so serious,' Eric pleaded. 'Aren't you pleased to know that businesswise I am doing very well?'

'Yes. Yes, I am,' she said slowly. 'As long as you aren't going to squander it all.'

He threw back his head and roared with laughter, until tears were trickling out of the corners of his eyes. 'My, but you're the careful one,' he gasped. He took a handkerchief from the pocket of his coat and wiped his eyes. Then squeezing her hand tightly he murmured, 'Oh, Joan, you baffle me. If I didn't know that there are times when you can and do throw caution to the wind and become totally uninhibited, wanton even, I'd say there was no hope for you.'

'Eric!' Feeling the blood rush to her cheeks, Joan punched his shoulder and turned her face away to look out of the window. She was more than relieved when she saw the signpost directing traffic to King George V docks.

Eric leaned across the seat and showed their tickets to the cab driver, who glanced at them and said, 'That's fine, mate. I've already dropped one fare at that dock today. If I'm lucky I'll be able to pull right by their landing stage. You jump out and find yerself a porter.'

Joan just stood there, taking in the different smells from the cargoes that were being swung aboard ships to be carried to distant destinations, savouring the noise, the hustle and the bustle of this busy dock. She watched Eric walk swiftly along the quay. He looked so dapper, so well dressed. There were several ships lined up in the inner harbour and Joan couldn't help but feel how lucky she was to be making this second journey to Malta on one of them. She did have a few misgivings. It had been such a good Christmas, and now she was leaving her staff to cope with her business and Martha, Sid and their family to see the New Year in without her. On the other hand, it was Freda, Martha and even Sid who had urged her to go with Eric.

389

She smiled to herself, admitting that she hadn't needed very much persuasion.

It was quite some time before Eric came back, a hefty-looking porter walking beside him pushing an upright trolley. The cab driver undid the straps that held Eric's two trunks and with what looked like ease the porter lugged them off and placed one on top of the other on the metal trolley. Meanwhile Eric was paying the cab fare and he must have tipped well for the driver touched the tip of his cap and said, 'Gawd bless yer, sir. You an' the lady 'ave a good time.'

Then, so suddenly that it seemed to Joan that they had appeared from nowhere, two police constables and another man dressed in a heavy dark overcoat came up to her and Eric.

'PC Christie,' one of the uniformed bobbies said as he laid a hand on Eric's arm.

PC Harris, the other constable, identified himself, looked at the crowd of onlookers that had gathered, and bellowed, 'All right, all right, there's nothing to see, so move on, please.'

The plain-clothes officer produced his warrant card. 'DI Mitchell.'

Eric looked grave-faced and muttered aggressively, 'Fucking hell.'

Joan couldn't believe that Eric had said that. She watched him close his eyes, doing his damnedest to control his temper.

'Going on a cruise, were you, Roussel?' DI Mitchell said snidely.

Joan stood rooted to the spot, her legs shaking. She was suddenly freezing cold; the icy temperature of the concrete she was standing on was penetrating right through the soles of her boots. She heard the inspector speaking to Eric but his voice seemed to be coming from a long way away. Suddenly he turned to her. 'Afraid you won't be going on any sea voyage today, ma'am. At least not with this gentleman.' He smiled slowly. 'Though I suppose there is nothing to stop you going on your own if you wish.' Swinging back to Eric, he said, 'You must have been barmy, Roussel, if you really thought you could get away with it. Anyhow, you'll have plenty of time down at the station to tell us what your plans were.'

Eric was ignoring him. He was trying frantically to make Joan understand that she should leave. PC Christie intervened. 'Your luggage hasn't been taken on board, ma'am. I suggest you take your case and go back home. Shame you got caught up with this . . .' He glimpsed the stern look on the detective inspector's face and let the end of the sentence remain unsaid.

PC Harris was worried. Every bit of colour had drained from Joan's face and she wasn't at all steady on her pins. He put out a hand towards her and asked, 'Are you sure you can handle this?'

She swayed a little but managed to answer him quite forcefully. 'Doesn't look as if I've got much choice, does it?'

'My trunks have been taken aboard.' Eric drew himself up to his full height as he protested, but the inspector's voice was like thunder as he answered.

'Well, *sir*, you won't be following them.' Then, with a smirk, he added, 'It's a dead cert you won't need all those fine clothes where you're likely to be going.'

Deliberately, Eric took a packet of his small cigars from his overcoat pocket, extracted one, placed it between his lips, set a match to it and inhaled deeply. 'Stop making assumptions, Inspector, and try acting like a gentleman. Call a cab for Mrs Baldwin and allow her to return home as your constable has already suggested.' His voice was as loud and aggressive as the DI's and everyone nearby stopped what they were doing to stare openly at the group. When he turned to face Joan, however, all the fight seemed to go out of him, though he did his best to smile as he said, 'Sorry, my darling. Please go now.'

Joan picked up her case and walked stiffly to the high boundary wall, where she stood with her back against the cold stone for about twenty minutes. Not once did she look to see what was happening to Eric. Her head was going round and round and her mind was screaming, how could I have been so gullible? It isn't as if I was born yesterday.

At last, she picked up her case and began to walk again, but nearly jumped out of her skin when she felt a hand laid on her shoulder from behind. Dropping her case, she turned quickly and the relief of seeing Jim Taylor was so great that the tears that had been burning at the back of her eyelids spilled over and trickled down her cheeks.

'Oh, Jim!' She let go her case. 'You gave me such a fright . . . I thought I was being arrested!'

'Come on, Joan, we'll find a café and get you a cup of hot sweet tea. It will make you feel better. It's the best thing for shock and I'm damn sure you have had a very big one of those.'

Joan looked up at this kindly, reliable man and blinked away her tears, but all she could think of saying was, 'Jim, you know I never take sugar.'

'Never say never.' He grinned as he bent and picked up her case.

'Hey, wait a minute,' Joan protested. 'How did you get here? How did you know where to find me, and why would you have wanted to?'

'I came here in my van. The rest of your questions I will answer one at a time when we get inside the café.'

Sure enough, there was the usual café to be found in the dockland area. Christmas made not the slightest difference; ships came into dock and others put to sea on the crest of the tide. Dockers and seamen all had to be fed.

Jim led the way down an alleyway. Joan could smell cooking and she made for a doorway but was pulled back by Jim. 'Come on. The café we want is about three doors down.'

Once seated inside a steamy room where the air was still filled with the smell of frying sausages and bacon even at this time in the afternoon, Joan asked, 'What was wrong with the other tea rooms?'

'Nothing at all, Joan, but it might not have been what you were expecting. It's a Jewish café, so I suppose you could have had a pretzel and lemon tea.'

'Oh,' was all that Joan could manage.

Jim left her staring into space and soon came back with two big thick mugs filled with a strong hot brew. Watching Joan slowly sip the dark brown liquid his heart ached for her. She was so smartly dressed, but her face showed how distressed she was and her hands were shaking as she placed the mug back down on the table. In a very quiet voice he asked, 'Would you like me to answer your questions now?'

Joan didn't even look up, just stared at the table top and nodded her head.

'Right, I'll start at the beginning. When you were in Malta, the police came into the Prince of Wales and showed Les Jackson a photograph and asked if he had ever seen this man in his pub. Les shook his head, and as I was standing at the bar having a drink with Les at the time the policeman shoved the photo towards me. I shook my head too and asked what the man had done. The two officers weren't that forthcoming, but one of them did say he had been released from prison when he shouldn't have been because there was another warrant pending against him.'

There was a faraway look in Joan's eyes as she asked, 'Did you recognise the man in the photo?'

Jim pushed his lips together and nodded yes.

'Was it Eric?'

'Um, I'm afraid so. Couldn't mistake him. Last bank holiday Monday I came to ask you to come out with me

393

for the day but just as I got out of my van I saw you leaving your place with him.' It was a sad silence that followed and Jim badly wanted to take her in his arms and comfort her. He didn't, though. As always, he kept his distance.

'You haven't told me how you knew where to find me.' Joan sounded so miserable even Jim felt a lump in his throat.

'Easy. Everyone knew you were going back to Malta the day after Boxing Day and so in the course of conversation I said to your brother-in-law I wonder what docks they are going from? Sid came straight out and told me – King George the fifth London docks did the Malta run.'

'That would have been easy enough to find out from a good many places, or you could have just asked me. But why did you want to know?'

'Joan, I honestly can't tell you. Right from the minute you started seeing him, I had the feeling that he wasn't all he made himself out to be. All day yesterday I had you on my mind, and this morning . . . well, I was jealous, if you want the truth. I thought I'd just come and see you off, though if all had been well I wouldn't have thrown a spanner into the works, truly. I wouldn't have said a word.'

Joan was staring at him, disbelief written all over her face. 'You said you were jealous.'

Jim looked a bit sheepish. 'We were getting on so well, going to auctions and so on. You even wanted to make me your business partner . . .' He hesitated, then said slowly, sounding disappointed, 'It hasn't been the same since Eric came on the scene.'

'Oh, Jim, nothing will ever alter between you and me,' Joan said sincerely.

'We'll see.' That was not the way he really wanted to answer her but it would have to do for now. 'Joan,' he began again, 'I didn't get here in time to see you walk away but one of the coppers did me a favour, said he'd felt sorry for you and had watched where you went. He pointed down the docks, said you were leaning against a wall down there. I came after you as quick as I could, saw you just before you started to leave.'

Joan had both hands cupped round her mug and didn't make any comment. Jim leant across the table until his face was nearer to hers. 'Don't you want to hear what else the copper told me?'

Joan shrugged her shoulders.

'All right, I'll tell you anyway. They will be keeping Eric at Leman Street police station for questioning before taking him to be rearrested. He said if we gave them time to take him from the harbourmaster's office we could call in at the station an' maybe, only maybe, the duty officer would allow you to have a few minutes with him. Do you want to do that or shall I take you straight home?' Endless time seemed to slip by without Joan's saying a word. She sat there, both hands clasped round the warm mug. 'Only you can decide.'

'Dear Jesus, if ever I needed help, I need it now.' It was a groan rather than a request.

Recently, Jim had been of the opinion that Joan would walk over red-hot coals for Eric Roussel. Now his heart went out to her and he said, 'You're still in shock.'

Joan continued to hang her head. Reluctantly Jim knew he had to take the lead. 'We can't sit here much longer. Only you can decide what you want to do, Joan. Either walk away now and put the man out of your thoughts and out of your life, or . . .' He couldn't go on because he couldn't find an alternative to offer her. Well, not one that she would even consider at this point.

It was still some time before Joan lifted her head and looked Jim in the face. 'You shouldn't be here with me. You should be at Martha's; I know she invited you for tea tonight. She'll be worried about you.'

Jim just had to laugh. 'If your sister knew the half of

what's been going on it wouldn't be me she'd be worried about, you know darn well it would be you.'

Even Joan managed half a smile. 'I know, I know,' she said, reaching out to take hold of his hand. 'I think I want to go and see Eric. It may not be the wisest thing to do but I owe myself that much.'

Jim was stunned. 'Are you sure?'

Joan nodded. 'Yes, Jim, I'm sure.'

Inwardly Jim was cursing himself for having mentioned that there might be a chance that she'd be able to see and speak to Eric. Still, he had to accept the fact that that was what she wanted and the sooner he got her to the police station and then took her home, the better it would be for all of them.

Chapter Forty-four

'DON'T YOU WORRY about anything.' Jim took Joan's arm as they walked towards the entrance of the police station.

A siren blared out suddenly, making Joan jump, and a second police car came to a halt beside the one that was already there. Joan shuddered, suddenly aware of where she was and what she was about to do. 'Who would have thought I would get myself mixed up in something like this?' she muttered, more to herself than to Jim.

Three steps up, Jim thrust his arm out and held the big heavy oak door wide open. Once inside the front office, Joan looked to her left and saw an endless corridor with many doors leading off it. Jim tugged at her arm and led her forward to a huge desk. Standing to one side was Detective Inspector Mitchell, and Joan smiled weakly at him, glad to see a face she recognised. Behind the desk stood a lanky young constable whom Joan immediately thought must be too young to be in the police force.

Jim spoke up. 'This is Mrs Baldwin,' he said, addressing the constable. 'If possible she would like to see Mr Roussel.'

The lad was given no time to reply. DI Mitchell stepped forward. 'Are you all right, Mrs Baldwin?'

Jim had to hold his temper in check, because he was capable of telling this bloke that no, she wasn't all right. He forced himself to remain silent.

Joan didn't answer the DI's enquiry. Instead, she said, 'Please may I see Eric, just for a few minutes?'

'Yes, Mrs Baldwin, I'll take you to him myself.' He nodded his head towards Jim. 'There's a chair behind you, you'll not have a long wait.' Then, taking hold of Joan's arm, the DI gave her a sympathetic smile. 'You had a nasty shock. I am sorry if I sounded a bit brusque with you out there at the docks.' He stopped walking suddenly, swung a chain from his belt which had a large bunch of keys dangling from it, selected one and opened a door.

Joan hadn't known what to expect, but it certainly wasn't this. She looked horror-struck. It was a bare cell, with just a long narrow bench attached to the far wall, on which Eric was sitting.

The DI looked down at Joan and said quietly, 'Five minutes, no longer.' His voice held a note of pity and that was something Joan felt she could do without. She was as much to blame as Eric for this unholy mess. He had got into whatever it was from choice and, when it came down to the nitty-gritty, so had she.

Eric rose to his feet, stunned. He hadn't expected to see her, and he didn't know whether he was pleased or not. For once in his life he was at a loss to find words to say. He clasped both of Joan's hands and they sat down beside each other on the bench.

'Oh, Eric.' The backs of her eyelids were prickling with unshed tears. Like Eric, she couldn't find anything to say, but she squeezed his hands tightly. He was immaculate as ever: snow white shirt cuffs, gold links, smooth light brown skin, well-manicured nails, onyx and gold signet ring on his little finger. 'You'll never alter will you?' she said, and Eric heard the sob in her voice. He couldn't bear her to see him like this and he really was sorry to have caused her such pain. But the devilish manner that Eric Roussel always showed to the world would not lie dormant and so he began to tease her.

'A few weeks ago you wouldn't have wanted me to, would you?' Seeing her smile, he withdrew one hand from her grasp and placed his arm round her shoulders. 'Now you listen to me, my darling. You've done nothing wrong. Nothing at all. You've just lived a little. Learnt that life doesn't have to be all sweat and toil. I made you realise that there is another side to life, didn't I?'

Choking back her tears, Joan murmured, 'You certainly did that!'

'Good, well you just remember the good times and only the good ones. Nothing ever came of constantly looking backwards. Try living your own life to the full. Will you promise me that much, Joan?'

'I'll try,' she whispered. 'But what will happen to you?'

He found himself thinking he really did love this woman. If only . . . but if onlys didn't figure in his life and he had to make a joke of it all even now. 'Joan, that is not your worry. Besides, if the gods are on my side I might get transported back to Malta. Can you imagine my family? Strings would be pulled and action would be taken. Who knows, one day you might even come and visit me.'

At that moment the young constable appeared in the open doorway. My, my, he said to himself, who'd have thought it? The posh old guy had that middle-aged woman in his arms and was kissing her! Not just peck on the cheek kisses, either, but long lingering ones. *Christ, they say there's many a good tune played on an old fiddle, and this guy could certainly teach me a thing or two.*

Discreetly, he coughed. 'Time t' go, missus,' he called, feeling a rotter for breaking the parting up.

It would have been hard to tell whether Eric was more upset than Joan as they drew apart and whispered goodbye! As Joan reached the doorway she heard Eric call out, 'I will always love you, Joan.' She couldn't bring herself to turn round and look at him.

She took a few steps, then leant against the cold wall of the corridor and handkerchief to her face she sobbed. Then, pulling herself together, she made straight for where Jim had parked his van, leaving him to jump to his feet and follow her. Outside in the cold air she blew her nose and wiped her eyes. Stony silence reigned during the ride back to Brixton.

Outside Distinctive Designs Jim pulled his van up to the kerb and turned off the engine. 'Shall I come upstairs with you?' he asked, leaning forward to look at her face.

'No, I'll be fine. But Jim,' she slowly put out a hand and placed it on his arm, 'thank you for coming to my rescue. You really are a good friend.'

He got out, went round to the passenger side and almost lifted her down on to the pavement. Holding out his hand he said, 'Give me the keys. I'll unlock the door and put your suitcase at the foot of the stairs, if you're sure you will be all right.'

'Yes, I will be fine. Thank you again, Jim.'

He got back into the van and drove off, cursing himself for not being more masterful. There was so much he could have said to her and done for her. Her big rooms would be cold, and she would be there all on her own. Rosie was still at her parents' house. If nothing else, he could have lit the fire. Why hadn't he insisted he stayed with her, if only for a while?

''Cos you're a loser, Jim Taylor. You've let so many opportunities slip past you.'

He was still upbraiding himself when he pulled up outside Martha and Sid's house. All he had to do now was tell them what had happened.

It was a task he was not looking forward to one little bit.

Chapter Forty-five

THERE WAS UPROAR in Martha's house.

Jim had just given them a rundown of the afternoon's events. He could see Martha out of the corner of his eye, her mouth hanging open in shock.

Suddenly everyone was talking at once.

Why did everyone have to be at home today, Jim was asking himself. Telling Martha and Sid would have been bad enough, but now he was getting an ear-bashing from both Lenny and Bernie, and there was young Rosie, the colour quite gone from her cheeks, repeating, 'Poor Auntie Joan, poor Auntie Joan.'

'Be quiet the lot of you!' Sid bellowed. 'Jim, I can't think why you didn't tell us where you were off to. You must have had some idea that things might go wrong for our Joan.'

'Yeah, I did,' Jim was quick to reply, 'but don't tell me that none of you had the slightest idea that Roussel wasn't all he cracked himself up to be.'

Sid had the grace to look sheepish. 'You're right, lad. I'd go so far as t' say yer could lay a lot of the blame on me and Martha, 'cos we egged our Joan on to going with the bloke.'

Martha found her voice. 'Hang on a minute, we did it from the best intentions and Freda was in agreement an' all. All we wanted for our Joan was a bit of spice in her life for a change. Didn't for a moment think it would turn out the way it 'as.'

'Why didn't you bring my auntie back here?' Rosie asked in tearful voice.

'I think she wanted a bit of time on her own, Rosie, to think about things.'

'Had enough on her plate on Boxing Day when old coals were raked over.' Lenny put his twopennyworth in.

'That's enough.' Bernie turned on him. 'Linda and our aunt have agreed to put the past behind them and that's good enough for me, so leave Linda and what happened with that rotter Bill Baldwin out of this.'

Martha shook her head, utterly bewildered by all the different turns of events that had taken place over this Christmas holiday. She couldn't believe the change in her youngest son. Blessed with striking good looks, he had always yearned to do well in life, but at the same time he'd played the field where girls were concerned. Mostly it had been young blonde ladies that he'd brought home before Linda Bradshaw turned up again. Seemed serious, her and him. Ah well, it was his life. To be fair to Linda she'd only been a slip of a girl when she'd found herself pregnant, and it seemed she'd been prepared to hold on to her little boy until what she thought was love had come along. What did any of us know about love when we were only sixteen years old? By God, from all accounts, she'd paid dearly for her mistakes. If Bernie thought she was the one for him then the least they could do was give them a chance.

Jim felt he was betwixt and between when Rosie asked if they could go and visit her aunt.

'No, love,' Sid said in his blunt way, 'we'll leave 'er be for tonight. Your aunt has a lot of thinking to do. Still, there's one good thing t' come out of all this. She'll be with us for New Year's Eve.'

Jim wholeheartedly agreed with that.

Two days had passed since Jim had brought Joan home and there were still two days to go before it would be 31 December. He just couldn't settle to any job no matter what he tried. He wanted to see Joan. There was so much that he wanted to say to her. You're mad, he kept telling himself. They talked about everything else, business, her family, even discussed what they ate, so why couldn't he put his feelings towards her into words?

'I love you' wouldn't cover it. He needed her, wanted to take care of her, wanted to wake up every morning with her beside him. How could he explain his feelings without getting everything wrong? What would he do if she rejected him? Well, he decided at last, there is only one way to find out.

He wasn't brave enough to call on her unannounced. He made a quick telephone call. Yes, she was on her own, and yes, she would be pleased to see him.

Dependable as ever, Jim arrived within twenty-five minutes of making the call. Joan opened the side door and together they went upstairs to her flat. He couldn't believe how downcast she looked.

'Not downstairs working then?' Joan gave him a funny look and he quickly added, 'Silly question.'

'Sit down, Jim,' she said, smiling, 'No, Freda is managing fine, tells me the sales have been even better than expected so I thought I wouldn't show my face. Not just yet. But I'm OK,' she insisted.

'Don't be daft,' he said firmly, holding out a Fuller's coffee and walnut cake that he had stopped to buy. 'You've had a tremendous shock; what happened was bound to affect you. You sit down, Joan, while I make us some tea.'

403

She had no choice but to sit still until he brought in the tea, then the coffee cake laid out on a glass plate with a knife beside it and two small side plates. Setting everything out on a small table he asked, 'Where do you keep the serviettes?'

'Second drawer on the left past the cooker,' she told him.

Maybe Jim thought she was suffering from delayed shock and in a way that was true. But not entirely so. In fact, her thoughts were centred on him. She watched him pour out the tea, then cut two wedges of the cake, expertly sliding each piece off the knife and on to one of the side plates. It was as he bent over to put her slice in front of her that she put out her hand and gently pulled his head down so that she was able to kiss his cheek.

'Thank you, Jim,' she said. 'Thank you for being there, whenever I need you.'

He caught hold of her hand and lifted it to his cheek, pressing it hard with his, and his eyes told her more than words ever could. Love shone in them. Nothing like the look she'd had from Eric. He came round from behind the table and sat down next to her. Slowly he took her into his arms.

Joan didn't move away. She couldn't. When she lifted her face, he lowered his head and gently placed his lips over hers. It was some while before he let her go and when he did he said, 'God alone knows how long I have wanted to do that.'

His kiss had been hesitant, as if he didn't believe this was any more than gratitude. But it was Joan who took the initiative now as she slid her arms round his neck to draw him closer still. Emotions that he had kept hidden for a long time stirred inside Jim. Nothing mattered other than that at last she was in his arms. The warmth of her lips was wonderful. Nothing existed at this moment other than the need to hold her and never let her go.

It was Joan that moved away first. 'What is it?' he asked.

Then, feeling her sigh deeply, he said, 'You're afraid it is too soon?' Without waiting for an answer he took her head in his hands, lifting it up so she could look at him. If she'd had any doubts before, they flew away.

'Tell me,' she said, knowing, but needing to hear him say it.

'I love you,' he whispered, his voice muffled on her neck.

Joan knew without any doubt that what he said was true. However mixed up everything else had become, this time and this man were right.

She had admired him for years, ever since she first met him on the market. Admired him for his talents, his patience, his intelligence. He had become first her workmate and then her loyal friend. Now they had both seen the light and she knew it was meant to be.

'You don't think I am taking advantage?' He smiled down at her. 'Because, Joan, I can't wait to ask you. Please will you marry me? Please, Joan, will you be my wife?'

Joan was a long time answering so Jim pressed his point. 'I mean it,' he said. 'You do believe me, don't you?'

She wanted to say yes but she was a little scared now. After a while she whispered, 'I do believe you, Jim. I'd be proud to marry you, but only on one condition.'

'And that is?' he asked, his heart in his mouth.

'Oh, Jim.' She leant against him, reaching for his hand. 'It is something we should have done a long time ago. Become business partners.'

Jim quietly considered her offer before answering. When he did speak, the words came from his heart. 'Joan dear, we neither of us are spring chickens, but to spend the rest of our lives together is all that I'm asking.'

'Only if we are partners in everything.' Now it was Joan's turn to push her point. And while she waited for his answer she smiled, really smiled, for the first time in days.

'Partners in everything,' Jim finally agreed, then added,

'I seem to have waited years for you and I would have gone on waiting, but it has been such a long, horrible couple of days and I couldn't bear to see you so upset. The times I have imagined myself proposing to you – but it was always over a wonderful meal and a bottle of champagne. Now I feel mean. I haven't even got a ring to give you.'

'Plenty of time,' Joan said.

'Oh no there isn't. There's no going back. I want a ring on your finger when we open a bottle and tell all your family on New Year's Eve. How does that sound to you?' He pointed to the cups of tea that had gone cold and the cake that hadn't been touched. 'If I make a fresh pot of tea, will this do till then?'

Joan reached up and kissed him. 'Very well indeed,' she whispered.

A LONDON LASS

Elizabeth Waite

A London childhood should be a time of happiness. But for Jane Jeffrey, growing up in Tooting in the early 1920s, life is anything but. For though Mickey Jeffrey is her mother's husband, he is not Jane's father, and for that he cannot forgive her.

Jane is sent to Winchelsea Lodge, a children's home in Sussex. It is the opportunity for her to start her childhood again: a world away from London, she feels as if she is among friends for the first time . . .

But as Jane's sixteenth birthday arrives, she faces the daunting task of returning to London. She settles in Balham, but struggles to find work, thanks to her past.Then Jane gets a job as a companion to a wealthy blind woman, and she feels as if she has struck lucky. And that is before she discovers the delights of love . . .

978 0 7515 3208 1

COCKNEY DIAMOND

Elizabeth Waite

London, 1964. It is a long time since the death of Patsy Kent's mother left her orphaned and facing eviction from her Tooting home. What followed was her first taste of the warmth and loyalty that Londoners do best, as they took in this cockney waif as one of their own. And later, as Patsy gained a husband and four children, she discovered this London spirit all over again, as Hitler tried – and failed – to break their resolve.

Now, as a mother, grandmother and even great-grandmother, Patsy is finding that it is her family who gives her the most pleasure, but also the most pain. Her daughter's marriage to doctor Robert Dellor is proving Patsy's instincts horribly right as it pushes Ellen close to breaking point and Patsy's younger son's wife Valerie seems determined to break David's heart. However, it is the next generation that is to give Patsy the most cause for concern . . .

If Patsy's family are going to pull through, they're going to need all the sparkle their cockney diamond can offer . . .

978 0 7515 3417 7

Other Elizabeth Waite titles available by mail

☐ Skinny Lizzie	Elizabeth Waite	£7.99
☐ Cockney Waif	Elizabeth Waite	£5.99
☐ Third Time Lucky	Elizabeth Waite	£7.99
☐ Trouble and Strife	Elizabeth Waite	£7.99
☐ Nippy	Elizabeth Waite	£7.99
☐ Kingston Kate	Elizabeth Waite	£7.99
☐ Cockney Courage	Elizabeth Waite	£7.99
☐ Time Will Tell	Elizabeth Waite	£7.99
☐ A London Lass	Elizabeth Waite	£7.99
☐ Cockney Diamond	Elizabeth Waite	£5.99
☐ Second Chance	Elizabeth Waite	£7.99
☐ Wheeling and Dealing	Elizabeth Waite	£6.99

The prices shown above are correct at time of going to press. However, the publishers reserve the right to increase prices on covers from those previously advertised, without further notice.

— sphere —

Please allow for postage and packing: **Free UK delivery.**

Europe: add 25% of retail price; Rest of World: 45% of retail price.

To order any of the above or any other Sphere titles, please call our credit card orderline or fill in this coupon and send/fax it to:

Sphere, PO Box 121, Kettering, Northants NN14 4ZQ

Fax: 01832 733076   Tel: 01832 737526

Email: aspenhouse@FSBDial.co.uk

☐ I enclose a UK bank cheque made payable to Sphere for £ . . . .

☐ Please charge £ . . . . to my Visa/Delta/Maestro

Expiry Date ☐☐☐☐   Maestro Issue No. ☐☐

NAME (BLOCK LETTERS please) . . . .

ADDRESS . . . .

. . . .

. . . .

Postcode . . . . Telephone . . . .

Signature . . . .

Please allow 28 days for delivery within the UK. Offer subject to price and availability.